The
Decoy Princess

❖

Dawn Cook

ACE BOOKS, NEW YORK

THE BERKLEY PUBLISHING GROUP
Published by the Penguin Group
Penguin Group (USA) Inc.
375 Hudson Street, New York, New York 10014, USA
Penguin Group (Canada), 90 Eglinton Avenue East, Suite 700, Toronto, Ontario M4P 2Y3, Canada
(a division of Pearson Penguin Canada Inc.)
Penguin Books Ltd., 80 Strand, London WC2R 0RL, England
Penguin Group Ireland, 25 St. Stephen's Green, Dublin 2, Ireland (a division of Penguin Books Ltd.)
Penguin Group (Australia), 250 Camberwell Road, Camberwell, Victoria 3124, Australia
(a division of Pearson Australia Group Pty. Ltd.)
Penguin Books India Pvt. Ltd., 11 Community Centre, Panchsheel Park, New Delhi—110 017, India
Penguin Group (NZ), Cnr. Airborne and Rosedale Roads, Albany, Auckland 1310, New Zealand
(a division of Pearson New Zealand Ltd.)
Penguin Books (South Africa) (Pty.) Ltd., 24 Sturdee Avenue, Rosebank, Johannesburg 2196, South
Africa

Penguin Books Ltd., Registered Offices: 80 Strand, London WC2R 0RL, England

THE DECOY PRINCESS

An Ace Book / published by arrangement with the author

PRINTING HISTORY
Ace mass market edition / December 2005

ISBN: 0-441-01355-4

ACE
Ace Books are published by The Berkley Publishing Group,
a division of Penguin Group (USA) Inc.,
375 Hudson Street, New York, New York 10014.
ACE and the "A" design are trademarks belonging to Penguin Group (USA) Inc.

PRINTED IN THE UNITED STATES OF AMERICA

10   9   8   7   6   5   4   3   2

To my parents,
who sort of gave me the idea . . .

I'd like to thank my editor at Ace fantasy, Anne Sowards, who helped make this a better story, and my agent, Richard Curtis, for without his efforts, there'd be no story at all.

One

❖

It might have been chance that kept my attention tight across the street and upon the mud-splattered gypsy van, but I doubted it. Nebulous coincidences like chance aren't allowed sway in my life, everything being planned to the moment if I didn't arrange for spontaneity. No . . . it was probably my thirst for something outside my ken, my wish to see what lay around the corner just outside my sight and understanding. Either that, or I was bored out of my mind.

"Look, Kavenlow," I said, squinting in the sun at the gaily painted gypsy van. "A palmist. Here." I dumped my latest purchase of fabric into his arms. "I want my fortune told."

"Tess." The man lurched to keep up with me as I started forward. "We should get back. It's not safe for you to be out this long."

"Oh, may God save you," I complained. "It's not even noon yet. I'm safer here than in my own rooms." Whether fortunate or unfortunate, it was true, and I confidently made my way across the busy street, a way parting itself for me as I cut across the narrow avenue for the wood-slatted, horse-drawn van parked in the shade of the closely packed buildings.

There was a huff of exasperation as Chancellor Kavenlow

hastened to catch up, and I slowed. I gave the thickset man a sur-
reptitious look to gauge his irritation as he came even. His lightly
wrinkled face was taut, his cheeks red from the sun's heat. The
fingers gripping my packages were strong from reining in unruly
horses, their tips stained from the ink I had spilled during my history lesson yesterday. His neatly trimmed black beard and hair
were grizzled with white, as were his thick eyebrows. But his jaw
yet carried the firm sensibility I relied upon. He was still my dear
Kavenlow, the one to whom I went first with my questions and
last with my complaints.

Right now, his brow was creased in bother. I winced, thinking
I'd reached the balance where my parents' anger at him for letting me stay out this long outweighed the scene I would make if
he bodily dragged me shrieking back behind stone walls. It
hadn't happened since I was thirteen, but the remembered humil-
iation still brought a warmth to my cheeks.

It had been cold when we started out, and he looked uncomfortable under his cloak; he had been carrying mine most of the
morning. His boots were dusty, as was the bottom half of my
dress, the street having turned the lace-strewn white cloth a begrimed yellow from my knees down. Seeing him so irate, I resolved to stop at a winery on the way home to bribe him into a
better mood. If the truth be told, the black leather jerkin and dagger on his belt made him look more like a master horseman than
a keeper of books and armed attendant.

"Tess," he said, his blue gray eyes pinched as he eased into the
slower pace. "I strongly suggest we go back. Your suitor has arrived early." He glanced behind us as he shifted my packages to
his other arm, squinting from the sun despite his leather cap.
"And he's brought so many soldiers. Twice as many as he needs.
They're thick in our streets."

I forced my expression into a carefree smile. I'd noticed that
as well, but since there was nothing I could do but watch and
wait, I hadn't said anything. And I knew Kavenlow was more
aware of the situation than he was of the fly currently trying to
land on his nose. "He probably heard what happened to Prince
Rupert," I said, thinking I could be safely married by now if the
dunderhead hadn't gotten himself killed a day's ride inside our
borders last year. Just as well. The man had a nose like a potato.
"I don't think we'll ever live that one down," I added, pulling up

short to allow a wagon whose driver didn't recognize me in time to rattle past.

Kavenlow looked pained as he took my elbow. "The point I'm making is that it's a mistake to risk meeting him prematurely in the streets."

"Of course I want to meet him prematurely," I said. "I won't see him for three weeks if my parents get their way." Eyebrow cocked in a rather saucy expression, I pulled out of his grip and made my sedate way to the gypsy van. "I won't be long," I said over my shoulder. "While I'm with the madam, you can get a drink from the tavern across the street. And I need a rest," I lied. "This heat is doing terrible things to my hair."

I fussed with the pile atop my head that I'd made of my waist-length curls. Apart from a few strands artfully pulled out for effect, the neat topknot was held together by not only hairpins but also needlelike darts. They were made from the bone of a bird and were hollow to hold a drop of venom. The short blowtube to launch them bisected the arrangement like a decoration. Kavenlow insisted I have them when out of the palace, though I'd never had to use them.

Kavenlow watched me check the position of my darts, his craggy face carefully neutral. I had been wearing them for the last seven years. Assassins plagued my mother's house. My first few years had been fraught with near misses, prompting my parents to give in to Kavenlow's insistence that he be allowed to teach me how to defend myself should I ever become separated from my guards. Hence the bullwhip I wore as a belt under a silk wrap and the throwing knife strapped to my thigh. Heaven help me if I ever needed it—I'd have to lift my skirts to reach it. The darts, though, were Kavenlow's and my secret. One sent a person either comatose or into convulsions; two brought death. The weaponry was very unprincess-like, but then, I was supposed to shatter the world if that damned prophesy could be believed.

The attempts on my life had slackened off after my tenth year when my parents began searching for suitors, but now that I was in danger of actually marrying someone, they had started up again. This time the assassins had switched from me to anyone I had shown a liking to. It made for very nervous suitors. I couldn't blame Prince Garrett for bringing so many men.

My eyes rose to search out the unfamiliar black and green

uniforms of the Misdev prince as I rose up onto the first step of the van. I wondered if Garrett was as young and handsome as his portraits made him. If they were anywhere truthful, I wouldn't complain. "Besides," I added, my gaze dropping to Kavenlow's as a thrill of anticipation flashed through me, "I want to know what Prince Garrett is like."

"Then let's go back to the palace, and you can ask the maids." Kavenlow's sea gray eyes were weary with a repressed exasperation. But the tiny scar above his eyebrow wasn't red yet, so I knew I had some leeway.

"The maids! They won't know anything except what color his stockings are." Giving him a wicked smile to dare him to stop me, I climbed the last two steps and knocked dead center of the red circle on the door. A flash of expectancy struck through me and settled to a steady burn as a tremulous greeting came from inside.

I'd been waiting what seemed like half my life for a husband. And by all that was holy, it wasn't fair to procrastinate into my third decade, shaky political situation or not. Papers had been signed, and now that I was mere days from meeting my intended, I was nervous. Gypsies were well-traveled. The madam might be able to tell me things about Prince Garrett my parents couldn't— or wouldn't.

I reached for the simple latch, hesitating when Kavenlow grasped my sleeve. I looked down, astonished not that he had touched me but at his troubled expression. The gypsy van had to be safe; he wouldn't have let me come down this street if he hadn't investigated it already. "I'm coming in with you," he said, worry tightening the corners of his eyes.

My lips parted in surprise. Kavenlow hated gypsies almost as much as he hated the ocean, always turning overly protective when I invited them to the palace to entertain. "It's just a foolish woman's fancy," I said, mystified that my harmless entertainment had him concerned. "Go have a drink. I'll be fine. Perhaps you could get me one as well?"

He made a small sigh of surrender. "Very well, little miss," he said, and I smiled. He hadn't called me that in years. He hesitated before leaving, looking up as if fixing me into his memory. His thick, salt-and-pepper eyebrows bunched, but it was the glint of apprehension in his solemn eyes that made my stomach clench. Something was wrong.

"What is it?" I asked, my gaze roving over the noisy crowd as I came down the stair, my instincts flashing into a wary caution at the tension he was trying to hide.

"It's nothing. Go on. I'll wait across the street."

Still unsure, I watched as he turned away and, with slow steps, crossed the street to sit at an outside table in the sun. I slowly mounted the stairs again, taking a long, appraising look at the street. I wasn't convinced all was as it should be anymore.

A puff of exasperation escaped me when I spotted the blue and gold of my father's soldiers tucked into the shadows. They were like rats; see one, know a dozen more were out of sight. Upon seeing my attention on him, the guard waved merrily. My nose wrinkled in bother, and I gave him a sour, pinky-wave back. They knew I hated them shadowing me when I was out of the palace, but I could ignore them if they remained hidden.

Kavenlow had settled himself, watching everything with his hands free and his eyes roving. Still not comfortable, I accepted the call through the door to come in. A chill enveloped me as I opened the door and stepped into the van's darkness. Immediately I moved from the opening to let my eyes adjust to the light of two candles. It was quieter than it ought to be, the noise from the surrounding market dulled. A forest bird fluttered against the bars of its cage. Vermillion curtains and drapes hung from the ceiling to insulate against the heat and noise. A red rug spread dusty and worn, the tassels tattered.

"Close the door," the madam whispered, and my attention jerked to a corner. She was in red, the gaudy color and her chains of jewelry blending into the bloodred background draped around her. There was a fox on her lap, and her swollen fingers gentling the animal and the tips of her stringy gray hair swinging were her only motion. I eased the door shut to seal myself in the ash-scented dark.

"Sit, girl," the heavy woman said, her ugly voice rasping.

My eyebrow rose, but I accepted the slur in the spirit of the moment, feeling her magic gave her more latitude than most. On a small table between us sat a lit candle, an empty dish, a jagged rock, and a feather. I eased myself onto the folding stool across from her. "You wish your fortune?" she said, her harsh accent pulling my eyes to hers.

I nodded, pausing at the creased, leathery look of her face. "Yes. I'm soon to be—"

"Be still," she muttered, shocking me. The fox flowed from her, and I watched, my anger dulling as it sniffed my foot. I wondered what live fur felt like but was too respectful of its teeth to reach. The old woman grunted when it curled up under the table between us. A wisp of its tail brushed my street-dirtied boots, and I froze, unwilling to move and make it leave.

Metal charms jingling, the madam stretched out a flaccid-muscled arm to light a stick of wood jammed between the slats of the wall. She blew the stick out, but it continued to smolder, sending the smell of wormwood to thicken the air. "Show me your hands," she said.

Not liking her tone, I nevertheless set them onto the knee-high table between us. She glanced at my left—mumbling derisively that love leads to peril—then took my right, gripping it with an uncomfortable firmness. Her paper-thin skin was cool and dry, showing none of the heat coming off the bay. She was from the forest and seemed to have captured its essence in her van.

"What are you called?" she said, gumming her teeth as she leaned over my hand and pulled her candle close. Her wrinkles folded in on themselves in a vision of ugly wisdom.

"Tess," I said, then gave her my proper name, trying not to sneeze at the fragrant smoke, "Princess Contessa of Costenopo-lie."

Her bird-bright eyes flicked to mine. "Oooh, a princess are we," she mocked, leaning to shift a curtain with a red-knuckled finger. A shaft of light fell over her worn face as she looked out across the street. The curtain dropped. "You aren't a princess. A princess wouldn't have one tired man looking out for her; she would have five young men with whips and swords. She would not be on foot, but have a coach to carry her. And her guardian would not be swilling ale while his charge allowed herself to be trapped in a van with a horse harnessed to it."

I stiffened. "I told Kavenlow to sit over there," I snapped, my ire rising. "And he's not swilling ale; he's drinking water. If your horse moves, it will die. If you threaten me, you will die as well. I'm Princess Contessa," I said, surprised to find her grip tightening until I couldn't pull away. "I walk alone because an entourage makes me a target."

She leaned forward, her bosom pressing up to look flabby and soft with age. "Oh-h-h," she mocked. "You're that Red Moon Princess, eh?"

I fought to keep a pleasant expression. The Red Moon Prophesy was not mentioned in polite company, having dogged my existence like a hungry cur since the month I'd been born.

"Yes," she murmured, eying me as if it was a grand jest. "A child of the coast destined to rule and conceived in the month of the eaten red moon will make an alliance of the heart to set the mighty as pawns and drive out the tainted blood rising in the south."

"So I'm told," I said, trying not to clench my jaw. *And if I ever find out who painted that in blood upon the doors of every royal family the year of my birth, I'll have them flogged, keelhauled, and spitted. Not necessarily in that order.*

She all but snickered at my bothered look, but I didn't find anything amusing about it. Many ruling families, especially those in the southern reaches, took that to mean I was going to grow up to war on them and decided to kill me as a child. Others were willing to chance that I would marry their son and bring them glory. All I knew is the burning-hell flight of fancy had made my life burning-hell difficult. Just try finding someone nice to dance with you with that hanging over your head.

"Bah," she said shortly, pulling my hand to her face and sending her cool breath against my palm. "You're going on a journey. Quite soon. You'd best prepare for it."

My anger dulled as she fell into the expected patter. Convinced she was going to say something worth hearing, I eased the tension in my arm, and she brought it closer. "A betrothal excursion?" I prompted, wondering if there might be something other than wood ash in that smoke. And why did she have a rock and a feather on her table? "My suitor has arrived early," I prompted.

"Do tell?" she said sourly. "Here." She trailed a begrimed nail down a crease in my palm. "Changes not of your doing. You'll be traveling by horse, then ship, then horse again."

I touched my throat and took a pleased breath. "We will be going to the islands? Oh, how splendid!" I couldn't help my smile. I'd never been on the water, since Kavenlow had an unreasonable fear of it. I thought it dreadfully unfair. It would be wonderful to see more of the land I would eventually be responsible for, especially if my future husband were with me.

My smile turned sly, quirking the corners of my mouth. Being out of the palace would make for far more opportunities to get to know Prince Garrett better, fewer eyes to catch us "talking," and a much better chance to make foolish, daring choices that we could laugh about when we were old and gray.

The woman had started to mumble incoherently, and thinking the performance was wonderful, I resolved to pay her extra. "What of my husband?" I asked slowly, frowning as my tongue seemed thicker than it ought to be.

"Husband?" she murmured, gazing at the rock as if it meant something.

"The man I'll be traveling with," I encouraged.

She looked at me, then back down, appearing to be confused. "He's dark like you. Brown eyes, like you. Brown hair, like you as well, though he has the decency to keep it short."

I stifled a surge of annoyance. I was a princess. I was supposed to have long hair.

"Good hands," she was mumbling. "Skillful hands. Tell him to watch what he does with them, or they will be the death of him."

I blinked. What kind of a fortune was that?

"He's closed, too," she said. "Hard to see. Here. Take this."

She released my hand, and I shivered. Picking up the rock, she dropped it into my grip. My fingers curled about it, holding it gently as I felt its roughness against my skin. "Mmmm," she said, her fingers brushing my palm as she took it back. "You won't be able to understand his pride. But he will understand yours. Best hope he's patient."

"Pride?" I questioned. This was the oddest fortune I had ever been told.

She grasped my hand again, and I started at her quickness. "I see—stone," she murmured, slumping as she fell into a deeper trance. "Marble and hay. Silk and red ribbons—"

"Gifts!" I jerked my hand from her, alarm jolting me out of the smoke-derived fog in my head. The fox at my feet yawned and settled itself further. "Saint's bells and incense. I forgot," I exclaimed. "I have to find a betrothal gift. Forgive me, madam,"

I said hurriedly as I stood and swung my coin bag from my wrist to my hand. "I have to go."

The stool I had been sitting on almost fell, and I scrabbled to catch it, flustered. She sat blinking at me, clearly struggling to shake off her interrupted magic. "Please accept this as a show of my gratitude," I said as I set a coin clattering into the empty bowl. She was quite good. "I'd ask that you come to the palace," I said impulsively. "I need another entertainer for my betrothal festival, and the women would enjoy speaking with you."

The folds in the old woman's face deepened. She took a sharp breath. Gathering her black shawl tight about her shoulders, she gave me a patronizing smile. "No."

I froze in surprise. No one had ever refused me outright before. I was too shocked to say anything and just stood blinking in the thicker smoke at the ceiling. I felt my breathing slow and found myself unwilling to speak or move. A tap at the door echoed in my head.

"Princess Contessa?" Kavenlow's voice filtered through the thick wood. "I have your water." He opened the door, the heat and noise seeming to pool in with the light. The bird in the cage fluttered to be free. The fresh air revived me, and I took a cleansing breath. Kavenlow's shadow eclipsed the light from the street. "I brought you a drink, Tess," he said, the van shifting as he entered and handed it to me.

Taking it, I gave him a bewildered smile and tried to shake the fuzziness from my thoughts. My search for the perfect gift would have to wait. Kavenlow's brow was furrowed worse than the time I broke the guards' practice scaffold, swinging on it. I knew without asking he wouldn't let me stop anywhere on the way home.

"If you want a token of love," the old woman said, "I have it."

Kavenlow's face went slack and empty. He gave the gypsy a curiously anxious look from behind his beard, then slowly— reluctantly—shut the door behind him.

"You don't understand," I said, glancing into my cup of water. "It has to be something unique, something my suitor has never seen."

"Something from far away," the old woman said, waving at the still-glowing stick of incense. "Something of value. Something small. Something you like as well?"

My eyes teared, and I tried not to breathe that foul smoke. "Yes. Exactly."

She chuckled, lumbering to her feet and reaching for a pouch hanging from the ceiling. "I know what pretty women like," she said, taking it down and untying the binding to show the bag was really a square of fabric as she opened it up on the table.

I leaned close: a bundle of silk woven with the likeness of sea-weed, a bone knife, a pointed rod of black metal the length of my forearm, a metallic cross inlaid with red wood, a flat black stone that seemed to draw in the candlelight, a plain ring of gold, a string of tiny bells, and a palm-sized puzzle box of colorful wood. But it was the knife my eyes lingered on.

"Not money," she said. "Give me something of yours."

A frown pulled my brow tight. All I had with me of value was the ring Kavenlow gave me last summer and my favorite necklace with blue stones and rubies—and she wasn't getting Kavenlow's ring. Bothered, I set the cup down and reached for the clasp of the necklace. But the old woman shook her head, her gaze upon the circlet atop my head. My eyebrows rose. She wanted my circlet?

I glanced at Kavenlow to gauge how this particular trade was going to go over with my parents. He was staring at the wall most helpfully, already trying to divorce himself from the coming furor when it was found I'd "lost" my crown again. But burning chu pits, I wanted that knife.

Knowing I'd pay for it later in spades, I took my circlet off and set it on the table. It was only a bit of twisted metal, worthless in my eyes. She nodded her acceptance, and I eagerly reached for the knife, pleased to no end. "Tell me about this," I demanded, knowing the story behind it was probably more valuable than the knife itself.

Immediately she bunched the fabric up, retied the binding, and hung it from the ceiling. My circlet was inside the im-promptu bag, and I felt oddly naked without it. She sighed heavily as she settled her bulk back into her chair, and it creaked in protest. "It's from the east," she said, apparently not minding the smoke she had stirred up. "It belonged to a young man searching for unfailing love. He became a sultan; that's a king of the desert. He found a good use for the ring I gave him in return. The knife of a king makes a fitting gift, don't you think?"

My fingers seemed slow as I turned it over in my hands, and I wondered if I ought to ask Kavenlow to open the door. But it seemed like too much effort. Engraved upon the knife were large beasts with noses as long as their legs and ears as big as their backs. Fanciful. It was perfect, especially with the story that went along with it. I blinked lethargically, trying to decide something. But I couldn't remember what my last thought was . . .

Her hand darted out, grabbing me. I gasped, jerking away as she pricked my finger on the blade. Shocked, I lurched to my feet. My stool crashed to the floor.

"Tess!" Kavenlow shouted. The van dipped as he put himself between the woman and me. The fox darted under the dresser. The table hit the wall as he flung it aside.

My heart pounded like the beating of the bird's frantic wings as it tried to escape. Instinct backed me to a corner. My face went cold, and my grip tightened on the knife still in my hand. The smoke swirled through me, numbing me. I should do something; I couldn't remember what.

"Get back, Kavenlow!" the gypsy cried shrilly as she rose. Her rough accent was gone. "If you dart me, I swear I'll pull your insides out through your nose!"

I clasped my throbbing finger to my chest. *She knows him?* I thought, forcing the concept through my muzzy head. She knew Kavenlow?

"How am I going to explain a cut on her?" Kavenlow exclaimed. Red-faced, he stood stiffly between the gypsy and me with his hands clenched at his sides.

The large raggedy woman sneered at him, her stubby fingers sending the jewelry about her neck clattering. "That's your problem, not mine. And you've made a mistake. She has no defensive reactions at all. Her thoughts revolve around men and buying things."

Kavenlow's shoulders were tense with anger. The smoke seemed to fill my bones. I couldn't move. I heard my pulse slow, and I forced my eyes to remain open. "Just recognize her so we can leave," he said tightly.

My lassitude deepened with every breath, and I wondered how I could still be standing. Concentrating fiercely, I shifted my head to see my finger and the drop of blood there. My knees felt shaky. The gray smoke pooled in my head. "Kavenlow?" I whispered, hearing nothing.

"Pick my table up," the gypsy woman commanded, and Kavenlow obediently righted it, replacing the candle and the shawl covering it. The rock and feather were sullenly placed in the center along with the bowl.

Grumbling in complaint, the gypsy settled herself in her chair and relit the candle from another. "Do you dream, woman-child?" she said, fixing a sharp gaze on me.

I blinked, dizzy. "How dare you address me like . . . that . . ." I whispered, my voice trailing off to nothing.

"Answer her, Tess," Kavenlow said as he pulled me from my corner.

"You want a fortune, dearie?" the gypsy woman said in a mocking falsetto. "I can give you a fortune to make your hair turn white." She leaned forward, running her eyes over my dusty clothes. "Tell me if you dream."

I swallowed hard. "Yes, of course," I said, hearing my voice as if it came from across the room. The smoke was turning my head, making my mouth work when my mind said to be quiet.

"Any of them come true?" she asked.

"No," I said, then hesitated. "No, of course not." *What an odd thing to ask.*

"Animals," the old woman said. "Do they do what you want?"

My brow furrowed, and a distant part of me wondered at the absurdity of the question. "I can ride a horse." I took a deep breath to dispel the fog in my head, but it only made it worse.

The gypsy shook her head in disgust. "Can you walk unnoticed?"

"I'm a princess. Walking unnoticed is pretty much"—I took a breath, willing myself out of the fog—"impossible." My finger throbbed as I gripped the bone knife. I wondered if the fox had run away, and my attention wandered until I found a pair of black, unblinking eyes watching me from under the dresser. It was panting, afraid. My water had spilled, and I wished I could find enough stamina to coax it out to drink from the puddle.

The gypsy followed my eyes to the fox. She made a rude sound and leaned forward. I made no protest as she reached out and plucked a loose hair from the shoulder of my dress. Holding it over the candle, she made a show of smelling the smoke when it flashed into light and was gone. "She can do little for the amount of venom you've subjected her to," she said sourly. "She'll hate you if you haven't told her the cost, which I'd wager six horses you haven't. What is she, eighteen?"

"She's twenty, and I chose that risk."

The woman harrumphed. "Breach the confidence, and you'll be ripped to shreds. The Costenopolie playing field will be destroyed to keep any disturbing ideas from taking root."

"I'm aware of that." His stance was stiff with no show of repentance. A part of me wondered who this woman was who thought she could treat Kavenlow as a drudge.

"She's weak-minded. I pulled her here easier than if she were a starveling child."

Kavenlow gritted his teeth. "She would have come without your summons. She likes gypsies."

"So do I," the woman said sharply. "But I don't go traipsing into their vans with no thought to my safety."

A spark of anger finally broke through my fog. "Kavenlow sees to my safety," I said hotly. "I don't need to think about it. And you will not address him in such a tone."

The woman's brow rose as if surprised I had broken my silence. "This is what you taught her?" she said, fanning that mind-numbing smoke at me. My anger died, all my efforts to pull from my haze gone in a breath. "Reliance on others? A smart mouth that runs without thought? You wanted a princess, Kavenlow? You have a princess. What you plan on making from this is beyond me." She leaned back with a shrewd gleam. "Either you are a moonstruck idiot or more cunning than even my master." Her eyes narrowed in threat. "He's dead."

I could almost hear the words, "I killed him," hanging unsaid between them. Kavenlow stiffened, his feet planted firmly and unmoving. "How I play my game is my business," he said through his gritted teeth. "Do you recognize her or not?"

A sigh escaped the woman. Her fingers played with the jewelry about her neck. I watched, unable to look away until the fox poured itself from under the dresser and slunk to the puddle by my feet. For a moment, only the small sound of its lapping could be heard, and then it slunk back into hiding. I smiled, pleased it had trusted me.

"Aye," the gypsy said grudgingly, eying the fox's nose peeping from under the dresser. "I'll recognize her. There's something there—though the package it comes in is worthless. You should burn your plans and start over. This woman is only fit for dressing in finery and resting on another's arm."

A flush of anger cut through my benumbed state, then died.

"Thank you," Kavenlow said, an irate relief in his voice.

"Thank you?" the gypsy questioned mockingly. "Whatever for? Go on. Get out. I want to leave before the crush."

Kavenlow hesitated. "Something is coming? Tell me."

A shaft of light stabbed into the smothering darkness as she shifted the curtain and peered into the street. "If you can't see it, you'll have to wait until it happens. I'm not your nursemaid."

Plucking her smoldering stick from the wall, she wafted it under my nose. "You won't remember any of this," she said to me, and I lost sight of everything but her eyes sharp with an old bitterness. They were blue. What gypsy has blue eyes?

"When I cut you," the woman said, "Kavenlow beat me with the flat of his sword, burned my van, and slaughtered my horse. Oh, it was a sight to remember," she said dryly.

"Burned your van?" I said, my eyes tearing and my words slurring at the sudden smoke.

The gypsy smirked at my loose speech, the folds of her face falling into each other. "Yes. Burned my van down to its wheels. It's what he wants to do. Can't you tell?"

Kavenlow pried the knife from my fingers. "That won't work with her," he said as he tucked it into the coin purse dangling from my wrist. "She will eventually remember. She's stronger than she seems. I've never been able to cloud her memory."

"It's a good thing I'm not you, then, isn't it?"

His lips pressed into a thin line behind his graying beard. Taking my arm, he moved me to the door. The rush of light and heat as he opened it was so sudden and shocking, it was almost a pain. I balked, unable to leave the cool rest of the van. With a smooth motion, Kavenlow hoisted me into his arms.

"Come see me again when you find unfailing love, dearest," she said sarcastically as he carried me down the steps, "and I'll tell you your children's fortunes."

Two

✦

"Not so tight," I gasped when Heather tugged my bodice laces. "I do have to breathe."

"Tish, tash," the young woman said, giving the laces a final yank before tying them off. "We have to make the most of what little you have. Heaven help you, Tess, if you took away the dress and long hair, you could be a boy. And you want to make a good impression if you see him in the hallways—by accident, of course."

My eyebrows rose at the blatant hint of scheming. "And passing out from lack of air will impress the chu out of him, won't it," I said dryly, but a stab of anticipation brought me straight.

Saucily humming the music I had picked out for my wedding, Heather helped me into a clean dress. She had joined the palace staff as a kitchen girl when I was seven and she was eight, but after borrowing her for a game of tag, I insisted she become a member of my "court."

Court had been a rather grand name for my loose gathering of companions at the time. I had been horribly obnoxious, demanding everyone play with me, noble and commoner alike. Heather, though, remained while others drifted away—a steady companion and extra set of ears keeping me informed of the palace gossip.

"Have you seen him?" I asked, worried as I sat in a rustle of fabric before my mirror in my outer room. She had been unusually silent while I'd washed the street dirt from me, making me think the news wasn't good.

"He who?" Her eyebrows were high with an artful disinterest.

"Garrett!" I said, pushing her away in exasperation as she tried to arrange my hair.

"Prince Garrett of Misdev?" She said his name around a languorous sigh that sent her ample chest heaving dramatically. "The entire staff met him after breakfast while you were out. He's been with your parents since, cloistered away with papers and maps. Dreary stuff. I don't know how he stands it, the poor man. I'm sure he'd rather be out hawking or riding."

Heather pulled a curl from my topknot, and I tucked it back. I didn't like her that close to my darts; she thought they were only a favorite bit of decoration. Lord help me if she ever pricked herself. I didn't wear my knife or bullwhip behind palace walls, either.

"And where did Kavenlow ride off to in such a hurry?" she continued. "The cook said he took the cold pork she was going to serve tomorrow and ran to the stables. Such a fuss that woman made. You'd think he stole a live pig the way she was bellyaching!"

I frowned. "Kavenlow left? By horse?"

"Right out the front gate." She teased out another curl. "Bilge scrapings, Tess. Let me put your hair down. Honestly! Why won't you let me pad you in front a little, too? Just for today? You're as tall and thin as a dinghy's mast."

Exasperated, I let the curl stay. Heather's preoccupation with my looks was because I didn't have any, and she did. She was shorter than me by half a head and pleasingly round where a woman should be, with rosy cheeks, blond hair, and wide, childbearing hips. Fine, good, Costenopolie stock, as Kavenlow would say.

"Kavenlow didn't tell me good-bye," I mused aloud. "That's not like him." Then I brightened. "Perhaps it has something to do with a betrothal gift."

"That must be it," Heather said. "Though why he raided the larder is beyond me."

"We didn't eat while we were out." I carefully took the darts from my topknot and placed them in the hairpin cushion. My hair tumbled down, and I reached for the brush.

The morning's excursion had been an obvious ploy to keep me out of the palace and prevent me from meeting Garrett. I thought Kavenlow was being grossly overprotective. Though our grandparents had warred upon each other, King Edmund had far more to gain by his second son marrying into the family, hoping to prosper by the Red Moon Prophesy rather than be destroyed by it. Our marriage had been arranged for almost a year, but Garrett and I weren't supposed to meet until a month from now at the summer festival, then be wedded this winter at the turning of the year. That he was early didn't bother me at all.

Heather pressed her lips and took the brush from me, struggling to get through the tangles the wind from the bay had made of my curls. "I don't like you going down into the streets. You're going to end up *dead*," she said, giving my hair a sharp tug. "And what's going to happen to me then? You couldn't pay me to go into the streets with you again."

"That was years ago," I protested. "Heather, bury it and find a new horse to ride."

A tinge of red came over her sun-starved cheeks, and her tugs grew sharper. In all honesty, it had been a near miss. The surrounding merchants and townsfolk had spontaneously retaliated, stoning the man to death under my and Heather's horrified eyes. To Kavenlow's fury, he hadn't been able to stop them. My people left nothing to question in their anger. Kavenlow had stomped about the palace for days. Two days later, he began secretly desensitizing me to the poison on my needles to supplement my growing whip and knife skills.

"You should have sent me," she said, tugging on my hair. "I know what you like."

I took the brush from her before she yanked my hair out entirely. "I was buying something for Garrett."

"Oh, that's right." A randy glitter came into her blue eyes. "What did you get him? A matched set of jewels?" Her eyes went wide with a mocking innocence as she fluffed my clean underskirt. "No-o-o-o? He probably has a pair already. Maybe a great, awful, long sword? No? He has one of those already, too." She giggled merrily.

"A knife," I said, meeting her grin with my own. Heather should have been married years ago, but had she accepted any of the numerous offers, she would've had to leave me until I was wed as well. And life beside me was too comfortable for her to give it up. Not to mention the court stipend.

"A knife?" Heather repeated. She played with the ends of her hair, her full lips falling into a pout that generally got her whatever she wanted from the cook's boy.

I nodded. "It used to belong to a desert king. Want to see it?" I reached for my coin bag atop the vanity, pulling out the knife and placing it in her palm. "Be careful," I warned. "It's wickedly sharp. The gypsy I bought it from accidentally pricked my finger on it. See?"

Heather dutifully glanced at the tiny spot as I held my hand out. "Kavenlow beat her with the flat of his sword," I said, a distant feeling coming over me. "He burned her wagon and slaughtered her horse. She had . . . blue eyes. Have you ever seen a gypsy with blue eyes?"

Heather's mouth fell open. "Kavenlow?" she whispered. "He beat her?"

"Oh, it was quite a sight," I said slowly, seeming to smell smoke. I felt odd, starting when Heather took my hand and pulled my finger closer for a better look.

"Chu, Tess!" she exclaimed softly. "Why didn't you tell me before?"

I pulled away, confused. "I don't know." Frowning, I turned to my mirror. "Do you think Garrett will like it?" I asked, tucking the knife in a drawer. "You saw him. What's he like?"

My pricked finger apparently forgotten, Heather sat on the edge of my dressing couch, her round cheeks pinched as she beamed. "You are so fortunate, it makes me ill. Of all the fat ugly men, you somehow find the single handsome one."

At least he isn't ugly, I thought. "Is he clever?" I asked her reflection.

"Clever? It matters? He's gorgeous!"

"Oh, how nice . . ." I said, trying to feign an air of indifference as I smoothed my hair. I'd seen portraits, of course. But portraits often lied.

"Yes, and he looks like he really knows how to use his sword," she confided. "Even the one buckled to his belt," she added, her blue eyes innocently serious.

I gave her a raised-eyebrow look. Angels give me strength. I'd been waiting for a husband too long. A girl can crochet only so many doilies.

"And he made the head cook blush with his praise of breakfast," Heather added.

That was impressive. Getting that old woman to color took some doing. "He can't be better looking than the falconer's boy," I protested, praying she'd say he was.

She nodded enthusiastically. "By a wagonload. Lord help me, his shoulders would make angels cry. And he has such a tight little—"

"Heather!" I cried as she dramatically fanned herself, falling back on the couch by the window.

"Oh . . ." she moaned. "You will have so many children, you will put the peasants to shame. To shame!"

I turned away, pleased. I was obligated to marry the most lucrative offer, no matter what the man who came with it looked like or how stupid he was, especially with the "Marry her for glory or murder her for safety" mentality the surrounding noble families were afflicted with. And the marriage offers had tapered off dramatically since poor Prince Rupert.

"Looks aren't everything," I said, running the brush over my hair and getting it stuck in a curl.

Heather's face was masked in a mocking horror as she met my gaze in the mirror. "Listening to you, one would think looks were nothing!"

I cocked my head. "If one thought that, one would be . . . half-right?"

She threw a cushion at me, which I easily knocked aside. "Your royal blood is showing," she said in disgust. "Looks are *everything.*"

I gazed at myself in the mirror, hoping Garrett didn't think so. "I want a husband as smart as I am," I said, thinking wistfully of Prince Rupert's witty letters still at the bottom of my wardrobe drawer. "One who can play a decent game of thieves and kings."

"Games," Heather said with a sigh as she came and took the brush from me. "Is that all you think about? Men are pigs rooting in the mud, royal and common alike. The sooner you realize that, the happier you'll be."

"A man with high standards," I continued, knowing she didn't understand. "Dangerous, maybe?" I said, and her eyes went bright with repressed laughter. "A man with power, not necessarily wealth."

Heather snickered as she brushed my hair. "You have a better chance to catch a punta by the tail than finding a man that meets your standards, Tess. Especially when you have such a small inlet to cast your net in."

I sighed. "Use a mythical creature to catch a mythical creature," I said, thinking that it was a good analogy—and not very encouraging. Puntas were large, ferocious cats with tufts of silver on their ears, able to vanish in a whirl of wind when surprised, which wasn't very often. They haunted the beach as well as the mountains, reputed to be able to heal the sick, bring rain to end a drought, or call wandering herds of goats to their doom. I'd seen a punta pelt before, dry and dusty, cracking with age. They avoided people to the degree that it was questioned whether there were any yet alive.

I stood, running my hands down my white linen dress. It wouldn't be my fault if Garrett and I met in the corridors. "Do I look all right?" I asked anxiously.

Heather sent her gaze over me, shaking her head in dismay. My eyes dropped, and my face went slack. It didn't matter how tall I stood or how courtly my accent was, I was not built right. My curves were too shallow and my figure hidden under the yards of fabric was too defined by my afternoons on horseback. It hadn't seemed to matter before. It did now.

There was a heartbeat of silence, then clearly realizing what she had done, Heather bustled close, fluffing my skirt. "Oh, your hair looks fetching," she asserted brightly, her face flushed. "I've never seen longer, and it's that lovely rich brown, like freshly turned earth. Just like your eyes. You look—nice. Princess nice."

I gave her a thin smile. I wasn't ugly, but we both knew I wasn't the one the palace guards were sighing wistfully after when we went down the hallways together.

"All you need is your circlet," Heather said as she turned to my vanity.

A small, pained sound escaped me, and I said nothing, keeping my eyes on my reflection.

"Tess!" Heather wailed, her shoulders slumping. "Heaven

help you, again? I swear, you'd lose your feet if you didn't use them to stand on."

"I didn't lose it; I traded it for Garrett's knife," I said defensively. "Could you slip out to the smith's for a new one for me? I'd be *ever* so grateful."

My voice was entirely reasonable, hiding my sudden flush of worry for what my mother would say if she found out. It had sounded like a good idea at the time, and it was my crown, drowned it all. I was tired of being told what I could and couldn't do. One would think that being a princess meant making your own decisions, but I never got a say in anything, always bending to do what was proper, what was expected. And I was weary of it. My thoughts drifted to the picture of Garrett hanging in the receiving room. Oh, I was so weary of it.

Heather stood with her hands on her hips, waiting. She wasn't supposed to leave the grounds unchaperoned, and I'd have to sweeten the deal for her to risk it. "I'll tell everyone you're cloistered away sewing," I offered, recalling her unending prattle this morning had been exclusively about her latest suitor, and how long it had been since she had seen him. Alone. In the spring air. Wink, wink. Nod, nod. Sigh, sigh.

My shoulders slumped. If I couldn't follow my desires, at least she could. And maybe she'd tell me about it in the morning. "Take as long as you want," I added. "I can get out of my dress tonight by myself."

I couldn't—at least not without hurting myself—but I knew I had won when a sound of anticipation slipped from her. "All night?" she questioned. "You won't tell anyone I'm gone?"

I nodded, relieved the price of Garrett's knife wouldn't be a lecture from my mother but an evening of sewing buttons back on my dress when I popped them off to get out of it tonight.

"Oh, pig feathers, it's a deal!" she said, licking her thumb and extending it. I did the same, and we pressed them together, sealing the bargain with spit as we had when we were giggling fools keeping secrets. Apparently not much had changed.

She looked to the door, clearly eager to be gone. "I hear there's a new fish in the solarium's pond," Heather said as she picked up the basket in which she had brought me my noon meal. "Very pretty. You should see it. All glittery with black and green . . ."

Black and green. The same color as the uniforms of Garrett's guards. I met her grin with my own. I would have been surprised had she not known where Garrett was.

Standing by my door, her smile faltered. "You aren't really going to force an introduction, are you?"

Seeing her troubled brow, I shook my head, bowing yet again to what was expected of me instead of what I wanted. Chu, I was so weak of determination, it was pitiful. But to do more than steal a look at Garrett would be a severe breach of etiquette. "No," I said. "Just look."

She gave me a satisfied nod and tugged open the door. Leaving it propped for me, she sashayed down the hallway with her empty basket on her arm, giving each sentry she passed a flirtatious hello, her mind obviously on—er—other things. I headed the other way, getting only cursory greetings until I turned the corner since most of the guards were watching Heather. All I had to do was get to the solarium before Kavenlow intervened. And he was gone for the day.

Nervousness began to creep up my spine like a wolf spider, and I gathered up my skirts so I could move faster. The halls were bright with noon, and my father's soldiers posted at the corners were wearing their best uniforms of gold and blue. They looked unusually dapper. I gave each a nod as I passed, and got more than a few encouraging winks in return. We had grown up together, and I felt as if they were overly protective brothers. They knew where I was headed, but only Kavenlow or my parents had the authority to stop me.

Anticipation tingled to the tips of my toes when I found four guards at the door to the solarium. Two were unfamiliar, dressed in the well-appointed uniforms of black and green that I had seen in the streets. Lavish hats with drooping black feathers sat perched upon their heads. I eyed them, thinking the gaudy things would blow off in the first breeze from the bay. The men were undoubtedly part of Garrett's personal guard. One looked too young, the other too old.

I shook my head at my father's sentries to tell them not to announce me. One smiled and opened the door, taking care to shut it softly behind me. The sun was glaring, and I squinted about the empty-seeming indoor garden. I heard my mother's laugh and placed them at the unseen table by the orchid pond. The space was draped in vines to make a private nook. I had often used it for a classroom, and there was an ongoing game of thieves and kings between my father and me on the fishpond's retaining wall.

Following the voices, I crept down the tiled path between potted ferns and lavish vines from the south border islands. The heat of the day was thick, caught between the stone walls and the high glass ceiling. I wished I had worn something lighter. My pulse quickened as I heard what had to be Garrett's voice. He spoke with great precision, hitting every syllable with a clarity that hinted at a clever mind and swift wit.

I eased around a large potted tree, well-hidden behind the captain of my father's guard and another, unfamiliar man in black and green. My father looked up across the distance when the sentries shifted to recognize and dismiss me. Brow furrowed, he started to rise but then turned the motion to that of resettling himself. "Leave now," he mouthed at me, distracting my mother and the young man standing beside her by shuffling the papers on the table.

I scrunched my face up in rebellion. I'd leave, but how fast I obeyed remained up for interpretation. Hunched with my skirts held tight to me, I studied Prince Garrett.

As promised, he was handsome, making a trim figure beside my squat, dare I say rotund, father. Garrett stood a shade taller than I, I guessed. His hair was straight and fair, cut short about his head. My brow rose in appreciation at his clean-shaven features. I liked a tidy man. Freckles scattered across his narrow nose made him look young.

He reached for a map, the black fabric of his uniform pulling tightly across his shoulders. I felt warm just looking at him. His attire wasn't flashy, using the cut of the cloth to hint at his wealth instead of distracting medals and jewels. He smiled at something my mother said, and I noticed his teeth were straight and even. My eyes ran down the snugness of his trousers as he turned his back to get a paper resting upon the pond wall, and my lips curved in a sly smile. Heather was right.

I rubbed my finger where the gypsy had pricked it as his pleasant voice joined my mother's in an easy laugh. It rankled me to be hidden away like a bauble to be brought out for theatrical effect. If I had half the fortitude of my father, I'd force an introduction now. But what I did was sigh and turn to leave. Protocol and diplomacy. They ruled me. *Coward.*

My foot scraped the slate tiles, and I froze.

"Tess," my father said as I spun and my mother met my horri-fied eyes. "What are you doing here?" He stood with a quickness I'd never seen in him before, dismay in his stance.

Garrett smiled as he straightened to his full height. Our eyes met, and my stomach twisted. I was knee-deep in the chu pits now. Trying to force my face into a pleasant expression, I squared my shoulders and came out from behind the sentries.

"Oh, Tess," my mother said, touching the yards of ribbon binding her yellow hair in its elaborate coiffure. "Why didn't you wait?" She and my father exchanged unreadable looks, seeming to be at a loss what to do.

Shaking inside, I curtsied low. "Good afternoon, Father, Mother," I said with a formal stiffness. "I do apologize. I was un-aware you were here." It was an outright, bald-faced lie, and I ap-proached slowly, praying I wouldn't trip on a slate tile and fall flat on my fundament. That would be about right for my day so far.

My pulse quickened when my father came forward, taking my arm in a show of ceremony. "I told you to leave," he whispered, looking unusually stately in his best receiving garb.

"I'm sorry," I whispered back. "I only meant to look." But my unease sharpened to a fine point when he answered me with si-lence. Together we halted before Garrett standing beside my seated mother. Her petite, wispy figure was tight with an unusual tension.

"Prince Garrett, second son to King Edmund," my father said. "This is our daughter, Tess. I apologize for her forwardness, but she has a mind of her own, as you can see."

A flash of emotion went through me as my father settled my hand into Garrett's. It was strong and lightly callused, telling me he had much practice with a sword. He held my hand gently, as if he might break it. "A woman who thinks is a boon to her kingdom," Garrett said, his voice mixing with the birdsong as if it belonged. "I'm pleased to meet you, Your Highness—under any circum-stances."

I flushed, thankful he didn't seem offended by me pushing up the courting timetable. "It's an honor to make your acquaintance, Prince Garrett," I said formally. "I trust your journey to join us was uneventful." The expected words flowed from me, a well-practiced litany. His nose was small, and his eyes were a riveting green. Both my parents had blue eyes, and I'd never seen quite their like before. They were beautiful, and I couldn't look away.

As tradition dictated, Garrett brushed the top of my hand with his lips. I smiled, welcoming the age-old promise behind that simple act and the feeling it pulled through me. "The honor is mine," he said. His voice was pitched low and his enunciation elegant. "Now that I have found you, the trials of the road have faded to a distant memory. It's truly a pleasure to see the claims of your beauty have erred on the side of modesty. But why did you have the portrait artist straighten your curls? I think they become you."

I met his smile with my own, glad to see he had a sense of humor. Straighten my curls, indeed. A flash of emotion went all the way to my toes, raising gooseflesh on the way back. *This is to be my husband? Oh, the trials of being a princess . . .* "Please call me Tess," I said, thinking my face must be red. "Life is too short to stand on formality behind palace walls."

Garrett glanced at my mother for permission before inclining his head in agreement. "Tess, then," he said. "I'd be pleased if you called me by my given name as well."

"Garrett," I repeated. "Of course." The formalities observed, Garrett escorted my pounding heart and me to the table. The tension eased as our court manners could now be dropped.

I glanced at the game of thieves and kings in progress upon the wall of the pool in passing. My father had finally shifted his pieces, putting one of his knights in danger to lure me into exposing my king. Pulling Garrett to a halt, I accepted the challenge of taking his piece in the hopes I could return my thief to safety before his second knight could make good his threat. My father made a sound of surprise as I set the black knight aside.

"Your princess is threatened," Garrett murmured as he helped me with my chair.

My hopes soared. He knew how to play thieves and kings! "Yes," I murmured. "But if he takes her, I will have his king in four moves."

"Clever," he breathed into my ear, adding to my fluster. A slow shiver filled me from the inside out. And I rather liked the way his hand lingered on the back of my chair. The mix of possessiveness and protection was something I couldn't find fault with at the moment. I knew I was behaving worse than a kitchen maid who had caught a nobleman's eye, but I couldn't help it. Saint's bells, but I liked him.

"There," my father said gruffly as he stood by Garrett. "Isn't this as nice as a day on the bay in summer?"

An awkward silence threatened, and my mother graciously stepped into the breach. "Tess?" she said, calm and self-possessed despite my social blunder. "We were going over the proposed exchanges. Would you like to see?"

Immediately I shifted my attention from Garrett's presence behind me to the map on the table. All fluster aside, I was keenly interested in what King Edmund was offering in return for taking their unnecessary, second-born son off their hands and out of their borders.

The map showed much of the lower part of the continent, my mother's large bays and several of her smaller ones clearly marked. We controlled the usable beaches for hundreds of miles up and down the coast, and thus most of the sea trade came from or through us. The shore we didn't actively use met the land in jagged cliffs. Farther inland were the hardwood forests where we harvested the timber for our homes and the sturdy, fast ships we were known for. Between the woods and the sea was a distressingly small tract of land fit for farming.

Beyond the forest was Misdev. King Edmund retained a slim portion of the forest we took from them two generations ago. The kingdom was thoroughly landlocked but made up for it by consisting of large tracts of farmland butting against the mountains. It was hoped the union between us would rub out the last of our grudges and increase the quality of food crossing into our borders.

My father leaned over the map and tapped a finger upon a small cove on the outskirts. "See here?" he said, leaning so his bald spot showed. "We would lose one of the minor, shallow harbors. Along with a generous ribbon of land so they can get to it."

A whisper of unease took me. The proposed section would drive a dangerous-looking wedge between us and our neighbors to the south. They wouldn't like that at all, and neither did I. "But a good portion of the populace pulls their fishing boats out there," I said, tugging the map from under my father's elbow. "I thought we would be returning the forest to them."

My father had a satisfied air about him as he leaned back and beamed, his gaze alternating between Garrett and me. "Didn't I tell you she was clever?"

Frowning, my mother touched his shoulder. I watched the exchange, not knowing what was being said. A sullen, almost defiant look flashed across my father's face before he focused on me. "You're right, Tess," my father said. "They will lose their homes, but they will be farmers."

"Where?" I asked, struggling to keep my voice mild and polite. "It takes a generation to turn woods into good farmland. What will they do in the interim?"

"They will farm the land we get in exchange for the harbor and boats," my father said, clearly pleased.

"Boats!" I cried. I looked at my mother, who nodded almost imperceptibly. A harbor *and* boats? We controlled the sea. Our armada was the only thing we had to fend off the greed of the surrounding kingdoms. "How many boats?" I asked warily.

"Dear, that's not polite," my mother said, and I pulled from her gentling hand.

"Neither is forcing your people to scratch the ground for their sustenance instead of pulling it clean from the ocean as they have for generations," I said hotly.

"Tess!" my father exclaimed as he flicked a glance over my shoulder to Garrett.

"Forgive me," I said, my words and tone contrite but my expression grim. I steeled it back to a proper, pleasant demeanor as there was a whisper of linen and the prince moved to the opposite side of the table so he could see me. His shadow fell over me, and I looked up.

"You have no reason to ask for forgiveness," he said. "You care for your people. I won't fault you for that. A queen puts her people first." He straightened, holding my gaze with his. "Your people will be justly rewarded on their first harvest, dear lady. The produce they bring to your markets will not have spent weeks drying on the back of a cart or being bruised in the belly of a ship. It will be fresher and bring a correspondingly higher price."

"Boats and a harbor?" I questioned my father, ignoring Garrett and his soothing smile.

My question clearly made my father uncomfortable, and his chin bunched behind his beard. He knew as well as I the threat another force on the water, no matter how small, would bring.

"Trust, Tess," he said. "Trust is expensive, especially with the history of—ah—your birth. The tracts of land we will receive will delve deep into Misdev. King Edmund deserves proper compensation."

Lips tight, I turned to Garrett. "And what will you gain from this, Prince Garrett?"

Garrett, though, didn't seem disturbed by my obvious ire. He sank down to a crouch before me. "Besides the satisfaction of knowing I've won a beautiful lady as my bride instead of an old hag with warts and an ugly nose?" he said as he took my hand. "Nothing. The boats and harbor will be managed by me only until such time as my brother becomes king after my father."

Beautiful lady? I thought. I was a flat-chested, narrow-hipped woman who looked like she should be tending fires, not lounging before them. His flattery fell flat, pulling me into mistrust. My heart pounded as I caught a dark emotion flickering behind his eyes. Jealousy. Garrett was unsatisfied with being a second son. That was dangerous. No wonder his father was so generous with his land. He wanted Garrett out of his kingdom and safely settled.

Garrett raised my hand to his lips, letting them linger a shade too long upon my fingers. My eyes jerked to his. A chill slid through me, and I struggled to not yank my hand away.

This wasn't right. None of it. But it wasn't as if I wouldn't be able to keep an eye on him. I would be queen after my parents; he would never be more than what he was now. With me, he would have at least the illusion of his own kingdom instead of a castle on the outskirts of his brother's realm.

I began a steady pull away from him, and annoyance flickered over Garrett as he was forced to let go of me or make it obvious I didn't like his touch. "Then it's settled?" he said, his tone light as he rose to stand over me. "Perhaps we can choose the boats tomorrow?" He smiled, but it no longer warmed my soul.

"Tomorrow?" my father said haltingly.

Garrett stood and drew me reluctantly to my feet. He was taller than I by half a head, outweighing me by several stone of sword-worked muscle. My heart gave a thump as I took in the faint scent of horse and leather, the familiar smell having lost all its comforting memories. "Everything is in place," Garrett said. "I suggest we move the wedding up to circumvent any possible retaliation concerning the Red Moon Prophesy."

Shocked, my breath caught, and I reddened. How dare he speak so cavalierly of my private heartache? That burning-fool fantasy was the bane of my existence.

"We can be married in place of the betrothal festival," he continued. "All the important guests will be here."

"No," came my mother's faint protest. She had a peculiar expression, dismay and . . . guilt? "The wedding has been planned for the turning of the year. We have set arrangements for informal parties, teas, and joint excursions to provide time to become better acquainted. That you're here early does not change our timetable. We have been fighting assassins for years, Prince Garrett. You are safe."

Garrett seemed unperturbed. "I insist," he said softly, and I stiffened when his grip on my arm tightened and then relaxed. "I will send my guards with news of the changes. They will be faster on horse than your ships. I'm only thinking of my bride's safety."

I stood stiffly beside him, disgusted at his impatience. He was thinking of my father's ships and harbors, not me. Slowly I tried to pull away. They wouldn't make me marry him if I didn't want to, would they? Then our ships and harbors would be safe. But even as I thought it, I knew what I wanted made no difference. It never did.

Brow furrowed, my mother gave my father a sharp look. Seeming reluctant, my father came around the table, taking me from Garrett and pulling me a step away. I went with him willingly, feeling as if I had to wipe my hands free of the Misdev prince.

"I understand your worries, Prince Garrett," my father said, placing himself between Garrett and me. "But as my wife says, we are skilled at fending off assassins. Having the wedding after the shipping season is to provide protection against a prophesy-induced attack. To have it earlier, even as a surprise, would invite violence. Our agreement remains unchanged. You will have your bride. But there will be no marriage for at least six months."

Garrett's stance stiffened as I stood beside my father, relishing his protection for the first time in years. "I believe you are stalling, sir," Garrett said, a faint flush coming over his pale features. "You have a lovely daughter, and I see no reason to wait for an assassin's knife when everyone is in agreement."

My mother sighed at my obvious ire. She gave my father a tight smile. "Dear," she said to me, patting the chair beside her. "Come sit. Gentlemen? I would speak with my daughter?"

My father slumped, turning from a sovereign to a father struggling to reconcile the will of a kingdom with the will of his daughter. "Leave us," he said to his guard. Still not looking up, he said tiredly, "Prince Garrett, if you would ask your man to join him?"

Garrett made a quick gesture to his guard, and the two sentries turned smartly and left. The silence was uncomfortable as we waited for the sound of the door. My resolve stiffened. Garrett wanted my father's ships and harbor. He didn't care about my safety.

"It's my responsibility," my mother said, her eyes sad upon my father. "I'll explain."

Explain what? I thought. I already knew I had no say as to whom I married. But I could make things difficult, drag the proceedings out, make sure everyone knew I wasn't happy. Papers had been signed, but if I set my mind to it, it could be years until the actual wedding took place. Who knew? Maybe if I stalled long enough, he would find a poisoned knife in his ribs.

Nodding with his head lowered, my father gestured to the prince. "Prince Garrett," he said. "Would you accompany me on a brief tour of our interior gardens? We can rejoin the women shortly, and all will be explained."

"Mother?" I demanded, feeling my stomach tense.

Garrett cleared his throat. "It's all right, Tess, dear. I have a desire to learn the history of that exquisite statue there. I won't be but a moment."

I scowled openly at his term of affection. My parents exchanged that same weary look, and my father escorted Garrett out of earshot to the most recent addition of statuary, a young woman in flowing robes. My father moved his hunched figure as if he would rather haul nets out of the bay than tell Garrett of the life-sized statue I pitched cherrystones at when avoiding my lessons. It's not nice to have a statue prettier than oneself.

Garrett gave me what was probably supposed to be an encouraging smile before he followed my father, standing so I could see him across the short distance. Thinking he was rather vain, I frowned and turned away. My mother took my hand and pulled me down into a chair beside her.

"Tess. Sweetheart," she said, her eyes showing deep lines at the corners. "I was expecting to have the next few weeks to tell you this. I am so sorry. Garrett arriving early has thrown everything into a quick coming-about, and now your impatience has complicated things beyond belief."

"You can't give King Edmund one of our harbors," I protested in a harsh whisper. "The man is a flop! A carp mouthing the top of the water for scraps. What about the Rathkey's proposal? They must need something, living way up in the mountains like that. Metal, maybe, or wool. I don't mind waiting until their son gets a little older."

"Tess, hush," my mother pleaded. "This isn't anything to do with Garrett or the marriage arrangements."

My next outburst died. Suddenly I wasn't so sure I knew what was going on.

"We do love you," she said, her thin hand looking pale atop my sun-darkened one, "and please don't take this the wrong way, but . . ." She hesitated and took a deep breath. "You aren't the crown princess."

Three

❖

"What do you mean, I'm not the princess?" I said, almost laughing. That was ridiculous.

My mother's eyes were sad, and her face drawn. "Dear," she said, her nervous gaze darting over my shoulder to the two men. "Not so loud. I know this is awkward—"

"How can I not be the princess?" I exclaimed, pulling away. Mystified, I glanced to my father and Garrett. It was obvious they had heard me. The prince was red with anger, and my father wore a look of pained determination.

Garrett stood with his hand upon his sword hilt. "You dare play my family as fools?" he said indignantly. "We offered you immeasurable tracts of land, and you give us insult? Using lies to null a signed agreement is craven. Wars have started for less, sir!"

My father's face darkened. "We do nothing of the kind. We fully intend to honor our agreement. We have a crown princess." He glanced at me with that same tinge of guilt. "She just isn't Tess, here."

Confounded, I stared blankly at my father. *What, by the three rivers, is going on?*

My father turned his back upon Prince Garrett and came to the table. I jumped as he cupped my chin, meeting my eyes with a sorrowful expression. "I'm sorry, Tess. If it was up to me, I'd let you be queen. You'd have made a good one."

He looked at Garrett standing by the beautiful statue. "Prince Garrett," he said, his voice carrying a weary weight. "Allow me to explain. There's been no breach of contract. I introduced Tess as my daughter, nothing more. Any judgments you came to are unfortunate."

"I am so the princess," I said, looking from my mother's pinched face to my father. A bad feeling settled over me. No one was laughing.

"No, sweetness," my mother said. "But you are our daughter. We love you very much. Please don't make that face."

Garrett hadn't moved. His eyes were fixed on me. I couldn't tell what he was thinking. "If she's not the Red Moon Princess, who is she?" he asked tersely.

My father winced. "Ah—we aren't entirely sure."

My eyes widened and I stared, not believing this was happening. "But I'm the princess!"

"It was troubled times, Tess, when your sister was born," my father said persuasively. "The assassination attempts began the week we found the prophesy painted on the wall, and we had to do something. There had been a lunar eclipse the fall before your sister was born, and it seemed she was the royal child of prophesy. We sent Kavenlow to find an infant to confuse the assassins, and after the first two babies perished, we sent your sister into hiding."

"I'm a *decoy*?" I exclaimed, feeling my face warm. "A moving target?" I looked at them as my disbelief whirled into outrage. "You're not even my parents?"

"Of course we're your parents," my mother protested. "We bought you honestly."

My breath seemed to freeze, and a wave of nausea swept me. I held my hands to my middle. Why hadn't Kavenlow told me? He had known, and never told me. I was a foundling? I was one of three, lucky enough to survive a prophesy that wasn't even mine to bear?

"We assumed the situation would ease, and we could bring her back and raise you together as proper sisters," my mother pleaded. "But things only worsened. Even to finding assassins among her suitors. We thought it prudent to wait until she was safely home before telling you so as to protect your sister while on the road, but between your impatience and Prince Garrett's early arrival . . ." Her hand reached out, and I drew away, unable to accept her touch.

Garrett was a blur of jerky motion at the edge of my sight as he paced. "Where's the princess?" He spun to a stop. "I was promised the Red Moon Princess. Where is she?"

My father stiffened at Garrett's callousness. "She is safe," he said coldly. "The chancellor has been sent this very afternoon to fetch her."

May heaven help me, I thought, going cold. It was true. And Kavenlow had known it. He had known and never told me. I felt betrayed, trapped. I wanted to run, but there was nowhere to go. It had all been a lie: the fancy dress, the privilege, *my entire life.* I was a beggar's unwanted child. I was bought and paid for. And Kavenlow, the only soul I trusted with my hidden wishes, had known it and let me live the lie, making myself into a fool.

My father stood between Garrett and me. "The joining of Costenopolie and Misdev will take place as planned in six months," he said firmly. "I apologize for your misunderstanding. There has been no intentional deception. You have a bride, Prince Garrett, the same you have been exchanging letters with this past year."

I felt I might pass out. I couldn't seem to get enough air. Who had gotten the letters I had written? Were the letters I had received in response even real?

Garrett's pacing came to an abrupt halt beside the pond. "Six months puts me on the wrong side of the shipping season," he muttered. "How far away is she?"

I stared, hearing but not understanding.

My mother's lips were pressed together, making her look severe and protective. "That is none of your concern," she said coldly. "Our chancellor is bringing her back directly."

"Who else knows?" Garrett said tightly. "Who knows this harlot is gutter trash?"

My eyes widened, and I gripped the arms of the chair. I was going to pass out. I knew it. My father's jaw clenched, and his round cheeks reddened. "Take care, Prince Garrett!"

"Who else?" Garrett exclaimed. "I have a right to know!"

My father was ramrod stiff. "Other than us and the crown princess? The chancellor."

"No one else?" he insisted, his brow furrowed. "Not even the people caring for her?"

"No," my mother said. "Chancellor Kavenlow told them nothing. The crown princess herself found out only recently of her true birth so she could properly answer your letters."

"I'm not the princess," I whispered as the nightmare forced itself into my reality.

"No, dear." My mother turned to me.

"I'm not going to marry Prince Garrett?" Somehow I sounded plaintive, as if it meant something. But there wasn't much left to my world at the moment, and I was trying to build on what I had. It was like making a castle with dry sand. Everything slipped away.

"No." Her eyes tightened. "And I thank God for that." Garrett's breath hissed in, and he spun. His smooth cheeks were spotted with red. My mother's face was grim with a repressed anger. "You speak like a snake, Prince Garrett," she said. "Your pleasantries are to lull the unsuspecting. You are far too eager to accelerate the marriage, couching it in a false concern for your bride. We will hold to our agreement of marriage, but I doubt if my body-born daughter will ever share a bed with you."

Clearly surprised, my father blinked. "Wife?"

"He calls Tess gutter trash," she said, gesturing angrily at Garrett. "He wants only the glory promised by the prophesy."

Garrett gripped the top of his sword, his knuckles white. "She *is* gutter trash! And you tried to pass her off as the Red Moon Princess. You wouldn't dare do that to my brother!"

Hand upon the hilt of his sword, my father stood before the man I almost wed, shaking in a repressed anger. "It would be best if you retired to your rooms, Prince Garrett. We will speak again tomorrow." His voice was frighteningly cold.

Garrett's fierce green eyes were unwavering from my father's. "As you say," he said. He turned to my mother. "Your Highness." Spinning on a heel, he strode up the walk to the door, his boots loud on the slate.

I sat in shock, blinking at nothing as his steps grew faint and vanished. My mother dropped her head into her hands and started to silently weep.

I'm not the princess?

Four

The creak of my outer door closing woke me. Eyes open, I stared into the dimness of the predawn dusk as Heather rustled about, trying to be quiet. A knot of worry loosened about me, and I stretched my feet downward to find the hot water bottle. Its warmth was all but gone, telling me as clearly as the lighter black outside my window that it was almost sunrise. Too early for me, but not for wandering, lustful members of my court.

A smile curled up the corners of my mouth. Heather was always sharp to spot a chance to escape the palace walls. As long as she didn't get pregnant, everyone would look the other way, and I enjoyed living vicariously through her. Reattaching buttons was a small price to pay for hearing how she had spent her evening. I just hoped she remembered what I had sent her for.

My flicker of anticipation died. I wondered if Heather would still like me after she found out I was a beggar's child.

"Heather?" I called, shame deciding for me that I wouldn't tell her until I had to. "What did you do, wait while the smith smelted the metal?"

There was a scrape of a foot on the floor inside my room, and I frowned. I could smell horse. That wasn't Heather.

Head throbbing with fear, I bolted upright, reaching for the knife under my pillow.

"Nuh-uh," a masculine voice said, and a thick hand gripped my shoulder in a painful pinch. A gasp of fear escaped me, and I struggled as the man swore and put a hand over my mouth, pinning me to the headboard. I froze, leaving my knife hidden when I heard the snick of steel against leather from a second man entering my room.

"There now, Princess," the man holding me said. "See, I tolds you she was a good girl. She only needs to know what's what."

The second man grumbled something, his black shadow shifting uneasily from foot to foot. My heart was pounding, and I was cold. Where were my guards? Why was I alone?

"Now," the first said, his moist fingers against my face stinking of mutton, "Prince Garrett sent us to fetch you. I can knock your pretty little head and carry you, or you can walk."

That was a choice? "Walk," I mumbled around his hand.

He eyed me in distrust, his grip on my shoulder tightening until I cried out.

"Clent," the second said, sounding worried. "Don't bruise her. He won't like it."

The fingers on me slackened, and he stepped back. My pulse raced, and my head throbbed. I wanted my knife, but it would be useless against swords. *Where are my guards?*

My face went slack, and my breath faltered. Garrett had taken the palace. He had enough men with him to take the palace! God help us . . . My parents . . .

The man standing over me gestured with his bare blade, and I scrambled out of bed before he reached for me. Stomach clenched, I drew myself up and forced my arms down from where I wanted to clutch them about myself in fear and cold. The second man motioned to the door, and I stumbled into motion. My thoughts were a sickening slurry as I went into my outer room, one guard before me, one behind. It was the first time I had ever felt imprisoned by swords, never having had them drawn against me instead of for my protection.

My nightdress wasn't enough to stop the dawn's chill from soaking into me as I paced the empty halls in my bare feet, becoming more afraid as I went. Most of the lamps had died, and faint calls and shouts echoed occasionally. We came into the main receiving room, as large and spacious as the banquet hall. You could get to anywhere from here, and I stared at a small archway beside the dais. *Please, no,* I thought. *Not the one leading to my parents' rooms.* My shoulders eased as the man before me went to the large archway leading to the solarium.

It was warmer past the heavy oak doors of the indoor garden, the moisture beading up on the inside panel. I could smell the night blooming vine my mother loved, mixing with the early roses. The damp air was a balm against my face. The sound of my father's voice raised in anger was both a relief and a fear. "Father," I whispered, darting round the first guard to reach him.

"Hey! Get her!" someone shouted.

I ran down the path to the glow of torches, jerked to a halt by a rough hand when I turned the corner of the path and found the fishpond. "Mother!" I cried in fear, struggling to push the hand about my arm away as the soldier who had caught me apologized to Prince Garrett. My mother was in the grip of a Misdev guard. *Angels save us.* There was a knife at her throat.

My attention flicked over the tiled patio. Garrett stood confidently with one foot upon the fishpond's retaining wall beside my game of thieves and kings. My mother was before him, looking small in her nightdress, pride in the set of her lips and the flash of her eyes. Two guards held my father. One had a bruise on his cheek and a cut lip. My father was sweating, straining against their restraint. His fear chilled me. I'd never seen my father afraid. It was quiet, with only the sound of water and the first twitters of caged birds. The sky beyond the glass was gray with the coming dawn. No one would hear us here. No one would see.

"Well," Garrett said as he pulled his foot down and straightened his uniform's coat. "Now we can start."

I said nothing, taking my cue from my parents. They looked vulnerable, pulled from their beds in their nightclothes with their hair rumpled and their faces bare. They were no longer a king and queen, showing only their deeper bond of husband and wife. I could see their love and fear for each other. And I knew Garrett could see it as well.

Garrett turned to my father. "I'm not going to be delicate about this. Tell me where the Red Moon Princess is, or I will cut her throat."

Shock took my breath away. "No!" I cried. I tried to break free, my knees buckling when the hand on me squeezed my arm with an unbearable pressure.

"Tess, no," my mother said, and the calmness of her voice pulled me back from the brink even as the knife under her ear glinted. "He won't do it. His father doesn't want a war with us."

Garrett blinked one eye at my father with a mocking slowness. "For once we are in agreement. My father is a coward. He and my brother. They'd quake in their boots if they knew what I was doing." He took a step to my father. "Where is the Red Moon Princess?"

My father went desperate. With a guttural groan, he fought to break free. The guards wrestled him to lie half upon the table, his arms pulled behind his back.

"I'm going to count from five," Garrett said, his breath fast as he came to stand before the table between my father and my mother.

"You won't," my father said, his face pinched as the guards kept him unmoving.

"Five," Garrett said, his hands on his hips and his back to my mother and me.

Chin against the table, my father sent his gaze over Garrett's shoulder to my mother. Desperation and fear showed from him. His breath came fast in indecision.

"Don't tell him, Stephen," my mother said, standing unafraid with a Misdev knife at her throat. The man holding her had wide, frightened eyes. His hands shook.

"Four." Garrett ignored her, fixed entirely on my father's fear.

"Don't tell. He won't do it." My mother's voice was strong.

Garrett stood unmoving. "Three."

My father's eyes shot from Garrett's to my mother's. "May?" he quavered, and the guards shifted to keep him down.

"Stephen. It's a bluff," she said, still calm.

"Two," Garrett said, the word short and clipped.

"May?" It was frantic with indecision.

"No, Stephen!"

"One."

The word was as devoid of emotion as the ones before. It settled heavy upon my ears. Garrett flicked his eyes to the guards and nodded.

I stood frozen as the Misdev guard ran his knife across my mother's neck with a silken sound. Her eyes widened. Red flowed, drenching her shoulder and side.

"Mother!" I shrieked, jerking into motion. Using nails and feet, I squirmed and twisted. I could hear my father's shouts, and Garrett's angry demand to hold him. The guard restraining me went to help them, and I ran to her, crumpled where the guard had dropped her.

"Mother!" I cried, falling to pull her head onto my lap. Her eyes were open, glazed.

"Tess," she whispered, her eyes unseeing. "Don't think—we didn't love you."

"Mother? Mother!" I looked down. There was so much blood between my fingers. I couldn't stop it. I couldn't stop it!

The tension eased from her, and she went slack. I looked up in delirium. My father was under a pile of guards. I could hear him angrily sobbing my mother's name over and over. Garrett stood over us. "This can't be real," I whispered. "This can't be happening."

Garrett's attention flicked down to me. He reached out, and before I knew what he was doing, he yanked me up from my mother. She slumped gracefully as if sleeping, her blood staining the moss between the flagstones. The white of my nightdress was crimson and warm. Garrett pushed me into the grip of one of his guards. "Her turn," he said softly.

"May," my father wept as the men pulled him to his feet. "May. You took my May."

Garrett strode forward and slapped my father smartly across the face. "And I'll take your gutter trull next if you don't tell me where the Red Moon Princess is."

A guard held me. Terrified, I looked at my father. His grief shone from him, beaten and overpowered. He slumped as the hands holding me tightened. "No," I whispered plaintively, too shocked to do more. My mother was dead. She had been alive, and now she was dead. The grief and loss in my father's eyes when he raised them to mine was like a blow to my middle. I struggled to find enough air.

I tried not to, but I cried out when the guard holding me put the knife, still red from my mother's throat, against mine. He stank of sweat and fear, and the knife trembled against me.

Garrett's smile broadened as my father hung unresisting. "She's at the nunnery on Bird Island," my father said, his voice cracking. "Damn you to hell. She's in the mountains on a peak called Bird Island. Leave Tess alone. Please . . . don't hurt my daughter."

Garrett leaned close, smug and confident. "Are you sure?"

"Yes!" my father shouted, beaten. "Yes. She's there. I swear it. Oh God, you took my May. She's gone." His head bowed to hide his eyes, and he slumped.

Garrett made a satisfied noise and motioned the guard to take the knife from me.

I took a shuddering gasp of air. My father pulled his eyes up. They met mine from under his mussed hair falling about his face. My only warning was the tightening of his jaw.

Crying in rage, my father struck at the guards. I broke free of the grip on me at my father's triumphant shout as he took another's sword and drove it deep into its previous owner.

"Run, Tess!" he shouted, magnificent as he fought the Misdev guards in his nightclothes. The softness I'd always seen was gone. He swung and parried, swirled and danced in a pattern of movement and sound given purpose and grace by the grief in his heart. His shouts were thundering vengeance, his blows carried the might of desperation of a loss never to be paid. He stood over his fallen love and fought as if mad, thinking only to assuage the pain in him. Three Misdev guards fell before him, and Garrett's brow furrowed.

"Father!" I shouted as a soldier he thought downed ran my father through from the back.

My father faltered. Horrified, I watched the second remaining soldier swing his sword in a smooth arc to land like an ax upon my father's neck. His breath escaping in a pained sound, my father reached upward. Blood flowed past his fingers. Face confused, he slumped from the table to the floor. His outstretched hand touched my mother, and he went still.

"No!" Garrett shouted, his beautiful face ugly with frustration. "You killed him! I needed him alive!"

"He attacked me, Prince Garrett," the man whined. "He killed Terrace."

"You bloody fool!" Garrett shouted, cuffing him with enough strength to send the man staggering. "He had to verify the true princess's birth!"

The man scrabbled backward, standing white-faced and shaking. The guard holding me tightened his grip. Heart pounding, I heard the distant sound of the door opening and feet on the path. Garrett scowled. Pulling me away from the guard holding me, he said, "Kill him."

The man who had murdered my father froze. His mouth opened and shut.

"Sorry, Kent," the soldier said, pulling his blade. "Better you than me."

Kent didn't even try to run. Falling to his knees, he whispered a prayer, his eyes fluttering closed, unable to watch.

I turned away, finding my head resting against Garrett's chest. I tried to shove him away, but he pulled me close. His breath caught as the sound of a sword meeting bone thunked through me. My eyes closed, and I thought I was going to vomit.

"His death is your fault," Garrett whispered, his breath moving my hair. "The last one there? He's dead, too. I can't use the real princess now. Who would believe me? Everyone who knows who you are is going to die. Congratulations. You're royalty again."

Horrified, I tried to break free. He held me tight, his strength far beyond mine. Sobbing, I stomped on his foot, and when his hand got too close, I bit it.

"Slattern!" Garrett exclaimed, shoving me at the remaining sentry.

I landed hard, crying out as the man brutally squeezed my arms. "Damn you, Garrett," I spat. Garrett's face showed a dark anger as he inspected his palm. It was his sword hand, and I had drawn blood. "I'll see more of your blood before I'm dead. *I promise you!*" The words raged from me, hot in vehemence. I couldn't look at my parents; I would collapse from the truth.

Garrett stepped close. Green eyes placid, he drew his arm back and swung the flat of his hand at me. His palm met my cheek with an explosion of hurt so unexpected I almost didn't recognize it as pain. I reeled and would have fallen had the last guard not been holding me.

"Keep her quiet," Garrett muttered as two guards came around the corner. Cheek burning, I gazed numbly at them, trying to make sense of it all. I couldn't.

The oldest paused as he took in the carnage, going ashen behind his salt-and-pepper beard. The other gave it only a brief glance. He was the only Misdev guard I'd seen who looked the part, being neither too old nor too young.

Taking off his overdone hat with long drooping black feathers, he stood beside the prince with a comfortable ease. He wore a black sash about his narrow waist that the other guards lacked, and I guessed he was the captain of Garrett's guards. He stood a good head taller than the prince, strong and broad of shoulders, in the prime of life.

"You said you weren't going to kill them," the captain said. His eyes lingered on me. I alone was unhurt in the room, the blood on my nightdress and hands clearly not mine. My eyes widened at the man's audacity.

"It was your men who did it," Garrett said tightly. "And I don't need a king or queen, only a marriage. We have the outer garrisons. In sixteen days, the rest of my men will be here, and we will have the town and harbor. Until then, we will hold the palace and continue as if nothing has happened. Do you think you can manage that—Captain Jeck?"

My eyes widened in understanding. Garrett was going to pass me off as the real princess. He was going to . . . He was going to kill Kavenlow!

Garrett flicked his fair hair from his eyes and frowned at the blood on his uniform's coat. "Have your men managed to find the last of the guards?" he asked as he took it off. Sweat stained his silk shirt underneath.

"Yes, Prince Garrett." It was a tight admission, and I could hear Jeck's frustration for having to take such abuse from someone so young.

Garrett's smile made a mockery of his handsome face. "Good. Something done right. Lock them in their own cells. They will be oarsmen when we need them."

I stood in shock. My betrothal plans had been nothing but a ruse. Garrett glanced at me and rubbed his bitten hand. "Has her room been searched?"

Jeck nodded. A part of me noticed his boots were as well-made as Garrett's, but heavier.

"Put her there," Garrett said. "And keep someone outside her door. I don't care if it's the Second Coming, there will be a guard on her. Is that clear, Captain?"

"Yes, Prince Garrett." Jeck's tone was heavy with repressed anger. "And the bodies?"

Garrett had moved to the game board, his breathing slowing as he took in the shifting of the pieces that had occurred. My father's careful plans to snag me had been destroyed, knocked askew in the slaughter. "Bury them in the gardens," he said as he tipped a piece upright onto the wrong square. "All of them."

My stomach twisted. Buried without markers, without rites.

"And, Jeck," Garrett said idly. "Have someone run down their chancellor. He's headed for a mountain peak called Bird Island." The prince nudged a pawn on the dividing line to sit dead center on a black square. "When he joins up with a woman with straight, fair hair, I want them, and anyone with them, killed."

"Yes, Prince Garrett."

My pulse quickened. I had known it, but to hear it said aloud made it terrifyingly real.

Garrett shifted to the opposite side of the board and reached for a black piece. "Knight takes pawn," he said, eying me as he removed the piece and set it aside.

"You're wharf slime," I said, knowing I would stay alive only as long as he needed me. "You're the muck we scrape from the bottom of our boats and throw into the chu pits. Starving wolves wouldn't eat you. Your insides will be drawn out through your nose. You—"

Taking three steps, Garrett closed the gap between us. My eyes widened, and I gasped when he pulled his sword. Panicking, I twisted to escape. The guard's grip on me jerked and went slack. I broke free and ran for the unseen door.

"Catch her!" I heard.

I fell, my feet pulled out from under me. Scrabbling violently, I twisted. The heel of my palm struck something. There was a pained grunt, and I was yanked to my feet. It was Jeck, the captain of the guard. The man held me up off the floor. My pulse hammered, and I froze as his grip bit painfully into my arms. This one would give me twice the hurt if I struggled.

There was a wet cough from the floor. My gaze darted from Jeck's eyes to the tiles. I took a frightened breath, unable to look away. The guard had dropped me because Garrett had run him through. The young sentry writhed on the floor, his blood washing the slate tiles as he struggled to rise with little gurgles, finally falling still.

"He was the best man I had!" Jeck exclaimed in frustrated anger. "Why?"

"I don't have to explain myself to you." A bright flush hid Garrett's freckles. "Get her to her room."

Jeck held me as Garrett wiped his sword clean and sheathed it. The Misdev prince walked past me without a glance, a frown twisting his youthful face into an ugly mask.

"Let me go!" I demanded when Jeck pulled me down the path in Garrett's footsteps. My fingers pried at his grip as Jeck pushed me stumbling through the door and into the hallway. It was quiet, with only one Misdev soldier standing guard. There was a soft shuffle as the old guard followed us out and closed the door to the solarium.

Garrett was disappearing around a corner, flanked by two of his own. I twisted, stomping on Jeck's foot. He grunted, his grip tightening on my arm. I went still. As his fingers loosened, I jammed my elbow into his gut, and his breath whooshed out. "Hold her," Jeck gasped, and the old guard grabbed my shoulders.

"Squirmy little thing, isn't she?" he said, then yelped when I lunged at him, only to be yanked back before I could reach his eyes. The third man laughed until Jeck barked at him to be silent.

As I fought to get free, Jeck wrenched my arms behind my back and bound my wrists with the black scarf he took from his waist. "Let me go!" I demanded, the pain from my shoulders making tears start. My hands were sticky from my mother's blood. It felt awful.

"Hold still," Jeck muttered, jerking me roughly around and flinging me over his shoulder.

Outraged, I kicked my bare feet at nothing. Jeck gave a little hop, resettling me as if I was a sack of salted fish. His shoulder cut into me, and I struggled for air. "Get the room cleaned," Jeck said tersely. "Bury the bodies in the garden. Make it deep enough so the dogs don't dig them up. I've got her all right."

"I said, let me—go," I wheezed, feeling my face redden as Jeck started down the hallway. "Put me down. You're a coward. A lackey for a spineless, gutless excuse of a man. Garrett is seaweed caught on my boat's keel. He'll kill you as quick as that soldier. He's a cur. A—"

Jeck turned the corner and shifted me from his shoulder to the floor. I made a tiny shriek as I slid from him, struggling to keep from falling while I found my balance. The hallway was empty, and I pressed against the wall in fear as Jeck stood before me. His arms were as strong and muscled as if he pulled nets all his life. His brown eyes were cold, and his jaw clenched under his closely cropped beard. He smelled like horse, and my mother's blood on my nightdress stained his shoulder. "Why did he kill my man?" he asked in a whisper.

"W-what?" I stammered, my fear faltering in surprise. He reached out, and a gasp slipped from me as he pinned me against the wall. The stones were cold on my back.

"Why did Prince Garrett kill my best swordsman?" he asked again.

My chin trembled. I wasn't the princess. If that became common knowledge, Garrett would kill me and use the real princess despite the problems of ill confidence it might instill.

Jeck saw my fear, and he jerked me up to push me back into the wall again. I bit my lip, refusing to cry out again as the stone hurt my shoulder. The man looked only a few years older than I was. He must be brutal to have gained captain so quickly.

"Tell me, Princess," he whispered, glancing down the empty hall. "King Edmund's second son is reckless. Ambitious, but reckless. I want to get out of this alive. If I like what I hear . . . I'll let you escape."

Hope warred with common sense. Hope won. "Prince Garrett killed him because he knew I wasn't the crown princess," I stammered.

Jeck's face went still. I felt three pounding heartbeats, and then he breathed, "The real one is on the road from Bird Island. The devil takes my soul. Who else knows?" I said nothing, and he shook me until my head snapped back. "Who else?" he demanded.

"The chancellor and the real princess," I blurted, frightened. I waited, hope making me hold my breath. He shook his head at my unspoken question. Despair took me. He wasn't going to let me go. "No! Please!" I begged as he bent, grasping me about the waist and flinging me over his shoulder again.

I cried and cursed, filling his ear with the foulest language I had overheard on the docks. He ignored me, not even puffing as he climbed the two flights of stairs to my apartments. There were two unfamiliar guards outside my room, and one held the door open. Jeck flung me onto the floor of my sitting room. I cried out as I hit the rug. The door slammed shut. Sobbing, I twisted and squirmed until I got my bloody, sticky hands free.

"Coward!" I shouted, flinging an empty pitcher at the door before I even rose. It shattered into six pieces. Running to the door, I locked it from the inside. I spun, looking over the empty room that was now my prison. There was nothing in it to help me. Giving up, I flung myself onto the couch and cried.

He had killed those I had called my parents. He was going to kill Kavenlow. And I was helpless to do anything about it.

Five

❖

Standing before my vanity mirror in my outer room, I tugged my skirt down over my narrow hips to try to make the hem meet the floor. The gray dress I had on was too short, but it and my red underskirt were the only things I could put on without Heather's help. My eyes closed at the reminder of her. I hoped she was safe with her young man beyond the walls. The front gates weren't visible from my window, but what I could see of the grounds looked normal, as did the streets. It seemed as if no one was even aware the palace had been taken over.

Slumping, I sat on the chair before the mirror with my elbows on the vanity—waiting. The night air pooled in my room, making goose bumps. I didn't care. Pulling my gaze up, I found my eyes red-rimmed and miserable-looking in the light from the fire. My stomach growled, and I turned away, angry that my body went on while my soul had died. Earlier today, I'd thrown the meal the Misdev guard brought me out the window lest it be poisoned. In hindsight, I probably could have chanced it. Garrett needed me alive until he was sure Kavenlow wouldn't be showing up with the real princess.

"Kavenlow," I whispered harshly, feelings of betrayal making my shoulders tense. He had known I was a foundling and never told me. The chancellor had been more available than my parents, in essence raising me as he filled my days with diversions when no one else had the time. *And his devotion had been a lie,* I thought bitterly. I had trusted him, loved him as a second father. I couldn't be angry with my parents. They were dead. The blood pounded in my head as I held my breath. I wouldn't cry. It had taken me all afternoon to stop the first time.

Hand shaking, I reached for my brush. My day spent wallowing in self-pity had left my cheeks blotchy and my hair a tangled mat. I welcomed the sporadic jabs of pain as I yanked the brush through my curls. It reminded me I could feel something other than grief and betrayal.

My reflection gray from the dusk, I began methodically arranging my hair. It seemed likely I would be dining with Garrett; I had a few extra preparations. Sniffing in a very unladylike manner, I piled my curls atop my head, binding the topknot together with a black ribbon. I wished I had a black dress to match it. Gingerly letting the arrangement go, I pulled my hairpin cushion close and plucked one of my decorative darts from it. I glanced at my door before I touched the flat of it to my tongue. Immediately it went numb. Satisfied the venom was still potent, I tucked the needle into my topknot.

I had never defended myself with my darts before, but I knew firsthand what the venom did to me. Kavenlow had spent the last seven years conditioning me to it until I hardly noticed when I accidentally pricked myself. The convulsions and nausea had been frightening and painful until I passed out, leaving me ill and weak for days until my body developed the ability to throw the poison off quickly. Even now my left leg turned sluggish when I was tired. I had risked death every time. More proof I was an expendable pawn even to Kavenlow, bought to keep the real princess safe. Angels save me, I was a fool.

I continued arranging my hair, finding only four needles from yesterday were still good. The last had chipped and gone dry. I threw it into my sitting room fire, nudging the remnants of my nightgown stained with my mother's blood into the flames. I had tried to wash, but with only a small pitcher of water, I still had a tacky residue on my hands and legs. I refused to look at my trembling fingers, knowing ugly black stains still lingered in the cracks of my skin.

Jaw gritted to seal away my grief, I closed my empty jewelry box. Garrett's guards had looted my room, finding not only my jewelry but also my bullwhip, the knife under my pillow, the handful of unadorned darts I used for practice, and the rope I used to sneak out my window when the moon was full and I wanted to walk in the garden.

I stood before the fire and fingered my dart pipe, wondering if it might be recognized as a weapon and lead to my hairpins being confiscated as well. Unwilling to chance it, I snapped the wooden tube in half and threw it into the fire. I'd have to get close enough to scratch Garrett. I didn't think it would be a problem. I was sure he would be here soon—gloating.

An unexpected pain prompted me to close my eyes. *They weren't my real parents,* I told myself. They used me, bought me in the village like a horse or dog. But even as I thought it, I knew whether bought or born, I had been their child. And they had loved me.

My throat closed in on itself, and I forced myself to breathe. Garrett had killed them. Tonight, I would return the favor, sending Garrett's body back to his father with my regrets, blaming it upon the assassins who plagued us. Kavenlow might suspect what had really happened, but I didn't care. The tears pricked, seducing a headache into existence as I refused to cry. I had thought Kavenlow loved me. It was all a lie. Everything.

My threatened tears vanished at the sound of a key in my lock. I spun, frightened, as Jeck strode in unannounced. Past him in the torchlit hallway were two sentries. He tucked the key into an inner pocket. "Your Highness," the imposing, square-shouldered man drawled, and my heart pounded.

"Knock before you come into my rooms," I demanded as I wiped the back of my hand across my eyes. "I may be a prisoner in my own palace, but I'm still the princess." I took a false strength in that he would have to treat me as such even though he knew the truth.

"My mistake," he said and smiled. It looked like an honest reaction, and I wasn't sure what to make of it. His gaudy hat with the excessive drooping feathers was missing, and I thought he looked better without it. "Prince Garrett has requested your presence for dinner," he continued, standing with his hands behind his back at parade rest. "I'll carry you if you refuse. You may want to walk, though. He's undoubtedly going to propose, and you'll want to look your best." He hesitated, his brow furrowing. "Don't you have anything nicer than that to wear?" he asked.

My mouth dropped open—part anger, part embarrassment. "Perhaps if the Misdev dog gave me my court, I could manage a decent appearance," I said stiffly. "Tell him if he wants a proper princess, he will have to supply me with the trappings. He should check with his guards first, seeing as they stole my jewelry."

A smile quirked the corners of Jeck's mouth, then was gone. "Prince Garrett has your baubles," he said. "Tell him yourself."

He reached for my shoulder, and I jerked back. Annoyed, he reached out again, gripping my shoulder with a painful strength through his soft leather gloves. My affront that he dared touch me warred with common sense, and I did nothing as he turned so the guards in the hallway couldn't see his face. "I also found a knife under your pillow, darts, a whip, and enough rope to tie down a bull," he murmured, a blatant question in his soft voice and brown eyes. They were the color of earth in the candlelight, with flecks of gold. "It's unusual for a princess to know the art of defense," he breathed, sending a loose strand of my hair to tickle my neck.

"But I'm not a princess, now, am I?" I whispered, my heart pounding as I shrugged out of his grip.

"So I've been told." A wary tone had darkened his voice, and he rested his hand upon the butt of his sword as he gave me a visual once-over. "Out," he demanded.

I draped the same black scarf that he had used to tie my hands with earlier over my shoulders like a shawl of grief, blew out my candle, and went before him. The way was darker than usual, with only every other lamp lit. We passed no one as Jeck and two sentries escorted me through the silent passages, and it felt cold. I walked beside Jeck, wondering why he asked the two sentries to slow when it was obvious I was having trouble keeping to their pace. He knew I wasn't the princess. Why did he bother with any kindness?

I was getting the distinct impression that Jeck didn't care if Garrett succeeded in his plans to take my mother's lands or not. It seemed as if Jeck was waiting, riding the waves until he knew which way the wind was going to shift. *Waiting for Garrett to make a mistake?*

My mind whirled as we passed from the corridor into the formal banquet hall. It echoed with a high blackness, but a warm yellow light spilled into the spacious room from the small dining room between it and the kitchen. Jeck took my elbow, his grip tightening when I tried to pull away. "Stop touching me," I demanded, and my face burned when he outright ignored me.

We entered to find the room empty but for the long table. There were only two chairs—one at either end instead of the usual three clustered in the middle—and a wave of grief almost buckled my knees. With more grace than I would've credited him, Jeck guided me to a chair and made me sit before the elaborate place setting. I was too upset to be amused that I didn't have a table knife. And sitting with my back to the archway to the kitchen instead of the hearth made me uneasy.

"I'll stay," Jeck said to the guards who had accompanied us. He shifted a step away from me and fell into a parade rest. "I want Olen as Prince Garrett's escort, then you're relieved."

The two sentries left the way we had come. Looking over the familiar room, a pang of heartsickness settled heavy in my middle. This was where I had eaten most of my meals with my parents. The room had no windows but was bright with oil lamps. Sitting between the kitchen and the large banquet hall, it served as a staging area for food on the occasions we had a large function. There was a fireplace we used in the winter. Right now the ugly black hole of the empty hearth was hidden behind one of the ceiling-to-floor tapestries that softened the room.

Jeck stood with a relaxed tautness, his well-honed body held still while thoughts unknown occupied him. I watched his square jaw alternately tense and relax, and I wondered if he would leave when Garrett came so I could kill the Misdev cur with no interference. "Are you the captain of Garrett's guard?" I asked suddenly.

Jeck shifted, seeming surprised that I had broken my silence. "I act in that position."

"What else do you do?" I persisted, hearing the lack of completeness in his words.

"Keep him alive when he does something foolish," he muttered.

Nodding, I shifted my empty wineglass to the proper side of my plate. He was charged with Garrett's safety just as Kavenlow had been charged with mine. Garrett had said he was acting without the blessing of his father. Perhaps Jeck might be open to working against Garrett's interests in order to maintain his king's? Starting a war with your neighbor is not undertaken lightly, and embarrassing if your son does it without your knowledge.

"Jeck," I said, hesitating as I fumbled for the proper term of respect. "Captain," I added. "I don't have the luxury of time to be delicate. Are you King Edmund's man, or his son's?"

There was a creak of leather as he looked at me, then away. "You are a nosy woman."

My boot tapped silently under my skirt. "I won't sit idly by and let Costenopolie fall to Prince Garrett," I said as I turned the plate so the pattern was right side up.

Jeck made a puff of amusement. "Prince Garrett's chances of success are excellent. And you have overestimated your reach, Princess. I'm charged by my king to protect his son. I'll kill you before I let you harm him."

It wasn't a boast—it was a simple statement—but I was too drained to be afraid. My eyes rose at the soft cadence of boots in the banquet hall. Garrett entered, accompanied by the old sentry from this afternoon. *Three men,* I thought as the older man took up a position behind Garrett. I had four needles—two of which would be needed to kill Garrett. The odds were not slanted enough in my favor.

I was shocked to find myself thinking Garrett looked all the more handsome. He entered the room with a poise and confidence that hid the ugliness of his true nature. His fair hair had been slicked back, and his jawline was firm. Moving with a predatory grace, his every motion screamed of his comfortable expectation of supremacy. But then I noticed his riding boots gave him more height than he deserved. And when he met my eyes with a cold distaste, my impression of him reversed from a powerful man to a spoiled child.

Garrett's brow rose mockingly as he took in my subdued attire and black shawl. He had changed into a more decorative uniform. Gold glittered from his sleeves and collar, and I wondered if they were my father's adornments. *Yes, my father,* I thought as grief pulled my eyes down. My entire life was a lie, but they had been my parents, and I would have my justice.

"Princess Contessa," Garrett said with no emotion. He went to the far seat, not bothering to take my hand in greeting as I deserved and so denied me the pleasure of kicking his shin. "How gracious of you to join me for dinner," he added as he shook out his napkin and sat.

I let mine lay where it was. I had no intention of eating, starving though I was.

"Olen, tell the cook we're ready," Garrett prompted irately, as if his sentry should know the niceties of polite dining as well as how to split an opponent with three strokes. My pulse hammered as the old guard went into the kitchen passage behind me. Two men; four darts. Olen would be back. I had to get Garrett alone. My foot under my dress jiggled nervously.

"Silent?" Garrett said, and my eyes flicked to his. "Good," he said as he poured a glass of wine for himself. "Stay that way."

I stilled my foot. "You are a cur," I said softly, knowing my words would carry in the small room. "I'm going to send you home in a box. There will be holes for flies. By the time you get to your father, he will see as clearly as I the maggots that infest you."

Garrett sipped his drink, his amused gaze going from mine to Jeck's. The captain shifted himself closer to me. His leather-gloved hand rested upon his sword hilt.

"I like you better silent," Garrett said.

"Your father will thank me," I predicted. "He sent you to marry into my family's blood, not destroy it. He won't like you altering his plans." Garrett's pale face colored, and I guessed I had found a sore spot. "Second sons are always a problem," I added, and he clenched his jaw. There was a scuff behind me, and I stiffened as Olen returned.

"It will be a few moments, Prince Garrett," the guard said as he took up his spot again.

"Good." Garrett's once-beautiful green eyes were ugly, and his smooth cheeks were red with anger. "I've something for you." He rose from his chair and set his napkin aside. My stomach tightened as he approached, and my fingers trembled at the chance to dart him. My eyes flicked to Jeck. He was watching closely, and I forced my breathing to slow.

Garrett took a handful of green, purple, and silver from his pocket. I recognized the familiar sound of sliding stones and metal as jewelry. I held deathly still as Garrett went behind me. I stifled a shudder as my scarf slid from me like water to make a black puddle upon the floor. He draped a necklace in its place. Green and purple stones so dark as to be almost black decorated it, making an obscene show of privilege. It was extravagant and heavy with wealth. My proposal gift. "That's for you," he said as he stepped away. "Now we can wed."

"Why a wedding?" I said, refusing to look at it. "You have what you want."

"By force," he admitted as he resettled himself in his chair. His elbows went on the table, and he leaned forward, looking entirely reasonable and pleasant. "I want it legally, as well. I won't leave an opening for my father to take my kingdom to add to his own. I will prove to him that I'm more worthy than my brother. Once the rest of my men get here, I will secure your ships and harbors. You will be coronated shortly after that, followed by our marriage."

"Then my death?" I said caustically, though I was shaking inside.

His face was sickeningly indifferent. "That's up to you."

"My parents are dead," I said, making my words harsh so I would feel nothing. "Do you think no one will notice?"

"Oh, I expect them to." He picked up his table knife and idly balanced it upon the tip of a finger. "I have their crowns, and that is what makes a sovereign." He smiled. "That and one's birth. But you know all about that, don't you? The survivors are the ones who write the history books. What does it matter to the common man who sits on the throne?" He set the knife down. "No one will care, Princess, as long as the goods keep moving."

Disgusted, I undid the necklace's clasp and threw the jewelry across the room. It hit the floor in a pile of glittering stone and metal. The old sentry behind Garrett shifted. Jeck never moved, quietly watching. Thin lips tight, Garrett rose to retrieve it. "How long you live after we consummate our marriage is up to you. There will be no children. You won't be allowed to carry them to term."

He paced the length of the table to me, his anger hidden but for the sharpness of his steps. Jeck was poised as Garrett replaced the necklace. I kept my hands in my lap with a white-knuckled strength. I'd never dart all of them. I had to get Garrett to make them leave.

"If you are troublesome I'll feed you to your dogs," Garrett whispered in my ear from over my shoulder. "Be agreeable, and I'll simply treat you like one."

My breath came and went. *Anger,* I thought, my hands beginning to sweat in their tight grip. Garrett was reckless when he was angry. If I could make him angry, he would want to remind me I was a guttersnipe. He couldn't do that properly unless the sentries left, especially his more valuable captain.

The beginnings of an idea set my heart to hammer. I waited until he sat down and took up his wine before I yanked the necklace off, snapping through the clasp. It reached the wall this time. There was a crack of a jewel breaking.

Garrett's face reddened. "Gutter trull," he snarled, standing so quickly his chair scraped against the stone floor. "You broke it!"

"Princess," I insisted, making the word as imperialistic as I could. "Put that on me again, and I'll toss it into the harbor's chu pits the first chance I get."

"It would suit you better then, wouldn't it," he said, his perfect hair shifting out of place.

"Look at you," I mocked. "Coming to the table smelling of horse and with dust on your boots. You're nothing but an unwanted extra son to be sold for your father's gain."

"Shut your mouth!" he cried, his refined voice harsh.

"Don't speak to me in that tone," I demanded. "I am Your Highness or Princess."

Garrett crossed the room in tight strides. "You two, get out," he said to the guards, but his eyes were on me. His fingers were trembling, and his freckles were lost behind his red face.

My pulse raced, and I worked to keep victory from my eyes. "Second son," I goaded. "Worthless but for what a *woman* can give him."

"Leave us," Garrett said through gritted teeth. "I have a few words of love I wish to speak to my bride, and I am—shy."

Olen edged to the door, but Jeck stood firm. Garrett took his murderous eyes from mine. "I said leave!" he demanded.

"Prince Garrett, I'm against this. She is—"

"A woman!" Garrett said, spitting the words. "Get out."

"This is a mistake—"

Garrett stiffened. "Get—out," he repeated. "Don't contradict me again."

A muscle near Jeck's eye twitched. I stiffened as he moved, not to the door, but to me.

"What are you doing?" Garrett exclaimed as Jeck took a cord from his pocket and began binding my unresisting hands in my lap.

"Securing her before I go, Prince Garrett." His words were clipped and seethed with frustration. I could smell his sweat of repressed anger as his one hand gripped both my wrists.

"*Get out!*" Garrett shouted, cuffing the larger man. His raised voice brought a Misdev guard from the kitchen, looking awkward wearing an apron in his new role of cook. "I don't need a woman tied up before me. Get out before you're whipped!"

I shivered, though the anger in Jeck's eyes wasn't directed at me. The cord slipped from my wrists and disappeared into Jeck's pocket. The guard from the kitchen eased back into hiding, and the old sentry stood uncomfortably by the archway to the banquet hall.

"Prince Garrett," Jeck said flatly, "my apologies." He turned on his heel and left with Olen going first. I didn't watch him leave. I couldn't. If Jeck recognized the victory in my eyes, I knew he would risk a whipping and stay. The sound of Jeck's thick boots was loud in the banquet hall, and I swore I heard the painful thump of something, or someone, hitting the wall.

"His father was a farmer," Garrett said scornfully. "The breeding always shows."

"Oh," I said lightly. "Your mother ran on all fours, did she?"

Garrett lunged, grabbing my arm and pinching it painfully. "You may want to shift your grip higher," I taunted, ignoring the hurt. "Most of my dresses show my arm there. It would be a shame to leave a bruise for everyone to see."

"Beggar's get!" he said, yanking me out of my chair, and forcing my back onto the table. "You're my play-pretty," the prince said, his beautiful face ugly. "Nothing more. Irritate me, and I'll hurt you. Even a queen is alone from time to time, and you will be alone more than most, stupid woman."

My eyes narrowed, my arm a flaming agony where he was gripping it. "Are you through?" I said, and his green eyes became choleric. He yanked me up. I reached for a needle. I jammed it into his chest.

Garrett stumbled back, releasing me. "Slattern!" he cried,

plucking out the dart and throwing it to the floor. "I'll beat you myself for that!"

I scrambled sideways along the table as he grabbed for me. But his stance wavered. Face ashen, his hesitated. He met my expectant expression in horror, realizing the needle was more than decoration. His mouth opened, and he clutched at his chest. He made a strangled moan. I watched, shocked and horrified at how fast he crumpled to the floor.

Heart pounding, my gaze darted from one empty archway to the other. *How much time?* I thought as I knelt by the convulsing prince. "You're a Misdev dog," I whispered, knowing from experience he would remember everything until he passed out. "You're foolish and ambitious, and your father will thank me for ridding him of such a dangerous combination."

"N-n-n-n-n," Garrett stammered, his eyes rolling back and his limbs jerking. Foam caught at the corners of his mouth. He was terrified, and rightly so. Not knowing if you would be able to stop jerking long enough to take a clean breath was enough to make one insane. I wiped the sweat of remembered fear from my hands, glad when he passed out, his limbs going slack and still.

"Cur," I muttered, feeling ill as I rolled him over so I could see his shoulder. Pulling another needle from my topknot, I lifted his collar. I'd take his life as easily as a rabbit's.

"Prince Garrett," came Jeck's voice from the banquet hall. There was the sound of boots.

I took a panicked breath. Jeck crashed into me, knocking me from Garrett. The scent of horse filled my senses. I jammed the dart into Jeck where his jerkin parted to show skin.

"Damn," I heard him pant, but his grip tightened instead of falling from me as expected. He pinned me to the floor. My arm was still free, and I scrambled for another dart. Why wasn't he going down!?

Panicking, I scratched his neck with the new dart to leave a trail of blood. His fingers went slack. My breath whooshed out as his deadweight fell upon me. His breath came in a quick heave. I could feel the beginnings of tremors in him.

I frantically shoved him off me, already gripping my last dart. Crouched, I waited a breathless moment, then gathered my skirts and crept to the archway. I peeked around the corner to find the dining hall empty and dark. Satisfied no one had heard, I turned.

Garrett was unconscious, but Jeck wasn't. Not only was he still awake, but he had pulled himself into a sitting position against the wall. He watched me through eyes weaving in and out of focus. His large body mass wasn't enough to explain how he could ward off the effects of two darts. He must have a shade of immunity, and I wondered where he had gotten it. The look in his eyes made it clear he knew I was going to kill his prince.

Shaking inside, I went over to where Garrett lay. I crouched and brushed aside a fold of cloth to show skin not yet toughened by age, still freckled and smooth. He was no older than I was. My fingers trembled. I had never taken anyone's life.

I was suddenly sickened. My eyes closed as revenge bitterly cried for justice. "He killed my parents," I whispered, trying to become angry. Garrett shuddered, unconscious. I cursed my indecision, my weakness. He deserved death for what he had done.

"No," I said with a frantic exhalation and pulled away. Killing him now was a mistake. Garrett's men had the palace and outer garrisons. Unless I had control of the palace, King Edmund would descend upon me in retaliation, finishing what his son started. I couldn't retake the palace alone. I needed help.

My eyes rose, and my stomach churned. I needed the chancellor. I needed Kavenlow.

Tucking my last dart back into my topknot, I went to Jeck. He was shivering from the venom. I was impressed; he ought to be dead. He watched me, his eyes showing pain but no fear, waiting to see which way the wind would blow. "I won't make my people go to war over a stupid man's death," I whispered. "I'm leaving to get help, not fleeing—and I'm giving Garrett the chance to escape. Tell your king I spared his son's life once. I'll kill him if he is still in my palace when I return." I glanced to the kitchen at the sound of the cook coming up the passage.

"But you—aren't—the Red Moon Princess," Jeck grunted, his mustache twitching as he forced the words past his lips.

He was right, and I blinked. I'd forgotten. I leaned close, knowing I only had a moment. "I am now," I said, shoving him over and making sure he had a good view of the wall.

A sound of outrage slipped from me as I saw the hilt of my bone knife showing from behind the hem of his jerkin. "That's mine!" I said, taking it in a flash of self-righteous anger.

It was light in my grip, but I felt safer for having it, paltry as it would be against a sword. Garrett's necklace I left where it was. I didn't want anything he had touched, and selling it would only start a trail to me.

The glow of approaching lights in the large hall brought my head up. "Chu pits!" I swore under my breath. This was not what I needed. I looked frantically at the kitchen passage. The cook was coming. I had nowhere to go. My eyes lit upon the covered fireplace.

I dove for it, settling the tapestry behind me with a silent prayer that no one would see the soft movement. I had hidden here a score of times while playing hide-and-seek as a child. I crouched, trying to slow my breathing. *Hide-and-seek,* I thought as the cook entered and shouted for help. Only this time, my life hung on the outcome.

Six

I heard the cook's boots falter. Stooping, I found the thin spot in the tapestry I'd made as a child. The peephole was lower than I recalled, and my knees complained. The scent of old ash tugged at me, threatening to tickle into a sneeze. I held my breath, stomach tight with tension.

"Guards!" the cook cried, retaining the presence of mind to slide the tray onto the table before lurching to Garrett. "He's alive," he whispered as he bent low over his prince. Jeck lay slumped beside him, ignored. I couldn't help but shirk back from the curtain when Olen and three sentries clattered into the room with drawn swords.

"Here," the cook called. "Get him up. Help me get him up! Up off the floor."

"We were only gone a moment!" Olen said as all five lifted Garrett to lay him prone on the table. The tray of food was almost pushed onto the floor. "Where's the princess?"

My legs trembled, and I tried to swallow as the soldier-turned-cook spun. His hand slapped his sword where it hung over his apron. "She didn't come through the kitchen! I swear it!"

Please, I thought, *don't look for me here.*

Olen pointed to the youngest of the three guards. "You," he

demanded, "roust the guard to find her." The sentry ran from the room, and I felt dizzy from relief. Olen knelt by Garrett. "Give me the wine. Let's get some of it into him."

"No wine," came a thin croak, and my gaze darted to where Jeck lay. "He might choke on it," he said, shifting himself upright on an elbow.

"Captain!" Olen said, his expression easing as he went to help him. "What happened?"

My stomach quivered. I was impressed. Jeck had more willpower than I had ever seen in a man. His clearing gaze darted over the room as he dragged himself into a chair. I clutched my dagger in one hand and my needle in the other, but he never looked at the tapestry.

Garrett's breath turned into heavy wheezes. Jeck leaned across the table to tilt the prince's head to the side. It was none too soon, as Garrett vomited, covering the table and floor with his last meal. I swallowed hard, forcing back my own gorge at the smell.

"Clean that up," Jeck said, taking control of the situation though he couldn't yet stand. The cook vanished into the kitchen. "He's going to live," Jeck said to Olen. Brow glistening with sweat, Jeck reached for Garrett's wine, gulping it.

"What happened?" Olen asked again as he refilled the glass with a shaking hand.

Jeck took a slow breath as if relishing the ability to do so. "She poisoned him."

Olen stiffened. "Poison!"

Jeck nodded, his face pale under his tan. "She must have had it on her when I searched her room." Jeck went still, and I could almost see his thoughts. *What else had he missed?* I wondered for him, my eyes narrowing in satisfaction.

The cook returned with a bucket and scented candle. He slopped up the mess as two guards tended to Garrett: loosening his clothing, wiping the vomit from his face, generally accomplishing nothing as the prince struggled to regain consciousness. His hands ineffectively tried to push them away. "She vanished into air," one of the guards said, his face drawn. "She didn't come through the kitchen or the hall!"

"Fool," Jeck said harshly as he took a swallow of wine. "She's just faster than you." He set the glass down as Garrett started to cough, his entire body shaking.

"Help him up," Jeck ordered, and Garrett was pulled into a sitting position atop the table. The prince looked repulsive, pale and vomit-strewn, still shivering from the venom. A swollen bruise was on his upper chest where the dart had punctured his skin. He would probably wear it for days, and I knew the use of his left arm might be impaired even longer.

"Where is she?" Garrett panted, his bloodshot green eyes weaving in and out of focus.

Olen stood at a stiff attention, worry clear in his wrinkled face. "We're looking—"

"Find her!" Garrett cried. He hunched into himself as his shout instigated a violent cough. Pushing the fumbling guards away, he rolled into a chair.

Garrett and Jeck were sitting at the same table, and my eyebrows rose. There was a heartbeat of silence before Jeck lurched to his feet. The large man leaned heavily on the table. "You and you," he said, pointing at two guards. "Escort Prince Garrett to his rooms. Keep the fire high. Stay with him. He may convulse again."

I nodded a hidden agreement. Garrett was coming out of it too fast not to have a relapse.

Jeck took another gulp of wine. "Olen, pull everyone not guarding the palace's sentries. Search from the walls inward. No telling how far she's gone. Keep the interior of the garden walls manned. Don't give them torches. They'll ruin their night vision."

"Yes, Captain."

Jeck's voice was steady and unhurried, seeming to make the air in my chest tremble. Garrett moaned and doubled in pain. My eyes narrowed in satisfaction. I'd done well letting him live. Death would have been merciful. When I did kill him, it would be painful. My eyes closed as I remembered the warmth of my mother's blood on my hands and the fear in my father's voice. I would make it painful. I would make him hurt.

"Get off of me!" Garrett protested as two guards tried to lift him. His words were badly slurred, and his eyes were glassy. "Get your—filthy—hands—off me!" The sentries backed up, too inexperienced to know what to do. "I want that whore now!" he demanded, focus wavering.

Jeck put his hands behind his back and straightened. His face was drawn, but it had already regained its normal color. His immunity couldn't have been an accident, and that worried me. "We're looking, Your Highness," he said. "I have set up a perimeter—"

"Worthless farmer!" Garrett shouted, startling me. I jumped, my shoulder bumping into the black stones. "You let her poison me! I'd be safer with a chu slinger."

Jeck's jaw clenched, and he stared fiercely at a spot over Garrett's shoulder.

"Who searched her room?" Garrett asked, his voice virulent and his head weaving.

"I did, Prince Garrett," Jeck said tightly.

A tremor shook Garrett as the venom began reasserting control. "Get me a whip," the prince said. No one moved. "I want a whip!" he shouted, lurching to his feet.

My mouth fell open as Olen strode out. Garrett was going to flog Jeck? I felt ill. I'd never witnessed a flogging, but I'd seen their aftermath in the streets.

The two young guards approached Jeck, backing off at the murderous look he gave them. Motions abrupt and short, Jeck removed his leather jerkin. It hit the table beside the cooling tray of food. His black linen shirt was next, but this he carefully folded. He stood directly before me with the table between us. I stared wide-eyed, blinking.

I had been raised as a princess. Was I chaste? Of deed, perhaps, but not thought. I had stolen my share of kisses and caresses in dark corners at elaborate functions when the laughter flowed and the music played. Usually the young nobleman was more inexperienced than I, anxious and stammering. Worried about being caught. Worried about not being caught. Worried about that damned prophesy. Even so, I was not such an innocent that the sight of a bare torso would fluster me. But Jeck . . . I swallowed and held my breath.

Burning chu pits. The man is magnificent. His shoulders were marred with old white scars, but they were as strong and smooth as the blacksmith's. His skin was dark from the sun, looking like well-oiled wood as his muscles bunched and eased as he moved. I could see every line that ran down his abdomen to vanish beneath his trousers. His power was clearly born from long hours with a blade. No longer hidden behind the disguise of clothing, his every movement possessed the unconscious grace of a predator. He was beautiful. And I'd never seen his like.

Olen returned and apprehensively extended a short black-stained whip to Garrett. The prince snatched it, his expression ugly. "Hold him down," he demanded.

Jeck shook his head, his hands clenched as he leaned over the table and braced himself. My eyes followed a puckered scar cutting a ragged path across his side. It hadn't healed as well as the others. There was a faint red mark on his chest where my dart had found him.

"Let me remind you," Garrett said as he staggered to stand behind him. "You are here to keep me *alive*!"

He swung the whip at his last word. It met Jeck's back with a crack. I jumped, startled. Jeck tensed, his eyes staring straight ahead at the tapestry. It was as if he was looking at me, and I backed up from the musty fabric. Olen reached to catch Garrett as he stumbled, thrown off balance by his swing.

"It's the only reason you are *here*!" the prince said. The whip descended, the blow harder this time. Jeck's eyes narrowed as his anger grew. My mouth went dry, and I bit my lip.

"Another lapse," Garrett said, "and you'll be chained with the slave detail, Captain *Jeck*!"

The prince nearly fell as the whip met Jeck again, the poison's effects returning. Olen caught him, and Garrett hung in his grip, his face white. "Find her. Bring her to me," he panted.

Garrett threw the uncoiled whip at Jeck's back. I started as it hit him and slid to the floor. "Finish whipping him," Garrett rasped. "Do it properly."

They weren't done? I thought in horror.

I didn't move as Garrett was all but carried out by a sentry. Olen looked at the remaining guard, then Jeck. "He's going to kill us, Captain," he said softly. "Taking a palace with boys and old men? We're spread too thin, and what we have are poor soldiers at that. Half-trained and better at guiding a plow or chopping vegetables than to stand where you tell them."

"He gave you an order," Jeck said. His voice was low with a barely leashed anger.

Olen edged the whip away from Jeck's boots before bending to pick it up. Taking Garrett's place, he pulled his arm back and swung, grunting with the effort. The leather hit Jeck with a loud, soul-breaking crack. My air hissed in, my hand going to my mouth. It was nothing like Garrett's blows. Jeck's head jerked, and his eyes bulged at the sudden, real pain.

Taking no pause, Olen swung again. Garrett had been weak from the venom; Olen was not. He was using all his strength to drive the cord into Jeck's flesh. It came away red with blood. My pulse pounded, and I watched, horrified but unable to look away.

A third strike, and Jeck grunted. His grip on the table went knuckle-white. The muscles in his neck became cords. His teeth showed as he gritted them. My eyes went hot with tears.

I looked away at the fourth strike, unable to watch Jeck's eyes glaze with pain. So it was that I only heard the fifth strike and Jeck's groan. I was shaking, holding a hand over my mouth to keep still. *It wasn't my fault. It wasn't.* How could someone do that to a person?

"Five strikes, Captain," Olen said somberly. There was a hesitation, then, "Get the surgeon."

"Wait." It was a breathy exhalation, and I looked through the tapestry, my eyes wet. Jeck lowered himself into a chair. He put his elbows on the table and leaned forward to keep his back from touching anything. "Put someone in Prince Garrett's rooms. I don't care if he threatens to have us burned alive. He's going to have a relapse. The venom isn't out yet."

"Captain?" the young guard questioned as he gingerly coiled up the whip.

"Go," Jeck said. He took a slow breath. "And put a guard outside the chancellor's room immediately. No one in or out. Send the surgeon to wait for me there."

"Yes, Captain." Olen nodded, and the two left.

Kavenlow? I wondered. Why was Jeck interested in a chancellor?

The room grew quiet as the sound of their boots in the banquet hall diminished. Sharp and bitter, the smell of vomit and blood mixed with the scent of cooked meat and the ash in the flue. Over it all was the candle the cook had brought in, adding pine and rosemary to the mix.

Jeck's head lifted. His face was haggard, but his eyes were intent. He was listening.

Blood humming in my ears, I eased back from the musty

tapestry, my grip on the dagger going sweaty. I was sure he could hear my pounding heart. Only cloth separated us.

"You should have killed him, Princess," he said, and I froze, panicking. Slowly Jeck levered himself up, his eyes on the table. My pulse slowed at his vacant stare. He was talking to himself. "You should have killed either him, or me, or both. I will wring your neck myself before I give you the chance to harm him again."

I held my breath as a wave of vertigo took me. *Don't find me. Don't.*

Jeck prodded his chest where my dart had hit him. He grunted in surprise as he plucked out the broken tip of the needle and flicked it to the floor. Slow from pain, he gathered his belongings, hesitating briefly before scooping up my scarf as well. Cradling everything in one arm, he took a slab of meat from the tray and shoved it in his mouth. He wiped the juice from his beard as he left, never looking back.

I waited a long time hidden in the hearth, wondering if Jeck was right.

Seven

❖

My eyes were on the archway to the kitchen as I slipped from behind the tapestry. The smell of roast meat lingered, though the platter was gone, taken to feed Garrett's men, I'd wager. It didn't matter. I was shaking too badly to be hungry.

Snatching a napkin, I wiped the soot from the soles of my boots, then bent to smear my footprints into a blur. I wedged the napkin in a crack in the chimney and turned. Heather was the only one to have found me in the hearth, and it had been my own fault, having left black footprints while checking the door. *Heather*, I thought, praying she was still beyond the palace walls and safe.

I held myself still, listening. It was surprisingly quiet, since the staff was dead or gone, and most of the soldiers were in the garden. Hopelessness pinched my forehead. I couldn't fight Garrett's men; I was almost half their weight and had only one dart and a decorative knife. I had to get out. The quickest way was through the kitchen.

Putting more faith in my dart than my dagger, I tucked the bone blade at the small of my back and edged down the tunnel until a muted conversation brought me to a halt. Breath held, I peered around the cold stone. The sword belted about the cook's apron made him look ridiculous. I was sure he and the sentry leaning casually against the table had been told to watch the door, but they were far more interested in the brace of squab over the largest hearth, the fat dripping down to spurt into flame.

Beyond them was the moonless night. The door was open to let the heat of the kitchen escape. I didn't know whether to be thankful or insulted they thought I was so little a threat. My gaze flicked from the door to them. It was so close, I could smell the dew.

The soldier-turned-cook spun to show a satisfied smile on his round face. "Leave your grubby hands off," he said sharply, looking far happier in his new position of cook than I would have expected. He held a pan under a squab and basted it. "Them's for the prince."

"Aw he ain't gonna miss a leg," the other said, leaning close with his fingers twitching. "You said he spilled his guts like a pregnant woman."

"You touch 'em, and I'll cut your burning fingers off!" the cook threatened as he turned to set the basting pan aside. "I want them pretty, not torn apart."

As I expected, the second man reached for the birds. Their backs were to me. I bolted to the door, shocked when a new wave of dizziness shook me. Muscles suddenly shaking, I skittered around the archway and put my back to the outside wall. My shoulders tensed as the cook shouted, then I slumped when I realized he was yelling at his companion.

Out, I thought as their argument grew louder. I had made it. Fingers gripping the cold stone I was pressed against, I listened to my heart pound, panting while the unreal feeling began to pass. The sensation was akin to having accidentally pricked myself on one of my darts, and I put my fingertips in my mouth, looking for the telltale bitter bite of venom. There was only the taste of ash. The dizziness must be from my hunger. I hadn't eaten all day.

The air was cold, and I shivered in my thin dress. Gaining the garden had been very much like my games of hide-and-seek as a child. Easier, almost, as it was night. It had generally come as a surprise whenever Kavenlow woke me from a sound sleep and bundled me off to a remote corner of the palace, announcing to all at breakfast that the first to find me got my dessert that night. I had usually spent all day skulking through the palace to reach Kavenlow's safe tree, pilfering my lunch from the kitchen or gardens as I went.

The working-class children who were my playmates were always delighted, since my hide-and-seek took precedence over their usual chores. Sentries replaced them when I was older, and Kavenlow got a lot of resistance until he told the captain it was good practice ferreting out assassins for his men. It had been then that my delight in the game blossomed into almost an obsession as I outsmarted the very men set to keep me safe. *But this time,* I thought as my smile of remembrance faltered, *if I'm caught, I won't forfeit my dessert, I'll forfeit my life.*

Taking a steadying breath, I tucked my last dart back into my topknot and crouched. The sound of approaching voices jolted me into motion, and I slid into the kitchen's outdoor firepit. Pushing up on the heavy oak cover, I slid it half over me. The sharp smell of ash and burned fat was an assault, and I kept my breathing shallow to keep from coughing. The pit was still warm from last night's dinner. Shifting uneasily in the defunct coals, I poked my head above ground level to see a pair of sentries.

They were halfheartedly beating the bushes with the flat of their swords as they complained loudly of their interrupted dinner and how this was a waste of time because I was probably crying at the back of a closet. If all of Garrett's men were this inexperienced, I'd have a chance. Even the stableboy had known the value of stealth while playing hide-and-seek.

The two passed. Feeling tense and ill, I waited until their voices vanished before I eased out of the pit. I stank of burned fat, and a dark stain of grease smeared my elbow. I was a mess.

Taking a steadying breath, I checked for lights and ran to a small grove of trees, skidding to a halt among them. The gray of my dress mixed with the shadows. Moonrise would be in a few hours; I had to be over the wall by then. Breathlessly I waited for any sound of pursuit. There was none.

Jittery and nervous, I gathered my skirts to keep them from snagging and eased through the small grove. Almost lost against the black sky was my goal: the only tree in the garden whose branches reached over the palace walls. It was Kavenlow's safe tree, and I frowned, realizing he had taught me the many paths to reach the one way out using games and diversions.

Lights and noise pulled my gaze up. My pulse quickened. They were far enough away for me to move, but not for long. I glanced the other way, then ran for a dull shimmer of rocks.

My breath came in time with my soft footfalls on the damp grass. I slowed to a hunched crawl as my boots scraped on the loose scree. The pile of rock was from a stone arbor, left where it had fallen after I had said it made a grand place for snakes and butterflies to overwinter.

Dropping down, I felt for the small depression I had scratched out nearly a decade ago. It was too shallow to provide much cover now that I was twice as big, and I felt exposed, crouched beside the rocks. They were warm yet from the sun, and I pressed against them.

The sound of a dog cheerfully barking seemed to freeze my heart. "Banner," I whispered in dismay, recognizing him. They had loosed the dogs to find me. And they would, wagging their tails and licking my face.

"Down. Down!" a sentry shouted, hardly a boy by the sound of it.

Please, no, I thought desperately, knowing if I moved Banner would find me all the sooner. I peered over the rocks to see a distant light. My hope sank as a sudden pacing and heavy breath came out of the dark.

"Dog!" I heard a deeper voice call, and the distant torch bobbed. "Whatcha find, dog?"

The large wolfhound stood poised, listening. His tail began to wag. I sank miserably down as he made a beeline to me from across the open space, leaving the sentries behind. His wet nose pushed into my hand, and he licked the grease from my elbow. "Go away," I hissed, but he wanted to play. "Bad dog!" I whispered, and his swinging tail faltered. He whined, his paws as big as my hand almost pushing me over as he wanted to know what he had done wrong.

"Oh, you're a good dog," I said in dismay, fondling his ears as I forgave the massive animal. "Good dog." Wishing he would be still, I peeked over the rocks. The lights were closer. I looked to the wall, then back. I couldn't run with him, and if I stayed, they'd find me.

"Dog!" the guard called, and Banner's ears pricked. He didn't move. It gave me an idea.

"Down," I said, and the large dog dropped, his eyes catching the faint light as he waited expectantly. I grabbed his bearded muzzle and brought it close to my face to remind him I was the leader of his pack. "Stay," I whispered. "Stay." He watched as I backed up, his tail swishing uncertainly. "Stay."

Stomach churning, I crept through the boulders until they gave way to pebbles and finally grass. I prayed Banner would do as told as I ran to a shack hidden behind a bank of roses. The scent of decaying weeds was thick. I circled the gardener's hut until I could see the palace wall and my tree. A shadow hiding a glint of steel shifted beside it. My eyes closed in despair. Leaning against the very tree I had to climb was a sentry.

A shout pulled my eyes open. They'd found Banner. Everything was falling apart!

"Here he is," one called to the other. "Here, dog."

"What's he got?" the second asked.

"Nothing. Come on, dog. Up. Up!" There was a pause, then, "He won't get up. Hey you. Move!" My eyes widened at the sudden yelp. "Fool dog!" the guard yelled. "Get up!"

"Good boy," I whispered, cringing as Banner yelped again. The shadow beside my tree moved. I watched, not believing, as the sentry left his post to see what was going on. A young, inexperienced guard, indeed.

"Hit him with your sword," a deeper voice said. "Get him moving." The sentry at the wall started to jog, passing me in a creak of leather. That easily, I was beyond their perimeter.

Cursing myself as a coward, I ran to the tree. Banner cried out in hurt, and the warmth of tears filled my eyes. He should have left, run to his kennel. Stupid dog. Why had he listened to me? But he stayed, his loyalty buying me time.

My hand touched the smooth bark, and I reached for a limb. Skirts catching, I levered myself up to the first branch. The bark scraped my palms, and dizziness washed through me, setting my arms shaking. There was a yelp of pain, and a stab of helplessness took me. "Good boy," I whispered as I went higher. I was a coward, running away while he was beaten.

Muscles protesting from lack of food, I finally reached the limb paralleling the top of the wall. Banner's cries turned angry. Tears pulled at me, and I risked a glance at the three lights circling him. More were converging on them.

The guards had begun to bait him, urging him to attack. One called out to kill him as they would never get a monster like him back in his pen. Hating myself, I turned my back on Banner, standing upright upon a wide branch. Banner's barks grew savage as I inched forward, arms out for balance. Tears flowed, unchecked. He trusted me, and I was abandoning him. I couldn't explain to him why.

The branch turned before coming close enough to the wall for me to jump, but another limb continued over my head, actually passing over the wall. Standing on tiptoe, I grasped it, closing my eyes to steady myself. Hunger sapped my strength; fear and worry made me dizzy. My feet left the branch, and I inched my way forward one hand width at a time. Banner's barks cut off in a heartrending cry of pain.

"Banner, just run away," I sobbed, my grip threatening to slip. The branch thinned. The soldiers cheered, and heartache gripped me. They had cut him. I was sure of it.

Another handhold, and I froze at the whine at the foot of the tree. *Banner! He was alive!* Then my heart sank. He had come to see what he had done wrong. They'd follow him!

My arms trembled as the guards rattled closer. Panicking, I lurched forward another handhold. I looked to see the shimmer of the wall under me. My fingers found a smooth strip of leather. It was the strap of a bag hanging in a thick tangle of branches. Yanking it from its hiding spot, I dropped the few feet to the wall to land in an unsteady crouch. My muscles trembled from overuse and cold. I felt as if I might pass out, dizzy and unreal.

"Thank you, Banner," I whispered, tears clouding my sight. "You're a *good boy*. Now, run!"

I slipped over the side of the wall and fell into nothing.

Eight

✤

I hit the ground hard, rolling into the street. A wagon was approaching, black and slow with a single torch. Favoring my ankle, I tucked back off the road and into the shadow of the wall. My pulse hammered. A long howl came from behind the wall, and my eyes closed in heartache. "Run, Banner," I whispered, hating myself. "Just run away."

I was out. It hardly seemed to matter. I lowered my head as the wagon passed, heavy with people and household belongings. Suddenly I was aware I was filthy, smeared with bark, grease, and dew. I'd never been past the walls alone before, and I felt naked without . . .

"Kavenlow," I said savagely aloud. *This is his fault,* I thought as I sat and massaged my ankle while the wagon creaked by. Kavenlow should have told me. I could have done something had I known. I had been so shaken by learning of my true birth that I blinded myself to Garrett. I'd seen his frustration at being a second son and his pride demanding he take a kingdom for himself. It had been there. I had ignored it, wallowing in self-pity. And now my parents were dead. Because of me.

"Footsore already, love?" rasped a voice.

My breath hissed in. An old woman with a cloth bag was

standing before me. I hadn't heard her approach because of her bare feet. "Beg your pardon?" I stammered, frightened.

"Footsore? Aren't you going? I'm going. Misdev soldiers thick in the streets," she mumbled over bad teeth. "Then suddenly, not a one. And Costenopolie men going to the palace and none coming to replace them? I don't like it. No, I don't."

I stood up, gingerly putting weight upon my foot until I was sure it would hold me. There were no cries coming from behind the wall, but I had to move. The leather bag in my grip was water-stained and old. I could hear the sound of sliding coins inside.

"And that poor woman," the lady said as I edged away. "Shouting at the gate, demanding she be let in, and the guards pushing her down. That's not Costenopolie men. No, it isn't."

Heather! I thought. "Is she all right?" I asked, stepping close. "Did they hurt her?"

The woman squinted. "I don't know. But I'm leaving. You should, too."

A wet cough spun me around. "Go home, Mabel," a thin man said. Holding a cloak tight to him, he crossed the torchlit street to join us. "The lights are up in the palace because of the Misdev prince. Don't be filling her head with your old-woman fantasies. It's wedding plans."

"Ha!" the old woman barked. "Then why did you pack your leaky old rowboat?"

"It never hurts to be prepared, I say."

I backed away from them, a false smile on my face. I didn't think they realized I was gone as they continued their discussion, each assertion louder and laced with more fond insults than the last. One thing was clear. The city was emptying. Somehow the people knew something was wrong, and fear had started an exodus. That was fortunate. I could get lost in a crowd, slip past the gates with the rest. I needed a horse, a cloak, food . . . I needed money.

Remembering the jingle of coins, I struggled with the knot holding the bag closed. A well-dressed couple passed me with what looked like all their belongings on a tidy cart. Two children were asleep in the back. I tried to hide the grease on my dress as the woman eyed me with contempt. Cheeks flaming, I went to the nearest light to look in the bag.

There was money, enough for a decent trip into the streets. My eyes widened as I recognized the bitter smell of Kavenlow's venom, and I wasn't surprised to find a small capped jar, the white crust helping to seal it. There was also a handful of un-adorned darts tied with a purple ribbon. A quick taste assured me they were potent, and I added several to my topknot in relief. It wasn't until I was replacing the bundle of unused darts that I found the folded paper tucked at the bottom of the bag. It was from Kavenlow, and my brow furrowed in anger.

My dear Tess,

>*That you have found this means I have taught you well. It saddens me I must rely on ink and paper to convey how proud I am of you.*
>
>*If you are climbing the walls to escape, I'm probably dead, and the stability of the realm is in jeopardy. Flee if you deem it best for the short term, but Costenopolie is now yours. I wish your game well. Whatever task the sovereigns have given you upon the return of their princess, use it to further your deception. I worked hard to keep the king and queen from knowing my real intention for you. Be satisfied knowing that though royalty holds the crown, we are the cunning and strength that keep the realm intact.*
>
>*You'll never know the depth of my grief for my lies of omission, but I want you to believe that you were never the king and queen's. You were mine, and I loved you as the child I couldn't have. You are the daughter of my heart, the in-heritor of my skills.*

Your loving mentor,
Kavenlow

The tears started somewhere in the middle, and they ran down my face unchecked. My chest was tight with an unbearable weight. *How could you do this to me?* I thought desperately. *Just when I was ready to hate you?* Choking back a sob, I stretched to put the note to the lamp flame and watch it burn. No one would see his words but me. I didn't understand all of what he meant, only that he loved me. I felt like Banner, howling at the wall as his source of strength slipped away, leaving him with an unheard promise to return.

I dropped my head as a handcart passed. Wiping my eyes with the back of a grimy hand, I numbly walked, heading downward to the docks and the inns. Kavenlow's absence made the once-comforting streets seem fraught with a hidden menace. Garrett's soldiers were absent, a situation I was sure would remedy itself tomorrow when they began searching the streets.

Much to my surprise, a good deal of the dock market was open as greedy merchants pandered to frightened people hoarding food and supplies. The lights were high, and so were the prices, but I wouldn't have to wait until morning to outfit myself. First, though, I needed a quiet place to draw my scattered soul together and find a sense of purpose.

The dizziness had passed now that I wasn't running, but exhaustion pulled at me as I angled for an inn set back two streets from the docks. It would probably be quieter. I glanced back at the palace before crossing the street. It glittered like a necklace in candlelight, high on the hill. My eyes closed in a pained blink, and I turned away. *They are dead. Both of them.*

Striving for an air of wealth rather than destitution, I resolutely smoothed my filthy dress and strode into the inn. The stagnant air smelled of overdone potatoes, but the low-ceilinged room was warm and almost empty. Three men were gaming at a table by the hearth. Another sat alone with a bowl, eating soup as carefully as if it were money to be counted. A surly tavern maid eyed me, but it was the man in a tattered cap leaning against the casks that I approached. A beggar would seek assistance from the tavern maid; a lady would demand it from the owner.

He gave me a once-over, the question clear in his eyes as to what a woman with good boots was doing alone with no coat, covered in filth, and her hair falling down about her shoulders. "I would like some supper," I said, pronouncing my words carefully.

The innkeeper took a breath to speak, but a shrill voice coming through a dark archway shouted, "Get her out! We aren't the palace to feed the city's laggards."

I gave Kavenlow's water-stained bag a subtle shake, sending the soft sound of sliding coins to him. The man glanced at the archway. "Tend to yourself, woman!" he yelled. He was smiling when he turned back, his work-reddened cheeks split to show he was missing a tooth. "Running away from our husband now, are we, ma'am?"

I looked at the empty tables. "Supper?" I asked as I set two coins down, glad Kavenlow had insisted I handle the money when in the streets and so I knew how much was needed.

"Help yourself to what's in the pot," he said, nodding to the hearth behind me.

"I left so quickly," I stammered, embarrassed, "I don't have a bowl."

Saying nothing, he leaned to reach behind a counter and pull out a wooden bowl and flat length of wood that might be considered a spoon—if one was desperate.

"She pays for that!" the unseen woman shouted, and the man's shoulders hunched.

I took them, feeling ignorant. "Would it be possible to have a bath?" I asked.

"I ain't doing any bath!" the woman exclaimed. The bar wench suddenly found something to do, vigorously scrubbing at a far table with her back to us.

I brought out two more coins. It was twice as much as I paid for dinner. My mother's blood still stained my hands; I would give him the entire bag if needed. "Shut your mouth, woman!" the man yelled over his shoulder.

"I ain't doing any bath!" she insisted.

"You'll do a bath," the man bellowed. "Shut yer mouth!" He turned to me, and I gritted my teeth to keep the tears from starting. "It'll be a while. You want it in a room?"

Head down, I nodded, though I wasn't planning to sleep in it, and he reached behind him to draw a tankard of dark liquid. "Here," he said, handing it to me. "Take your pick of the rooms in back. The second one has a lock, ma'am."

My face went cold. "Thank you," I managed, a sick feeling thundering down upon me. I was so alone. There was no hidden escort, no friendly guard behind me. I was alone after sunset with a bag of money in a tavern two streets up from the docks, dressed in rags and covered in pig grease. The only thing that could make this worse was if it started to rain.

Knees feeling like wet rags, I crossed the room to a table near the hearth and sat with my back to the wall. I set the heavy tankard down, and with Kavenlow's bag over my shoulder, I found the pot held a fish stew. The thought of eating was repellant, but having nearly passed out from hunger, I took some. Eyes were on me. I didn't like it. I'd never eaten by myself before.

The men turned away as I sat down. Slowly my fear eased, warmed away by the creamy soup. The spoon was hard to manipulate, and I felt like a fool as I struggled to keep anything on it. I found my appetite quickening—until I realized the gelatinous blob I was pushing around in my mouth in question was probably twin to the fish eye that was now staring up at me.

Gagging, I hunched over the bowl and spat it back out. My face was warm as I looked up, but no one seemed to have noticed. I stifled a shudder and pushed the bowl away, my gaze falling upon the old man eating. He didn't seem to care that his soup was looking back at him, but I did.

The gaming table grew noisy, and my attention went to them as they played three rivers. The oldest man at the table was graying at the temples and had a kind, noble-looking face despite the weary slump that put him as a laborer of sorts. He was dressed simply but clean. A stick was tight between his teeth, and he shifted it from one side of his mouth to the other.

Closest to the hearth was a soft-spoken man, tight with both his money and opinions. He was dressed like a merchant with clean boots and a good cloak.

The last had his back to me. He wore a nondescript shirt and trousers of brown cloth. Unlike the other two, he had no beard, and his brown hair was cut severely short as the younger sentries like to keep it. His jests were quick, as was his speech, and he seemed to be winning a lot. I watched him pull a few coins to himself with pleasant, encouraging words to the others. His hands were too clean to be a laborer, and his clothes weren't good enough for a merchant's. *Soldier?* I thought, but dismissed it as his build—though nicely muscled and sturdy with a broad back and trim waist—was clearly used to casual exertion rather than the discipline of swinging a sword. He had a dagger, though, its outline showing at the top of his ragtag, thin-soled boots.

Then I saw him draw a card from his collar and replace it with one from his hand, disguising the action as a stretch. My breath hissed in. He was a cheat! That's what he was!

Outraged, I felt my cheeks warm, then checked my upward motion. *What the chu pits was I doing?* I was worried about a thieving cheat when my life was balanced between my quick feet and Garrett's anger?

Chilled by the thought of Garrett's soldiers, I pushed my bowl farther away and looked into my bag to estimate what I could purchase. There was enough for supplies but not a horse, too. They were expensive in a coastal city where the little fertile land was used for growing food for people. They would be even more costly with half the city surging through the gates.

How was I going to get a horse? Worried, I took a sip from the tankard, almost choking at the acidic taste. It was near spoiled. God help me, this was the worst meal I'd ever not eaten.

I spat the ale back and frowned as the cheat laughed at something the merchant said. My gaze rose, lighting upon the money on the table. My eyes narrowed in speculation.

I could play cards. Kavenlow had taught me. As a rule, he cheated. The first time I caught him, I swore I'd never play against him again. He had laughed uproariously—which made me so angry I could have had him stuffed and turned into a rug— then changed the stakes. If I caught him cheating, I got his dessert. If he won without me spotting the deception, he got mine. It had been a very enjoyable winter.

The flash of pleasant memory died. Depressed, I wound a stray curl back around my topknot. I would find Kavenlow. But I needed a horse.

Leaving my uneaten soup, I rose with my tankard and bag and approached the table. The talk fell to nothing as the men looked up. I flushed for my forwardness; I hadn't been introduced, but I didn't think it mattered. "Three rivers?" I said. "May I join you?"

The silence grew uncomfortable. The merchant glanced at the innkeeper, and he shrugged. It was the cheat who broke the tableau by shoving a bench away from the table for me. I ignored it, my face warming. Immediately the merchant rose with a quickness undoubtedly born from pandering to customers. The other two men got to their feet as well.

"Let me help you, madam," the merchant said, taking my tankard and setting it on the table before assisting me onto the rough bench with a practiced ease. "My name is Trevor."

"Thank you, Trevor," I said, breathing easier now that someone had finally said something. I eyed him speculatively as I adjusted my filthy dress. "I believe I have visited your shop on high street. You sell threads and cords, yes?"

"Yes ma'am," he said with a smile. He didn't recognize me, and for the first time all night, I appreciated the fact.

"Collin," the second man said. His stick shifted between his teeth as he sat back down.

The cheat had hardly risen from his bench and was already back to shuffling the cards. "Ma'am," he said, giving me no name, and I nodded at him.

"I'm . . ." I hesitated, not knowing what to call myself. "I find I'm in need of a distraction tonight, with all the excitement in the streets. What version are you playing?"

As one, the men relaxed. "Stones dam the river," the cheat said, sliding a card to me. "Forest blocks the sun."

I nodded. I'd played that. Pulling an appropriate coin from the bag atop my lap, I set it in the center of the table with the rest. I took up the cards and bit my lower lip. Play circled from me to the cheat, exactly how I wanted it. If I couldn't win what I needed, I could blackmail the cheat into losing to me. That is, if I could catch him cheating and show him I could prove it.

There would be two circles of the table, each of us trading cards with a visible waste pile or the unseen remainder of the deck. At the end, each could fold and lose their coin, or throw in another to buy the chance to win it all. The strongest hand won. It was a simple game.

We played our first turns in silence. My dislike of the quiet prompted me to turn to the merchant, the most refined of the three. "Trevor," I said, eyes watering as I pretended to sip the awful ale. "You sell that marvelous thread made by insects, don't you?"

"Yes ma'am." He discarded a sword card into the up-facing pile. "I don't think I will be selling much silk for a time. I would be wise to shift my inventory from domestics to the thicker cords that can be used in ropes for warships, but I have yet to find a supplier."

"Warships!" I said, my surprise genuine. How could he have even guessed such a thing? It had only been this morning that Garrett began his bid for my lands.

"Rumors," Collin growled around the stick between his teeth. "Costenopolie won't go to war over a damned-fool marriage."

I blinked. But my unease went unnoticed as the merchant took up his tankard and said, "No, but the Misdev dogs might. May they rot in hell."

With loud agreements, the other two men raised their drinks in salute. All three took a draught, slamming their tankards onto the table with undue force. I watched Collin in fascination as he didn't have to take the stick from his mouth to manage the lip of the cup.

"You deal in cords and string?" Collin questioned as he picked up the merchant's discarded sword card and put down a red pawn. "I make twine for nets."

The two exchanged shrewd looks as I chose an unseen card. Anything was better than the pawn I discarded. It was a black stone, useless with the cards I had, but I kept it, casting aside a valuable queen. I had three reasons for giving it away. One, it would imply I had an excellent hand and perhaps I could bluff my way to winning. Two, if I was right, the cheat would take it, squirreling it away for future use. Or three, it would lead the table to believe I was a simpleton. Any of the results would be favorable. My heart gave a pound as the cheat hesitated for the barest moment before picking up it up.

Collin leaned toward the merchant, his eyes carefully away from the man's cards. "With incentive, I could pull my workers from nets and shift them to ropes. Ropes will be in high demand if we war with Misdev."

"To the Misdev dogs!" the cheat said loudly. "May they rot in hell."

"May they rot in hell!" the men returned. The man eating soup weakly joined in, and I belatedly raised my tankard, pretending to drink the swill. Excitement tingled my toes as the cheat slipped the queen into his sleeve and replaced it with another while we drank. It was very quick, and I never really saw it, but my games with Kavenlow assured me that's what happened.

"Pay the pot or fold?" the cheat asked, his brown eyes innocent as he discarded.

Collin chewed furiously on his stick before tossing in a coin.

"Fold," said the merchant, placing his cards unseen on the table.

"Me, too," the cheat said, unable to show his cards and risk someone recalling he ought to have the queen I had thrown away.

Immediately I put a coin in to join Collin's to further the illusion I was foolish. After losing the queen, I had a very bad hand. Collin won, and he gathered the coins, looking pleased.

The cards went to the merchant, and he shuffled them. "I'm surprised you aren't at your shops," I offered as he slid my cards to me. "The town seems to think it's noon at midnight."

"People fleeing war do not buy spools of flax," he said shortly.

"All this talk of war is foolish," the cheat said. "What does it matter who she marries?"

His stick clamped between his teeth, Collin picked up a card and threw a black wolf down with enough force to almost send it off the table. "I'd rather the princess marry a goat keeper than one of King Edmund's spawn," he muttered. "My grandfather came back with his hand black and stinking from the last Misdev war. He lived long enough to touch the sea, then died among the nets he could no longer even mend. And what did he die for? A strip of forest."

The bitterness in his voice surprised me. "It wasn't for a strip of forest," I said as I took up the wolf. "He died to keep the Misdev devils out of our harbors."

"May they rot in hell!" the men shouted, and I found myself joining them. My attention wandered as I realized my father almost put King Edmund in our harbors, the very thing my grandfather had fought so hard against. Distracted, I never caught the man cheating, and he won.

"And what do you do, sir?" I asked the cheat as Collin dealt a new hand.

"I'm in trading," the young man said without hesitation, his eyes on his cards.

My eyes flicked over him. "Trading?" If he was in trading, I was a dock whore. Which I wasn't. So far. Despite what I presently looked like. "What do you trade in?"

He glanced at me. "Black sheep. When I find a farm with such an animal, I buy it."

"Black sheep," I repeated. I discarded a priest, taking up the red sun. I was betting the cheat would take the priest. Instead, he chose from the unseen pile.

"And what is it you spend your daylight hours upon?" the cheat said sarcastically.

My mocking mood went bothered as I realized I didn't do

much of anything. "Purchasing," I said. "I purchase large amounts of goods for sundry reasons."

"You tend house," he said, his tone making it an insult.

"You would be surprised at the amount of planning that goes into one," I said hotly. "But you wouldn't appreciate it, seeing as you don't stay in one spot for the span of a moon's life—chasing black sheep as you do."

The merchant glanced at Collin. "Ah, I'm sure you keep a fine house, ma'am."

"Then why is she leaving it?" the cheat asked.

"The Misdev curs," I answered, unable to keep my eyes from dropping.

"To the Misdev curs!" the cheat asserted.

"May they rot in hell!" the other men returned.

I watched closely as they drank, but the cheat didn't shift his cards. I wondered if he knew I was watching. On my final turn, I was lucky in picking up a river card. I had a strong hand containing all the elements. No longer needing my king, I discarded him. The cheat's eyes crinkled at the corners as he picked it up. I waited for him to pocket it, but when the game ended and I had won, he still held all his original cards.

It was my turn to deal, and I almost missed his treachery in the rush of cards upon the table. The cheat only returned four. The fifth went into his boot as I pretended to slop my ale and Trevor solicitously blotted it up. My eyes narrowed. I was sure it had been the king. It was the only good card he had held.

"Gentlemen," I said, intentionally shuffling the cards so they threatened to spill from me. "My—husband used to play a game with me when we were first wed." I grimaced, putting a tone of irritation in my voice. "We used to play for sweets. Of late he refuses to play anything with me at all. I still recall it fondly, though. Do you know spit in the wind?"

The table went still in speculation. The pot built upon itself quickly in this game, reaching dangerous proportions with four or more players. I knew the cheat would be unable to resist. The two honorable men looked at each other, clearly unwilling to take advantage of a woman with a tankard of ale in her. But the cheat nodded. "I know it," he said. "I'll play one hand. More would be too rich for me tonight."

"Well," Collin hedged, "if it's just one hand."

"One hand," the merchant agreed.

I dealt out the six cards per player, a thrill of warmth starting in my middle. Taking a steadying breath, I picked mine up, planning out how to use them. My pulse increased as I anticipated the end, and I concentrated on keeping my breathing even.

There was a jingle as we all contributed a coin. Spit in the wind was too fast for sleight of hand. The cheat's cards would stay right where they were. Everyone simply played the card of his choice. The highest card won, pulling in the coins along with the cards. The winner then had not six cards to chose from but nine. The losers had five. Play repeated with additional coins being bet until one person had all the cards—and all the money. The winner would have taken six coins and turned it into twenty-four at the very least. I had an even chance of walking away with the pot. I would either win it outright or blackmail the cheat into losing it to me.

The cheat won the first round, then I won the second. The merchant won the third, setting everyone to seven cards except for Collin, who had three. "I've got fish offal for a hand," the man said, knowing he couldn't come back from such a low position. Spitting his stick onto the floor, he threw his cards on the table. "I'm done. I'll buy my cards out."

I stifled a smile. I had been hoping he'd do that. What it meant was he would contribute three coins to the table, one for each of his remaining cards, instead of playing to the end. My pulse hammered as the coins hit the table. I had to win this.

The cheat won the next, and I the next two, then the cheat again. It brought the merchant down to three cards to the cheat's and my nine each. "That's as far as I'll go," the merchant said, easing his cards down and emptying his tankard. Three more coins joined the center of the table. He remained watching, as did Collin. Both wanted to see the end.

Together the cheat and I laid down our chosen cards. My jaw clenched. I hardly bested his by the color, and the man's mocking brow shifted to concern.

The merchant leaned toward Collin. "When this is done, I'd like to talk with you. I might be willing to loan you money to hire more workers if they make cord for my shops."

Collin's eyes went distant in thought. "I'll starve if we go to war and I'm making nets."

I was ahead by two cards. I should act before I got behind, making his concession look forced. "Do you think it will come to war?" I said, surprised at the quaver in my voice.

Immediately the merchant became reassuring and jovial. "Not at all, milady," he said, his reassurance falling flat on me. "King Stephen dislikes war as much as the merchant guild. Princess Contessa will be wed in such a manner that no one will think to go to war. I can't see the king abandoning his comfortable slippers to put on boots and march or sail away. Still, it is best to be prepared, eh?"

The cheat made a rude noise and reached for his tankard. Clearly he didn't care. "Ah," I said cryptically, thinking of the card in his boot. "But a *king* can find himself in the oddest of *boots* occasionally." I looked at him squarely, eyes wide and innocent. "And a *queen* often finds herself on the strangest of *arms*—from time to time."

The cheat froze as he took in my carefully accented words. His tankard slowly descended to the table, and he stared at me. "Is that so?" he said, shoulders tense.

I nodded slowly, confidently, as he forced his shoulders down. "It is. I've *seen* it."

His clean-shaven chin was thrust forward, and I wasn't surprised when he jostled my ale to spill it as he reached to place another coin. "The cards!" the merchant called, and as he and Collin pushed the discard pile to safety, the cheat leaned close to me.

"What do you want?" he muttered, his eyes almost black in the dim light.

"Lose to me," I whispered breathlessly, "or you'll lose your hands."

The barmaid sighed at the spill so loudly I could hear her from across the room. The cheat kept his eyes upon his cards as she blotted at the mess. I knew he was trying to decide if I would call him on his cheating, and what would happen if he couldn't escape. He eyed the coins on the table. His breath quickened as his gaze went to the door. I narrowed my eyes in threat.

"Fold or play?" the merchant prompted. The cheat reached for a card in his hand.

"Innkeeper?" I called loudly, my eyes riveted to the cheat's brown ones. My heart pounded. I knew that I couldn't turn him in; they might cut off his hands. But cards was a game of not just skill but bluff—and Kavenlow had taught me well.

His mouth twitched, and his thumb rubbed the second finger on his hand. "Ah, hell with it. I fold," he said, grimacing as he threw his cards to mingle with the others.

The two men leaned back with a sigh. I didn't reach for the coins, surprised when my exhaled breath shook. I jumped when the innkeeper bumped my shoulder, brought by my earlier call. "I'm buying the table a round of ale," I said. "It was a wonderful game, gentlemen. If you will excuse me?" I sat on my bench and smiled at each in turn as my pulse slowed.

The merchant rose immediately, knowing from experience a lady wouldn't put such a large sum away while anyone was watching. "A pleasure, ma'am," he said, inclining his head and going to the casks where the innkeeper was drawing four tankards.

The bench scraped loudly as Collin rose with a pained slowness. He had a new stick between his teeth already. "Ma'am," he said shortly, almost hobbling as he went to join Trevor. I wondered if he suffered from bone-ache, and the stick was from a willow.

I turned to the cheat. For all of three seconds I resisted the urge to cock my eyebrow, then gave in, making him scowl. There was no joy in taking his money. I had been lucky.

"That's my money," he said as he placed seven coins atop the pile to pay for his loss.

Immediately I stiffened. "Not anymore, it isn't."

He leaned closer, clearly going to say something. I could smell horse sweat on him, and earth. Glancing at the door he muttered, "Purchasing? You're good. You're very good."

On edge, I shifted all but one coin into my bag to pay for the ale. "If you mean I know how to play cards and spot a cheat, yes. If you mean I cheat? You are sadly mistaken. I could have won it all from you honestly, but I'm in a hurry."

Silent, he glanced at my bowl of soup before he pulled the king from his boot, the queen from his sleeve, and a priest from behind his collar. "We made a good team, didn't we?"

My jaw dropped. "This is my money," I said as I stood. "All of it. Get out of my sight before I tell the innkeeper and you're thrown into the pillory."

He stood slowly, clearly not alarmed as the cards were now upon the table and not on his person. Gathering them all, he wedged them in a stiff leather box and tucked it behind his shirt. The man had his own cards. How could he not be a cheat? "Good-bye, Lady Black Sheep."

I frowned at the connotation as he went to get his ale. He said a few words to the merchant and cord maker before he left, swallowing his tankard in two breaths to make his Adam's apple bob.

My bag was substantially heavier, and knowing the target I was, I motioned for the innkeeper. The flush from my win vanished as he brought me a new tankard. "Do you have a son who can accompany me as I shop tonight?" I asked.

He nodded and took the coin I had left on the table. "I'll fetch him, ma'am," he said. "Though if I were you, I'd wait until morning."

"Everything will be gone by then," I said, clutching my arms about myself. He walked away, his head nodding in understanding.

The merchant and Collin were deep in conversation as I waited for the innkeeper's son. I felt ill, the fish soup sitting uncomfortably in my knotting stomach. My first stop would be to get a new dart pipe. I expected the cheat was a thief as well, and despite the assurance of an escort and a topknot of deadly darts, I was alone and vulnerable.

My eyes closed, and my jaw clenched. My parents were dead, I was a beggar's get, and the only person I had left in the world had let me live a lie. And there wasn't a soul I could tell.

Nine

❖

"No horses!" I flicked my gaze past the stableman to the stalls. "What are those?"

The man took the lantern down from an overhead hook and rubbed his whiskered face.

It was blessedly warm inside the stable, but my arms were still wrapped around me. To my disgust, the innkeeper's son had been half-drunk in addition to being half-witted. After fending off his groping hands, I had left him on a corner singing of women to finish my shopping alone. I was safer without him. And I wasn't as out of place as I had originally feared.

Scores of people were in the streets shopping by lamplight. Being under a terrible time constraint and too dispirited to care, I had accepted inferior everything: my blankets were one thickness not two, my cooking utensils were made of copper and wood instead of clean metal, and the change of clothes shoved dismally into the bottom of my pack had been worn before.

At least my boots were my own, and the gray cloak bumping about my ankles was fresh from the loom. Even better, I again had a whip coiled in supple loops and fastened to my waist. It was eight beautiful feet of leave-me-alone, and it gave me more confidence than I deserved. No knife, though. Clean steel of any length and strength was nearly as expensive as a horse.

I had been to two other liveries already. If I didn't find a horse here, I wouldn't have time for my bath and find a mount both. And leaving without a horse with the hope to buy it from a fellow traveler wasn't a promising proposition.

"Come back tomorrow," the man said as he shuffled to the wide doors. "I've got a few at pasture. Seems horses are in demand now. Damned wedding has everyone jumpy."

The last was muttered darkly, and I reached out after him. "Wait. Please?" I said, and his eyes widened as he caught sight of my whip. I clutched my cloak closer, hiding it. "What about one of those?" I stepped from the ring of light his lamp made to where two magnificent black horses—a perfectly matched mare and a gelding—stood sleepy and nodding.

His brow was furrowed, his mind clearly on my whip and not the horses. "Ah—you can't have those," he said. "They belong to someone in the palace. A gift for the princess."

I took a breath to explain, then let it out in frustration as I gazed at my beautiful horses I couldn't have. He wouldn't believe me. Probably take me to the palace gates as moonstruck. Lips pursed, I went to the last stall. "What's wrong with this one?" I said, surprised to see a child curled up in the corner, almost under the mare's feet. Her body was thin from growing too fast, covered by a grimy, too-short dress. I couldn't tell how long her hair was as it was a mat of tangles and straw, and her toes were black with filth.

The man leaned over the edge of the short wall. His gaze fell upon her, then rose to the horse. "Can't sell you Dirt." His voice was oddly flat.

"Why not?" The brown mare looked sturdy, though a little short. Almost a large pony. My irritation tightened, knowing in a seller's market, he could demand almost anything. When he didn't answer, I entered the stall. The mare's whiskers tickled my palm when she dropped her head to greet me. "Is she yours?"

"Bought her this spring," he admitted, clearly not pleased I was in with her.

Good, I thought. It was a matter of finding the right price, and I was going to make sure it was one I could pay. I ran my fingers down the mare's leg and lifted a hoof. Kavenlow had taught me to ride, insisting being able to choose a good horse was as important as being able to keep your seat in a jump. Letting the man stew for a bit, I looked her over. "There's talk of war in the streets," I said calmly as I patted the mare's shoulder. "You can sell her to me tonight or give her to the palace when they assemble their cavalry troops in the morning."

"Costenopolie doesn't have a mounted army," the stableman said quickly.

"I imagine they are going to need lots of horses, then—aren't they?"

The man looked like a trained bear as he shifted from foot to foot. The girl woke, and I scraped up a smile to soothe her frightened stare. She couldn't be more than thirteen, gawky with adolescence. I'd been enamored of horses at that age, though I'd never been allowed to sleep with them. "She has a cracked hoof," I said, trying to keep the price reasonable, "and is out of condition. I'm willing to pay you a good price, regardless."

The girl's eyes widened. "You can't," she cried, scrambling up. "You won't!"

"Shut yer mouth!" the stableman bellowed, and I, the girl, and all the horses jumped. "I'll sell the worthless thing if I want!" He turned to me with a smile. "You leaving tonight?"

I hadn't liked him shouting, and I nodded curtly. My curiosity took on a tinge of confusion as he beckoned me out into the small stable yard. Giving the mare a pat, I latched the stall shut behind me and followed him to where he waited just outside. He leaned close enough for me to smell the sour pork he had eaten tonight, and I backed away. "If it were just the horse, ma'am," he said, "I'd sell her to you and be done with it. But it's the girl."

My eyebrows rose, and I glanced behind me into the lit stables.

"I bought the horse after her family died in a fire," he continued. "It used to belong to them, and she won't leave the mare. Screams as if the devil himself were after her if you try. She won't stay with the folks that took her in and gave her work, either. They quit coming to fetch her, seeing as she's old enough to be on her own. If I sell the mare to you, she's going to follow you sure as chu pits stink. She's a wicked thing, but I get too much work out of her to let her go for nothing. Maybe if you added a little something . . ."

My face warmed. He had himself a slave. I recalled her haunted eyes watching me from her narrow face. She was what I would have been had Kavenlow not bought me: a beggar beholden to filth like this man for everything she had.

Kavenlow had kept me from such misery as this, I thought, unable to be angry with him. He had lied to me, but his love had been true. I had to find him before a Misdev soldier did. And though it would complicate my life immeasurably, I couldn't leave this girl here to accept whatever this man forced on her. Right now, her grime protected her. That might change if he ever got drunk and found her. "I'll take both," I said, praying I had enough.

"She'll make a fine servant, ma'am," he said, his eyes fixed on the money I was stacking on a fencepost. "She jest need a good whipping. I can't bear to beat a woman. But seeing as you are one . . ." His grin turned ugly. "She'd make a fine lady a good servant," he repeated, his eyes dropping to the coil of leather on my hip.

She wouldn't, and I fought to keep from sneering that he would pander to me like that. The man was vile. I'd known such commerce took place in my streets. God save me, I was one of the commodities. I would make it clear to the girl that I bought her freedom, not her. "I want the girl, her horse, and the tack for it," I said, disgusted as I gave him everything but a few coins.

"Done," he said greedily as he snatched them up in a thick-fingered hand.

We spun at the sound of hooves. "Look out!" the stableman shouted, stumbling back as the brown mare clattered into the yard. The girl clung to the horse's back like a brown shadow. "Addie!" he cried as the mare took the low fence. "Come back here. Wretched girl!" He ran to the street's edge, coming to a frustrated halt. Dogs barked, and a candle flickered as a curtain was pulled aside. I stood in shock as my horse ran into the dark and was gone. "Addie!" he shouted again. He turned to me, anger hunching his shoulders. "I'll get her ma'am," he all but growled. "I'll get her and tan her hide so well she won't be able to go horseback for a fortnight."

"My horse," I said, outraged. "You let her steal my horse! Is this why you're the only one in the city with horses to sell? How many times have you done this tonight?"

The man's face went ashen in the light spilling from the barn. "No, ma'am!" he cried. "She run off on her own. Ask anyone; I'm an honest man!" He took a step to the gate, then turned back again. "Wait—wait here," he said, his words seeming to stumble over themselves. "I'll get your horse. She couldn't have run far."

My eyes narrowed as he jogged to the street. He turned and gestured for me to stay, then lumbered into the dark. Dogs barked at his shouts, and I stared in disbelief at the empty street. He had my money. I had no horse. I had to leave. Now.

Not knowing what else to do, I went into the stables to pick out my saddle. There wasn't a sidesaddle, but I could ride astride. Kavenlow had insisted I learn, despite the stares of the stable-boys. Worried, I sat on a bale of straw and tugged my dress hem down. The gelding flicked his ears back and then up, clearly not sure whether he liked me or not. "That girl is halfway to the forest by now," I said aloud, and his ears stayed pricked.

I frowned with a sudden thought. I had paid for a horse, its tack, and a girl, much as the idea revolted me. It wasn't my fault he had allowed all but the tack to run out the barn door and into the night. The horse I bought wasn't coming back. I had every right to take one of these. After all, they were intended for me.

Making soft noises, I entered the mare's stall and made friends with her. I liked the more flashy gelding, but the mare would have more endurance. "Why shouldn't I take you?" I whispered, my fingers arranging the silky strands of her mane. "You're my horse. That I haven't been presented with you yet is a formality. He should be thankful I paid for you at all."

I flushed in shame for what I was going to do as I got the saddle and pad and tightened the cinch. The mare tossed her head as the weight of them hit her back. She looked as eager as I was to leave. Her stablemate stamped and blew; he knew he was being left behind.

My expectation that the man would come bursting back in at any moment kept my pulse hammering. Guilt made me choose the bridle in most need of repair, and I slipped the bit in between her teeth. The bag of belongings I had purchased went into a tattered saddlebag I found. I hadn't exactly arranged to purchase it, but I was stealing a horse; the bag was incidental.

Fingers trembling, I turned the oil flame down and led my mare out into the yard. The noise of her hooves was loud, and I cringed. I had paid for a horse. I was taking one. My gaze roved over the empty yard, listening for the stableman. Nothing. I couldn't wait. I had to go.

I gazed up at the stars, unseen behind the smoke of a hundred fires. Asking for forgiveness, I swung up into the saddle. Pitch— as I decided to call her—shifted a step, then settled as I adjusted my new cloak to best cover my legs.

"She's my horse to take. I'm not a thief," I said as I shifted my weight and sent Pitch into the street. But somehow I couldn't seem to still the small, nagging voice that said I was.

Ten

❖

I pulled my cloak tighter about my shoulders, relishing the clean smell of the wool and glad for its warmth as the cold slipped in from the bay to fill the town. Having decided careening through the streets on a galloping horse was a sure way to attract attention, I was again on foot. Slow and hypnotically relaxing, the noise of Pitch plodding behind me at the end of her lead echoed against the buildings. I was sensing alarm in the few knots of people huddled under the puddles of flickering light, and I wondered what the rumors had shifted to.

I warily eyed a group arguing as I passed. The street traffic had dropped off with an alarming suddenness, but the people who were left were noisy. "Lady Black Sheep," a masculine voice called sarcastically, and my breath seemed to freeze in me. A shadow pulled itself away from the lamp. Chu pits, it was the cheat. I looked up at the hazy heavens, wondering why it wasn't raining. Everything else seemed to be going wrong.

He angled away from the small group, a gray horse trailing behind him. My hand plucked a dart from my topknot and I held it hidden in my palm. I wondered if I should risk making a scene by darting him or if there were enough people about that I could tolerate his presence. I decided on the latter but kept the dart where it was.

"Sir Cheat," I said tightly as he came even with me. His horse wore a patched riding pad instead of a saddle. A bedroll and pack were tied behind it, filthy with use.

"My name isn't cheat. It's Duncan."

"I don't care," I said, eying the street. Pitch made greeting noises and accepted the gray gelding in the easygoing manner of equines. I, however, wasn't pleased.

"Look . . . lady," he said, "and I'm being generous with the title. I have to talk to you."

My jaw clenched. "I don't owe you anything. Go away."

"Hey," he said. "Hold up." He matched his pace to mine. "Ah, no one has caught me cheating since I was fourteen."

"Congratulations." My eyes were on the next pool of light. Perhaps I should have tolerated the innkeeper's son after all.

"Will you listen to me?"

He grabbed my arm, stopping me. Shocked, I tugged away from him. "Don't touch me!" I said, feeling my face go hot. Angry, I continued on, my pace quick and stilted. If he grabbed me again, I was going to drop him where he stood.

The cheat took a breath and surged after me. "All right, but listen. What you did in the inn was incredible. I've never built up such a stockpile of cards before. Not that fast. You fed them to me," he said, sounding grudgingly impressed. "Offered distractions so I could move them. And you did it so you could blackmail me into giving the winnings to you."

"What if I did?" I said, not proud of myself.

"Don't be such a snot," he said, and I stifled the urge to slap him. "I'm not mad. Not anymore, anyway. It was as beautiful a bit of trickery as I've ever seen. You took the table's money and kept your lily-white hands spotless."

"Must be my breeding showing," I muttered. Why was he still here? I had made it obvious I wanted him to go.

"Will you stop?" he demanded. "We can do far better together than we can alone."

My feet halted, and I stared at him. He thought I was a thief. He wanted us to work together? "I am not a thief!" I said loudly, and he pursed his lips in bother and glanced over the empty street.

"Of course you're not," he said, with a hurried quickness, eyes still roving. "Neither am I. I'm a cheat, and I only take from those who can afford it."

"Oh," I said dryly. "A noble cheat. That makes it so-o-o-o much better."

Duncan didn't seem bothered by my scorn, actually touching the brim of his dirty hat. Angel's Spit, was there nothing clean outside the palace? "So what do you say, Lady Black Sheep? Shall we find a quiet table and have a quiet conversation?"

"No," I said sharply. "I'm not interested in your paltry little schemes . . ." I hesitated. "What did you say your name was?"

"Duncan."

". . . Duncan," I said, gripping Pitch's lead tight. "I want to leave the city, not fleece it."

"Good idea. Leaving, I mean." He lurched into motion as I strode briskly forward. "This damned betrothal has everyone jumpy. But you've got a star-shining play with your act of fallen wealth to soften their guard, little girl. Pit that with my skills at cards, and the excess coinage we could alleviate is incalculable."

I seethed at being called "little girl," but as I put my eyes on the next puddle of light, my throat tightened in fear. I forced myself to keep moving and not draw attention by changing my pace. A soldier, in my father's colors, but I could tell he was Garrett's man by his stance alone.

Not so soon! I thought, my knees going weak. They couldn't be looking for me in the streets already. Swallowing hard, I shifted the dart between my fingers. I could probably put the sentry down from here using the new dart tube in my hair, but it would tell Garrett where I was.

There was an alley to my right, and I took it, heading away from the docks and toward the western gate up a street and over. A flash of annoyance colored my fright as Duncan matched my move. He glanced behind us with a casual interest. "Where are we going?"

"*We* aren't going anywhere," I said, distracted. "Will you please leave?"

The alley opened into the next street. This one was still lit and busy as it led to the gate. I forced my pace to slow, matching that of those around us. My pulse raced. Duncan walked beside me, his silence worrying. I put the back of my hand to my face, carefully wedging my palmed dart into my sleeve. My cheek was cold. How was I going to get past them?

"I don't think you realize the extent of my talents, Lady Black Sheep," Duncan said. "I am the best carder up and down the coast. Maybe you've heard of me?"

"No. And stop calling me that."

"What do you want me to call you, then?"

"Tess." I glanced ahead to a guard questioning a haggard woman with a heavy pack bowing down her shoulders. They were looking for me: a woman traveling alone.

"Well, Tess," Duncan continued, watching me watch the woman. "I can assure you there's few as good at cards as I am. It's a mistake to walk away. You owe it to yourself to at least see what you're turning down."

The woman was dismissed, and she shuffled to the gates with an uncomfortable haste. *They are looking for me!* I thought, my mind whirling. "Take my hand," I said, feeling ill.

"Your hand?" he said slyly, the surprise I'd have expected utterly absent. "Of course."

My stomach dropped. Shifting his horse's lead, he slipped his hand into my free one. It was warm and dry, and he twined his fingers into mine with a grip that wasn't tight but comfortably firm. A surge of unexpected emotion warmed the pit of my belly, mixing with my fear in a spine-tingling slurry of feeling.

I kept my head lowered as we approached the sentry. I thought of my dart up my sleeve and the whip on my waist. *Don't see me. Don't see me,* I thought, the litany setting my blood to pound through my head. Vertigo came from nowhere, rising to set my limbs trembling as we passed him. But we continued, unchecked. The city gate was ahead, the night black beyond it. "What is he doing, Duncan?" I asked softly, thinking I should have eaten that soup, whether it was staring at me or not.

Duncan tipped his hat off, looking behind us as he picked it up. "Watching us," he drawled with a questioning, confident lilt to his voice.

"Hold me," I whispered, feeling unreal and distant. "Keep walking."

"Of course, Tess." His tone had a sly understanding, and he put an arm over my shoulders and pulled me close. I could smell the stink of ale on him, mixing with woodsmoke, crushed grass, and his own sweat. My blood tingled, and I cursed myself for a fool, thinking how heady his arm felt about me while my life hung by a thread. He wasn't a nervous young noble. His hands weren't ready to fly from me at the slightest sound. They gripped me with a dominating sureness that carried a promise I'd never felt before.

"Mmmm, a whip?" he breathed as his featherlight touch of his fingers slipped down my shoulder to find my hip. "You are full of surprises. Anything else I can do for you, love?" An unstoppable shiver shook me. "A kiss, maybe?"

Oh, God help me. He knew what he was doing to me. A wisp of my hair pulled against the stubble on his cheek, and I stared at him, seeing his eyes go intense. I heard the guard hail someone behind us, and I pushed Duncan away.

His soft chuckle said more than words. I could tell I was flushing and was glad the dark hid it. My heart was pounding, and my knees were weak. *It's from the danger,* I thought, *not because a man's arms were about me.* But I knew I lied. I'd been held by men before and stolen flirtatious kisses behind the roses. I knew how easy it was to confuse the thrill of danger with the stir of desire. And I knew what I felt was not born from the guards but Duncan.

Duncan glanced behind us, then leaned close. "They're looking for you," he said, his breath on my cheek warm. "What did you do? Correct their manners? Tell them their stockings needed mending?"

"Nothing." I forced my thoughts from him, recognizing them for the folly they were.

"Well, there's another guard. I'd wager he knows. I'll ask him."

Fear pulled my head up. "No."

Duncan's look turned almost angry. "Spill it, pretty thief. What did you do?"

Taking a quick breath, I eyed the gate ahead, counting four sentries, two on either side of the opening. I couldn't tell Duncan who I was. "They might think I stole a horse," I improvised. "Just help me get past the gates."

His anger turned to a manipulative understanding. "Ah. This one here?" he asked, not appalled as I thought he should be. "Not smart, Lady Black Sheep. They hang you for that in the capital. Well, they'd hang me for that. You, they'd probably strip and flog." He eyed me. "That might be entertaining."

"I didn't steal her," I nearly hissed, frantic he might turn me in. "I paid for her. The man let the first one run away. I had every right to take another! And you are a disgusting pile of chu, you know that?"

We slowed as we fell into the line before the gate. My face went cold when his expression changed, becoming darker, more intense as he ran his eyes slowly over me, lingering on my shallow curves and face, never reaching my eyes. I'd never been looked at like that before, and I stifled a shudder.

"I want everything you won at the inn," he said, finally meeting my eyes.

My breath caught. "I spent it. All of it."

"In an hour?" he protested. "You had—" His brow furrowed in bother. "You couldn't have spent all of it!"

"I'm good at spending money," I said bitterly. "It's all I've done for the past ten years." We were starting to attract attention, and I lowered my voice. "Please. Help me get out. I'll give you whatever you want—except the horse."

The press of the people at the gate had increased, and Duncan's gray horse tossed his head and fidgeted. The cheat soothed the flighty animal with a surprising gentleness. His eyes caught the torchlight, glinting in greed. I waited in a breathless anticipation.

His gaze flicked to the sentries at the gate, then over my shoulder behind us. Nodding, he pulled out a clay flask. Uncorking it, he took a swallow. My lips curled as he spilled some on his front. "Get back, woman!" he suddenly shouted, shocking me. "Before I beat you blue."

Wide-eyed, I gripped the dart hidden in my sleeve. A wash of vertigo took me, dying to nothing as he rolled his eyes toward the sentries in exasperation. My tension eased, then swelled back to life.

"Damned wench," he said, hunching into himself and slurring his words. "Get behind me where you belong."

I flushed. But the cart ahead of us trundled through the gate. Freedom beckoned, barred by sheathed swords. The night shimmered in the hazy moonlight, its darkness and cooler air welcoming compared to the crush of people behind me. I shirked back between the horses, trying to stay unnoticed. Nausea rose high, and I forced myself to breathe.

"Trouble?" the sentry said as he looked past Duncan to the people lined up behind us.

"Cursed wife spent all the money," he grumbled. "Left me with hardly anything to put ale in my belly. Why do we have to wait? We've never had to wait before."

Duncan leaned heavily against the sentry, breathing his stale breath over him. The sentry pushed him away. "What was your business?" the other guard asked in a bored litany.

"Selling my culled rams. She bought a cloak with the money." He turned to me, spittle flying as he shouted, "You don't need a cloak! You never stir your ugly hide out of the house!"

Don't see me, I thought, pulse hammering. *Don't see me at all.* My head felt thick, and I stared at the ground and held onto the saddle as my knees threatened to give way. Something was wrong. I was afraid, but it wasn't fear that was making my muscles tremble and my head spin. The sensations were reminiscent of when Kavenlow had been building my immunity to the venom on my darts. *Why was I so dizzy?*

"She keeps me from my ale," Duncan slurred. "Shouldn't keep a man from his ale." He lurched, falling into the sentry again, holding himself up by the man's shoulders.

The sentry shoved him away. "Go," he said in disgust. "Go on. Get out."

Duncan fell back into his horse's shoulder. The frightened animal shied, and I reached out. "Woman!" he shouted. "Help me onto my horse."

"Get out," the sentry demanded, drawing his sword. I cried a warning as it descended, smacking into the rump of Duncan's horse. The animal lunged forward through the gate, dragging Duncan since he refused to let go of the reins. I jogged after them with Pitch. When I caught up, Duncan shoved his horse's bridle into my hand and stumbled to Pitch's side.

"I said, help me up!" Duncan slurred.

The guard's eyes were on me. Leaning close, I whispered, "Get on your own horse!"

"A man wouldn't let his wife have a saddle before he had one," he said softly. Then he broke into song, singing lustily as he tried to get up on to Pitch's saddle. The mare spun in a quick circle as he fumbled and lurched, finally gaining her back.

Outraged, I flung the reins over Pitch's head to him. His horse's reins were in my hands, and I looked up at the gray's tall back. The monster stood too high for me to get up on without a stirrup, so I angrily paced beside them. Duncan gave a loud, wet belch, disgusting me. My jaw clenched, but as I glanced back at the city's walls, I realized I was out. I had done it! Somehow we had done it!

The night air felt cooler, and a great deal cleaner. Heart pounding, I fought the urge to move faster. All of the visible traffic before us had turned west to the little arable land we had. My ears warmed as I abruptly understood the words that Duncan was singing. Even worse, he kept starting over every time he got stuck at the same phrase. Finally he remembered it, yelling it at the top of his voice. The silence as he quit seemed all the more profound.

Slowly the noise of the horses' hooves became loud. We were alone, the trees arching over us protectively, hiding us from the stars. I tucked the dart back into my hair with shaking hands. My dizziness had gone, leaving my hands trembling with only my spent fear.

The shadow that was Duncan looked down at me, his smug satisfaction obvious even in the blackness. "There you are, Lady Black Sheep," he said. "I got you out, safe and sound."

"Thank you," I said tightly, my worry at my vertigo coming out as anger. And I didn't like him riding when I was forced to walk.

"Thank you?" he said, sounding affronted. "I got you past four—no, five guards—and all I get is a thank-you? You ungrateful brat! You think that was easy? It wasn't as if it was raining and we could have simply walked past them."

My eyes narrowed as he swung down, putting us back on more even terms. The knots in my belly eased. It lasted for all of three heartbeats until he said, "So, about my fee . . ."

I rocked back a step. I had nothing. My offer, while not empty, lacked a certain promptness. My face burned. "I said I spent it. You'll get your money as soon as I do."

"Oh-h-h-h," he laughed. "I've heard that before. And I've got a burning-hell good idea on how you can pay me back."

The appraising way he was eying me made my pulse race, and a new fear set my stomach to roil. He was three stone over my weight and stood half a head taller than I did. Remembering the warmth of his arm about me, I backed up. If he touched me, he would die with three darts in his belly. "Take my supplies," I said, cursing my voice as it quavered.

"I don't want your supplies. I want to know how you saw me move my cards. A week working together ought to do it. And I keep everything until you pay me back what you took in the inn."

My breath came in a gulp of surprise. *A week working together?* "I told you I'm not a cheat. I appreciate your help, and if you don't take your fee from my supplies, it's not my fault."

Saying nothing, he shoved Pitch's lead at me, and I stepped back out of his reach, heart pounding. He hesitated, eying me. "Kinda skittery, aren't you?"

I stared, not believing this was happening as he dropped Pitch's lead and reached for her cinch. "What are you doing?" I finally managed, snatching her reins up and gripping them along with his horse's lead.

"Taking your saddle until you pay me back."

Pitch's ears flicked as her cinch swung free. "What?" I exclaimed. "I never . . ."

He turned, his stance going aggressive. "You said if I helped you past the gates, you would give me anything except your horse. I can't believe you were stupid enough to steal a horse! Or do you make a habit of using your womanly charms to win your innocence? God I hate that. You women get everything for nothing."

"You chull bait!" I exclaimed. "I've never stolen anything in my life! I paid for her!"

"Yeah. All right." Undoing the knot holding the pad to his horse, he handed me the blanket. I held it blankly. "You can have my riding pad," he said magnanimously as he moved my saddle from Pitch to his horse.

Dumbfounded, but realizing the only other option was to cowardly dart him and run, I did nothing as he took the blanket from my loose grip and fastened it atop Pitch. Giving his horse a reassuring pat, he made the half jump to his horse's back, not even using the stirrups. I dropped his horse's reins, and Duncan leaned forward to gather them up.

"Where to?" he said, looking very pleased with himself as he sat tall in my saddle. "Saltwood is the only thing in this direction, and finding a fisherman willing to risk a coin on cards is like finding a virgin in a brothel." He hesitated, his face lost in shadow. "There're the sailors, though. They don't have much money, but they're free with it. That might be a good place to start. Work out the tack we're going to play out before we hit the bigger towns." He hesitated, looking down at me. "You gonna walk the whole way?"

I led Pitch to a fallen tree and scrambled up the best I could. Duncan's eyes widened as he saw me with my feet to either side of the animal. He opened his mouth, then looked away as I flushed and pulled my cloak to cover my legs. I sniffed, trying to make it as haughty as I could. "Keep the saddle. I'm not working with you," I said, nudging Pitch into motion.

"No, no, no, my pretty thief," he said as he pulled even with me. "You owe me. And I want to know how you spotted me moving my cards. If you caught me, someone else could."

"I'm not a thief," I said, wondering if I dare try to outrun him in the dark. I'd never ridden without a saddle. The movement of muscles under me was odd, and not entirely uncomfortable.

Duncan's words caught at me, reminding me who I really was. Within hours of losing my crown I had shown my true birth, becoming a thief with frightening ease. The princess had taken everything from me. I was nothing, thanks to her.

I felt the warmth of tears and held my breath, refusing to cry. I had to find Kavenlow. He was all I had left. He would know who I was.

Eleven

✤

I rubbed at my neck in time with Pitch's motion as I watched the flight of birds winging their way to their evening roosts. The mat of needles and dead leaves muffled the sound of hooves. This far out, the path was a thin ribbon, but it was still clear where it ran, circling the rocky places and running beside narrow, deeply cut streams until a good crossing was to be had.

We had passed only a few people today, on foot and slow with their belongings. They had been frightened and unwilling to talk. It seemed my unrelenting pace had put us ahead of the crush, though, and we hadn't seen anyone since noon. Duncan had said nothing about traveling deep into the night yesterday; I had waited until almost dawn before collapsing by the road like the beggar I was. He probably thought I was trying to leave him behind. He'd be right. The man was sticking tighter to me than a burr, and I had resigned myself to his presence. At least until I found Kavenlow and the chancellor paid him off and "encouraged" him to leave.

Pitch stumbled, and I winced when my cramped knees flamed at the jolt. I was hungry, exhausted, and the pain from riding too long was almost unbearable. But I'd sling chu in the careen pits before I said anything to Duncan. I'd stopped several times today to shift my legs, blaming the halts on checking Pitch's feet for nonexistent stones or watering her. Duncan seemed obnoxiously fine, perched on my saddle and probably used to the travel.

I brushed a wisp of curl out of my eyes and tucked it behind an ear. The continual jarring had loosened my topknot, and as I wound my hair back up for the uncountable time today, I spotted a maple leaf impaled upon a stripped twig. Kavenlow had put it there. I had been following his markers since sunup—though Duncan didn't know it—Kavenlow's modified garden game of hide-and-seek paying off in an unusual way.

The way the branch that held the marker was growing showed direction. The height of the leaf told me he was on a horse. An upside down leaf would tell me he had lingered and moved on, or camped in this case. We had just passed one like that. Despite my pace, I was almost a full day behind him. I'd never catch him before Garrett's assassin did. But Kavenlow had kept me alive for two decades. I had to believe he could survive one Misdev guard.

I'd been watching the markers closely for his path to leave the trail and strike out southwest. Saltwood was a harbor town, and though it would be faster by nearly several days to cross the large bay between us and the mountaintop called Bird Island than to go around it, Kavenlow hated the water and would most likely take the longer way.

The thought that I should have tried to free a garrison instead of chasing after Kavenlow flitted through me, quickly dismissed. It would precipitate an armed attack, ending scores of lives, soldier and commoner alike. Garrett was the only one I wanted to kill, and with Kavenlow's political skills to convince King Edmund his death was justified, that's what I'd do.

I shivered in the chill of the coming evening. The sun was behind the trees, and it was growing dark. We were passing beside an open field, gray in the low light, and after flicking a bothered glance behind me at Duncan, I angled off the path and into it.

"Stopping already?" he said. "You went till almost dawn yesterday. What about the hundred men following you?" he mocked. "Seeing as you stole your own horse and all."

"I didn't steal Pitch," I said tightly. "I paid for her."

"And that's why I had to sneak you out, yes?"

My breath quickened, but I tried to ignore him. There wouldn't be a hundred men hunting me. There would be one: Jeck.

Depressed, I shifted my weight, and Pitch obediently halted. My feet hit the ground, and pain almost buckled my knees. Clutching at the riding pad, I breathed slow and shallow. "I'm camping there," I said, pointing to the edge of the field.

Duncan swung from his horse—I'd found out today he had named the gelding Tuck. Both of them reached for a tuft of grass, the cheat contenting himself with a single stem, the horse taking a mouthful. "That's a god-awful place to camp," he said around the stalk of green. "If you want to sleep on soft ground that's going to leave your blanket wet again, fine, but I'll be over there." He gestured to a crumbling rock face that looked as appealing as sleeping in a dog's kennel. "The fire's warmth will be reflected by the rock, and it will be drier."

I was too tired to try to disguise my ignorance. "You're right. I'll get wood for a fire."

"I don't suppose you know how to start one, do you, Lady Black Sheep?"

The arrogant mockery in his voice pushed me beyond my tolerance. Jaw clenched in a flash of anger, I flicked the bone knife from my waistband and sent it spinning across the space between us. His horse shied as it thunked into the tree next to him. "My name is Tess! Use it!"

Duncan blinked at the hilt of the knife quivering a foot away from him. "Uh, sure, Tess," he said, reaching to wiggle it free from the wood soft with spring sap. My anger took on a healthy dose of exasperation when avarice joined his surprise as he looked it over. "Hey, I've never seen a knife like this. What is it? Bone?" He grinned. "Find it lying about, did we?"

Insulted, I snapped, "I bought it."

"Just like your horse?" he challenged, eyebrows high. "All right. How much, then?"

My lips pursed. "For more than you'll ever have to lose," I said, knowing he wouldn't believe me if I told him I bought it with my crown. Literally, it seemed. I was embarrassed for having lost my temper. He was still turning it over in his hands, and the thought crossed me for the first time that he might not be willing to give it back. Worried, I hobbled closer and extended my hand. Eyes distant in thought, Duncan gave it back, and I tucked it away.

Making an "uh-huh" of disbelief, he led Tuck off the path to the rock face. Slow and pained, I followed, trying to keep my limping as unobtrusive as possible. My left leg had gone sluggish as it did when I was tired, and I tried to hide its hesitancy.

Seeming unconcerned that Tuck would wander, Duncan took my saddle off his horse and gave the gray a fond slap on the rump, letting him graze as he wanted. I collapsed beside the black circle of a past fire, thinking longingly of the bath I'd paid for but never used.

"Get up," Duncan said, pushing the toe of his soft boot into my ribs. "You'll go stiff."

"Stop it," I said irritably. "I'll get the wood in a moment."

He squatted beside me and brushed my dress up to my knees. Shocked, I bolted upright. "What the chu pits are you doing?" I shouted, jerking my leg out of his hand.

"Rubbing the life back into your knees. Even a blind man could see they hurt."

Again, he reached out. Appalled, I drew back and kicked him square in the chest.

Duncan fell backward. His rump hit the earth, and his breath whooshed out. My pulse pounded. I scrambled up, my fingers tingling as I fought to keep from reaching for my darts.

"What the devil is wrong with you?" he gasped from the ground, his fingers splayed over his chest as he struggled to breathe. There was a wet print of my boot on his lower chest.

"Don't touch me!" I demanded, face tight. He was a grasping lowlife of a man. How dare he presume I wanted his hands on me? *Even if I had. Once. By mistake.*

Duncan staggered to his feet. His face was red, and his eyes were watering. "You ungrateful brat!" he exclaimed, hunched into himself. "I was trying to help."

"You're a filthy liar. And don't you *ever* raise your voice to me again!"

Still red-faced, Duncan made a sarcastic bow, sweeping his raggedy hat off and running it along the dirt. "Whatever you say, Princess."

My face went cold and my anger shifted to alarm. "What did you call me?"

"Princess," he mocked, his eyes bitter as they dared me to throw my knife at him again. "That's what you seem to think you are: talking in that fool accent, checking your hair six times a day, unable to show an ounce of gratitude for someone who helps you. Your act may work on half-drunk merchants and fisherman, but I know who you are." He pointed, and my breath caught. "You're a cheat and a thief, no better than me, so bury your airs and shovel chu like the rest of us!"

"A thief and a cheat," I said, hearing my voice shake. "And if you touch me again, you'll find out if I'm an assassin, too."

He pulled his narrow face into a smirk, thinking I was making an idle threat. Tugging his water sack from his pack, he affected a mien of indifference. "I'll find the water," he said over his shoulder as he swaggered into the brush.

Full of a flustered anger, I removed Pitch's tack and rubbed her down. The horse arched her neck and nickered at my overly aggressive touch, leaving to join Tuck before I was done. Eying Duncan's pack suspiciously, I arranged my things to claim some space. Knowing the horses wouldn't likely stray from a meadow surrounded by trees, I left to search out some wood.

My knees felt like embers as I struck out across the field in the opposite way Duncan had gone. Slowly my muscles loosened, the pain almost feeling good. Firewood was only one of my goals. What I really wanted were the flowers from the stand of torch plants growing in the field where the sun shone most of the day. It was too early in the season, but I gathered the spent blossoms from last year's tall spikes lying flat on the ground. When dried and powered, the yellow flowers made a tea to ease pain and act as a mild sedative. It wouldn't help me tonight, though, and so after putting what I gathered in Kavenlow's small bag tied to my waist, I went to search out a willow.

I found one in a rill that was probably dry in high summer, cutting several twigs and a good portion of the underbark. Working my way back to camp gathering deadwood, I vigorously chewed a sap-rich twig, thinking of the man in the inn.

My cloak snagged on a briar at the edge of the meadow, jerking me to a halt. Dropping my wood in exasperation, I worked to free it, hesitating when done. I was exhausted, and breathing in the evening-cooled air, I looked over the meadow. Last year's dead vegetation was already dew-wet and purple in the graying dusk, and there was a definite chill in the air. No rain, though, and I was thankful for small favors.

My face went slack when I realized the field was empty.

"Where are the horses?" I whispered. "Duncan?" I cried, not seeing him. Then I went cold. "He took them," I breathed.

Wood forgotten, I ran to camp, fear making me feel unreal and disconnected. *Had he played me like one of his marks? Following me until he could steal everything?* Not a day from the city, and I lose everything. I was such the fool!

I skidded to a heart-pounding halt by the rock face. My things were where I'd left them. He hadn't robbed me. But the question still remained as to where the horses were.

"Hey! Here!" came a faint call. I spun to find Duncan emerging from under the far trees. He was leading Tuck; Pitch followed obediently behind. "I found good water," Duncan said when he was close enough. He slipped the rope from Tuck and shooed the horses into the field. Looking up at my silence, his face darkened. "I'm a cheat, not a thief," he said hotly.

"Can you blame me?" I all but shouted. "I come back to find you and the horses gone. I don't know you from a hole in the ground. You should have told me you were taking them!"

Duncan coiled up his rope and tossed it at his pack. "Get off your pedestal, Princess. I'm sorry if I scared you. I was only watering them."

"Don't call me that," I said, my heart beginning to slow. "And you didn't scare me."

"I think I did." He crossed his ankles and sat down in a smooth motion. His eyes were amused, watching me from under his tatty hat. An emblem had been torn from it, and I wondered where he had gotten it. Taking up a stick, he peeled the bark from it for kindling. "You look like that net maker with that stick stuck between your teeth."

Aghast, I stiffened. "It's to ease my soreness," I accused, refusing to throw it away. "I'm not accustomed to riding without a saddle."

"I can tell. It won't be long before you are, though. You smell like a horse already."

My jaw dropped. *The gall of him!* I stared, not knowing what to do. Feeling six times more filthy, I sat down across the fire from him and took up a stone to pound my willow bark with. "Better that than the chu pit you smell like," I belatedly muttered.

"I think it's an improvement," he said. "Better than that soapy smell you had before. And I like the smudge of pollen on your nose."

Immediately I wiped it off and took the stick out from between my teeth. My face warmed, and I pounded at the willow bark, thinking I'd like to do the same to his smirk.

Making a scoffing noise deep in his throat, he pulled a wad of fluff from his pack. Using a striker rock and flint, he set a spark to a triangle of charred linen. The burned fabric held a faint glow of ember until the healthy wad of waste flax caught. "What are you making for dinner?" he asked as he tried to get the sudden burst of flame to catch his grass and twigs.

"I'm not making you dinner," I said flatly. "I don't even like you."

His fingers were among his infant flame. "Camp tradition," he said as if not having heard the last part. "One person makes and tends the fire, the other makes dinner."

"I got the wood," I said quickly. A wisp of unease floated through me. I'd never made anything to eat in my entire life.

He eyed me from under the brim of his hat. "What wood?"

I took a breath to explain, then let it out. Saying nothing, I lurched to my feet. The bottom half of my dress darkened with dew as I stomped across the open field to pick up my dropped sticks. I struggled to get it all back in one trip. Duncan just sat and watched, the lazy cheat. "Here," I said as I dropped it beside him in a clattering pile. I had bits of lichen all over me, and now my dress was wet. *Angel's Spit, will I ever be clean again?*

"What did you find for us to eat?" he asked lightly, and I stared at him. "Whoever gets the wood has their eyes on the ground," he said slowly as if explaining something to a child. "Did you find anything to eat?"

I unclenched my teeth. "No." I was sure he was making it all up. But seeing as he had eased himself back against the rock face with his hands behind his head, I knelt and hesitantly pulled out my small stewpot. "I've got a few things from the stores. What do you have?"

"Travel cake, cheese, dried fish. The usual. Help yourself." He tossed his patched bag at me. It landed at my knees, and I reached for it. His claims of the division of work were chu in a pit, but I was starving, and he wasn't showing any signs of doing anything.

At least he didn't expect me to furnish all the food, I thought as I opened his bag to find it contained what he said and more. Convinced if I protested he would have me brushing his horse and mending his shoes because I sat on the west side of the fire, I silently warmed things up, burning my fingers twice.

I would be the first to admit my quiet compliance was partially due to my thoughts being full and worried. Finding the horses gone had struck me with a mind-numbing blow. I'd never been so vulnerable: out in the woods with a man I knew to be a cheat and a vagrant. Always I'd had guards and Kavenlow. I checked my hair, vowing to keep my darts close.

Duncan industriously cleaned my saddle as I prepared my torch flowers and put them to dry beside the fire. With luck, they would be crisp enough to powder by morning. The decoction from the willow bark would do tonight.

It was fully dark when I irresolutely decided there was nothing more I could do to dinner and pronounced it done. Duncan eagerly filled his bowl from the pot over the fire, then after tasting it, emptied it reluctant spoonful by reluctant spoonful. Clearly it wasn't what he had expected. I would've been angry, but even I admitted it was tasteless. Without a single word of thanks, he put his back against the rock face and pulled out his leather box of cards.

I could feel him watching me, and I tucked myself closer to the fire. It only left me too hot in front and too cold behind. The branches moved incessantly, the rustling continually drawing my gaze to the edge of the firelight. My eyes widened at the screech of a bird or animal. Duncan didn't seem bothered, but I wished the horses were closer.

The cheat silently manipulated his cards in and out of hiding, blatantly watching as I emptied my pack to rearrange it into some semblance of order. We hadn't said but a few words to each other while on the trail, but now that we were face-to-face, his quiet irritated me. It had been a difficult day. I wasn't used to silence and wanted someone to talk to. Finished with my repacking, I cleared my throat. "I'm . . . sorry for kicking you," I said.

Duncan wiggled a stick into the fire until sparks flew up. "Forget it." He rubbed his nasty stubble and glanced at me. "Like you said, you don't know me from a hole in the ground."

It was the first halfway intelligent thing I had heard him say, but I didn't know what to come back with. We had nothing in common.

"Play a hand with me?" he asked, his thin fingers sliding a card into his sleeve as slow and unhurried as a musician playing scales.

Or so I thought. I met his eyes briefly. He made an odd picture of slovenly attentiveness as he sat in his travel-stained clothes, poised and alert as he practiced his craft. "No, you cheat."

"I'll let you win," he offered, a new smile on him, the first that wasn't at my expense.

My shoulders eased. "Then I especially don't want to play."

Duncan shuffled the deck, keeping the same five cards on top. "Then I'll let you lose."

I ducked my head to hide my smile. "No, thank you." The spring night was cold, and I set some water to warm for tea. Dinner had been awful, but how hard could it be to make tea? "Do you have any honey?" I questioned. He looked at me in bewilderment, and I added, "For tea." He shook his head with a cautious slowness, and disappointed, I dug out my tea and dropped a handful into the cold water. Duncan was staring at me. "Do you want some?" I asked, trying to be nice.

"Um, yes," he said hesitantly, and I added another handful. His brow furrowed. He leaned forward as if to say something, then sat back. "Do you want to head inland after Saltwood?" he said, his words clearly not what he originally intended. "It'll be warmer."

I pushed my fingers into my forehead as if in pain. "Duncan," I said wearily. "I'm not a cheat. You should take my saddle and just . . . go away."

His eyebrows arched slyly. "You won't find anyone better," he persisted.

"I've seen street performers who can move cards like you," I scoffed.

Duncan went cocky. "Can they do this?" he asked, bringing one of my needles out.

My jaw dropped. "W-where . . ." I stammered. My hand flew to my topknot, my fingers counting to find a dart missing. "When did you take that?" I demanded, going frightened.

"Earlier." He was smug, almost frightening in his confidence.

"When?" I said, unable to think of a time when he had been close enough.

Duncan put a finger to his nose and grinned. "I'm not saying, Lady Tess."

I watched the dart, thinking Lady Tess was marginally better than Lady Black Sheep. "Fine," I said cautiously. "You're clever and quick. Give it here."

He heard the threat in my voice and pulled away. "Is it valuable?" He looked at it with a new interest, grinning to show his teeth. "Did you lift it where you got that knife?"

"Duncan . . ." I warned. "Give it to me."

He shook his head, thinking it was a grand game. I lunged around the fire to take it, and he pulled away. Jumping, his fingers jerked apart. "Damn," he said, eying the needle by his knee. "That's wickedly sharp. I can't believe you keep it in your hair."

I went cold. "Duncan, listen," I said, knowing the venom's effects would be slowed if his heartbeat stayed slow. "You're going to be all right. I promise I'll see you out of it."

Duncan looked at me as if I was insane. Then his humor left his face, replaced by a sudden pain. "Wha—" he started, then bent double. "Chu pits," he moaned. "What is it?" Then he fell over, curled up about himself.

Lips pursed, I leaned across the camp and snatched my needle up and tucked it where it belonged. I was more irritated than worried. Shifting around the fire, I checked his pulse at his neck. It was fast but steady. "Idiot!" I berated him. "I told you to give it back." He moaned, and I sighed in resignation. "You'll be all right," I said, scraping up my empathy and awkwardly patting his shoulder. "I promise I won't let you stop breathing."

Apparently it wasn't the right thing to say, as a violent spasm shook him, and his jaw clenched until his neck muscles turned to cords. Remembering the cold, I pulled his blanket over him. He had curled into a ball, his eyes closed and his face tight with an agony he didn't understand. His breath came in quick, harsh pants.

I bit my lip in concern and poked the fire for more light. He looked awful, a tinge of purple edging his lips. The venom seemed to be acting harsher than usual. His gasping breath hesitated, then resumed. My mild concern shifted to alarm. That wasn't good.

"Duncan?" I said, knowing he could hear me. I watched his pulse at his neck. The wild pounding had frightening hesitations.

"Duncan, you're all right," I lied. He was having a bad reaction, made worse by his fear. "Listen to me," I said firmly, trying to keep what little presence of mind he had left, focused. "I have to look at your finger." I reached for his right hand, clutched to his middle. "Let me see it," I coaxed. "You need your hands for your trade."

Frightened for him, I yanked his hand from his shivering huddle to find it swollen grotesquely. His middle finger was purpling. A stark white upraised circle showed where the dart had penetrated. It would be easy to slow the venom's spread with a tight bandage from his elbow to his finger. But doing so might cause irreparable damage to his hand.

"I'm sorry," I whispered, feeling nauseous. "I have to bandage your hand. It's going to hurt like the devil's dogs are chewing it, but it will slow the poison down." I hesitated, having to be honest with him. "You might lose your finger, but if I don't, you might lose your life."

He jerked. "N-n-n-no," he moaned, yanking his hand out of my grip and curling around it. Sweat beaded up on his forehead, glistening in the firelight.

"Duncan!" I tried to sound authoritative but was scared to death. What if he died out here? "It's either that or you might die. I told you to give it back. Let me see your hand!"

He clenched into himself, trembling and sweating. He managed another guttural moan, and I touched his shoulder, turning alarmed at how his muscles had locked up. His shoulders were like rocks. "Let me have it!" I demanded, tugging at his arm. He gritted his teeth, and his eyes were clenched shut. Even under the throes of the venom, he was stronger than I was.

Frustrated, I sat back on my heels, watching. If he fell unconscious, his hand was mine.

Anxiety prompted me to pick up Duncan's cards, dusting each one carefully before I put it back in his box. Listening to his painful rasps of breath, I wished he'd pass out, then prayed he wouldn't as he might never come out of it. I sat at his shoulder, worrying as I built up the fire.

"You're doing fine, Duncan," I said as the first hints of rhythm returned to his breathing. His blanket was soaked in sweat, and I draped my second blanket over him. "That's it. You're going to be all right," I whispered, falling into a soothing pattern of voice. "I'm right here. I'll see you through it. I promise."

The words sounded eerie coming from me. They were nearly verbatim to Kavenlow's whispers when I had struggled to throw off the venom. I wondered if he had been as worried as I was now, when he watched with only his voice to ease the pain. The memory of Kavenlow prompted me to run a hand over Duncan's head. Kavenlow's touch had always made the pain easier to bear, as if he knew and understood. Duncan was an idiot, but his pain was my fault.

His shortly cropped hair was softer than I had expected, a pleasant whisper on my fingertips. My tension loosened as the warmth of the fire finally soaked into me, making my hands tingle in relief. I let one rest atop his shoulder to feel his muscles slowly ease. "You're going to be all right," I whispered as the hurt finally left his face.

He took a shuddering heave of breath. It was his first grasp at conscious control, and my shoulders slumped. They ached, as if I had been the one struggling to breathe, not Duncan. His gamble to save his hand had worked. Tucking a wisp of hair from my eyes, I moved away, stiff and sore from the day's ride.

I reached for the forgotten tea, black and boiling over the fire. My hands were shaky as I pulled it from the fire and poured two cups. I set Duncan's within his reach and moved to my bedroll. Experience told me he would want something to shake the cold that gripped him. And I needed something to steady myself as well. Watching his misery had brought it all back. Until I had built my resistance high enough to suit Kavenlow, he had repeatedly subjected me to that same pain, that same fear. The reminder left me heartsick. What had it all been for?

"Who . . . are you?" Duncan rasped.

My attention jerked to him, finding him huddled under the two blankets. His eyes looked black as he stared at me over the low fire, his long face haggard under a day's growth of stubble and his struggle. I wondered if he hated me the way I hated Kavenlow the first time I had gone through that hell. I looked at the fire, trying to find an answer. "No one," I said, believing it. My eyes closed so they wouldn't fill, and I felt the fire's heat on my cheeks.

"That's a pit full of chu," he said harshly, and I opened my eyes. Taking two attempts, he propped himself up on one elbow. He hunched as he coughed violently, then wiped the spittle from himself. "I saw you repacking. Everything you need for extended travel, but you've never slept in the open before. You ride like a man but have the manners of a lady." He held his breath as he shook with a repressed cough. "And though you know what to do with torch flowers, you can't cook worth a tinker's damn. Who are you?"

"I'm no one," I said, recalling Garrett's face twisted in disgust as he learned of my true birth. My eyes flicked to his and away. "I'm a beggar's child," I whispered, afraid.

Duncan clutched the blankets tight about his shoulders. He shivered, eying me over the flames. "A beggar's child wouldn't walk away from a bowl of uneaten soup. They don't have poison on their hairpins, either. Neither do thieves."

He raised his tea to his lips with shaking hands. Hesitating, his face drained of what color it had. "You *are* an assassin," he said, dropping the cup. Tea soaked into the ground. "I thought you were—who did you kill? Sweet mother of God. I helped you escape! They saw me! They're going to come after me, now!"

"I'm not an assassin," I asserted, depressed.

"Then what are you?" he demanded. He tried to raise his arm, becoming panicky when it didn't move as well as it ought. "What did you do to me?" he cried.

Frustrated, I shouted, "Next time listen when I tell you to do something!"

He hesitated, then settled back on his blankets, showing a wary respect. I waited until I knew he was listening, then added, "My hairpins have poison on them. I've been conditioned to withstand it. One scratch usually won't kill a person. Two will, unless you work hard to keep them breathing." I recalled Jeck retaining enough control after two darts to talk. "Usually."

"Only an assassin would be immune to poison," he said, shivering.

I sighed as I gathered my thoughts. Perhaps he'd believe the truth now. "You were right, earlier," I said in a flat voice. "Well, almost. I'm—" I took a breath, forcing the words out as my betrayal rose caustic and strong. "I'm the princess's decoy, bought to shield her from backlash caused by that damned Red Moon Prophesy. I'm immune so as to extend my usefulness."

And I'm stupid, I thought bitterly. I should have seen it. No one risks the life of a princess to make her immune to poison.

And you don't leave her upbringing to the chancellor, however well he keeps her occupied and prevents her from bothering the royal family.

I closed my eyes against the hurt. In that instant, I hated them. Hated them all: my father, my mother, Kavenlow, the princess I had unknowingly protected, all of them. When I opened my eyes, I found Duncan watching me with a mix of disbelief and mistrust. "Listen," I said, deciding he needed to hear it all. If Jeck found him with me, he might be killed by association. "King Edmund's second son, Garrett, is making a bid for Costenopolie's land and ships. He could have had it all but in name had he bided his time and married the real princess at year's end, but he wants it now. He took the palace and the outlying garrisons, and when the rest of his men get here, he'll take the city, the harbor, and all the ships in it."

Grief broke through, and I caught my breath. All I cared about and thought was true had died in the name of Garrett's meaningless conquests. Nothing had arisen to replace what I once thought real. "Prince Garrett killed my parents," I whispered. "After I find Kavenlow, I'm going back to kill Garrett."

"You can't kill a prince of Misdev," Duncan whispered, his knuckles white where he gripped his blanket.

"I almost killed you," I said, weary of everything.

"But it will start a war," he protested, hunching into his blankets.

I dropped my gaze. "Kavenlow can stop it."

"Kavenlow?" he questioned.

"The chancellor." My face twisted as I struggled not to show my emotions. "He went to fetch the real princess. He's the only one I have left—" My voice had risen to a squeak, and I cut my sentence short. "He doesn't know what happened," I said flatly. "I have to find him."

"You're the Red Moon Princess?" he said, a hint of belief in his long face.

"Not since yesterday." I said the words carefully, refusing to feel anything. My life had been ruined, and all for nothing. I glanced up at the branches and the clear skies beyond them. *Where is the rain? My life can't get any worse. It ought to be raining.*

Numb, I took a gulp of tea and set it aside. It was bitter. "Drink some tea to keep your heart strong through the night, and don't even think about swallowing any of that vile ale of yours," I said. Not caring if he had more questions, I lay down, wrapped in my cloak, and drew my last blanket over my head. I wanted to sleep, exchanging my reality for dreams if only for the span darkness ruled the sky.

Twelve

The light on the inside of my eyelids was a restful gray, not the bright glare I usually woke to. And I was cold. Confused, I tried to separate myself from my dream of shifting waves. I smelled horse, and the surprise of that, not the stick poking repeatedly into my shoulder, brought me fully awake.

My pulse leapt as I bolted upright. Duncan was crouched on the far side of the fire. The stick that had been poking me was in his grip. My hand dropped from my darts, and I clutched the prickly wool blanket to my neck. Sitting to curl my legs under me, I blinked at the man.

The dim light of morning made him look more unkempt than usual. He had a brown cloak over his shoulders that I hadn't seen before, its hem black from use. "Morning," he said as he dropped the stick and pushed the rim of his hat back. "I'm going to water the horses. I thought you'd want to know."

"Thank you," I said, then coughed at the coldness of the air. The birds were noisy, and I wondered how I had slept through them. Saying nothing, he rose and went to Tuck. He wasn't using his right hand much as he coddled the gelding into taking the bit. "Can I . . . see your hand?" I asked.

He hesitated. Dropping Tuck's lead, he eased down into a

crouch beside me. Silently he pushed his shirt up to his elbow. I leaned close. His deeply tanned arm was still swollen, and the purple and red streaks across his palm and finger were downright ugly. Still having not said anything, he flexed his poison-bloated hand, wincing.

"Can you move your cards?" I asked, knowing he must have tried.

His eyes were fixed upon his shifting fingers. "No."

It was flat and emotionless, and guilt made me drop my gaze. "It will get better, but your fingers might always be slow when you're tired." I hesitated. "Do you want some willow tea?"

"No." Rising, he turned his back on me, sliding the bit into Pitch's mouth with a practiced ease. The horse mouthed it noisily.

Shivering, I bent to tighten my bootlaces. I felt bad about what had happened, but at least he wouldn't be following me anymore. "You'll be heading inland, then?" I asked, not sure I was happy to see him go. I didn't like being alone.

He turned, his nasty stubble unable to hide his surprise. "We aren't going to Saltwood?"

"We?" I blinked up at him. "After last night? I nearly killed you!"

"Really . . ." Motions stiff with what I thought was pride, he set the saddle pad on Tuck, quickly followed by my saddle. He rubbed his right shoulder before cinching it as if noticing a general weakness there.

"There's no reward for helping me," I said. "Just take my saddle and go." Miserable, I removed my needles and let down my hair. "I can find Kavenlow on my own," I whispered as I set my black ribbon aside and forced a comb through my curls.

Duncan's rough bark of laughter pulled my head up. *He was laughing at me? The nerve!*

"Tess," he said as he stood by Tuck's head. "Let's say you are the princess's decoy and not a lunatic." His eyes flicked to my darts beside me, then the whip on my waist. "You don't owe that man anything. The king and queen bought you with the sole purpose of keeping their daughter alive. And you want to help her? Wake up," he said bitterly. "Your dream is over."

"They loved me," I said hotly, surprised to find myself defending them, even though the same thought had filled my head for the last three days.

"They used you." His narrow face was harsh. "Don't you know how the story goes? The lost princess returns, saves the kingdom with the help of a goat boy, then marries her rescuer to live happily ever after. There's no room for you! If you're lucky they'll banish you from the kingdom. If you're not, they'll tuck you away, and you'll never see the outside of the palace walls again. You," he said, his eyes fierce as he pointed at me, "should be running hard and fast. And I'm going to run with you until you go hungry long enough to realize it's better to be well fed than spotlessly honest. You have a hard-won skill, Tess. And I'm not going to let you hide it under morals too expensive for commoners when we could be living like royalty in two years!"

Angry, I gritted my teeth and swung my length of hair in front of me. I tugged my comb through it, heedless of the sharp jolts of pain. "You think I should run away," I said as I picked at a snarl in frustration. "From Garrett. From everything. He killed them right in front of me!"

My pulse hammered, and an upwelling surge of anger knotted my stomach. "He had my mother's throat slit while I watched!" I exclaimed. "I couldn't keep her blood inside her, Duncan! It's still under my fingernails!" I held my hand up, almost screaming at him. "My father died to protect me! I promised I'd kill the murdering dog, and I will!"

My anger and grief poured through me, tightening my throat. I dropped my head as I realized I was almost in tears. Duncan stared, clearly shocked.

Catching myself, I dropped my head and bound my hair up off my neck. It was hard without Heather's help, but I managed. Duncan silently finished with Tuck and put the riding pad on Pitch for me. I brought out my venom and refilled the needle Duncan had darted himself with, adding it to the four in my topknot. I was cold, and I hated it. I hated everything.

"But it's not your kingdom," Duncan said, jerking my attention up. "Why do you care?"

My lips pressed together as I put the venom back into Kavenlow's pouch and tied it shut. "I'll sleep in a chu pit before I let Prince Garrett think he can have Costenopolie."

His shoulders shifted in an audible sigh as stood beside Tuck's head. "Tess, you're a commoner. And there's no shame in it. Let the royals bicker over what they will. It makes no difference who sits on the throne. You have to look out for yourself. No one else will."

I said nothing, putting my eyes on the brightening sky showing behind the spring leaves.

The uneasy silence was heavy as he took up the horses' leads. "I'll bring some water back so you can wash," he said, leading the horses away. "I have some soap—if you need it."

At the mention of soap, my feeling of filth seemed to increase tenfold. It was more than the earth beneath my palms and the blood staining my nails. I miserably got to my feet as he left, feeling all the aches from yesterday come to life. Today ought to be a joy as I added to them.

I wondered at Duncan's new respect. I didn't think it came from me having nearly killed him, and I was sure it didn't stem from a reverence for the crown—of which he had none. I was hoping it was born from a respect of me and me alone. It was something I found rarely enough among the fawning nobles, and I found my feelings toward him softening. After two days of fending for myself, his simple offer to get me water meant more to me than it should.

The sound of the horses in the brush faded. I gazed listlessly after them, wondering if Duncan was right and I should just keep running.

Numb, I folded my torch flowers into a cloth and tucked it in Kavenlow's pouch before tying it to my belt. The stink of last night's onions was thick on me, and when I took care of my morning ritual, I found my inner legs had a layer of grime on them from rubbing against Pitch yesterday. It had gone clear through my underthings.

"God help me," I whispered as I dropped my skirts, wondering if there was anything clean in the world. Duncan's water wasn't going to touch the black mix of horse sweat and dirt.

There was a movement at the far end of the field, and I hurriedly checked that my skirts were in the right place. A sharp pinch in my shoulder brought my hand up, and I slapped it.

My hand hit not the expected insect but the smooth feel of wood. Heart in my throat, I plucked out a tiny wooden dart ringed with back.

I was found.

Panicked, I looked up. A black horse bolted from the trees and across the field. Hunched upon him was Jeck with his cloak flapping like Death himself.

"Duncan!" I shrieked, lunging into the woods. Hidden behind a tree, I fumbled for my dart pipe. I peeked past the oak, my face going cold as I loosed one, then another, to no effect. I fumbled for my whip, but the black monster of a horse was upon me. Gasping, I ran, stumbling as my will was faster than my feet.

"Duncan!" I cried as I spotted him. He was too far away. Branches snapped as the black horse came to a four-posted stop. "No!" I shrieked as an arm wrapped about my waist. I jammed a dart into Jeck. Swearing, he dropped me, pulled the bone needle from his thick leather jerkin, and snapped it in two with a leather-gloved hand.

I hit the ground hard. Jeck followed me down. I held my last dart like a dagger as I tried to rise. Jeck caught me halfway up, grabbing the back of my neck so tight I yelped. His other hand went about my wrist, squeezing. My fingers opened. My last needle fell to the ground.

"Princess," he growled, and I was flung like a sack of fish over the horse's shoulders. "He-ya!" Jeck shouted as, with a lurch, he sprang onto the riding pad behind me. My stomach hurt. I struggled to breathe as the horse bolted.

"Let me go," I panted. The vegetation was a blur as we raced down the trail. Taking a jolting breath, I kneed the horse. It squealed, rising up to almost spill us.

"Relax, Princess," Jeck said as the horse's feet hit the ground and we continued. "Can you fight a little less energetically?"

He sounded almost casual, infuriating me. "Let me go!" I shouted, bending awkwardly to punch him in the gut. The man grunted, but I hadn't been able to put enough force behind the blow to do more than annoy him.

"Stop it," he said. "You asked for this meeting, not me. Your trail was clear enough."

Trail? I thought, going limp in surprise and wheezing for breath. Kavenlow's trail of leaves? Jeck knew what they were?

"So you're Kavenlow's apprentice," Jeck was saying, confusing me further. "It's a pleasure."

Jeck knew Kavenlow? I tilted my head, bouncing with the horse's movements. Jeck was smiling behind his trim black beard. I felt his leg tense as he put the horse into a slower gait.

"I thought it was your servant girl, first, seeing as she had disappeared," he said, his eyes on the trail back to the palace. "But only a player could escape the palace as quickly as you did. And no one but a player would have dart venom. Hard luck Kavenlow being sent on an errand just when he needed to be here. He must trust you if he is willing to let you speak for him. You're being a shade paranoid, though. Dragging me out here to talk settlements? The tower would have been fine."

I took a grateful breath of air as the horse's pace eased. What was he talking about? He knew I wasn't the princess and would have nothing to do with making treaties. "Let me up," I demanded, feeling my face redden from being upside down.

"'Course." He glanced behind us. His gloved hands tightened about my waist, and it was with great relief I found myself upright and set gently down upon the horse before him, sidesaddle, as was proper. His arm stayed around me, and my pulse pounded as my chance of escape dimmed. The man had arms thicker than a fence post.

He grinned at my cold face. "Surprised? Being the captain of King Edmund's guard is risky, but it works." His grip on my waist tightened as he glanced behind us at the empty trail. "Kavenlow is either moonstruck or planning a game I won't live to see the end of if he's taking someone so close to the throne as his apprentice. Hell and damnation, what if something happened to the real heir? You'd be pulled down before the ink dried on the coronation invitations. The man has more gall than I'd give him by his milksop looks."

He looked behind him again. "So, out with it," he said. "Leaving Prince Chu-head alone this long isn't wise. What are Kavenlow's thoughts on Garrett's bid for your land? I'm tempted to back the dunderhead, though his father will have to annex the kingdom as his own before I can use it in play." His white teeth showed strongly behind his beard. "I'm going to enjoy tending Costenopolie's harbors as well as Edmund's farms. Hard luck having to start over."

I stared dumbfounded at him. He was talking as if he stood higher, had more power, than his king's son. "Don't you mean, King Edmund's farms?" I stammered.

"King? Since when does a piece warrant king?" Jeck paused, taking in my silence. His face went empty, and his grip tightened.

"You didn't leave the trail; you were following it. Damn it all to hell," he swore. "He hasn't told you who you are yet. You're not a player, you're still a damned piece."

Panicking, I squirmed. "Duncan!" I shouted, slamming my heels into his horse. The black horse squealed and lurched. Jeck scrambled for control as I slid to the ground.

Three darts hit me in quick succession as I ran into the woods. Bark bit at my palms as I clutched at a tree, staggering under the venom. Lungs heaving, I fought off the vertigo, quickly regaining my balance. Nausea rose high. Jeck crashed after me. Panic gave me a renewed strength. I struggled forward, running.

"Sorry, Princess," Jeck said breathlessly as he yanked my arm and brought me to a spun-about halt. "I'm not wasting any more darts on you."

I gasped as the butt of his sword arced toward me. There was an instant of white pain in my temple, then nothing.

Thirteen

My head hurt. It pounded from somewhere over my right temple. That was the first breath of awareness to wedge itself past my muzzy blanket of unconsciousness. The second was that I was sitting on something sharp. It felt like a thorn, but I had a suspicion it was one of Jeck's darts. A filmy black cloth stretched across my face, cutting into the corners of my mouth. I tried to raise my hands, finding my arms were bound behind me. A familiar chalky taste coated my tongue—the flavor that an overdose of venom left behind. I pried my eyelids apart, blinking.

It was well past noon by the sun's position; I had been out most of the day. My boots and stockings were gone, which would explain why my feet were so cold they ached. A cord was about my ankles. I was propped against a tree, its bark pinching my knuckles and back. Before me was a small camp. Jeck's, I assumed, since it was his horse tied nearby. The black gelding still wore his riding pad, and he looked annoyed as he flicked his tail at it.

A metal pan steamed over a small, smokeless fire. Beside it were my black hair ribbon, my coiled whip, my bone knife, and Kavenlow's bag. I went cold as I realized Jeck had searched me while I was unconscious. He had taken my hair down in his search for more darts, and the tips were trailing in the sticks and leaves. Where else had he looked, I wondered, and why had he taken my stockings off? My head slumped back to hit the tree. I was tied to a tree in my bare feet. It wasn't raining. That meant it was going to get worse. Somehow.

Gathering my resolve, I wiggled to get free. The horse turned to watch. "Mummph," I grunted in frustration around the gag, but the horse didn't care. Ears pricked, he looked over my shoulder. I heard the thuds of approaching hooves. *Duncan!* I thought, squirming to make as much noise as possible.

Wiggling and twisting, I peered around the tree to find Jeck, not Duncan, leading Tuck through the brush. My struggles stopped, and I slumped. Tuck eagerly paced to join Jeck's horse. I closed my eyes in misery. The gray still wore my saddle; Jeck had probably stolen him so we could reach the palace sooner. Worry pinched my brow, and I hoped Duncan was all right. A single dart might kill him so soon after last night.

"Princess."

My eyes flew open at the soft word. It was entirely devoid of emotion, either sincerity or mockery. Dressed in black leather and linen, Jeck looked more like a highwayman than the captain of King Edmund's guard. His black cloak was clean, showing only a dusting of grass and dirt. He eyed me from under the brim of a simple black hat. It appeared far more functional than the one decked with feathers he had worn when I first saw him.

Crouching by the fire, he took off his riding gloves and poured the liquid from the steaming plate into a bowl. My eyes darted from the near-boiling water to his eyes. Whatever was in that bowl probably wasn't soup. And I was sitting here, pretty much helpless.

"I'm glad you woke," he said as he stood. "I didn't want to move you until you had."

"Mummph," I said, making it as belligerent as I could. My defiance faltered as he crossed the camp and knelt beside me. Lurching, I swung my bound feet up to hit him.

Balance never shifting, he grasped my knees with a thick-knuckled hand and pinned them. "Easy, Princess," he said, sitting upon my knees and tugging the scarf from my mouth.

"Get off me," I demanded, taking a grateful breath of air. "Let me go!"

"I don't like being kicked." He dipped a square of cloth into the water, and I squirmed, tilting my head away as far as I could. "Hold still," he muttered.

I flinched when he touched me, but his fingers were gentle as he dabbed at my forehead. Slowly I let out my held breath, watching his brown eyes. I could almost believe it was concern that pinched his quiet face. The cloth came away with crusted blood and the faint smell of figwort. It would reduce the swelling, and I wondered why he bothered.

"My apologies," he said, his attention on what he was doing. "I hit you too hard. Prince Garrett wants you in good health, not feverish with infection." He rinsed the cloth, and the water turned red with my blood. "He'll have my hide should I bring you back in too sorry a condition." Leaving the rag on the edge of the bowl, he leaned closer to inspect his work.

His shirt brushed my cheek, and I could smell woodsmoke and two days in the wilds on him. He eased back, and I started to breathe again. "How gallant of the Misdev dog," I said sharply. "Wanting me in good health before he weds me, rapes me, then kills me." I would have called for Duncan, but Jeck wouldn't have removed the gag had he been close.

Jeck made a noise of agreement and moved to sit before the fire on a decaying log. Watching, I pulled my knees to my chin to hide my dirty feet as much as to try to warm myself. I thought I'd been vulnerable sleeping across the fire from a cheat. Now I knew what vulnerable was. Jeck rubbed a sword-hardened hand over his tidy beard and looked at his horse. "What am I going to do with her?" he asked the animal as if I wasn't sitting in front of him.

"Let me go?" I prompted.

His gaze flicked to mine. "No."

"Untie me? At least my hands? It's not as if I can run away from you. Not without my boots." My thoughts went to my knife and whip beside the fire. "And I'm sitting on something sharp," I complained to move him into something foolish. "One of your darts, probably. One would think you would have realized I had some immunity right off. But no-o-o-o, you just keep darting away, wasting them until you *hit* me."

He reached out. Before I realized his intent, he shoved me over. I shrieked as my cheek smacked the leaf mold. "Get your hands off me!" I cried as a hand fell heavy on my hip, forcing me down. A scream escaped me as he flung my skirts over my head.

"Hold still. I see it."

The light was a crimson tint from my red underskirt as I wiggled, fighting him. There was the twinge of something sharp being removed from my behind. "Get off me!" I yelled, and his weight on my hip vanished. I gasped as a hand gripped my shoulder and yanked me upright. By the time I flung the hair from my eyes, he was back before the fire holding one of his tiny wooden darts between his fingers and eying it for damage.

"What luck. It's not broken," he said as he tucked the sliver of wood into his hatband, showing me where he kept them. His eyes went to mine, and his eyebrows bunched. If I got loose, they would be the first thing I would head for, and he knew it.

"You uncouth Misdev *barbarian*!" I shouted, trying to spit the curl of hair out of my mouth. "Don't you *ever* do that again! I'll have you keelhauled and thrown into the chu pits!"

He gave me a speaking look, his eyes going to the gag still loose about my neck and the rope about my ankles. My dress wasn't exactly where it ought to be, and face flaming, I tucked my legs up to hide them.

"You are the most vile man I have ever met," I said, my heart still pounding. "You abduct me, knock me out, search me while I'm unconscious, and tie me up. Then you shove me down and nearly pull off my dress while my hands and feet are bound. Untie me. Right now!"

A rude snicker came from Jeck, infuriating me. "I didn't pull off your dress. I pulled out a dart. Would you rather I left it in?" I stiffened as he rose to his feet, flicking a knife out from somewhere. "You do anything I don't like, I'll knock you silly again," he said.

I held my breath, pushing back into the tree for leverage. If he got close enough, I could kick him unconscious, now that my skirts were about my knees. But before I even had a chance, he put his big hand on the back of my head and shoved my forehead to my knees. I took a breath to shout at him, my impetus dying as there was a firm tug on my wrists, and my hands were free. His hand lifted from me. My outrage vanished and I pulled my aching arms forward. A groan of pain slipped out before I could stop it.

Jeck eyed me carefully from three steps away as I rubbed my wrists and the red marks left by the bindings. Tingling jolts pulsed through my fingers with a steady hum, hurting them with the sudden heat of circulation but soothing my wrists where I held them. My feet were still tied, but I had my hands. I was halfway to freedom. Soldier he may be, but he was a fool for believing threats of violence would keep me docile.

"Thank you," I said sullenly. The gag was still about my neck, and I picked the knot loose and dropped the spit-soaked rag to the earth.

"If you try to escape, I'll tie you up again," he warned as he coiled the cord he had used about my wrists and shoved it in a saddlebag along with my whip and knife. His face lost its emotion when he saw me sitting cross-legged, holding my wrists. "What—ah—what are you doing?"

I looked up, doing nothing to hide my disgust. "My wrists hurt!"

"Um," he said, his lips pressing together to almost disappear behind his beard and mustache. "It's just the circulation coming back. You'll be fine."

"I know that." My eyes narrowed when he turned away. I remembered my hands had the same, humming-tingly feeling when I had been comforting Duncan. They hadn't been tied at all then. But my wrists felt better, and I let them go.

I purposely kept my gaze away from the horses. As soon as I could, I'd be gone. "May I have some of that warmed water?" I asked, embarrassed that my face was streaked with dirt.

Attention on an unvoiced thought, he set the high-walled pan within my reach. I edged closer to it and the fire. Everything but my hands were cold, the tingling having subsided into an ache. "Did you kill Duncan?" I asked, unable to keep the worry from my voice.

"The man with you?" he said, seeming to jump to the present. "No. I had no reason to."

"Then how did you get his horse?" I asked.

Jeck smirked and sat down across from me. "He fell off when

I spooked his horse. The beast is more flighty than six deer. I thought the gray was yours. The stableman said you stole a horse and a saddle—"

"I *paid* for them," I protested, then hesitated. "You talked to the stableman . . ."

Nodding, Jeck pulled a travel cake from his saddlebag. "Getting out as one of two," he said around a mouthful of fat and grain. "Nice. How did you convince a vagrant to help you?"

I said nothing, feeling sullen. My stomach rumbled at the smell of honey.

Apparently unconcerned, Jeck brushed a crumb from his beard. "I knew you'd want a horse, and the man wouldn't stop talking about you. How his girl ran away with the mare he sold you. How you stole the one that belonged to the palace, and what was he going to tell the palace when they came to collect them? Oh, woe is me," he finished in a mocking voice.

I felt ill, realizing I'd left a trail as clear as Kavenlow's. My eyes flicked to the black gelding. It was the twin to my mare. "That's my horse," I said. "He was holding them for me."

Jeck's narrow mustache rose as he grinned. "He's a fine animal, and a great deal more rested than my horse. Being the captain of King Edmund's guards has its privilege."

He had taken my horse when it came right down to it. Turning the hem of my dress up, I looked for a fold of less-begrimed fabric I could use to clean myself.

Jeck leaned to his pack and tossed me a wad of cloth. It arched over the fire and landed squarely in my lap. I picked it up—fully intending to throw it back into his face—but it was soft and clean, smelling of soap. Abandoning pride for comfort, I dipped it into the warm water.

Jeck set his travel cake aside and picked up Kavenlow's bag. My mouth opened as he undid the tie and upended the pouch. "That's mine," I protested. His eyebrows rose as he took in my anger, and I added, "Get out of it!"

Ignoring me, he ran his fingers over everything. "Fishhooks," he said, dropping them back in the bag. "Candle, needle and thread, flint." He glanced at me from under the brim of his black hat. "Dry tinder, cord . . ." He held up my packet of dried torch flowers. "What's this?"

"A mild sedative and pain relief," I said, seeing no harm in him knowing. His soft cloth felt like heaven against my travel-torn fingers, and my hands were humming from the hot water.

Never dropping my gaze, Jeck slipped the torch flowers into an inner pocket of his jerkin. Outraged, I stiffened. "Put that back!" I cried. But my anger shifted to alarm when he opened Kavenlow's venom and took a sniff.

"Still a liquid?" he murmured. "Interesting." As I watched, unable to stop him, he removed his hat and slipped a tiny dart from the hatband. I knew he used a dart pipe, but I had yet to see it. He dipped the dart into the venom, then touched it to his tongue. "Chu," he swore, recoiling with a grimace. "No wonder you put me down with two." The skin about his eyes wrinkled as he replaced his dart into his hatband. "And why you were still running after four of mine. What does Kavenlow do to keep the venom from coagulating after you kill it?"

Kill what? I thought as I struggled with my desire to either smack him for pawing through my things or thank him for the information. He recapped the small jar when I remained silent, tucking it into his saddlebag. My face flamed. "That's mine," I said.

"What's yours?" He meet my eyes with a blank expression.

"That's my dart venom. Put the jar back in my bag."

He gave me a handsome grin. "What jar?"

Giving up, I scrubbed the cooling cloth against my face. Keeping even my hair ribbon, he shoved everything into Kavenlow's bag, which he then knotted to his belt. "You're a thief," I said, unable to think of anything more derogatory.

His eyebrows rose. "I prefer 'using my means to their fullest potential.'"

"And a coward," I added, coming up with something vastly better.

Jeck's face emptied of all expression, and I wondered if I had gone too far. "No," he said softly. "Not a coward." I couldn't tell if he was angry, and somehow that frightened me.

"What are you going to do with me?" I asked as I braided my hair, despairing of the sticks and leaves my fingers kept finding.

He scuffed a boot into the leaf mold. "Return you to Prince Garrett as ordered."

I looped the braid about itself, shaping the entire arrangement into a decorative ball at the base of my neck. It would hold as long as I didn't move about much. Sniffing at him, I tried to find the air of misplaced confidence that worked so well on the palace guards when they caught me where I shouldn't be. "This morning you seemed to be acting on your own. And now you're back to taking orders from a spineless, sniveling, worthless excuse of a royal who has as much right to rule as a barnacle worm." Excitement went through me as Jeck stiffened in unease. I'd found a sliver of truth, but how did it fit?

"This morning I thought you were someone else, Princess," he said.

"Don't call me that," I demanded, pretending disinterest as I scrubbed between my toes to turn the cloth brown. "We both know I'm not."

Jeck rose to take the saddle off Tuck. "People act within the expectations they're given. I say you're a princess. Act like one. And keep your burning hands away from those knots."

Disgusted he had known I was working my way to them, I made a face and dropped the cloth into the water. "I'm her double, that's all," I said tightly. But Jeck never noticed my frustrated anger as we both turned at a scuffling in the leaves. My breath came fast in hope, but I slumped when I spotted a squirrel, not Duncan. There was a thump and a squeak. A knife pinned the rodent to the ground, dead.

Shocked, I spun back to find a second knife in Jeck's hand, his arm cocked to throw it. Frowning, he slid the knife behind his belt. "But I'm in no hurry to get back to Prince Chu-head," he said. "And you look hungry. Skinny. All legs and arms."

Ignoring his insult, I sourly picked the mud from my hem. *He could throw a knife. How wonderful.* And though I was starving, I wouldn't eat. He might tamper with my food.

"Well, I'm hungry," he continued as if I had said something. "We can't make it back by sundown, so we'll leave in the morning. Garrett can stew for a while. Maybe he'll realize what he has started." Putting the last of his travel cake in his mouth, he went to get the squirrel.

The captain's casual disregard for Garrett's standing still shocked me, serving as more proof that Jeck held more power than he ought. He had said I was a player, that I was Kavenlow's apprentice. What the devil was a player? A specialized body-guard, maybe?

As Jeck butchered the squirrel, I finished washing my feet, thinking about that. Kavenlow had taught me my letters and numbers, and countless ways to dally the hours away, but nothing about protecting anyone except myself. Then again, Kavenlow had kept me alive my entire life through a score of assassination attempts. A chancellor.

Feeling as if I was close to figuring something out, I dried my feet on my red underskirt. Jeck had hinted at a huge conspiracy. His few words—at first glib and bewildering, then hesitant and obscure—had filled me with unease. Things weren't as I thought. My ingrained beliefs—the beliefs of my entire society—were based on a veneer that even the royals thought went all the way through. I had very little to shape my new wisdom upon.

Fingers slow, I placed my damp cloth on the rim of the pan. Kavenlow's note had said that though the king and queen held the crown, we kept Costenopolie intact. It went along with what Jeck had implied about him controlling Misdev. But I had grown up in the palace. I knew the king and queen ruled. Didn't they?

A wash of unreal feeling coursed through me as I recalled how often my and Kavenlow's diversions had been interrupted by private councils with men of importance, the letters without the royal seal passed by Kavenlow's hand, and his excursions to the docks at all hours. Suddenly Jeck's hints of Kavenlow pulling hidden strings sounded not only plausible but obvious.

I raised my head to find Jeck butchering the squirrel at the edge of camp. "You said I was a—a player," I said, trying to pull more information from him. The familiar word felt odd as I said it, and Jeck's first expression of shock melted into a fierce look.

"Don't," he said with a frightening harshness. "Don't ask me."

I leaned forward, feeling as if I almost had it. I recalled Jeck's whipping, the frustration in his eyes—and the control. "You aren't just the captain of King Edmund's guard," I said, thinking I was closer to the truth than I had been my entire life. "You're a player."

"No," he said, raising a protesting hand, fingers red with the squirrel's blood. He saw it, and put his hand down. "It was a jest. A very bad jest. I'm the captain of King Edmund's guard, charged with keeping his second son alive until he's safely married. That's all." But his brown eyes looked too determined.

"No, you're more. You're a player," I prodded.

"Princess . . ." His shoulders shifted as he took a deep breath and slowly let it out. Returning to the fire, he flicked my damp rag into his grip and wiped his hands clean. He looked worried as he stood before me. "Damn it, Jeck," he swore. "Your big mouth finally caught up with you.

"Listen," he said, crouching down before me. "Do us both a justice and keep your thoughts to yourself. Kavenlow is going to be angry enough with me as it is for letting Garrett make an unannounced bid for Costenopolie. But forcing his timetable with you?" The corners of his eyes crinkled, and he took off his hat, making him look younger as it tousled his hair. "I'd rather swing from King Edmund's rope as a traitor than interfere with you. That it was an honest mistake means nothing. I'm going to salvage what I can and get out." Clearly worried, he carefully set his hat on his bedroll and moved the pan of bloody, brown water out of my reach.

My pulse raced. He was more concerned about what he had told me than about Garrett killing the king and queen? I was learning bits and pieces, each one more confusing than the last. "You're afraid of him," I said. "You're afraid of Kavenlow?"

Jeck looked up from the squirrel, his wide shoulders tensing. "No. I'm not."

"I think you are, Captain."

He turned around. "No, Princess. I'm not." He hung the rodent upside down to drain into the pan. "It's not all my fault, though. Why he kept you in the dark this long is beyond me. You have a considerable tolerance to venom. He should have had you recognized years ago."

"Recognized," I whispered. An image of fox lapping water drifted through me. I could smell burning wormwood. My heart hammered as memories flooded back.

Kavenlow had been angry, but he hadn't burned the gypsy wagon. He had carried me to my room, kissed my forehead, and went to talk to my parents. Why hadn't I remembered that before?

Suddenly frightened, I met his eyes. "What is going on, Captain Jeck?"

"Nothing," he said, staring at me.

"That's a lie," I said, knowing it was.

Jeck carefully wiped his fingers clean. "You keep telling yourself that, Princess, and we both might survive."

Fourteen

It was cold. The clear skies had allowed the heat of the day to abandon the earth quickly once the sun set, and even the spring frogs were too numb to sing. Everything I owned but the clothes I had on were in Jeck's saddlebags or with Duncan, thoroughly out of reach. I wondered if "my thief," as Jeck had come to call him, had taken Pitch for his own and headed for better pickings. A part of me hoped he had. The more frightened part of me hoped he hadn't.

My head throbbed dully where Jeck had knocked me. There was a lump the size of a walnut, but it didn't seem feverish. Feeling sorry for myself, I scooted closer to the fire and licked the last of the grease from my fingers. The previous empty ache in my middle—and watching Jeck prepare the squirrel—had convinced me it was safe to eat.

"Thank you," I said as I glanced over the fire. I froze, embarrassed; I had bolted down my meal before he had even finished half of his. He sat on his log well back from the fire, looking plenty warm with his boots, coat, and heavy cloak. My eyes lingered on his blanket folded neatly beside him. I wouldn't ask for it. I had my pride.

"You're welcome," he said. "I've never seen anyone eat the meat from toes before."

"Dinner last night wasn't very good," I muttered. A sudden sneeze shook me, and I clutched my arms around my drawn-up knees and pulled my thin cloak tighter. The tight band about my ankles had been replaced by a length of rope that hobbled me like a horse. It was humiliating. If I had my knife, I might loose my bonds. If I had my boots, I could run. If I could knock Jeck unconscious, I might elude him entirely. If, if, if . . .

"So," I said hesitantly, not liking the silence, "you learned to cook while a guard?"

Jeck laughed, and the pleasant sound of it startled me. "No," he said. "My father taught me, but I'll be damned if it wasn't his cooking that got me my position of captain."

"How could cooking do that?" I asked, not liking his rough language.

He pulled a bite from a tiny bone and chewed thoughtfully. Wiping his mouth, he said, "King Edmund sends his foot soldiers into the field for a month every fall. You know that strip of forest you left him?" I nodded, and his eyes went distant. "They camp there and fend for themselves. At the end of it, there's a contest. Fighting, climbing, swimming, that sort of thing." He flicked the stripped bone into the fire. "The best join the palace guard."

"And you won it your very first year."

I couldn't keep the sarcasm from my voice, but Jeck's eyes held laughter, not anger. "No. It's generally the big hulks of men who win. After two years of being beaten black-and-blue, I befriended one. Fed him the entire time. I invented so many ways to cook squirrel, you wouldn't know you were eating the same animal for a week. He agreed to hoist me up the rope, push me over the wall, and fight beside me in the final melee if I kept his belly full until then."

"You cheated," I said, not surprised.

"No." Jeck gave me a sideways smile from behind his beard, his eyes glinting in the firelight. "You have to have rules to break them, and there weren't any. I couldn't do it by brawn, so I did it by brain." Jeck wrapped a cloth around a pot of boiling water and pulled it from the fire before adding what I thought was a ridiculously small amount of tea leaves.

"I had a life expectancy of about forty in the army if we never went to war," he said softly. "I didn't like the idea that my life was that close to being half over. Being in the castle guard would have increased it dramatically." He met my eyes. "It did increase it dramatically."

I clutched my knees to myself, uneasy. "Have you ever killed anyone?" I asked.

"Of course." He frowned, then added, "I don't enjoy it, if that's what you're asking."

I thought of Garrett and the shudder of lust I'd felt in him while he watched his guard kill another. He had enjoyed it. My throat tightened as I remembered watching my parents die. How could I have let him live? Next time I would be strong. "Does it get easier?" I whispered.

"The doing? Yes. Much as I'd like to think otherwise, yes. It does. The afterward, though, gets worse." His eyes met mine. "Why? Do you wish you had killed Garrett?"

Defiance mixed with fear and anticipation in a nauseating mix. "He deserves to die."

Jeck nodded in an absent fashion. "True, but that doesn't mean it's in everyone's best interests that he should. But I won't let you kill him. I'm not eager for another pointless Misdev war, which is what you'll get if Garrett dies."

"There won't be a war. Kavenlow can convince King Edmund I was justified," I said.

"Justified . . ." Jeck stretched his feet out to the fire and loosened his bootlaces. "So the contest ended, and I and my dinner companion were left," he said, continuing his story. "I hadn't yet grown into my height, and I lacked the power that the men who lost had, but I was smarter. It wasn't long before it was recognized, and after I got my growth, I moved up to captain. Life became interesting after that." He met my gaze from under his hat, the firelight flickering to make shadows. "How about you? How did you become the princess's decoy?"

"Uh," I stammered, caught off guard. "I was bought in the streets. The only one of three decoys to survive the earliest Red Moon Prophesy assassination attempts." I tucked the hem of my dress under my feet to keep them off the damp ground. "I'm a beggar's child, I suppose. I didn't know until"—I thought for a moment, surprised—"four days ago. Before that it was the usual princess tasks: reading and sums, how to draw a map, how to play a tune, how to step a dance, how to seat visiting dignitaries at dinner so no one is beside the person who snubbed them last spring." I flicked my gaze to his and then looked away, seeing a worried confusion in his eyes.

"That's it?" he asked. "He hasn't taught you anything. Anything of value, I mean."

"Who are you to know?" I snapped, but it lacked conviction. I had a feeling Jeck was right. Kavenlow had been responsible for my schooling, and most of that had revolved around the political niceties of being a princess. Perhaps because there was always the chance I might end up on the throne if anything happened to her. *Like her royal snotship meeting the soul reaper on her way home,* I thought, almost hoping she would.

An animal screeched, the same as last night, and I edged closer to the fire. Kavenlow hadn't taught me anything special. If he had, I wouldn't be sitting here with my feet tied together, shivering. I would have chewed my way free when Jeck had been digging a shallow privy, whipped him into submission when he returned, then stolen the horses to run away.

"I was bought for silver, too," Jeck said suddenly. I looked up at his quick-worded admission. His brown eyes held a hint of vulnerability, and I didn't think he had ever told anyone before. "Before that, I lived with a childless farmer. A passing priest saw me throwing rocks at the birds to keep them off the corn. He took me right there, yanking me onto his horse and shouting for my father. I was eight."

Shivering, I pulled my cloak tighter. Jeck must mean his surrogate father. He had said the farmer was childless.

Jeck looked tired as he gazed into the fire as if searching for his past. "I remember my father clutching my leg as I sat before the priest on his horse," he said. "My father told him I was all he had. The priest kicked him in the mouth—broke one of his teeth—then threw a pouch of coins into the dirt." Jeck poured the brewed tea into a metal cup. "He died three years later from too much work and not enough food. I didn't know until he was in the ground until grass had grown over him so thick I couldn't tell where he was. He was the only father I knew."

"You don't remember your real father?" I asked, feeling an odd kinship.

"He was my real father." Jeck's lips pressed together, all but disappearing behind his mustache. "He took care of me. We worked together to build his farm so he would have food when he was too old to work and I would have food until I was old enough to work. If he wasn't a father, then what is one?"

I said nothing, feeling foolish. Apparently satisfied with my attitude, Jeck took a sip of his tea and brushed away the drops left on his beard. "The priest left me with the army, and I already told you the rest. God help me, I thought it was such a waste at the time."

"You were eight?" I asked, appalled. "King Edmund puts eight-year-olds in his army?"

"No," he said in annoyance. "I was a glorified slave to the enlisted, but I joined when I was old enough. I never saw the priest again until I made captain. That was when he—" Jeck cut his thought short and poked at the fire.

That was when he gave Jeck his first dose of venom, I guessed, and told him about players. But I wouldn't say it. If Jeck realized how much I was gleaning from even his casual words, he would return to his stone-lipped self.

Stretching to his stack of firewood, he set a thick piece on the fire. "Do you want some tea?" he asked, clearly changing the subject. "I don't have another cup, but you could drink it out of a bowl."

"Do you have honey?" I asked, and when he shook his head, I gestured no. It wasn't tea if it didn't have honey in it.

His cup almost lost in his big hands, Jeck tilted his head and eyed me from under his hat. "I'm curious. How old were you when you first tasted venom?"

I tucked an escaped curl behind my ear. "You admit there's such a thing now?"

The flash of white teeth as he grinned was unexpected. "I do nothing of the kind. But you have quite a tolerance. If you don't mind my asking, when did Kavenlow first initiate you?"

I hesitated. He was charming information from me, but if it kept him talking, I might learn something myself. "Thirteen," I said. "An assassin found me while I was in the streets. Almost got me with a dart." I picked at the grimy hem of my dress. It had been awful. I couldn't blame Heather for not coming into the streets with me. I hoped she was all right.

"Kavenlow wanted to give me a better weapon of defense," I

continued, "suggesting the very thing that almost reached me. He said I had the ability to become immune to it, that it wouldn't kill me." Stomach clenching, I remembered my first dose of venom. I hadn't died—though at the time, I wished I had. The convulsions had left me weak and in tears. "He said I'd never see the outside of the palace again if I didn't. It was outright blackmail, even to keeping it from—from my parents. They never knew the cause for my occasional lethargy."

Jeck made an understanding noise. His eyes, when I met them, were very intent. I shut my mouth. I was talking too much. He reached for a stick, his cape pulling against his broad shoulders. Stirring the coals, he left it to burn. "Do you like him?" he asked, shocking me.

"Kavenlow?" I said, affronted. "He's like a second father to me."

His eyes fixed to mine. "Why?" he asked, the word making me uneasy. "He poisoned you countless times, made you go through the hell of building your tolerance. For what? To protect someone you never met? To force you to suffer the weight of a prophesy that wasn't yours to bear? He has lied to you your entire life. And you trust him?"

"Kavenlow saved my life more times than I have fingers," I said hotly. "He sat with me every time I took the venom. And he always had something nice planned for the next day to make up for it. A rare outing into the hills or—" I abruptly went silent, thinking. "Or a good game of hide-and-seek," I breathed as I pondered Kavenlow's diversions with a new outlook. I had never guessed they were more than games. What had Kavenlow made me into? My eyes flicked to Jeck's. I had to stop talking.

"At thirteen?" Jeck's voice overflowed with disbelief. "You were playing *games at thirteen*? I was learning how to kill a man at fifteen paces with a knife when I was thirteen."

"How splendid for you," I said dryly. "But I didn't have to kill anyone to get past the palace walls. Could you have done the same?"

Jeck grunted at that, seeming pleased rather than annoyed as I would have expected.

"Stop talking to me," I said in a huff. "I'm going to sleep."

"You do that. We leave before sunup."

I shifted my shoulders to show I had heard him, pushing the dirt smooth where I was going to have to sleep. Leaves and dirt clung to my palms, and I looked at the filth on them in disgust. I'd be leaving tonight if I could sneak away with the horses.

He wadded up his blanket and threw it at me over the fire. "Sleep on that," he said.

Relief filled me as the coarse wool rasped across my fingertips. "Thank you."

"Take this, too," he said as he undid the clasp of his cloak and carefully handed it to me.

I accepted it with some surprise, my eyebrows rising as I found the black wool lined with an even blacker silk. It was beautiful, and I wondered that he had something this exquisite. "What will you use?" I asked, seeing nothing left to him but his coat.

"I'm staying awake for obvious reasons." He took a sip of tea. "And before you get any ideas, I'm bigger than you, I'm stronger than you, and if you try anything . . ."

I made a face as I remembered the shriek of the dying squirrel. His eyes were on me while I struggled to arrange the blanket with my ankles hobbled. Finally giving up, I covered myself in his cloak, pulling the hood up over my head as I lay down.

The smell of horse and woodsmoke filled my senses—it seemed to warm my chill as much as the added weight of the cloak—but the masculine smell of Jeck mixing with them stirred me back to vigilance. I took a shallow breath, then a deeper one, pulling in his scent and studying it as I might a new concoction from the kitchen. Much to my disgust I decided it was nice. Manly nice, as Heather would say. I sighed, wishing I was of a strong enough mind to convince myself it stank.

I could see Jeck across the fire, his image distorted from the flames. He was . . . He was taking his shirt off! My pulse hammered, and I sat up.

"Don't flatter yourself, Princess," Jeck said, his brow furrowing as his shirt stuck to his back. "Not every man is trying to get under your skirts." His shirt pulled away with a sharp suddenness accompanied by a tight grimace. My stomach clenched as I remembered his whipping. He dropped his shirt, leaving him bare to the waist. Pulling the hood of his cloak over my face, I settled down, propping my head on my folded arms so I could watch the bunching smoothness of his muscles. I had a feeling he knew it.

Jeck took a rag and dipped it into the water left from making tea. Twisting awkwardly, he tried to sponge the dried blood from his back. It didn't take long to realize he couldn't manage it. "I'll do that," I said, not knowing why I offered.

Jeck's attention flicked over the fire to me and away.

"You got them because I escaped," I prodded, sitting back up and letting his cloak fall from me. "I'll clean them for you."

He wrung out his rag in the water and stretched to reach the center of his back, coming short. "Why would you help me?"

"Why would you bother to feed me and give me your blanket and cloak?" I answered.

Jeck sighed, his entire chest moving. "No. Soothe your conscience some other way. Like not annoying me with trying to escape."

"They'll get infected," I said. "And what can I do to you? It's not as if I can hurt you. You took all my darts and tied my feet as if I was an errant goat."

Jeck's jaw clenched. "True. But I might have to hurt you. And it's harder if—"

I felt the blood drain from my face. He wouldn't hurt me. He couldn't.

He scowled as he took in my expression. "Hell and damnation," he swore. He rose, and while my pulse hammered, he brought his pot of hot water and tin of paste to my side of the fire. Feeling ill and unreal, I slid down the blanket to make room for him. He sank down beside me, stiffly showing me his back. "Behave yourself, or I'll knock you so hard you won't wake up," he threatened. "Don't think I won't."

I swallowed hard. "I know." His back was very broad and smooth, the skin dark from long hours in the sun. The five brands looked raw, rimmed with red and their edges swollen. With the right ointment, they'd heal. Garrett's marks were faint welts, nothing more.

The water was hot on my chilled fingers as I wrung out the cloth. I reached forward, then hesitated. Angel's Spit, I'd never done anything like this before. Taking a breath, I decided I'd pretend I was Heather. *She'd* know how to wash a man's back. God help me, I was pathetic.

Steeling myself, I dabbed hesitantly at the highest bloody mark and worked my way carefully down. His shoulders were different from those I'd seen at the docks, bunching with strength gained from swinging a blade rather than pulling a rope. He smelled like horse, same as his cloak. Scattered between the whip marks were a sprinkling of old white scars.

I continued to work, running the cloth carefully over each rise and fall of muscle, feeling the difference in each of them. I'd never had this opportunity to unhurriedly touch a man, this soft exploration that was made right and proper by way of an offer of help. It was heady, and the cool detachment I touched him with seemed to make it all the more intense.

Jeck started as I touched the small of his back to catch a rivulet. I suddenly realized I had gone over his entire back and had needlessly started over again. *What the chu pits am I doing?* Embarrassed, I draped the rag over the edge of the pot and opened the tin.

I risked a sniff at the white ointment, recoiling at the stench. Garlic and horseradish, with a healthy dose of thyme to try to counteract the smell, mixed in what looked like wax and fat. It was a nasty concoction, undoubtedly guaranteed to remove infection. I hesitantly dipped my fingers. I looked at his back, thinking it was beautiful with power, even marred as it was.

A grunt slipped from Jeck as the cold ointment hit his back. "Sorry," I said, shifting to kneel behind him. His skin was warm where I smoothed the paste over the brands. The muscles in his neck turned to cords, and his shoulders tensed. "I'm not going to try to escape," I said, trying to get my mind off how my fingers felt sliding over the smoothness of him.

"I'll believe that when I have you in the palace," he replied, his voice strained.

"Well," I admitted, a finger tracing a brand from his shoulder to the small of his back. "I didn't mean I wouldn't try to escape. Just not while tending your back."

"Oh-h-h-h-h. A noble-minded prisoner. I'll rest easy tonight."

"I'm not a prisoner," I said quickly. "Prisoners are helpless."

"No?" he said with a strained-sounding laugh. "What are you, then?"

"All right. I'm a prisoner, but I'm not helpless." My fingers were humming, almost hurting, really, and I looked at them. "What's in this ointment? It's making my fingers hurt." Annoyed at how easily his back could distract me, I roughly smeared the paste across a red line.

Jeck's breath hissed in over his teeth. Turning where he sat, he snatched my wrist.

"Hey!" I shouted, surging to my knees and trying to tug away. His grip was like sun-warmed metal, hard and unyielding. I lurched back, the length of my arm stretched between us. "Let go," I demanded, frightened. "I'm sorry. I didn't mean to push that hard." But it was the look on his bearded face that shocked me to stillness. Wonder, fear, and—speculation?

"They're humming, aren't they," he said, making it a statement. "Your hands. Almost enough to hurt."

My mouth opened, and I twisted my arm until he released me. The tingling in my palms swelled, tiny spikes exploding from my skin. I made fists of them, willing the sensation to go.

He took a breath to say something. Clearly changing his mind, he extended his hand toward me. I drew back, and he aggressively shifted closer. I spun away, lurching to get to my feet, and was pulled back to my knees when he gripped my shoulder. "Let me go!" I shouted.

"Sit," he demanded, jerking me back onto my blanket.

A cry escaped me. In that instant, Jeck frightened me as no one ever had before. He knew I wasn't a princess and held no respect that I once had been. I was a beggar, to be treated as such. He could hurt me without even trying—and he didn't care if he did. Panicked, I froze in fear as he gripped my upper arm. My heart pounded, and I shirked back as he hesitantly, almost reverently, reached out and touched my jawline.

My lips parted and my shoulders eased at the tingling sensation where his fingers rested. I met his eyes, seeing flecks of gold hidden within the deep brown. In his touch was the heat of the sun, soothing. His hand dropped, and I reached to feel my face in wonder. I looked at my hands, then his, knowing he had felt that same warmth coming from my fingers.

"It's the venom," he said. "I dosed you up beyond your usual levels. Even so, I've never heard of anyone beside me who could . . ." He drawled to a stop. Eyebrows raised, he confidently waited for me to ask the expected question.

I swallowed, afraid at how well he was manipulating me. "Could what?" I whispered.

He picked up the tin I had dropped. Picking out a flake of

bark, he recapped it. "Agree to leave Kavenlow and be my apprentice, and I'll tell you."

My breath came in a knowing sound. "You are chull bait, Captain," I said, frightened.

His face gave me no clue as to what he was thinking. Breaking our gaze, he took his water and tin of paste and returned to his side of the fire. Silent, he pulled a clean shirt from his saddlebag and put it on. Ignoring me, he sat on his log and took up his tea.

I settled myself uneasily on the blanket. The tingling of my hands had retreated to a dull throb, and I tried to wipe the stink of garlic off on the hem of my dress. Strong and heady, the scent of Jeck's cloak assailed me, thoughts of his smooth skin flashing unbidden into my mind. Eying him over the fire, I promised myself I'd stay awake, but my full stomach and the warmth of Jeck's cloak put me asleep faster than if I had been lost in my sheets and pillows safe at home.

Fifteen

❖

It was the birds that woke me up, screeching and squawking as if only they could convince the sun to rise. They were unusually noisy, and I stretched my feet downward in search of my bottle of hot water. My toes poked from under the covers to find the icy morning instead of a warm spot. Jerking my feet back, I remembered where I was and that my pillow hadn't slipped to the floor but was missing entirely. *Chu,* I thought, keeping my eyes closed as I listened for any movement from Jeck.

The sun wasn't up yet, I decided as I slit my eyelids and found only a faint brightness. I had woken on three occasions during the night. Each time I'd found Jeck awake—not watching me but alert. Once, he had scratched out a grid for thieves and kings, populating it with finger-sized pieces of black and white. Now, though, when I rolled my head to see him, I found him sitting before a neglect-extinguished fire with his chin slumped to his chest.

My pulse hammered. I slowly brought my knees to my chin, moving my hands down to my ankles. If I could worry the knots loose, I could slip away, barefoot or not.

"Get your hands from your feet, or I will lop them off," Jeck said, his head unmoving.

"Lop what off?" I asked sourly as I sat up. "My hands or my feet?"

Jeck's head rose. "Care to find out?" he said irately. "Get up. We're leaving."

"What? Now?" I complained. "The sun isn't up. I haven't had my breakfast."

A sigh shifted his shoulders. He slowly rose, stretching. As he collapsed in on himself, he unexpectedly snatched his cloak off me. Gasping, I clutched at my cloak still wrapped around me. "Aren't you a basket of sunshine in the morning?" he said as he draped it over his shoulders. "Show me your feet."

Feeling shrewish, I poked my toes out from behind my cloak. My feet were nigh frozen.

"Farther . . ." he demanded, "and put your hands in your lap."

I sullenly pulled my palms from where I had braced them on the dirt to give myself leverage should he come close enough for me to kick. Only when I was unbalanced did he lean over my feet. "You were a good girl," he said, satisfied.

"I could have gotten away," I boasted, "but it was too cold. Can I have my boots back?"

Jeck grunted. Before I could take a breath, he flipped his knife from somewhere, darted forward, cut the rope between my feet, and leaned back. He stood still, as if he hadn't moved. His knife was gone. The blood drained from my face at how fast it had been.

"If you have to do anything, do it now," he said. "I won't stop until we reach the palace."

I shivered, shocked by how easily he could have cut my throat instead of my bonds.

"No farther away than that, Princess," he warned, pointing as he brought Tuck closer to make him ready for travel.

My head bobbed loosely. Worried, I took care of my morning ritual as best I could, horribly glad women wore dresses. As Jeck finished readying the horses, I alternately picked at the leaves in my hair and the rings of rope about my ankles. The knots were too tight, and I could do nothing with them. It was humiliating. A frown pinched my brow when I realized Jeck had put my saddle on his horse. Men were thieves, all of them. Feeling sour and unpleasant, I glanced over the camp, my gaze landing on the game of thieves and kings he'd scratched out.

My heart seemed to stop. It was the game I had been playing with my father.

Misery closed my throat as I saw the layout wasn't quite right. "I didn't take the pawn," I whispered in grief. "I took the knight." Jeck looked up from folding his blanket in confusion. "The game," I said, my voice high. "I'm the white side. And I took the knight before Garrett—" I caught my breath and held it. *Angels save me, they were dead.*

Jeck glanced from me to the game and back again. "That puts your thief in danger."

"I know." It was almost a sob. Standing with my thin cloak clenched tight about me, I watched him crouch to adjust the pieces. He then moved his king to threaten my thief. I stared at him, my mind swirling with a sickening slurry of emotion. "Just let me go," I warbled. "My parents are dead. Kavenlow used me. There's nothing left—"

"Tell it to Prince Garrett." Face tight, he swept the pieces up into his palm and dropped them into a saddlebag. It was the last of the camp. Jaw clenched in what looked like anger, he cinched Tuck's riding pad so tight that the flighty gray tossed his head and squealed.

"I'm going to pick you up and put you on him," Jeck said as he came forward. He was so much taller than I was, and I stared up at him, numb. "If you kick me, I'll break your toes. If you hit me, I'm going to drop you. Put out your hands so I can tie them."

I was too miserable to move. With a jerky quickness, Jeck snatched my hands and wrapped a cord about my wrists. Garrett had killed my parents. He was going to kill Kavenlow. I would be dead when Garrett grew tired of me. I should have run. I should have listened to Duncan.

I gasped when Jeck's gloved hands went around me and he picked me up. Tuck snorted as I landed gently on him, my feet to either side of the tall gray. The horse danced, and I almost fell. Jeck shoved me upright, and his rough touch sparked my anger, cutting cleanly through my grief.

I might be a beggar's child, I might have lost my kingdom to a woman I'd never seen and then to Garrett, I might have been betrayed by the man I thought of as a second father, but I would sling nets and shovel chu from the careen pits before I accepted being treated like this. My face burned as Jeck brusquely tugged my cloak out from under me so it lay right. "I need my hands to hold on," I said, forcing a half cry into my voice though I was seething.

"You'll hold on as you are, or you'll ride the entire way on my lap," he said calmly. My eyes darted over everything, and I weighed my chances to escape as he knotted Tuck's bridle to the black gelding. After a final check on the extinguished fire, Jeck untied his horse and led us to the trail. I balanced easily, ducking the low branches.

Frustration kept me silent. My fingers twined in Tuck's mane in a white-knuckled grip. I could not let Jeck take me back to the palace. Stomach clenching, I assessed what I had to work with as we edged down onto the sunken trail and Jeck swung onto his horse.

I had no boots. My wrists were bound. I'd have to escape by horse, and mine was tied to Jeck's. My shoulders were tight with tension as we shifted from a walk into a smooth canter. I licked my lips, glancing at Jeck riding beside and a little before me.

I had to get him off his horse. It was all I had; the rest would come as I needed it.

"Captain!" I cried out as I let myself slip. "Jeck!" I shrieked, clenching my eyes shut as I fell. I let go of Tuck's mane lest I get dragged under him. I hit the ground in a painful thump, my shoulder taking most of the hurt. A stick bit into my thigh, and I snatched it, tangling it into my hair. It was only the length of my finger, but it would be enough.

Tuck danced aside, not liking his rider falling off. Jeck's gelding, too, was spooked, and it took a moment for Jeck to calm him before he could turn him around and dismount.

The fall had shaken me, and my confusion wasn't entirely faked as he grasped my shoulder. "That was a foolish thing to do," he said roughly. "Don't do it again."

I hid my disgust that his knife was on his saddle and out of my reach. He had put his hat and its darts on the saddle as well. "I hurt my hands," I said, allowing my eyes to fill as I held them out to show him. "I can't hold on if they are tied."

Jeck pulled me up, and I wobbled until I found my balance. With an excessive force, he put me back on Tuck. "I'm not going to free your hands," he said, squinting up at me from under his hat, his jaw tight and his shoulders tense. "Do that again, and you'll ride with me."

I nodded, making my face sullen to hide my excitement. I was on the trail. I was on a horse pointed away from the palace. And in this splinter of time—Jeck wasn't.

He turned his back on me. As he reached for his hat, I tore the stick from my hair and jammed it into Tuck's hindquarters.

"Heyah!" I shouted. The flighty horse squealed, bolting into a run. Gasping, I clutched his mane and crouched low. Jeck's horse was tied to us and had no choice but to follow. Jeck's tenuous grip was torn away. The horses and I fled. Surrounded by trees, there was only one way to go. I didn't need to do anything but hang on.

"Tess!" Jeck shouted. "Damn you, woman!"

I grinned, encouraging Tuck with wild, hissed words. I was free and running.

The wind in my hair had never felt so glorious. The aches from my night on the ground melted into victory. The thudding of eight hooves pounded into me, making me wish I could go on forever.

But horses are stupid beasts, more inclined to fill their belly than run from a pain they quickly forget. Tuck began to slow, and judging I was far enough away to get out of my bindings, I sat up, murmuring until he came to a jolting, arched-necked stop. Jeck's horse obediently halted since they were still tied together. As they vied for the same spot of green, I looked behind me. Jeck was rapidly closing the distance, pounding down the path.

I stretched for Jeck's knife tucked into the saddle. Fingers bent awkwardly, I tugged and sawed. Finally the cord parted. Heart pounding, I looked to see Jeck scooping up his fallen hat. I could almost make out what he was saying, hollering at the top of his voice. The black horse watched him with pricked ears. Jeck should have stuck to his own tired mount instead of stealing a rested one who didn't know him.

I put the knife away. My pulse hammered and I slipped from Tuck. Ignoring the twinge in my ankle, I quickly made friends with the black gelding. As Jeck yelled at me, I swung myself onto my saddle and arranged my filthy dress. "What am I going to call you?" I said as I patted the gelding's neck. I glanced behind me to Jeck. Unable to resist, I pulled the black up into a squealing, two-footed half turn. "I'm not a thief!" I called merrily as his front feet thudded down and he pranced. "I'm using my means to their fullest potential!"

Leaning forward, I screamed into the black horse's ear. He surged forward, willingly charging ahead with a reckless abandon until our pace was neither safe nor stoppable. Tuck thundered alongside, urging the black into a faster pace.

Jeck will never catch me now, I thought in satisfaction. I would go to Saltwood. I would find Kavenlow. He would explain to me why he had taken a beggar's child and made her into a player. And then he would tell me just what the devil a player was.

Sixteen

❖

The stableman watched me as I counted the money he had put into my hand. It was obvious by his glances into the yard where Tuck and the black gelding stood blowing at the smell of grain that he thought it suspicious I had them. I didn't care as long as he bought the saddle. A part of me regretted selling it, but I needed money for passage across the bay.

Satisfied the coinage was correct, I wrapped the money in a cloth and tucked it away. The relief I felt surprised me. Money had never been important until I didn't have any. "Thank you," I said, trying to sound as coarse as my dress and hair were. Five days in the wilds with little water had left me so filthy I could hardly stand myself.

He grunted in acknowledgment as he took my saddle and moved it to the tack rack. "We don't see much leatherwork from the capital," he said. "Leastwise not for *sale*." He hit the word hard, as if expecting me to confess it wasn't mine.

Last night had been miserable. Duncan hadn't been at our abandoned camp. Alone and depressed, I had kept the horses plodding forward most of the night. There was no moon because of the clouds, making traveling difficult. I wasn't willing to risk a fire when I stopped, and between the cold, the dirt, the misery of my dead parents, and waiting for Jeck to catch me up or the wolves to take me down, I hadn't slept. Morning found me moving before the sun had risen. I was wretchedly tired, but I wouldn't rest until a ship was carrying me across the bay.

I took a slow breath, letting my anxiety go as I brought the musty smell of hay and horses deep into me. I liked stables. I had often hidden in the palace livery to avoid my studies, until Kavenlow realized what I was doing and switched my lessons to horsemanship, pushing me so far into exhaustion that I would willingly sit with paper and ink the following day. Looking back, I realized he had been very good at such persuasion, invariably getting his way without calling upon my parents to force my obedience.

A memory swirled up unbidden, of Kavenlow squinting from the sun and smiling proudly the first time I made my pony jump a fence. I had been seven, and so full of myself one would think I'd jumped the cracks of hell. The stableman cleared his throat, and I brought myself back.

"Maybe you could help me," I asked. "I'm trying to catch up with my father. Tall, gray-bearded man on horse? He'd be dressed well. It would have only been a day or so ago."

"Haven't seen him," the man muttered, rubbing a filthy rag over my saddle.

"Thank you," I said, edging away. "I may be back to buy food for my horses."

"I'll give it to you cheaper than the inns in town," he said, his voice eager.

Nodding, I stepped from the still warmth of the stables into the late afternoon. Jeck's horse pricked his ears, his eyes begging me to scratch the underside of his massive jaw. The silly beast stretched out his neck like an enormous cat, a low moan escaping him as my fingernails raked through his stiff hair. My hand pulled away with dust and sweat under my nails. I looked at them, sighing. I wanted nothing more than a good meal and a bath. But I didn't think being on foot would slow Jeck appreciably, and I felt as if any moment a dart would find me.

Taking the two horses' leads, I walked into town. The dock street was a dirt track, widening where thick wooden pilings jutted out into the bay and a scattering of ships rested. Barnacle-encrusted fishing boats were pulled out onto the rocky beach. Most were empty and abandoned, having processed their haul already, but one latecomer was busy. A vicious flock of seagulls and crows circled and dived as the man threw out the offal of his catch. The harsh noise of the birds and the dog chasing them were loud. By the looks of it, the tide was almost in.

Jeck's horse called out, startling me. Another answered him. My gaze went to the hard-packed yard of an inn, the Seasick Pony by the placard showing a wide-eyed, pathetic beast with green spittle coming from it. My heart gave a pound when I saw Pitch tethered outside.

"Pitch!" I cried, not caring that I was attracting stares as I jogged to her. The black gelding behind me was nearly as enthusiastic, neck arched and tail raised. "Oh, don't you look fine," I murmured as I tied Tuck and Jeck's horse beside her.

A small stableboy with a broom taller than he was watched me suspiciously, and I took my hands off her. A flush of guilt for selling the saddle went through me when I saw that my gear was on Pitch, right beside Duncan's. But if Pitch was outside, then Duncan was inside.

Leaving the three horses to their reunion, I eagerly stepped over the dice game on the front steps of the inn and entered. The room was stuffy and dim, noisy with too many men struggling to fit months of entertainment into days. My gaze roved over the throng, my eagerness dulling as the stares of the women grew hostile. Nervous, I checked my bedraggled topknot.

"Gone!" I heard a familiar voice moan, and I spun to the bar. "Vanished like a meat pie from a windowsill in spring."

A smile pulled up the corners of my mouth as I found Duncan sprawled miserably across the counter, monopolizing the innkeeper. Not wanting to attract more attention by calling out to him, I edged through the tables with an intentness that would hopefully tell the watching eyes I had my own business to attend to.

"She was going to make me rich," Duncan said as I gave a grasping sailor a nasty look and sidled out of his reach. "And now she's gone. I looked for her. God knows I did, but I couldn't find a trace. Vanished like a punta in a whirl of wind."

"Ah," the innkeeper said. "Don't chase the women that run

from you, lad. You'll find better. Have another ale?" It was clearly a well-practiced litany by his bored countenance.

"No." Duncan pulled his tankard close. "You don't understand. I could look a lifetime and never find another like her. I didn't even care her cooking was like the scrapings from under the stewpot and her tea was like rabbit piss."

I grimaced, startled to find the innkeeper looking me over with a derisive interest. "Did she have curly brown hair to her waist with sticks and leaves in it?" he asked.

"Aye." Duncan sighed, sounding angry. "Full of leaves and wickedly sharp darts. Damn it all to hell, it was perfect. Now I'm back to nothing."

My hand went up to check my hair. I hadn't brushed it in hours. I must look as if I had been pulled through a knothole backward.

"And was her dress too short?"

Duncan's head bobbed. "God help me, but she had a red underskirt. I saw it when she was on horseback. And she rode like a man." Hunched over the bar, he stared up at the innkeeper. "Like a man, I say!"

I frowned and tugged at my dress. How else could I ride if I didn't have a proper saddle?

"And does she have a temper about her?" the innkeeper asked, looking from me long enough to spit on the floor.

"Slap your face as soon as give you the time of day," he said morosely. "You sound as if you've seen her."

The man shifted his eyes from me to Duncan. "She's burning well standing behind you."

Duncan spun so quickly, he nearly knocked his stool down. "Tess!" he cried, shock on his face as he rose. "You're alive!" A score of unvoiced thoughts cascaded over him, too fast for me to recognize. Then he settled on one, and beaming, came forward with his hands outstretched.

Alarmed, I held out my hands to keep him away. Duncan pushed them aside and gave me a hug that forced the air from my lungs. His stubble had turned into the beginnings of a nasty-looking brown and red beard, and it scraped my bruised forehead. "Stop!" I protested, unable to keep the grin from me. He had missed me. I didn't think anyone, except Heather, had missed me before.

"You're all right!" he said, smiling as he put me at arm's length. "I thought I'd lost you."

Embarrassed, I glanced over the room as the noise resumed. The innkeeper had made his escape to a table, but I couldn't help notice he kept an eye on us.

"What happened?" Duncan asked, trying to lead me to his stool. "Who was that? How long were you standing there?" He frowned, reaching out to my head. "Hey. You're hurt."

"Don't." Flustered, I pulled away, and his frown deepened. "It's just a bump."

He took my shoulders and peered down at my scalp. His eyes hardened. "He hit you?"

I looked up, surprised at his anger. "Yes," I said, "and tied me up and sat on me. But I got away—with your horse and his—so I guess we're even."

Hope lit Duncan's eyes. "Tuck! Is he outside?" He strode out the door, and I stood for three heartbeats, unbelieving. *The man was as skittish as his horse,* I thought, decidedly put out. I followed him into the street, trying to scrape my dignity from the floor as I went.

Squinting in the brighter light, I found Duncan running his quick hands eagerly over Tuck. "Hey, boy," he said, his eyes alight with pleasure. "Look at you. Not a scratch. Stupid beast. It was only a tree." He slapped Tuck's neck fondly, and I sourly wondered if Duncan's attempt to find me had been out of concern for me or his horse.

"Tess," he said earnestly. "Thank you. I raised him up from a foal when he was born out of season and abandoned. I can't imagine where I'd get another like him."

"You're welcome," I said, forgiving him for leaving me standing alone in a tavern.

"What happened?" he said as I started to move his gear off Pitch and onto Tuck. "Who was that who grabbed you?" He leaned close until I could smell the smoke from the inn on him. "You stole his horse?" he asked, clearly exasperated. "Tess, you've got to stop doing that."

My anxiety flowed back. "I've got to go," I said as I tied my pack onto the black gelding.

"Good idea." He started to take his things off Pitch and put them on Tuck with an unhurried quickness. "Now for the third time, who was that? You think he'll follow you?"

I started to help him, hesitating as I tried to decide what I should do with Jeck's things. Now that I had mine back, it didn't feel right to keep them. "Oh, he's following me all right," I said, feeling a pinch of urgency. "He's a—" A new caution stopped me from saying player. "He's the captain of King Edmund's guard," I whispered, not sure how much was lie and how much was truth. "It was luck that got me away, and he's as angry as a stingray on a deck. I have to find a boat to take me across the bay. I've got to find Kavenlow."

"Us." Duncan pushed Tuck's bony head out of the way to see me. "You have to find a boat to take *us* across the bay."

His stance was determined as he squinted in the sun at me. Though as tall as Jeck, he lacked the captain's bulk, replacing it with a lanky quickness. His hand was still swollen from the dart that had nearly killed him, and it made him look vulnerable in my eyes. "Duncan," I protested softly, "this isn't one of your schemes. He's not going to stop until he finds me. I know I promised I'd give you anything for helping me get past the gates, but a week of my time is going to get you killed."

"You got away," he said just shy of belligerent. "How bad can he be?"

A sigh escaped me. I looked down the street, worried. "You don't believe me, do you?"

"Beat me with a dead carp, Tess. I believed you when you first told me! That's why I say you should keep running. He'll stop if you go far enough. I should know." He grimaced, looking angry at some past injustice.

My attention followed his to the light foot traffic. My pulse increased. Jeck was out there. He was getting close. I could feel it. "I can take care of myself," I said.

"I know you can. That's one of the things I like about you."

Shock struck through me, jerking my eyes to his. We were caught between two horses, closer than proper decorum allowed, hidden from casual eyes. I swallowed, unable to find the will to pull from his grip as he took my hands and exerted a soft, subtle pull. *He liked me?*

"Work with me," he said softly, making my heart pound. "Say you will. I'm looking farther ahead than you, and Tess, I know you feel like you owe them something, but there's nothing left for you in the capital. Nothing. Come with me . . . and I promise I can have you living like a princess again in three years."

I tried to swallow, finding my throat too dry to manage it. "Duncan . . ."

His long face turned pained. "I thought I lost you, Tess. Just . . ."

My breath caught. *He thought he lost me?* Suddenly frightened, I tugged from his grip.

Duncan stiffened as my hands slipped from his. "I'm sorry," he said, ducking his head. "I didn't mean how that sounded. It's just that . . ."

I forced myself to smile up at him, my hours spent in diplomatic conversation coming to the forefront. "It's just that you want to make lots of money," I said, the stupider part of me hoping that he had meant it exactly how it sounded. *I was an idiot; but at least I knew it.*

His breath escaped him in a relieved, half laugh. "Yeah," he said. "You got me there."

Relieved that we had sidestepped whatever he had almost said, I ran my gaze from his grease-stained hat to his squalid, worn boots. What was in between was unkempt and coarse. But his words still resonated in my mind. He cared about me, Jeck frightened me, and I needed a friend. I didn't care if his motives were a little skewed. *Or were they?*

"I have to find Kavenlow," I said softly. "He can pay you back for what I took from you in the inn. And if he doesn't, he can get it for you." I felt embarrassed as I looked up, knowing Duncan heard the unspoken *please stay with me* in my words.

"Kavenlow, huh," Duncan said. Lips pressing together for an instant, he licked his thumb and stuck it out. My thumb was in motion before I knew it. Jerking to a halt, I watched his eyes as I finished the motion to lick it and press it to his thumb, sealing our bargain. I wondered if he put the same weight as I did on the silly bond. "Fine." He was scanning the street again, shifting back to put space between us. The rims of his ears were red. "I'll stay with you until I get paid."

"If you'd rather, you can take one of the black horses," guilt prompted me to say.

He shook his head with a nervous smile. "I'd sooner sleep in a chu pit than take one of those horses. They're stolen, remember?" Then he paused, frowning as he looked them over. "Where's the saddle?"

Seventeen

I flushed and dropped my eyes. "I sold it," I admitted. "For ship fare."

His long, stubbly face suddenly empty of emotion, he moved to shield me from anyone passing by. "How much did you get?" he asked as his shadow fell over me.

Wondering why he wasn't angry for me having sold a saddle he had considered his, no matter how loosely, I handed him the impromptu bag. He unfolded it in his cupped hand, his head bowed over it. "Chu," he breathed in admiration. "You all got this? For that saddle?"

My smile turned relieved. "I know how to bargain."

"Huh," he grunted, and my eyebrows rose as he handed it back to me. "Nicely done."

I looked askance at him. "I thought you'd be angry."

He turned to Tuck, seeming to want to ignore that he was doing something nice. "I don't need a saddle. And now we can cross the bay in comfort."

"Uh, Duncan? A saddle won't get two people and three horses across the bay. Especially since we'll have to charter a ship. There's no regular run from Saltwood to Brenton."

Duncan's brow lifted. "Who says?"

"Three summers spent sketching the trade routes," I answered, thinking that though the information was now proving useful, it still seemed like a colossal waste of time.

Duncan turned an appraising look at Jeck's horse, and I shook my head. "I'm not selling him. The other one either," I said with a grimace. "They are a betrothal gift."

Frowning, he took Jeck's pack off Tuck. "Maybe we could sell his things, then."

I'd been through Jeck's pack yesterday, finding my boots and stockings—I had no clue as to why he had taken them off in the first place—but my venom was gone, and I'd found only a handful of my darts. My whip, though, was again at my waist. "I thought you weren't a thief," I said. "Besides, the only thing he has of worth is a bunch of knives, and if we tried to sell them after I sold the saddle, someone would say we stole them."

He grinned and touched his hat's brim. "That's what you did, Lady Black Sheep."

I fought the urge to kick his shin. "So you'll understand then why I'm leaving everything but the knives at one of the inns for him to find," I said.

"What? Tess, he kidnapped you. He owes you. A blanket, a bowl. Pick something!"

"I'm not a thief." I yanked the bag back and slung it behind my things for the time being. Not meeting his eyes, I untied the two black horses and backed them up with soft words.

Duncan looked at the inn. "Why don't we eat while we're here."

"Tide turns in a few hours. We need to arrange passage, first. Then we can eat."

A groan escaped him. "Good. I'm famished. You look at the boats. I'll stay here." His eyes were bright, and he hunched closer. "How about my share of that saddle?"

My shoulders tensed, and I touched the fold of cloth with the money, reassuring myself I still had it. "We need it for getting across the bay. We're short coinage as it is."

"Give me an hour, and I'll double it. Play with me, and I could double it again."

I felt an instant of fear in that a flicker of temptation burned in me. "That money is to get us across the bay, not gamble with," I said, hushed though no one was near enough to hear. "Especially after what you told that innkeeper about me making money with you."

"We won't get caught," he said, starting to sound angry as he pushed his filthy hat up.

My stomach clenched. How could I go from dewy and soft to irate so quickly? "You want the money? Fine. Take all of it. But you're only three days from all but dying from the venom. Your fingers can't be fast enough yet. And there isn't enough money in town to keep your hands attached to your wrists if you're caught." He said nothing, and guilt prompted me to add, "We can eat, though, and maybe buy a bath."

"A bath!" His face lengthened in disgust and he scratched his jawline under his scraggly beard. "You don't smell that bad. You look like you need sleep more than a bath."

Cringing, I led Jeck's horse and Pitch into the street. Duncan hesitated a moment before following with Tuck. My dress was too short, my boots were dirty, and I had slept in my clothes four nights in a row. "I may be a beggar, but I don't have to look like one," I said as he came alongside. "And if I smell at all, then it's not all right."

Duncan snorted as he paced beside me. As peeved as I was, it felt good to have someone beside me again. I didn't like being alone. Over the bay, a bank of rain clouds was building. We were at slack tide, and it was chancy that we'd be able to leave yet today. Jeck was moving while we stood still. I could lose half a day because we were an hour too late.

Fatigue forced me into a slower pace as we came to the first dock. Sun warming my back, I evaluated the handful of ships berthed and the precious few more at anchor in the close, deep water that Saltwood boasted. Seeing them with their sails wrapped and anchors trenched, my thoughts went to the scores of ships at the capital. They were fish trapped in a tidal pool, trusting the twenty-year peace of the harbor. I could do nothing to warn them. I could only hope that I could find Kavenlow and get back before the bulk of Garrett's men got to the capital.

Worried, I focused on the few docked ships. I'd rather hire one of them since the captain would likely make me pay the docking fee if he had to tie up to take on the horses.

I passed the first without comment. Duncan glanced once

behind us as we continued. "Is there anyone we can ask what boat is going where?" he questioned.

"No," I said. "If it's like most small harbors, the inns put up and maintain their separate docks. They cater to the captains, knowing their crews will come to their taverns first when given leave. There's a fee to pay for the dock's upkeep, which the captain arranges with the innkeeper, sort of as we do when we stable our horses. It's based on how big the boat is and how much trouble the crew generally gives the innkeeper's ladies." My cheeks warmed as I remembered the hostile looks in the Seasick Pony. "It's the innkeeper who collects the taxes on the goods coming ashore, passing them to the king's collection boat." My eyes dropped at the memory of my father. "At least, that's the theory," I finished, my throat tight.

Duncan made a rude noise. "I'd think the innkeeper would keep some for himself."

"That's your first thought?" I accused, depressed. "How to cheat someone?" He gave me a telling look, and I dropped my gaze. "In the larger ports, there's a palace-paid bookkeeper," I admitted. "But it's not worth the salary in the small harbors—as long as the innkeeper isn't too greedy. And in most places there's enough traffic to warrant two inns and docks. They watch each other's purse strings better than the most loyal servant to the king."

That seemed to satisfy Duncan, or perhaps he was trying to devise how one could get around even that. "How about that boat?" he said, pointing. "That one looks big enough."

I shook my head. "See how low it's riding? They already have a cargo and destination, and I doubt it's Brenton, seeing as it's carrying grain, and Brenton has its own farms."

"That one?" he asked, sounding hopeful as he pointed to the next.

"Too many crewmen sitting doing nothing. It looks like they're leaving tonight, though. We can check later where they're going. Maybe we can convince the captain to make a detour."

"Chu, Tess," he swore. "We're running out of boats."

Worried that he was right, I bit my lip. I was so tired. My left leg was growing sluggish, and I was nigh starved from the smells of cooking food. "We want a ship that's big enough to handle the open sea but small enough to make a profit harbor-hopping," I said. "One that's riding high and empty, and whose crew is ashore, saying the captain has no prospects yet but isn't willing to move his boat to anchor and incur another docking fee to take on cargo."

Duncan eyed me. "You know a lot about boats for a princess."

"I'm not a princess," I said tightly. The road turned to wooden planking, loud under the horses' hooves. Kavenlow took me whenever a shipment came in at the palace dock. I hated the idea that my food was better traveled than I was, and he knew I enjoyed hearing where everything came from and why some things were twice as expensive other times of the year. It was a wonder Kavenlow had done anything with me, I pestered him with so many questions.

My feet slowed as we came to the second, nicer dock. "There," I said, pointing. The end of the pier was overwhelmed by two large ships. Stuck between them looking like a toy was a trim little schooner. I liked it. Its two masts were gaff rigged, giving it the ability to run close to the wind. Its timbers were black with age but clean. There was a small shack in the bow where I imagined the galley was, a long, thigh-high rise in the middle above the hold, and a second, shorter but slightly higher rise breaking the deck at the back right before the wheel.

There were six catapults for lobbing flaming tar against pirates, twice as many as usually found on a boat this size. The ropes were neatly coiled around the dock cleats; the captain was meticulous—and in port too long. He was probably anxious to be under way as much as I was. I read the name, smiling. The *Sandpiper*.

Duncan's eyebrows bunched worriedly at my pleased look. "It's small."

"Only because it's between those two hulks," I countered. Turning to the silent boat, I cupped my hands. "Ahoy, *Sandpiper*!" I called. I glanced up and down the dock, not liking to have to shout. No one answered, and I frowned. "You try," I said, gesturing for Duncan. "You have a screamer of a mouth."

He grinned. "*Sandpiper!*" he shouted, his voice echoing. "Hey! Anyone aboard?"

A dark head rose from the fore hatch. "Hoy," a gaunt man called back. He was dressed in faded red, and he squinted at us as if wondering why we had bothered him.

"We're looking for your captain," I said loudly. "Is he about?" The man stared at me, and I repeated, "We're looking for your captain?"

The man looked at the top of the mast, outright ignoring me. Anger warmed my cheeks. Sailors were superstitious fools. I'd never been treated like this at the docks when with Kavenlow, and though I knew it happened, to have it happen to me was a shock. "You ask him," I muttered, giving Duncan a nudge. "He won't talk to me because I'm a woman."

Duncan smirked and took a cocky stance. "You, sir," he called. "Is the captain aboard?"

I seethed as the sun-darkened man turned back to us. "He's at the Three Crows, but if you're looking for the sheepskins they're gone." His voice was rough—wind-torn almost.

"Thank you," Duncan said. "I need to speak to him all the same."

"Ask him where it is," I said, peeved when Duncan turned Tuck and headed up the street.

"I know where it is," Duncan said, pointing. "See? Right there."

He swaggered beside me, finding something funny in that the man had talked to him and not me. *What a fool bunch of simpletons,* I thought. I hated being dirty. It was the dirt that had done it. The dirt, the leaves, my filthy black hem, and my muddy boots. They wouldn't dare treat me like that if I was clean. But as Duncan angled us past the shop fronts to a sprawling building, my temper eased.

This inn had a fenced yard, and even what looked like a separate building for the louder guests. It was obviously the better of the two inns. The plaque hanging above the open double doors showed three crows fighting for a perch on a fence post or mast. One had his wings open to land, another was falling off with feathers splayed, and the last was perched safely, his eye eerily watching everyone passing under him. The smell of cooked meat almost made me dizzy. It had been days since my last good meal, and I felt, more than heard, Duncan sigh.

"Let's put the horses behind the fence," I said, thinking of Jeck. "Mmmm, smell that?"

A limping stableboy came to take the horses. I handed over Pitch and Jeck's horse, dismally thinking that the boy's clothes were cleaner than mine. Duncan dug through a bag and pulled out his bowl. "Chu, is it beef?" he asked.

My eyes shut in anticipated bliss as I sniffed. "And potatoes, and carrots, and onions." My bowl in hand, I followed Duncan as he boldly strode under the sign and entered.

I found fewer eyes on me than when I had burst into the other inn by myself, but I still ran a hand down my grimy dress and checked my topknot as I followed Duncan to the counter where a bookish-looking man and a well-endowed woman were slicing potatoes for an empty stewpot. The short man was keeping a tight eye on the loudest table. His beard was cut so close it was almost not there, and his apron was stained from long use between washings.

"Two for supper," Duncan said cheerfully, seeming to think this was a grand event when all I wanted to do was slink to the back and hope no one saw me in my grime and filth. Duncan looked expectantly at me, and I grudgingly laid out the proper coinage, my reluctance at parting with money new and disturbing.

"Help yourself to the stewpot at the hearth," the man said, his eyes shifting from the noisy table to the coin and me. His gaze took us in, lingering on the bump on my head. A flicker of concern crossed him. "The new bread is almost done. I imagine the lady would like a bit of bread, eh? Keep the color in your cheeks and the curl in your hair, ma'am?"

I dropped my eyes and blushed, having discovered a new appreciation for being called a lady the last few days. The plump woman next to him sent her knife through a potato with a thump, and the innkeeper sighed. "I'll bring you your bread," he said blandly. "For a bit more, you can have ale instead of water."

Duncan bobbed his head, then seeing my disapproval, he frowned. "One ale won't turn my head so far I can't do business."

"I was thinking of the cost," I muttered, warming with an unexpected mortification.

The man in the apron straightened. "Ah, well. I know everyone hereabouts. I can help you there if you need it."

Duncan put an elbow on the counter and leaned forward conspiratorially. "We were told the *Sandpiper*'s captain was here?"

I cringed inside. He was doing it all wrong. Because it was the first thing out of his mouth, the woman was not only listening, but she would remember us for months.

The innkeeper's eyes shifted to a corner by the fire. "Aye," the man said. "That's him. But if you have business with Captain Borlett you should wait until he gets a few pints in him." The man smirked to make his spotty beard bunch. "He's doing his books, or trying to, the poor sod."

Duncan grinned in understanding. "We'll talk to him now."

I kicked Duncan's boot in disgust, and he gave me a black look. In fifteen minutes, the entire room would know we were in a hurry. The cost of our fare just went up, thanks to him.

The innkeeper shrugged. "As you want it."

His eyes went to the table at the back. They had started to sing, and a heavy man in a calf-length blue coat seated in a quiet corner slammed his fist down. "Shut yer mouths, you bilge scrapings!" he shouted with enough force to carry over storms. "Can't you see I'm thinking? Get out! Get to the wench house where you belong."

The group quickly broke up. Most left the inn with quiet words of apology, leaving one of their own dead drunk at a table in his own drool. The men passing before me were thin and wiry, or bulky and muscular, but they all had an untamed look about them that wasn't entirely unattractive and made me glad Duncan was beside me.

The innkeeper took up a tankard and wove through the exodus to the squat man in the corner with the blue coat. It had to be Captain Borlett. The innkeeper whispered a few words into the captain's ear, and he eyed us from under a faded blue hat. I shivered, unable to say why.

"Books?" Duncan grunted. "His mood won't get better no matter how much he drinks."

I sourly agreed, and I followed Duncan across the quieter room. The song started up again in the yard. The captain visibly sighed and ran a hand across his eyes and down his face, ending with a white-knuckled grip on his short, graying beard.

"Keep your mouth shut," I said as we neared. "I'll do the talking."

Duncan made a noise deep in his throat. "I can do more than play cards, Tess."

I gave him a raised-eyebrow look. "I'm sure you can, but all I've done the last ten years is purchase things."

He took a breath to protest, then nodded, his face blank in thought. "Will he talk to you?" he asked. "The sailor wouldn't."

I nodded, fairly sure he would. The captain of a reputable merchant ship was generally a book-learned man who had developed an unfortunate taste for adventure. Educated and from an affluent family, he was a step up from his superstitious crew. He could read and write, and had some skill with sums as he had to prove to his backers that he was making a profit. He was often set apart from his crew, so much so that many captains maintained quarters to entice passengers for long trips, hoping for the diverse conversations he couldn't get from his crew.

We came to a standstill before Captain Borlett. An oil lamp shone over the scattered papers, his tankard making a blurred smear out of the notes under it. The mess was atrocious, and I couldn't imagine anyone working in such a haphazard way.

"Captain?" I said when he didn't look up. I pronounced the word carefully to tell him I was educated despite my slovenly dress.

"What do you want?" he barked, eyes still on his papers.

I jumped in surprise, elbowing Duncan into silence when he opened his mouth. I would wait to be recognized properly. The captain's jaw clenched, then relaxed. His shoulders shifted as he glanced at me from under his hat. His eyes seemed tired, and the wrinkles about them vanished under a shaggy frazzle of a beard. "Yes," he said with a sigh.

It was likely the best I would get, and I extended my hand. "Good evening, Captain," I said, and he took it for a moment. My hand felt lost engulfed in his, thick with knobby knuckles and salt-parched skin. "May we join you? It won't take but a moment. I can see you're busy."

Captain Borlett's gaze flicked behind us to the innkeeper. Leaning back in his chair, he made a puff of amused acceptance and gestured for us to sit. Duncan grabbed a stool, but I waited with a growing warmth. I wouldn't sit unless someone helped me. It was imperative the captain think I was a lady despite my true birth being lower than everyone's in the room.

Grimacing, Duncan got to his feet. The innkeeper chose this moment to intrude with a basket of warm buns from the kitchen and two tankards of murky water. "Unknot your hair, Tess," Duncan whispered as he helped me sit. "This isn't how normal people act."

"I have to make up for you telling everyone we're in a hurry," I nearly hissed back.

"I only told the innkeeper," he protested.

The bench slid smoothly beneath me and I sat down. "And his wife," I said. "Who told the dock women, who told the stable-man, who told every burning soul outside."

Duncan slumped to sit beside me in exasperation. By unspoken agreement, we silently waited until the innkeeper left. The moist smell of hot grain drifted to me, and I forced my hands into my lap. I wished I could take a roll as Duncan had, but I didn't want to look hungry. "We would like to get to Brenton," I said as my stomach rumbled. Angel's Spit, I was tired.

Captain Borlett dipped his quill into his ink, dismissing me.

"Two passengers," I continued, undeterred, "and three horses."

Never looking up, the squat man muttered, "If you have horses, ride it."

"If I wanted to ride it, I wouldn't be speaking with you," I said, putting the proper amount of arrogance and irritation into my voice. "The *Sandpiper* is empty. Your crew is spending the last of their pay. What will they do tomorrow except cause trouble? You're harbor-tied, sir, unless you want to sail with half your hold empty." He looked up with a mix of surprise and worry, and I smiled. "We would like to get to Brenton," I repeated pleasantly.

The captain set his quill aside and put a thick hand atop his papers. A thrill went through me. He would consider it. "You two," he said, his gaze taking in our dirt and exhaustion, "and three horses." He hesitated. "Expensive."

Duncan shifted, and with that telling him we didn't have enough, I vowed to leave the man in the stables the next time I had to buy anything. Cheat he may be, but he was ruining everything. "May I?" I asked as I reached for the captain's quill. I had an idea of how I could make up the difference in our fare, but if the captain thought it was his idea, then all the better. Under his watchful eye, I wrote out a sum that would leave an unsettlingly few coins in my pocket. The amount wasn't as important as much as him knowing I knew my numbers.

He made a long, "Mmmm," as I pushed the paper to him. I had just elevated myself from a beggar to a lady of stature down on her luck. His weary blue eyes were a shade softer, and he took his hat off as he leaned back with the beginnings of interest. "You're right," he admitted, smoothing his greasy, graying hair. "I'm in a bind. But I would rather be cargo-light at Saltwood than at Brenton." He tapped the paper. "This here will pay for the horses."

Duncan stiffened. "Come on, Tess," he said. "There're other boats."

I ignored Duncan as he stood and grabbed the bowl of rolls. "Captain," I said, trying to insinuate Duncan's opinion wasn't mine. "I like the *Sandpiper*. She's small and fast."

"In a hurry?" he asked, chewing his lip to send his mustache dancing.

I nodded since the damage had already been done. "There's a storm breaking upon the capital," I admitted. "We're six days ahead of it."

Captain Borlett leaned forward until I could smell the ale on him. "Aye," he said softly. "You look it. What happened?" Fear crossed him. "Plague?"

I shook my head. "Worse. A wedding, sir. An unexpected hastening of the wedding with Prince Garrett by month's end." Captain Borlett's eyebrows rose. Clearly the news hadn't come this far yet. It was a valuable piece of information that could make fortunes. "They will want wine at the capital," I continued softly. "Good mountain wine from Lovrege. It's a two-week sail from Brenton this time of year. It would bring a fine price in the capital harbor."

"If the timing was right," he breathed, his mind clearly thinking as was mine. Duncan sat back down. I squashed my guilt for sending the captain to the capital, but it would be won or lost by the time he got there.

Captain Borlett shook his head, but the gleam in his eye told me he wasn't saying no. "Good advice," he said. "But I can't take advantage of it. My backers will beach me if I don't have my year-end figures to them soon. I can't think on the water. There isn't enough time to make the run from Lovrege to the capital and do my books as well."

I smiled. We had passage. It was only a matter of the formalities—if Duncan didn't make a chu pit of it. My pulse quickened. "I have a small skill in figures," I said. "Perhaps I could do your books for the price of passage?"

Turning over a paper, he scrawled two rows of numbers. "Show me."

Duncan leaned to watch as I rewrote the numbers in tidy rows and added them up. He sat back with a puff of disgust. A flash of memory sent the smell of gardenias through me, a memory of me by the solarium pond, sunlight warming my back as I frantically scribed what Kavenlow shouted at me from across the garden. He nonchalantly trimmed greenery while I struggled to work out on paper what he added in his head.

"That will gain one of you passage," the captain said, jerking me back to the now. "But you?" He pointed to Duncan with a stubby finger. "I'll take you if you work."

Duncan's eyes went alarmed. "Me? I can't do sums."

Captain Borlett took a long draught of his tankard and carefully wiped his beard. "I'm short a hand. He didn't duck fast enough last night. He needs a day or two to remember how to focus. You filling in for a short hop won't be too dangerous—for you or my crew."

"I don't know how to sail!" he exclaimed. "I've never been on a boat before!"

The captain snorted as he capped his inkpot and shoved everything pell-mell into his satchel. "I'll be the one sailing, not you." Suddenly somber, he leaned close, and I held my breath against the stench of ale. "She wasn't supposed to wed till the new year. Are you sure?"

I nodded, thinking it wouldn't happen. Someone would die first. Or shortly thereafter. And it wouldn't be me.

Captain Borlett rubbed a hand across his belly and looked to the innkeeper. "No more for my crew!" he shouted as he rose. "We leave with the tide."

The innkeeper bobbed his head to show his bald spot. There was a groan from the hearth and the card game. Duncan had been eying them throughout the conversation, worrying me. "Be at the dock within the hour," Captain Borlett said. "I want to see how your horses take to the water. I'm not feeding them or you, ma'am. But he can eat with the crew." He pointed to Duncan. "He can sleep with the crew, too." His eyes pinched. "I don't know what to do with you, and that's the honest truth. Putting you under the deck is asking for trouble."

"I'll sleep by the horses," I said. I'd rather be on deck than in a rank hold, though if it rained, I might change my mind. My thoughts returned to the dark clouds building. Rain. I had escaped Jeck, found Duncan, and gained passage across the bay. It was about time for fate to swing my luck back around, and sleeping on deck during a storm while Duncan was comfortable below had a certain poetic justice. Then again, it might be the only way I'd ever get my bath.

"So . . . the horses' fare?" Captain Borlett said pointedly.

Embarrassed for having forgotten, I pulled out the cloth and counted it out. Twice. Captain Borlett pocketed the money and put on his hat. "I'll set you up with the books after we cast off. If you aren't done when we get to Brenton, you aren't leaving my deck."

I nodded, and he put on his hat and left. Duncan went to the stewpot with our bowls. Shifting chairs, I put my back to the wall as Captain Borlett talked to the innkeeper. Their eyes landed on me once during the conversation. Two of the men carding left with the captain, dragging the drunken man between them. There were shouts from outside as the news spread.

"An hour," Duncan said as he returned and set my bowl before me. I slumped against the wall, and he stared. "What?" he asked. "All you have to do is scratch a quill across paper. I'm going to be ruining my hands scrubbing decks for the next two days."

"An hour isn't enough time to buy a hot bath," I complained.

"So take it cold." Sitting down beside me, he put his elbows to either side of his bowl.

Disgusted, I watched him slurp, deciding it would be pointless to ask him to remove his elbows. And I was so tired it didn't seem to matter. I wearily reached for a roll. "You know," I said as I broke it in two and breathed in the heavenly scent of new bread, "there might be time to wash our clothes, at least. And maybe you could buy a shave."

Duncan nearly choked on his stew, standing with a harsh scraping of his stool. "I'm going to check on the horses." His eyes darted to the door. Taking his bowl in one hand and two rolls in the other, he left, making me wonder if it would be possible to civilize him.

Eighteen

❖

The last hour waiting for departure was nerve-racking. I had gotten us passage. We had arranged for supplies. The tide was running. And Jeck, I was sure, would find me. I was waiting for his voice, expecting his arm to wrap around my waist from the shadows, and I found myself watching for his silhouette against the lowering sun as we stood on the dock before the *Sandpiper*. Rumors had begun to fly about the small town like embers from a bonfire, and Captain Borlett was as eager as I was to go.

I had left Jeck's pack with the innkeeper of the Three Crows along with a description of Jeck and a coin for his trouble. All but the knives and game pieces. The knives were safe in the bottom of my pack, and the pieces were set up on a board scratched on one of the inn's tables.

Jeck had made a bold move by shifting his king to the middle of the field. It freed me to take it before his remaining knight took my king—if he didn't see the trap before it was too late. My imagination put Jeck at the inn right now, hunched over the table, pondering his next move.

I alternately fussed with the mane of Jeck's horse and glared at the crew as they lowered a ramp for the horses. The men were being unconscientiously noisy with it, uncaring that the horses were watching. I knew they wouldn't like walking on something they'd just seen boom and rattle.

The sun was a mere two hours from setting. To the bay side, a featureless bank of clouds threatened, purple and even. Behind me over the land, the sun set in a clear sky. The strong beams of light outlined everything with a silver-edged shadow. If I had been less nervous, I would have enjoyed the unusual look to the sky. As it was, I was more concerned with Tuck balking at the ramp shifting under his front hooves.

"Hey! Hup!" Duncan shouted, giving an impatient tug on his lead. "Get up here. Flaky beast." Duncan was in a foul mood since the innkeeper hadn't sold him any ale, cutting him off with the rest of Borlett's crew. It had come as a nasty shock, dreadfully unfair in his eyes.

Tuck took another step, then flung his head, almost pulling the rope from Duncan's hand. The horse's eyes were wild. He backed up nearly into the water as Duncan alternately shouted soothing words and curses. The crewmen ignored us, carrying aboard the bundles of hay we had dropped shipside earlier. It had gotten noisy. We weren't the only ones leaving, and the dock had become busy surprisingly fast as last-minute details were found and dealt with.

Anxious, I sent my eyes over the ship, starting as I found a crewman scowling at me from the railing. He wore a red cap, and he seemed to be important enough to not have to be working. *First mate?* I thought, sure of it when the captain pulled him aside. Our locked gaze broke, and I turned to Duncan. "Let me take Pitch up first," I said. "Tuck might follow a mare."

"Go ahead," Duncan said crossly, clearly not expecting it to work.

I dropped the lead to Jeck's horse and headed up the ramp with Pitch. Duncan fell into place. I looked behind me to see Tuck's ears flattened at the sound of his hooves echoing on the ramp, but he followed the mare's sedately shifting rump up and onto the ship. Jeck's horse pricked his ears and followed Tuck by himself. I waited breathlessly by the railing, hoping he wouldn't step on his dragging lead and scare himself, but the black horse took the incline like an experienced war animal.

Duncan muttered a curse when he realized Jeck's horse was boarding without direction, but I was delighted, especially when the black horse came to find me, dropping his head into my hands. My palms were tingling again, and the horse seemed to enjoy the warmth on his sensitive nose. "You are a sweet horse," I murmured as the first mate strode toward us.

"Duncan?" the man barked, and Jeck's horse laid his ears back for an instant. The man never looked at me, his animosity plain enough.

I glanced at Duncan, seeing his entire body shift as he sighed. "Yes," he said flatly.

The first mate frowned. "That's 'Yes sir,'" he said. "Or you'll miss your ale rations."

"Yes sir," Duncan muttered, not as excited about the ale as I thought he would be.

The man grunted, apparently satisfied. "Tie the horses against the galley wall, stow your things, then find me," he said. "Captain says I'm to keep you busy and out of the way."

"Yes sir," Duncan repeated sullenly.

The first mate ran his eyes from my filthy boots to my topknot falling apart. He made a sniff of distaste and turned away. It was his sole acknowledgment I existed. Where I would have demanded an apology and lorded over him for the rest of the trip, I now felt more inclined to hold my tongue. I found it easier than I imagined. They were all fools, except the captain.

"Where's the chu pit of a galley?" Duncan said, surprising me with his bad temper.

I gave Jeck's horse a final pat. "Probably up there," I said, and headed for the small shack at the bow with my horses clattering behind me. I wondered what was bothering Duncan, not thinking anymore that it was the ale.

We found precious little space for them between the galley and the second mast, but at least they would be out of the wind. And there were rings already in the wall telling me they had carried livestock before. Ignoring Duncan's not-so-soft comments of who was likely going to be cleaning up after them, I took off the packs and dropped them in a pile.

"Where?" Duncan asked shortly as he stood with his riding pad and pack in his grip.

A shout from the wheel brought us spinning around. "Down below!" the first mate shouted, gesturing at the rise that took up much of the middle deck. It was about thigh high to give the area below some headroom. A doorlike hatch was at one end, and it was here that the first mate was pointing to. "And hurry up!" he added.

Jaw clenched, Duncan stomped across the deck. Growing more unsure, I hastened to follow with my things. The crew moved around us with very little direction as they prepared to cast off. Duncan tossed everything down the opening before turning to go backwards down the steep ladder. Waiting for my turn, I tried to remember if I'd done something to make him angry.

I headed down after him, my feet faltering on the steps when the clean smell of wind and salt turned dank: wet rope, mold, unwashed man, damp wool—and rats. I had known it was going to be bad, but this was awful. I shot a look at Duncan, glad I would be shivering on deck tonight.

Duncan muttered under his breath as he looked for somewhere to put his things. Slowly my eyes adjusted to the precious little light that came in slatted vents in the sunken room's sides. There was a cleared space where a table was fixed to the floor. Around it were a handful of narrow, low bunks built right into the walls of the ship. The few personal belongings I saw were carefully arranged, and most of the beds had a locked chest beside them.

Both fore and aft of the living quarters was storage, and I left Duncan so I could investigate. Barrels lined the center of the ship, the symbols burned into them telling me some held water but most had ale. Bags hung from the ceiling like fruit. I spotted a few sheepskins piled in a corner, and I wondered if the captain was keeping them for a favored customer. Actually, I decided as I investigated further, the captain seemed to have kept a little of everything from past shipments.

There was a small cask of very good wine with a Lovrege stamp, a crate of pottery from the lower islands, and three bags of sand, pure and white for making glass. It was rare in the rocky beaches that made up most of the kingdom. Clearly the captain was well traveled.

There was a sudden commotion of voices and thundering feet followed by a series of chants and rhythmic clatters. Something bumped the side of the ship. The calling voices didn't turn angry, just louder. I felt the floor move, and my breath hissed in from excitement.

Duncan saw my thrill and gave me weary look. Lips pressed together, he clambered back on deck, grumbling about his hands. I hastened after him, refusing to let his mood ruin my first sail. Kavenlow had never taken me on the sea despite my pleading. Costenopolie's strength was on the water, and I had always thought the situation grossly unfair.

As I emerged after him, blinking into the odd, silver light of sunset, my gaze went to the rigging. The mainsail was up and full with a light wind. Dizzy, I dropped my eyes. We were already free from the dock, and I watched it fall away with relief. There was one more obstacle between Jeck and me, one fewer between Kavenlow.

Before us with their masts showing sharp against the clouds were two ships. Beyond them was only the black line of the wide bay's horizon. The evening sun shimmering on the flat skin of the ocean against the backdrop of the purple clouds was breathtaking. My shoulders eased from the beauty of it. "I should've been born a man so I could go to sea," I murmured.

"Aye," came the captain's voice behind us, and Duncan and I spun. I put a hand to my face, feeling the warmth of embarrassment. "It's—nice," the squat man said haltingly, clearly loath to divulge his feelings. "I always thought the sea, in any weather, was a sight not to be taken lightly. But I can't tell those louts." He glanced at the crew divided into two teams to hoist the second sail. Before I could say anything, he straightened with an official air. "Got your belongings stowed?" he asked, and I nodded.

Duncan opened his mouth to say something, but someone was calling his name, and he turned. "What?" he shouted, then realizing it was the first mate, added, "I mean, yes sir?"

"I talk to the captain, not you!" the man yelled from the wheel. "You're crew, not passenger. Get on one of those ropes!"

Duncan's shoulders hunched. "This is why I do what I do," he muttered for my ears alone as he moved away. "I hate people giving me orders."

My breath slipped out in a sound of sympathy as I realized where his bad mood was coming from. It was going to be a long two days for him.

Captain Borlett gazed intently at the larger boats in front of us. "We've time afore we catch their backwind," he said, gesturing for me to accompany him. "I'll show you my desk."

I couldn't help but notice the captain's squat stature suited him well as he moved with confidence across the level deck. The first mate's stare was heavy as we approached the wheel and the second half-sunken room before it. Skin prickling, I ignored him as I passed him to get to the hatch. Captain Borlett went down before me, his mood splendid as he offered me a hand. Remembering the stink of the other room, I held my breath as I descended. But my first hesitant sniff drew a smile from me. The small room smelled of leather, twine, and metal polish.

A small table and two chairs took up most of the tiny space cluttered with charts and shiny instruments I didn't know a thing about. A marvelous map showing the entire coast and the four kingdoms bordering it took up much of the fore wall, and I envied him in that he'd probably been everywhere on it. There were two doors, one on either side of the common room, and Captain Borlett opened one. "This one is mine," he said. "The other is my first mate's."

I lifted my skirts as I stepped over the raised sill. He didn't come in but remained in the outer room, and for that I was thankful. It wasn't that his room was small as much as it was so full of things both wonderful and odd that there was no room for him. If I hadn't guessed it before, I would have known now that the captain liked collecting expensive, beautiful things.

Captain Borlett leaned in. Lifting a coat from the cluttered desk, he tossed it to the narrow bed built into the wall. His attempt to tidy made no difference, but now I could see the papers hiding the desktop. There were three small windows at head height looking out at a shin-high view of the deck, but it was a gimbaled oil lamp that lit the clutter. I swallowed, feeling a slight alarm. If this was any indication of how he kept his books, I was in trouble.

"Some of the records are in the bag there," he said, pointing. "But most are on the desk. There's paper in the drawer—I think." Not looking at all embarrassed for the mess, the stocky man rubbed his hands together as if pleased. "I'll be on deck if you can't read my writing."

"Yes. Thank you." I picked up a scribbled note. Five cases of granite, no, grain from Geants. I frowned. It had to be granite if it was from Geants. "Captain?" I asked, as he disappeared into the small outer room.

He poked his head back in, looking eager to escape. "Yes, yes. What?"

I brought my attention up from the pungent ink. "The barrels in the first hold . . ."

His eyebrows arched. "The ale? I told you that you'd have to feed yourself."

"It's the water I'm asking about," I said patiently. "How much am I allotted?"

"What you can drink, I suppose. No washing or cleaning." A smile came over his round face. "Your man can ask my first mate for the leftovers from his work if you want any of that. He'll be scrubbing the deck soon enough. But Haron is stingy with his water. He got caught in deep ocean without once and would have died had he not snared birds and rats. He won't let any water go over the side until its blacker than my beard used to be."

My brow furrowed as I found myself hoping for rain. I had very little money, but I had been trying to take a bath for the last four days. "Can I buy some?" I asked. "I can pay for the trouble of replacing it at Brenton."

Now it was Captain Borlett's turn to frown. "I don't rightly know how much that would be," he admitted, rocking back. "I'll ask Haron and tell you when you finish the books."

It wasn't a threat—more like a carrot. I suddenly felt like Tuck, lured into finishing a distasteful act by the promise of a nicer one.

A series of shouts came through the walls, and the captain looked up as if able to see through the low ceiling. "That'd be *Sky Dancer*," he said. "We're passing her. That tub is so heavy, she would sink in waves I could make in my washbasin. I'll be on the wheel deck."

"Thank you, Captain," I said as he backed away. "Perhaps when I'm done, we can find some diversion together. I can play cards or even recite poetry."

He smiled. "Aye," he said. "Some company who doesn't think with their stomach would be nice." The door snicked shut behind him. I turned to the desk, blushing at the sailors' catcalls as we passed *Sky Dancer*. Clearly the rivalry I had seen at the palace docks was commonplace.

I shifted a stack of papers to find the desktop was a dark

wood. "This is going to be nigh impossible," I whispered as I leaned against the wall. Sighing, I spun the oil lamp up high and set to finding the desk under the mess. It was going to be a long night.

Nineteen

❖

My shoulder hurt. Pulling the strand of my hair out of my
mouth yet again, I balanced against the swaying of the boat and the
force of the wind, focusing on the three chicken feathers stuck into
the rope coiled and tied to the railing. Exhaling, I drew my whip
back. With a practiced motion, I flung it out and back in a series of
rapid motions. All three feathers exploded with a satisfying, *crack,
crack, crack*. From behind me came a scattering of muttered oaths.

I grinned, not looking behind me as I heard money exchanging hands. The crew had been watching since I'd come on deck
after finishing the captain's books this afternoon. Their conde-
scending banter had since turned to respect.

The squat form of the captain came forward from where he
had been watching, and I met his smile with my own. "Ma'am,"
he said, nodding to the whip. "You have a right nice skill there.
Don't think I've ever seen a woman wanting to know how to do
more than whip her horse or her servant."

"Thank you," I said. "I haven't practiced in a while, and it
helped me find the balance of the boat." A pained twinge came
from my shoulder as I coiled the whip up and tied it to my hip. I
should have quit an hour ago, but the scornful laughs of the crew

and my desire to find the accuracy I was accustomed to kept me practicing long past where I should have stopped.

His head bobbed in understanding as he stood with his hands clasped behind his back, looking embarrassed. I squinted up at him, wondering what was bothering him. The splash of a stingray pulled my gaze to the waves, and I wished I had been quicker so to have seen more.

"I've been over my books," he finally said, his words halting and reluctant as he drew my attention back to him. "I hope my notes weren't too difficult."

I coughed to cover up the beginnings of a hysterical laugh. "Oh," I hedged, "it was easier after I started using the map in your common room. I simply followed the dates and made guesses at the next harbor if I couldn't read something. It wasn't hard, seeing as I knew the cargo you had just picked up and where you might be going with it."

He ran a hand over his beard in an endearing motion of chagrin. "Aye," he muttered. "That's what I usually do."

The sun was bright, but now that I had stopped moving, I felt cold. The threatened rain of last night had never materialized, but I could feel the chill in the air being pulled off the water. Taking my filthy cloak from where I had dropped it, I settled it about my shoulders. My sweat was cooling rapidly, and I felt awful, sticky and cold all at the same time. "Captain," I hedged. "Have you had a chance to talk to your first mate about the water?"

"Yes ma'am," he said quickly. "That's why I came to talk to you. He's not pleased, and he set a price so high I'm shamed to tell you. Haron is in charge of the stores, though, and a good man. I'd hate to drive him to another ship over this."

A sigh slipped from me as I held my cloak closed at my neck while the wind stole what little heat I had under it. I understood too well the politics of small groups. The captain could overrule his first mate's decision, but it might cause a rift between them. My comfort came out a distant second to that. "To be honest," I said as I looked askance at him, "I was thinking that instead of outright purchasing the water, I might try to win it from you over a hand or two of cards? Perhaps tonight?"

The captain blinked. A slow smile curved over his face, and his attention went to the helm where the first mate stood with the wheelman, eying the ribbons trailing from the edges of the sails. "That'd work," he said.

I felt a thrill of anticipation. "I'd be willing to wager more of my time. Perhaps tidy your room or help Duncan organize your hold. Seeing as he's not much good with the rigging."

His blue eyes grew brighter in what I thought might be avarice. "Yes ma'am," he said. "I would play a hand or two with you tonight. Why don't you get yourself out of the wind, meantime? The crew seems right impressed by you, but I'd stay out from under the deck anyway. Your man Duncan is in the galley, though."

"I will, thank you," I said, chilled to the pit of my being from the wind and my exertions.

"Good," he said shortly. "Have some tea. You look cold, if you don't mind me saying."

Nodding emphatically, I held my cloak to me and headed across the sloping deck.

The glow of acceptance warmed me as much as the sudden lack of the wind when I peeped round the archway and into the small kitchen. Duncan was alone, and he looked up from where he was leaning against a wall, keeping himself steady as he plucked a chicken.

"Tess." He wiped his stubbled chin with the back of his hand, only managing to stick more feathers to him. "I saw some of that. Very nice."

"Thank you." I touched the familiar loops on my belt. Holding on to the archway, I moved inside and perched myself on the tiny counter space to get out of his way.

The minuscule fire in the gimbaled pan kept the small space plenty warm, and Duncan had stripped down to only a worn pair of trousers and a thin shirt despite the wind whipping just beyond the archway. It was a shade too small for him, pulling tight to show the curve of his shoulders as he worked. Haron had put him here after he had loosened the wrong rope and brought a sail halfway down. I had a suspicion Duncan had done it intentionally. His mood had lightened considerably since he had taken over the galley and put some distance between himself and the first mate's barked orders.

"The captain said I could have some of the crew's tea," I said, looking around for a pot.

Duncan flopped the messy bird onto the counter and wiped his hands on his pants. "I'll get it," he said, finding a pot from somewhere in the mess. "It should still be warm."

He poured out a dark stream of liquid into a thick-walled mug, and I murmured a grateful "Thank you," as I took it. The boat's motion was rougher closer to the bow, and I tucked myself back on the counter until I was wedged into a corner. A patch of sun moved from the floor to the cabinets and back again as the *Sandpiper* took the waves. My one hand went to rub my shoulder, and I thought pride was responsible for the hurt, nothing more.

Duncan picked the chicken up, turning so he could watch me. "I won a bet with one of the crew," he said. "I knew you'd be hitting all three feathers before you quit."

I smiled as I took my hands from my neck and sipped my tea. It was bitter without honey, but I drank it greedily, glad for its warmth. "It took longer than I thought to find the boat's balance," I admitted. "I don't know how they walk about like they do."

His long, expressive hands worked fast against the damp bird, and the cleared patch rapidly grew larger. "I knew the moment you found the pattern of the waves," he said. "Crack, crack, crack."

My smile deepened. I liked being on the water, glad I hadn't gotten seasick as Kavenlow had staunchly claimed I would. "It's like being rocked by your mother, or the kingdom's chancellor in my case," I said, half-serious.

"I wouldn't know." Gathering a wad of feathers, he dropped them in a bucket.

Embarrassed, I eyed him over a slow sip. "Sorry."

"About what?"

"That you don't remember your parents."

He laughed harshly. "I remember them all right. But as the eighth child out of nine, I was never rocked. More likely told to 'Stop yer bellyaching and go to sleep!'" he said, shifting his voice to a harsh, low-street accent on the last word.

"Oh." I set my cup aside and swung my hair to my front, running my fingers through my curls to get the worst of the tangles out. "Sorry. Where are they?"

A shrug shifted his shoulders. "They have a farm on the edge of the forest about a week from the capital. I left when I was twelve." His voice was bland. "Gone before the sun set on the day they buried my grandfather. See, I was at the end of the children. Kind of scrawny. I should've been in the fields, but someone had to look after my grandfather, and I didn't mind spooning soup into his toothless mouth. My sister thought he smelled. He didn't like her either and wouldn't eat unless I fed him. So while everyone else worked, I took care of him. He was the one who taught me cards. I left the day he died."

"Sorry."

His eyes were dark with irritation as he pulled them up. "Will you stop saying that?"

My fingers stilled themselves in my hair, moving instead to rub my stiff shoulder. "You must have loved him very much," I said, my sympathy mixing with the grief of my own loss.

There was the sound of boots, and a crewman passed the open archway. "Nah. See, once he was dead, they were going to make me work the fields. That's why I left."

I made a small sound. He was lying; we both knew it. Sighing heavily, I continued to work at my neck. Angel's Spit, I was sore. And dirty. If the filth I was covered in didn't keep me awake tonight, the pain in my neck would. And I wasn't even going to think about rain.

"Stand up and turn around," Duncan said suddenly as he rinsed his hands clean and dried them. I stared, not understanding as he tossed the towel into a dry sink. "It's your neck, right? You haven't taken your fingers off it since you came in. I'll rub the knot out of it for you."

I hesitated, my fingers dropping. My thoughts went back to having kicked the breath out of him when he tried to do the same thing with my knees. Then they darted to his words said outside the inn. I froze in consternation, not knowing what to do. Despite my better judgment, I liked Duncan, but the last thing I could afford to do was give him the wrong impression.

He puffed in exasperation. "Go ahead. Hurt all night, then," he said, sounding wounded.

"No," I said as I slipped from the counter. "I'd like that. You—surprised me. That's all." Still unsure, I got to my feet and turned to show him my back. I regathered my hair in front of me. Head bowed, I heard the tension ease from him as he exhaled.

His hands touched me, cool from their fresh wash. The gentle pressure of his thumbs steadily increased until it had me almost moaning in relief. He was silent, and I relaxed. It did feel better, his coarse motion lacking the seductive feeling I was worried about. The square of sunlight coming in the door shifted from the waves, and I reached for the counter for support.

"So you've been on your own since you were twelve?" I asked. No one came up to the bow much unless it was time to eat, and I felt the need to maintain the conversation to keep the situation from growing intimate.

"For the most part, though I'd have died that first week if it hadn't been for Lan." He sounded irate as his fingers found a knot between my neck and shoulder and concentrated on it. God help me, but it felt good, and I had to stifle a sigh. Kavenlow had often rubbed aches and pains from me. Duncan was right; it didn't mean anything.

"Lan took me in," Duncan said as he worked. "He kept food in my belly, taught me how to beg properly. I never knew why we never spent more than a few days in any one town until I got too well-fed to beg, and he took me off the street and taught me how to move cards."

I didn't know what to say, keeping my eyes on my hands braced against the counter.

"I was so stupid," Duncan whispered, his ceaseless motion moving outward to my shoulders. My eyes closed, my body shifting slightly under his hands. "By the time I'd figured it out, I didn't care. I saw him as a big brother. Better even, as he never hit me unless I deserved it. He always dressed well. He always knew what to say. Always had money. I was so bewitched with the desire to be like him, I never saw how he was using me."

The boat dipped and hit a wave wrong. My eyes flashed open as Duncan reached to steady me. "What happened?" I asked as he let go.

He turned me around, and I pressed back against the counter. His sudden nearness gave me pause until his hands began rubbing away the deeper tension in the front of my shoulder. My hands dropped, and I didn't know what to do with them.

"Lan was more than a cheat," he said. His gaze went distant, and I noticed he had a tiny scar above his upper lip. "He was a thief, and a very good one, or so I found out. But one night he was caught and somehow slid his thievery onto me. I had no idea what was going on." The strength in Duncan's fingers grew less, and his face lost its expression. "He laughed with the rest when they dragged me through town in chains and burned a thief-mark into me."

Anything I might say would sound trite. My life looked suddenly worthless, my childhood worries and disappointments petty.

"The man Lan had robbed wanted me hung, and they would have, but it rained like the flood that night, and Lan broke me out of the pillory. Expected me to thank him."

"I'm sorry," I whispered. I was so self-absorbed, it sickened me.

He shrugged, seeming far too at peace with himself. "Someday. Someday I'll find a way to get back at him. Make him pay for what they did to me." His voice was calm and relaxed, standing in a sharp contrast to his words. It was an old hate, spoken without passion. It almost seemed as if he wasn't listening to what he was saying. His hands, too, had gentled their motions as my muscles loosened.

My face lost its emotion. The intent behind his touch had changed. It was deeper, slower. And it now held an unspoken question of the possibility of more.

A spark of warmth flickered through me. My eyes darted to his, seeing anew how close he was. They were dark and one thought ahead of me, waiting to see what I would do as I stood against the counter, clearly having felt the difference in his hands, yet not moved.

His motions slowed, his touch becoming firmer, more demanding. My heart pounded. I was suddenly filled with the desire to know what it was like to kiss a thief, a dangerous, clever thief who wasn't fumbling or worried. Someone who knew what he was doing and felt no shame.

He was taller than me, but I would only have to tilt my head a little. Breath held, I leaned forward. My chin lifted, and my lips parted.

Only now did the heat in his eyes falter and his hands on me go still. "You're a princess," he whispered, clearly having recognized the invitation. "You're not serious."

"I haven't been a princess for the last seven days," I said. "And I've kissed men before."

He said nothing, but his look of doubt prompted me to reach

up and cup my hand behind his neck, pulling his head down to mine. It was only a kiss.

His beard was scratchy against me, a delightful contrast to his lips, soft as they met mine. Relaxing into the kiss, I let the warm feeling take me. My eyes closed, and I found my tension easing under his hands gripping my shoulders. He pressed into me, prolonging it. I willingly responded, parting my lips and pushing gently back against him. My hand ran down his back, stopping just above his hip.

Slowly I pulled away, and Duncan leaned after me until our lips parted. Opening my eyes, I found him waiting for me. Heart pounding, I kept my hand where it was, feeling the heat of him through his thin shirt. It had been a very nice kiss. Much nicer than my last, even if he did smell like chicken and potatoes.

Duncan's eyes were bright with surprise. "You *have* kissed a man before."

A sly smile hovered over me. Did he think that royalty was any less randy than common folk? We were perhaps more so since we had to be so discrete about it—especially princesses. "It was just a kiss," I said, believing it.

He nodded, his brown eyes dark with an unsaid emotion. "Just a kiss."

Yet I was holding my breath when he cupped my cheek in his palm and leaned close. I let him draw me in, and my eyes closed as he tilted his head and met my lips again. Stronger, the feeling of warmth rose in me. My breath slipped in, gathering my will and seeming to melt me into him. I sent my fingers to link behind him, pulling him closer.

So slow it was almost unnoticed, his gentle kiss shifted from inquisition to a deeper heat. The growing hint of his restrained need was like a spark, jumping from him to me. The feeling crashed over me in a warm wash, shocking me to stillness as it drew from me a surprising, almost desperate need I'd never felt before.

Shocked, I pulled away. My hands dropped from him, and I stood with my back to the counter, frightened. I knew better than to let a kiss become more than a kiss.

Duncan looked at me, seeming to have to catch himself. "You started it," he said, his voice low and husky as he stood with his arms at his sides, a heady mix of want and restraint in his stance.

I swallowed hard, frightened that I had slipped so badly. "I shouldn't have done that," I said softly. "I'm sorry." Unable to meet his eyes, I headed for the open door.

"Sorry?" A jolt went through me as he grabbed my upper arm, halting me. His eyes were angry, and I let him pinch me, thinking I deserved far worse for having mislead him like that. "You can't tell me you didn't like that."

"Of course I liked it," I said. "It was the most—" My words caught. I couldn't tell him it had been the most sensuous, the most passion-lost feeling I'd ever let myself experience and that I'd do almost anything to feel it again. "I can't do this, Duncan," I whispered, frightened. "I can't do this, right now." His hand loosened, and I continued out into the sun. The wind beat at me, seeming to take the last of my certainty with it.

"Well then, when can you?" he called belligerently after me. I clutched my cloak about myself and went to stand at the railing. I would have thought he was no better than an animal, but that I was wondering the same thing about myself.

Twenty

❖

The breeze was glorious up on deck, lifting through my hair in a wonderful sensation. The curly strands were smooth and silky against my fingers—and about a foot shorter since I'd cut them to fall midback instead of to my waist. I was finally clean, and it felt *so good*. My dress clung uncomfortably to my shoulders, the waistband of my red underskirt was positively damp, and my stockings had fallen apart to rags in their wash, but I didn't care. I was clean.

I stood between the water and sky on the deck of the *Sandpiper* adrift off Brenton. The faint noise from the small cluster of buildings was lost behind the excitement of the horses being winched over the side, and it was only knowing I would be leaving the *Sandpiper* that dulled my satisfaction.

I had finally gotten my bath this morning, taking it in the captain's quarters since the crew would have mutinied had I bathed elsewhere. Duncan had toted the buckets of water across the deck from the galley. He was sulking, now. I had confronted him about his mood, thinking it was from our kiss. I had said that I was sorry, that he had every right to be angry but that he would do better to forget about it. He had turned belligerent then, telling me not to flatter myself and that he was angry I had gamed with the captain without him, not about some fool kiss from a tease of a woman who couldn't control herself.

I had soothed my injured pride by throwing the soap at him, thinking he probably believed that. And he had good reason for being upset about my card game. As crew, Duncan wasn't allowed to play cards with the captain. He hadn't even been allowed to watch, since only the first mate was allowed into the captain's common room. The small chamber had quickly become my favorite spot on the boat, a cozy oasis from cold looks and cutting wind.

Thankfully, the captain's fatherly coddling had vanished as soon as he realized my skill at cards rivaled his. By the end of it, I not only had the water for my bath but the fuel to heat it.

The captain and I were on excellent terms now, having shared much conversation and tea. He had a tea leaf equaling the quality I had grown up on and, saint's bells preserve us, the honey to go with it. I found he was quite the learned man, eager to tell an appreciative ear of his stories: dark-skinned women who went about half-naked under a sun strong enough to strike a man dead, warriors bedecked with feathers, spices that burned from the inside, clever animals with tiny faces and hands like men, and music beaten from drums to drive one mad.

In return, I entertained him with anecdotes from the palace. He readily accepted my story that I was a member of the court fleeing the possibility of war. It explained my skill at sums and why I spoke the way I did. I thought the randy behavior of men and women of noble standing boring, but he listened with a rapt attention. Of the darker news of the capital, I was circumspect. I couldn't bear that Captain Borlett would become an officer and his trading of salt and grain would turn to flaming tar and metal. I said nothing of my parents' death, only that the Misdev prince was making irrational demands, forcing the wedding to take place immediately. It wasn't a lie, just a very large omission and a drastic understatement of Garrett's actions.

I would say nothing to start a war. The memory of my people stoning the assassin to death in the streets eight years ago was very clear in my mind. I didn't want them to take matters into their own hands when diplomacy and a well-placed knife could end the problem with no loss of life but Garrett's.

"Tess!" called a voice behind me, and recognizing the captain's bellow, I turned. Smiling, I pulled the hair from my eyes, only now realizing I hadn't worn my topknot and darts since the first night. "Tess," he repeated as he came close. "You're looking . . . clean."

"Thank you." I squinted up at him, a hand held over my eyes. "It's a charmer of a day."

He nodded, his gaze going up the mast to where his flag fluttered. "Aye. We'll be heading out of the bay from here, and then to Lovrege."

There was a warning shout, and we both looked to where Duncan was struggling to fasten a looping harness around Tuck. The poor animal was near panic, his eyes wide and wild. Pitch had already gone over the side, winched to the water and left to swim to the shore. Jeck's horse would be last. The rude shouts of the crewmen in the unseen dinghy floated up.

"I should go," I said regretfully. "I don't think the black gelding will give you much trouble. Pitch is almost to the beach. One of us should be there to make sure no one takes her."

"My crew will keep an eye on her," he said. "I've two ashore buying water and wood."

Tuck whinnied when the straps tightened about him and his feet left the deck. I reached out, relieved when the animal went stiff, all his legs into a four-posted position.

"See?" Captain Borlett said. "I knew he'd be all right. My lads know what to do."

Duncan shouted a nervous encouragement from the railing as Tuck was swung out over the water and three crewmen began slowly winching him down. The horse's feet touched the water, and he exploded into helpless motion. He was frantic, and the weighted ropes tangled.

"Hey, hup!" a sailor in the dinghy called. "He's caught! He's gonna drowned himself!"

"Tuck!" Duncan cried, his voice cracking in fear. He watched in horror as the horse struggled. Lunging over the railing, Duncan fell into the water. I ran to the side, but the horse calmed as Duncan touched him. Talking loudly to Tuck, he untangled the rope, and the two started swimming for the nearby shore.

"I should go," I said, halting my motion to leave as the captain cleared his throat.

"Ma'am," he said formally, extending an envelope sealed with a drop of wax. I took it, mystified. Seeing my confusion, he added, "It's a recommendation. A written one." He looked embarrassed as he ran his grip over his graying beard. "You did a capital job with my books. That's my recommendation that any captain would be lucky to trade your figuring with numbers for passage." His eyes crinkled. "In case you find yourself in a hurry again."

I beamed. It was the first time I had done something on my own, and I had done it well. "Thank you," I said, tucking the valuable paper away. He had no idea how delighted I was.

"And this," the squat man said, handing me a cloth-wrapped package. He stood ramrod straight beside me and rocked on his heels, his gaze on the forested hills before us.

I unfolded it to find a small jar of honey. But then I noticed what it was wrapped in, and my lips parted. I glanced from the square of fabric to the flag atop the highest mast. "It's your flag!" I breathed as the standard—a gold field with three black slashes—fluttered in the breeze.

"Aye," he said. "It's so I can find you this winter, wherever you might be—if you like. I'll be looking for it. And you can do my books again. I may have to go out to the southern islands. It will be a long trip. You can bring your man, there. Just not his horse."

My throat went tight. If only I could. "Thank you," I said, suddenly loath to leave.

"Fly it from a pole in sight of the dock," he said, staring off into nothing. "I'll find you."

I wrapped the honey back in his flag, unable to say anything. Throat tight, I gathered my skirts and one-handedly levered myself over the railing and down the rope ladder. It was Haron who helped me make the jump to the rocking dinghy. His small hand was rough in mine, and I appreciated his grudging help. Jeck's horse reached the water the same time as I did. The weighted ropes slipped smoothly from him, and the levelheaded horse set out for the beach.

The *Sandpiper* fell from me in even, rhythmic surges of motion. The lump in my throat surprised me. My hands drifted upward to bind my hair in a topknot with a bit of twine. By the time the dinghy scraped the rocky beach, my few remaining darts were in place.

Miserable, I stood to disembark. Haron stepped into the water, and with no warning, scooped me off my feet and sloshed the few steps to land. "Thank you," I said, flustered, as he set me down. He smelled of wind and sweat. I glanced at Duncan making baby sounds at his shivering horse. The men threw our packs to land out of the surf. They were replaced with a bundle of wood and cask of water that two crewmen had rolled forward.

"I still think women on water are unlucky," Haron said at my elbow, and I spun, surprised. "But the captain . . . He says you can hear it. The sea, I mean." His gaze flicked away, then back to mine. "Can you?"

Vision blurring, I looked at the *Sandpiper* and nodded. I had felt safe there. And free.

"It don't seem right," he said as he touched his red cap and stepped barefoot into the surf. "Why would God let a woman hear the sea if she's not supposed to brave the waves?"

He pushed the boat into deeper water, the scrape of the keel seeming to grate across my soul, wounding me. His question wasn't a taunt; he was confused. I'd cracked his beliefs.

Taking a quick breath, I wiped a hand under my nose and turned my back on the sea.

Brenton lay before me, small and disorganized. I nervously checked my topknot to see that all was as it should be, and my worry about Jeck thundered down. The wind in the leaves became threatening, and the slightest twitch of the horses' ears caught my attention. There seemed to be an animosity or cunning in the curious stares of the few passing townsfolk. They were dirty, and I had yet to see anyone with shoes. The entire town stank of fish. I had never seen anything as filthy and poor as Brenton. I pulled my cloak tighter about my shoulders, wondering what else I had missed living behind my walls.

Slipping awkwardly on the stone beach, I went to Duncan. "Is Tuck all right?" I asked, but he didn't answer, the back of his neck going red as he continued to fuss over his horse. *Chu,* I thought. He was worse than Heather, thinking he could punish me by ignoring me.

Frowning at his infantile behavior, I led Pitch and Jeck's horse into the stream that bisected Brenton. My skirts tied high to keep them from going damp, I dumped water over the horses using the bowl from my pack to get rid of the salt. I used the remnant of my stockings to dry the back of Jeck's horse before arranging my pack and riding pad on him.

Duncan said nothing, keeping with his cold silence. He stomped into the stream, sitting up to his armpits to let the current wash out the salt. Dunking himself, he slicked his hair back as he came up. Still dripping, he splashed off Tuck and led him up the steep embankment to the street. I followed, and we silently headed into town. There was no dock, but there was probably a tavern where I could ask after Kavenlow.

I didn't look back at the *Sandpiper.* My chest was tight with a confused frustration. With Captain Borlett's letter, I had freedom. I had no earthly reason not to abandon my position as the princess's double. Except that to flee would allow Garrett to live. And I wanted him dead.

"Look at her," Duncan said crossly to Tuck as we found our place among the noise and stink of people again. "Did I tell you she made me carry fourteen buckets of water across the deck of that burning ship? Madam princess wants to burning wash her hair. Madam princess wants to burning wash her clothes. It's burning unfair. And what's worse, she didn't even let me watch her win it. She burning well cheats, Tuck. Otherwise, she would've let me watch."

"I didn't cheat," I said, frustrated. I still thought it was the kiss, not the cards.

"Hear that bird singing, Tuck?" Duncan mocked. "Have you ever heard such an annoying twitter in all your life?"

I frowned. Duncan's feet squished in his wet boots, keeping exact time with my pace.

"No one wins at cards that often unless they cheat," he continued, speaking to his horse but talking to me. "She cheats, Tuck, sure as you're a gelding, poor sod. But how she does it, I can't tell." He was silent for three heartbeats. "If she told me, I might talk to her again."

"Duncan . . ." My shoulders slumped. "I don't cheat. I grew up playing cards with someone who does. I had to learn how to read people just to win my fair share. The captain was good, but he was careless. He touched his beard when he had to think about which card to throw away. He leaned forward when he thought I had a better hand than his, and he took a drink when he pulled a card higher than a sword. If you would spend as much time watching your opponent as you do the cards, you wouldn't have to cheat."

"Listen to her," Duncan said to Tuck as he squashed the biting fly that landed on his horse's neck. "Such pretty stories." He glanced at me, his infant beard making his ire look ugly. "You make a good storyteller, Tess. Ever think of changing your profession?"

Ignoring that, I angled to a hard-packed dirt yard that was as indicative of a tavern as much as the sign above the door. "You don't have to come in if you don't want to," I said, tired of inns and ale and loud voices of men raised in tone-deaf salutations of friendly women with full tankards and ample breasts.

Duncan pushed Tuck's head out of the way so he could see me. "Do you have enough for something to eat?" he asked, apparently having forgiven me already at the prospect of food.

"You spent the last two days in the galley, and you're hungry?" I said feeling a jolt of nervousness. "Jeck's behind us. We find out if or when Kavenlow was here. Then we leave."

"Yes," he drawled. "I can hardly wait to watch you go in there and ask if they've seen a wise old man and a princess."

My brow furrowed. "You have to go through Brenton to get to Bird Island. Either he's in front of us or already on his way back. I have to know which direction to take."

"And Captain Jeck will do the same thing, won't he," he said. "He's either chasing behind us by boat, or waiting for us to walk right into him on the way back."

For a moment, I could only hear the pounding of my heart in my ears. *Why hadn't I thought that far ahead?* "Shut your mouth, Duncan," I said, the pit of my stomach cold.

"For a talented woman, you aren't very bright."

My lips tightened, and I tied Jeck's horse and Pitch to the post outside the inn. The stable was nothing more than a shaky-looking lean-to propped against a tree. I glanced back at the bay, fighting a pang as I found the *Sandpiper* in full sail heading toward open ocean without me. The fear—the need to be moving that had been absent from the time I has set foot on the *Sandpiper*—filled me again. I didn't want to advertise my presence, but I had to know if Kavenlow had been here. Garrett's reinforcements would reach the capital soon. I was running out of time.

Duncan entered the inn ahead of me. I followed, a small sound of disgust slipping from me as I took a shallow breath. The place stank of soured fish and musty potatoes. Even Duncan wrinkled his nose as he looked to the hearth and the cluster of too-thin men drinking. I took in the slovenly dressed woman draped across the loudest man and grimaced. The inn was nothing like the Three Crows. Not having any competition, the inn did very little to attract customers. "It's a wonder anyone is here at all," I muttered. "It reeks of fish."

"Oh, someone new. Whatcha want?" a woman said as she came out from a back room. Her eyes roved over Duncan's damp attire. "A late noon meal? Perhaps a room? Eh? Yes?"

My heart gave a pound as Duncan eyed me in speculation. "Two ales, please," I said, laying out the proper amount of money. *Maybe ale would soften him where my words couldn't. It would distract him, if nothing else.*

Her brow rose at my accent. Duncan took the first tankard. Holding my breath, I tried a tentative sip, my eyes meeting his when I found it surprisingly pleasant. Duncan's gaze slid from mine to the men by the hearth. "I'll be over there till you're done," he said shortly, drifting toward them as if flotsam on the tide.

"Yes, go," I encouraged, thinking if he was over *there*, he wouldn't foul up my careful questions over *here*. "Ma'am," I said, "you brew a good ale."

She sent her gaze over me again, clearly wondering what I was doing here. "My husband, he taught me," she said, dragging a rag over a table as she pretended to clean it. "It brings the ships in when nothing else will, it does. You out from the capital?"

I thought back to the bitter ale in the casks on the *Sandpiper* and nodded. "We're just off the *Sandpiper*."

"You and your husband, there?" she interrupted, nodding toward the hearth.

"Ah, yes," I stammered. "I was wondering—"

"Tymus is taking on passengers?" she blurted. "That's not like him."

Tymus? I thought, not liking that Captain Borlett and this woman were on a first-name basis. "It took a fair amount to convince him," I said. "I've been trying to meet up with someone. An older man, well-dressed? He was headed this way."

The woman brushed her hands on her skirts, her eyes roving over the patrons. "I didn't hear the call of a boat coming in. Where's Tymus's crew? Is it a big cargo? Any fabric?"

"No," I said in exasperation, realizing I had lost what little control I had. "No cargo. He's already headed out. He only stopped to let us off."

"Oh." The woman slumped. She eyed Duncan across the room. "He made you swim?"

"Just—my husband." Her eyebrows rose, and I surged ahead. "I was hoping you might be able to help me find my father. He might have my sister with him?" The lies came out so easily, it was frightening.

"You don't know if your sister was with him or not?" She looked at me as if I was stupid. Flushing, I glanced at Duncan, his hands waving in conversation. I didn't like that tart of a woman touching his shoulder. Neither did the man whose lap she was currently sitting on.

"Ah-h-h," I said, remembering the innkeeper had asked me something. "He's fetching her back to the capital. He wouldn't have gone by boat, and I don't know if I passed him in my rush to catch up with him."

She nodded knowingly. "Oh. Old man with graying beard? Attractive, if you don't mind me saying so? Dressed up real fancy?"

I felt a wash of relief. Garrett's assassin hadn't found him. "Yes, that's probably him."

"Aye," the woman said, wiping out a bowl with the corner of her apron. "You just missed them. He came through two days ago off the *Sea Mist*. He bought the Ellisons' horse and rode out of town like the devil himself were after him."

"Two days!" I exclaimed softly. I would never have guessed he would cross the bay.

"Shame you didn't come in earlier," the woman said. "He left this morning."

My head rose, and I looked at her in confusion. "But you said . . ."

"With your sister and her man," she added, and my brow smoothed in understanding. Kavenlow was on his way back to the capital. Then I hesitated. *Her man?*

"They spent the night," the chatty woman was saying. "Took my two best rooms. She's a beautiful little thing, ain't she? Hair long enough to sit on, and as fair as sunlight on water."

I grimaced, touching my dull-brown hair. "Yes. That's—her."

"I can see why your father dotes on her," she said. "Never left her alone. Kept everyone away. Waited on her hand and foot. I hardly saw the frail wisp. She looks a mite ill, the tiny thing. So sad and melancholy. Was she away for her health?"

"She's fine," I said, trying to hide my anger. Kavenlow *waited* on her? He wasn't a servant. My growing aversion for the princess shifted to a real dislike.

"It was a sight. The both of them tending her as if she was a queen," the woman said.

"Queen. Yes," I muttered.

"I tell you, if my husband had given me half that attention, I might have worked harder at keeping him alive when he fell sick."

Ill with jealousy, I put my ale down. "Yes. Thank you. I have to go now."

"I expect if you hurry, you might find them yet tonight. Wagons are slow things."

A wagon! I thought. No wonder she was taking so long to get to the palace. Little princess perfect couldn't ride. She needed a wagon. "I expect so," I said, no longer trying to hide my bitterness. "Thank you."

"Good luck finding your father and sister."

"Yes. Thank you." I turned away before she could say anything else, stomping across the room to Duncan. I stood behind his chair, seething. The men ignored me, making me even angrier. "Come on, Duncan," I said, tugging at his sleeve. "We have to go."

Duncan rose with a mocking slowness, tipping his hat at the unsavory woman in parting. She all but leered at me, thinking I was his jealous wife, no doubt. Why would I be jealous of her? She had dirty feet the size of a duck.

"They were here last night," I said as I pulled him to the door.

Duncan tilted the bottom of his tankard to the ceiling and finished his ale in one swill. "I know," he said when he came up for air. "Chu, that's good."

"How did you find out?" I said, glancing behind me as the group sprawled about the hearth laughed, probably at me.

"Thadd likes to roll the dice."

"Thadd? Who's Thadd?" I took his empty tankard and set it on a table as I hustled him back out into the sun and to the horses.

"Thadd is her goat boy," he said. "A sculptor, really. He's delivering a statue. That's why the wagon."

"Goat boy?" Bewildered, I squinted at him in the bright glare.

Duncan untied Tuck and belched, earning my disgust and the admiration of the boy nearby throwing pebbles at the chickens in the road. "Yeah. Goat boy. You know, the hero in the stories who helps the princess save the kingdom." Smirking, he added, "He's sweet on her. Poor sod. I wonder if he knows who she really is?"

Goat boy? Deep in thought, I swung up onto Jeck's horse and arranged my dress and cloak. What was the princess doing with a sculptor?

We headed out of town at a fast pace. Behind me I heard small belches coming from the stableboy as he tried to outdo Duncan. "Look what you started," I said, disgusted.

Duncan grinned, his nasty red and black beard looking awful. "Don't you know how to show the proper appreciation for such a fine ale as that? Who ever heard of an assassin who didn't know how to belch?"

My stomach tightened, and I looked over my shoulder to see if anyone had heard him. "You're a stark-raving idiot, you know that?"

"And you're an assassin, Tess," Duncan said cheerfully, as if he rather liked the idea. "Not a thief or a cheat. You're an assassin. And together, we're going to make a fortune. After you save the kingdom and all."

"Some cheat you are," I scorned. "One ale, and you lose what little sense you had."

"I'm not drunk," he claimed, and the clear look in his eye made me believe it. "Think about it. What else are you good for?"

What else, indeed? I thought as we left the smelly harbor of Brenton behind, slipping into a mile-eating canter headed back to the capital. I wondered what it said that the skills of a princess and that of an assassin were so alike that no one had noticed the difference.

Twenty-one

❖

What am I going to do about the princess? The thumps of Jeck's horse's hooves pounded the thought into me as we cantered up the path to the capital. Though rutted with the imprints of hooves and wheels, the trail was blessedly empty. Jeck's horse never stumbled, and the gentle motion that usually soothed me only made things worse. Each hesitation of hoofbeats seemed like the gathering of breath, tightening me until I was ready to break. My mind kept circling back to the question I had blinded myself to. *What am I going to do about her?*

If the princess took the throne, I'd never be able to convince King Edmund that I was justified in killing his son for the murder of my parents. Only if I was a fellow sovereign would he listen to me. Only by taking the throne could I find my revenge for the murder of my parents.

"But it's not my kingdom," I whispered, hearing my voice quaver.

It should be, a selfish thought whispered. A tremor took me, and I hid it by tapping the horse with my heels to get him to step it up. She might be heir to the throne, but she would lose it in three years, taken by Misdev or any of the other kingdoms watching the wealth pass through our harbors. War would erupt up and down the coast whether I killed Garrett or not. Captain Borlett would carry soldiers, not grain. People would starve. People would die.

I angled Jeck's horse to a branch impaling one of Kavenlow's leaves. It ripped from the branch with a wet sound, and anxiety tightened my stomach. They were close. Perhaps as little as just out of sight. Fingers trembling, I dropped the leaf.

"Duncan," I said as I pulled Jeck's horse to a standstill. "We're stopping."

He brought Tuck to a neck-arched halt, his shoulders bunching as he reined the horse in. "Now? Look at those ruts. They're right in front of us." His eyes were wide in the early dusk under the trees.

"It's getting dark," I said. "They'll have stopped, too. We'll catch up with them tomorrow." Face flaming at his questioning silence, I dismounted and walked Jeck's horse and Pitch off the trail to a small clearing beside the path.

"All right," he said slowly and dismounted. I could feel his eyes on me as I wound the reins of Jeck's horse into a bush and started up the trail. I had to see her. I had to see the princess. Perhaps she wasn't as frail and stupid as the woman had made out.

"Tess? Where are you going?"

Duncan's voice brought me spinning around. "To find something to eat," I lied, not knowing why I did. "I'll be right back."

He scratched a finger through his vile, sparse beard. "You never have before."

My lips pressed together, and I belligerently tossed a stray curl out of my eyes. "Would you rather have me try to cook again?"

Misdirected anger made my words harsh, but instead of reacting in turn, he stared at me. "What about your horses?"

"Oh," I said, returning. "Yes." With abrupt motions, I removed the riding pad and packs from Jeck's horse. Leaving them where they lay in the dirt beside the trail, I dusted my hands and backed up three steps. "There," I said. "I'll be back."

I strode down the path. The hairs on the back of my neck pricked, but I wouldn't turn around. My pulse quickened. "Hey!" he called, and I spun. My hands dropped from my topknot to catch the water sack he tossed me. "See if you can find running water, too."

"Yes. Fine," I said, hastening down the trail. As soon as I was around a bend, I gathered my skirts and went faster. My tension didn't dissipate with the motion; it worsened.

A low murmur of voices pulled me to a standstill. One was high-pitched, the other low. Hunched, I edged off the trail and continued. My heart pounded, and my hands trembled. I smelled the smoke from their fire before I saw them. In a low crouch, I crept forward. The canes of wild berries caught at my skirt and hair, and the sharp stabs of thorns were like guilty accusations for my spying. I stifled a cry as my sleeve ripped to leave a long scratch in my arm. I brushed at the pain, a sliver of motion making me go still.

Shifting a small branch, I peered through the vegetation. My eyes narrowed. A young woman sat on a log beside a fire, huddled under a thick woolen cape. Her arms were wrapped around herself. She looked cold and lost. And beautiful.

The tips of her yellow hair brushed the ground as she sat. It was straight where mine was curly. Her skin was sun-starved while mine was dark. She looked unfit for anything useful, with ample curves where I only had suggestions. She smiled up at the short, powerfully built young man who draped a blanket over her shoulders, and I hated her. I was no princess. *This is a princess,* I thought as I wiped a hand under my nose. I was a fool to ever think I had been one.

"Goat Boy" crouched beside her to arrange the fire. He was too muscular to have any sense in him. His feet were bare, and he had broad shoulders and thick legs, looking as if the cold couldn't touch him. I frowned when he flicked the black bangs from his eyes.

Pulled off the trail in the shadows was a narrow wagon holding a box the shape of a coffin. There was only one horse to pull it. The draft animal was enormous, looking as if he had pulled stumps from the ground the day he fell from his dam. No wonder it was taking them forever to get to the capital.

My attention returned to them as the man murmured something to get her to smile. Anger filled me. Where was she when Father died on a sword? Where was she when Mother's blood stained my fingers? I was their daughter, not her!

I watched her take a comb from a small sack and brush her hair. The curve of her cheek and her position struck me as familiar. With a shock that twisted my stomach, I realized the statues in the solarium were of her. The beautiful statues in the garden were of her!

Goat Boy leaned closer and rested a hand on her shoulder. "Do you want another blanket, Contessa?" he asked in a slow country drawl.

I felt as if my breath had been knocked from me. She had taken my future, she had taken my parents. How *dare* she take my name?

Stomach churning, I stood. Thorns caught at my skirts, the soft sound of them ripping adding to my anger. "That's my name," I said softly.

Goat Boy spun, his eyes wide and his mouth open.

The princess stood, her blanket falling to almost catch fire. "It's you!" she exclaimed, a weak-looking hand going to her neck. "You're her!" She hesitated, and my face burned as she ran her gaze over me, taking in my scratches and travel-stained clothes. I drew myself straighter, refusing to touch my hair or dress to straighten them. "What are you doing here?" she asked, her country drawl a hint under her attempt at a noble accent. "You're supposed to be at the palace."

My breath came in a shuddering sound, I was so angry. "You have no right to question me," I whispered, drawing on every ounce of hard-won protocol to not shout at her.

The princess pursed her lips, her chin rising. "I'm the princess, not you. I can ask you anything I please. Why aren't you at the palace?"

My hands trembled, and I took a step toward her, my motion not as graceful as I would've hoped because of the thorns. Jerking free of them, I stumbled into the clearing. Though her words had been bold, the princess went pale, clutching Goat Boy's arm. She made a conscious effort to let go, nervously smoothing her dress. The woman at the inn was right. This was a weak-minded nothing. Costenopolie would fall under her.

"Don't question me again," I said, matching her highbrow speech though I was seething inside. "You are a little country bumpkin who doesn't know the first thing about ruling a country. You're going to lose it without my help."

"It's my kingdom, not yours," she asserted, her chin high and spots on her cheeks. "And I'll do just fine without you. Be sure you remember that."

I took another step forward, and Goat Boy shifted uncertainly. "Your kingdom?" I said, and she sniffed, clearly thinking my soft voice meant a soft temper.

"Yes, my kingdom. Thadd was right. You're a grasping little beggar, angry that you aren't the princess and I am."

I struggled to keep my breathing even. "I kept you alive for twenty years," I said, my voice rising despite my efforts. "And you call *me* a grasping beggar? I didn't ask for this. You ruined my entire life with that damned Red Moon Prophesy of yours!"

Face tight, she looked me over. "Your speech is foul, and you've torn your dress. Mother wrote and said I was to speak to you as my sister, but you're not worthy to be her daughter. They never thought of you as anything but a way to protect me. You aren't their daughter. How could they ever love you?"

"You . . . you little . . . chu mouth!" I stammered, standing before her, shaking. *My mother, not hers. My father, not hers.*

"I'll have the chancellor beat you for your insolence," she said, her nose in the air.

My breath hissed out. A flash of fear crossed me that she could make him do it. Anger washed it away. If Kavenlow was going to beat me, I'd give him something to beat me for.

Striding around the fire, I swung the flat of my hand to smack sharply onto her cheek.

She gasped, taking a step back. The imprint of my hand showed an ugly red. Shock froze her for an instant, then she flung herself at me, crying out in rage.

I backpedaled, but not fast enough. We went down in a tangle of skirts and flying hair. She hit my eye with her fist. Stars exploded in my vision, and I rocked my head back. Her grip tightened in my hair, and I smacked her again, hitting her ear by the feel of it. She fell back, and as the stars still danced before me, I grabbed her shoulders and rolled her over to the ground.

Straddling her, I sat on her back. "They are my parents!" I shouted, forcing her pretty little blond head into the dirt and leaf mold. "Don't you *ever* try to take them away from me again. Do you hear me? I'm their daughter as much as you are! I am. I am!"

The princess was crying, her arms reaching behind her to find me with the sleeves of her dress down about her elbows. Her hair was full of sticks and leaves, and I thumped her head into the ground, jerking when Duncan grabbed my shoulders and pulled me off her.

His eyes were bright in amusement, and I wondered how long he had been watching. Goat Boy was wisely staying out of it, standing at the edge of camp, pale and shaking. Laughing, Duncan shook his head, his hand still gripping my elbow. "Tess, what are you doing?"

"Let me go!" I cried, and when he didn't, I punched him solid in the stomach.

Clutching his middle, he rocked back with a breathless, "Ooof."

I swung the hair from my eyes and looked for the princess. She was tripping on her skirts and cloak as she tried to rise and get to Goat Boy. Her dress was mussed, and her hair was in disarray. She was sobbing, and my eyes narrowed. "I don't think you fully understand the situation yet," I said, lunging for her.

A shadow darted between us, and I ran right into Kavenlow.

"Kavenlow!" I cried, jerking to a stop. He was dressed as a huntsman in black linen and leather. His dagger was in plain view instead of hidden, and his dart pipe was tucked into his hatband, already loaded. Worry pinched his brow, but his lips were firm in disapproval.

Fear flashed through me, then anger. "You lied to me!" I shouted, the heartache of the last eight days thundering down upon me. "You lied—then left me!"

His face melted into understanding, and he put a hand on my shoulder. "Easy," he soothed. "I never meant for you to find out this way. But do you really think slapping the princess is the best way to make her acquaintance, Tess?"

At the sound of my name, something in me broke. "That's not my name!" I shouted, furious. I hit his shoulder to drive him away, but he wouldn't let go. "It's *her* name!" I cried, shoving his chest with my palm. "I don't even have my own name. You lied to me. My entire life is a lie!" My throat closed, and I felt the tears threaten, hating myself for them.

"Hush," he soothed as the first one trickled down. "It will be all right."

"No it won't!" I exclaimed, pushing against him to get away, but he pulled me closer. The familiar smell of horse and ink drew from me memories of books, and riding lessons, and long evenings of idle diversion and talk. My angry resolve faltered as I admitted it was all gone. Everything.

I held my breath, my head pounding. My throat ached for release, and a cry broke free. My parents were dead. My life was gone. He was the only one left to me. I clutched at his coat, burying my head against his chest. Sobs shook me as the last of my will dissolved.

"Shhhh," he said, bringing my head against him as he used to when I fell from a horse. His hand brushing my hair was soothing and familiar. "It's all right. It's going to be all right."

"But I don't know who I am," I wept, unable to stop. "Why didn't you tell me? Why?"

Twenty-two

❖

Kavenlow set a cup of tea within my grip. I took it without looking. My hands were stiff with cold, but the warmth of the cup did nothing to shift the chill that had taken me. Feeling numb and drained, I sat upon the log beside the fire. The princess was at the edge of the camp, glaring at me from behind the wagon as she brushed her hair to get the dirt out of it. Goat Boy, or Thadd rather, was standing beside her looking laughably out of place. Her face was red where I had slapped it, and she had a bump on her forehead where I had pummeled her into the ground.

My breath eased from me. She had snapped my temper as if it had been a dry twig, and I had acted like the gutter trull she claimed I was. But she had said they hadn't loved me.

Duncan was talking with Kavenlow in a hushed, intent voice. It took a decisive sound and went silent. There was a rustle of fabric, and Kavenlow sat beside me. "You cut your hair," he said by way of greeting, distress heavy in his voice.

My heart seemed to clench, and I wondered if he would beat me. I certainly deserved it. "Kavenlow, I'm sorry," I whispered.

He stopped my words with a raised hand. "I'm not the one you need to apologize to."

I glanced at the princess. She sneered at me, showing no

control of her emotions at all. "She is the one who should apologize," I said. "She said I was filthy. A grasping beggar."

He stretched his legs out to the fire, pulling his long cloak away so the flames could warm him better. "You are filthy."

My throat closed. Her insults weren't why I had slapped her, but I couldn't make myself tell him that my parents were dead. It should be raining. It couldn't get any worse. "She said they didn't love me," I breathed.

"Of course they loved you." He tried to meet my eyes. "You were their daughter."

"Kavenlow . . ." I took a breath to tell him they were dead, then hesitated. He had put them in past tense. Eyes warming with unshed tears, I looked to see his face gentled in shared sorrow. "You know?" I warbled.

He nodded, his gaze deep into the fire. "Duncan told me. I'm sorry. I had guessed as much by the assassin I found yesterday. They were good people, deserving of far better. Tell me what happened? Of Garrett's reasons, if nothing else."

I could do that. "Garrett is acting on his own," I said, wondering at my even tone. I must be dead inside. "He killed my mother to force my father to tell them where *she* was." I glanced at the princess. She couldn't hear me, but her face had gone blank at my obvious misery. "Father died . . . to avenge her death and give me the chance to escape." I took a slow breath, remembering the guard's knife shaking against my throat. "Garrett wants to make his claim to the throne legal by marriage so his father can't take the ships and harbors through an act of war started by his son."

"Garrett gets a kingdom by his own hand," Kavenlow breathed. "Clever . . ."

"My parents are dead!" I exclaimed. "There is nothing clever about it!"

There was a gasp, and the princess's face went white. "Dead?" she quavered. Her beautiful face twisted with panic as she stood. She clutched at Thadd's arm, her eyes on Kavenlow. "You said I wouldn't be queen for years and years," she cried. "You promised!"

Kavenlow slumped. "Tess . . ." he murmured. "You have the timing of a hurricane." Straightening, he turned her. "I apologize, Princess Contessa," he said formally. "I was unaware Prince Garrett had planned treachery."

My heart sank deeper. "How could you let them give me her name?" I whispered. *Wasn't anything mine? Was she going to take everything, even down to my name?*

"You promised!" the princess wailed as Thadd fussed over her. "I want to go home! I don't want to live in a city. I never wanted to be a princess. I'm not going to marry a prince. I don't care how handsome he is!" she blubbered, her straight hair falling to hide her face.

I sighed, finding myself agreeing with her. Kavenlow rubbed his temples with his fingertips. Glancing between me and the panicking princess, he stood. "Tess, come with me to get your horses. You're not on foot, are you?"

Numb, I shook my head and set my cup aside. Thadd and Duncan were hunched over the princess, trying to soothe her as she sat by the wagon in tear-strewn hysterics. Kavenlow's neck was stiff, and he refused to look at her as he took my elbow and hustled me down the dark path.

I settled into his pace, pulled into matching him stride for stride. It was comforting, his hurried gait, which he had often strode about the garden with. The realization he chose to walk with me in the dark rather than console the princess was more of a comfort than it should be.

"I'm sorry, Tess," he said as soon as we were out of earshot.

"Don't call me that. It's *her* name," I said, scraping up enough feeling to put some weight behind it. "I don't even have my own name."

He harrumphed. "Stop feeling sorry for yourself. You have your own name. I gave it to you. The king and queen christened her after you, adding to it to get Contessa."

It was a small thing, but I fastened on it greedily. Kavenlow had named me? I had been named first? Then my shoulders slumped. What did it matter, really?

"If I could do it over, I would have told you before I left," he said.

"Tell me what?" I said bitterly. "That I'm a whore's get or that you're a player?"

Kavenlow gripped my arm and pulled us to a stop. "H-how . . ." he stammered, his white face a blur in the chill darkness under the trees. "Who told you that?"

His surprise gave me strength. So it was true. Jeck hadn't lied. "You're a player," I said, trying to pull away only to find his grip tighten. "That's all I am to you, a piece in a game."

"Who?" Kavenlow demanded, but his anger wasn't directed at me. "Who told you?"

"Jeck," I said. "The captain—"

"—of King Edmund's guard," he interrupted. "What else did he say?" he demanded.

His fervor shocked me, and I took a step back, still in his grip. "That you control Costenopolie," I said, suddenly afraid. "That he controls Misdev. That there are more of you, and the rule of the kings and queens are a sham that even they don't know—"

"The fool!" Kavenlow exclaimed, wire-tight as he dropped my arm.

My eyes widened. I had never seen Kavenlow this angry. Except the time I hid in the palace well and couldn't get myself out. I had shouted myself hoarse before Heather found me. "It wasn't Jeck's fault," I said, only wanting him to calm. "He thought I was a player, seeing as I downed him with darts and escaped right under his nose. He didn't tell me anything once he knew I wasn't one, but I pieced it together from what he didn't say as much as what he did. And with the note I found hanging in the 'safe' tree—"

A flash of pride crossed him, banishing his anger. "You found it. I knew you would."

"How could I not?" I said bitterly. "You trained me like a dog to find it. Bent my life for escape and murder. You made me fit for nothing but frivolous games and dealing out death, and I'm not even good at it. *Why didn't you tell me?*" I exclaimed, desperate for answers.

His head bowed, he started slowly up the path. "I couldn't," he said as I followed him. "There was a chance the real heir wouldn't live to see her coronation, and you'd be put on the throne. I couldn't risk that happening with you knowing who you are."

"Why?" I asked, angry as I paced beside him.

Pain crossed his brow. "If you reached the throne knowing you were destined to be a player, I would have broken one of the strongest-held rules of the game. A player can't sit on the throne.

It would give them too strong an advantage. The rest would have banded together and swamped us until there was nothing left of Costenopolie but a tattered flag hidden under a straw mattress." He frowned. "Just building your resistance to the venom was a risk, but one I was willing to chance. The danger was minimal until Captain Jeck fouled it."

My arms swung in quick, short motions as I paced beside him. "My entire life has been a game for you," I said caustically. "All of it."

Kavenlow avoided a low branch and my eyes both. "Aye," he said, "a game, Tess, but a very real, complex, deadly game, and I'd like to make you a willing participant."

"Then you admit you used me! I'm nothing but a pawn to you!"

He drew me to a stop, his eyes pained. "You're not a pawn. I made you a thief. The most powerful piece in the game. The only one not of noble birth that can take the king."

"A thief! Don't you mean an assassin?" My breath caught, and I turned away, refusing to cry again. I was frustrated, angry, and very confused.

"Tess . . ." Taking my hands, he led me off the path to a fallen tree. I sat stiffly, listening to the frogs, unwilling to look at him, as I was sure whatever he might say would be a lie. Jeck was right. How could I ever trust Kavenlow again?

Still standing, he ran a hand down his beard in thought. "When the first assassin gained the princess's chambers, the queen asked me to find a child," he said.

"Me," I said, though it sounded much like a sob. My head hurt, and I held my breath.

"You were one of three that I found that day and took behind palace walls," he said, not sounding at all repentant for it.

"Who were they, my real parents?" I managed.

The darkness hid his eyes. "I don't know. I found you with a woman who took you mewling from your dead mother's arms two days previous. I had no intention of finding my successor, but you were strong, Tess. Clinging to your short life as tight as a soldier. I lost myself to you the moment I held you."

"How much silver?" I said bitterly, determined to know my worth.

"I don't remember."

"Yes, you do."

He hesitated. "Enough for a loaf of bread," he said, and I made a helpless moan. "I don't know my parentage either," he said, trying to catch my gaze. "No player does. I came from the docks. My mother was a tavern wench and my father probably a sailor."

I sniffed, miserable. I didn't want to hear any more. None of it.

Kavenlow took my chin and turned me to him. The lines of his face were softened by shadow. "The king and queen bought you, Tess, but I stole you from them." He made a short, unhappy laugh. "Perhaps it is more accurate to say you stole me. I was completely unprepared."

My eyes rose to his, and I saw the love in him.

"You were so clever and bright," he said with a faint smile. "You were the daughter I could never have. And when you survived the assassin's darts that killed the others?" His smile turned full with a soft memory. "That was when I convinced the queen the only way to insure her daughter's survival would be to send her away. I had found my apprentice, and I would have her raised with all the skills and grace of a princess."

"Apprentice?" I whispered, my hope almost painful.

"The king and queen are legally your parents, but I raised you, Tess," he said, pride crinkling the corners of his eyes. "You're more my child than theirs."

The tightness in my chest loosened, and I took a breath. In my soul, I knew he was right. Our long hours spent in diversion, his attentive interest in my studies—these were not faked, put on to lull me into thinking he cared. I was not his plaything. I was not the princess's decoy to be cast aside. I was Kavenlow's apprentice.

He nodded, seeing the beginnings of forgiveness in my eyes. Shoulders bowed in relief, he moved us back to the path. My thoughts were spinning too fast to say anything, and we went to fetch the horses in an awkward silence until he cleared his throat. "Did Captain Jeck tell you anything about his plans?" he asked, his voice mixing with the singing frogs.

"No," I said, amused at the intentness in his voice. Imagine, Kavenlow looking for information from me. "Garrett has only enough men to hold the palace and outer garrisons, and they aren't very good. He expects more in about . . . ten days. Jeck did say he thought Garrett could manage it and that he wouldn't mind tending our ships as well as Misdev's farms."

Kavenlow frowned. "Then he thinks King Edmund will claim Costenopolie when the dust settles. A player can only manipulate one kingdom. If Jeck wants to use Costenopolie in play, King Edmund will have to take it first." He was silent, his movements going jerky as they did when he was worried.

"Just how many rules are there?" I questioned, not liking the idea.

His teeth gleamed from the dark. "Very few, of which I'll acquaint you in due time. Some are self-imposed and can be broken, such as knowing who another player is in reality, like Captain Jeck. Others can't and will result in being pulled down should you flaunt them."

"Like putting yourself on the throne," I said, and when he nodded, the fear slipped back into me, twice as strong. "Yes, but if I'm not on the throne, how will we keep the royals from swamping us? You saw her," I accused, walking almost sideways as I pleaded. "She is a pathetic, soft know-nothing."

His eyebrows rose. "Don't be harsh. Her life has been upended as much as yours. She may be having hysterics, but she wasn't the one pounding her sister's head into the ground."

"She's not my sister," I said, flushing. "She doesn't even want to be the princess."

"She is Costenopolie's heir, and she will be put on the throne." His jaw was set.

"But she can't control a kingdom!" I protested. "She can't even control her mouth! When it's made common knowledge that Prince Garrett murdered my parents and the princess was raised in a nunnery, the assassination attempts will redouble. That's assuming our neighbors don't declare outright war on us. Garrett should be sent back to his father in a box. You can convince King Edmund that his death was justified. That's why I came looking for you! You have to smooth the political waves after I kill him."

"Political waves!" Kavenlow said, aghast. The horses were just ahead, and he pulled me to a stop. "Tess. We can't kill Prince

Garrett and not expect retaliation under any circumstances. It doesn't matter how much blood money we give them."

My lips pursed. Kavenlow didn't understand. Garrett was going to die. He couldn't be allowed to think his actions would go unpunished. "The easiest way to end this is to kill Garrett," I said sullenly.

Kavenlow shook his head. "No. I won't start a war over one person's pride."

I stiffened. "Pride! He murdered them! If that's not justification, what is?"

"It's not necessary, and I won't let you."

"Kavenlow!"

"No. Costenopolie is mine, not yours. There can't be two players for one kingdom. Technically, you're still a piece. I'm the player. And you won't kill Prince Garrett. I forbid it!"

Embarrassment covered my surprise at him giving me a direct order. I was no longer the princess, even in play. I was his apprentice. I didn't mind as much as I would have expected—seeing as I had spent the last few days being nothing. "But they're dead," I protested, and we shifted back into motion. I could say the words, now that I'd found Kavenlow.

His face was sad as he glanced from the shadows of the waiting horses and back to me. "Tess, Costenopolie's player before me wasn't a pleasant man. He used people badly, and it was because of him Costenopolie and Misdev warred upon each other."

"What does that have to do with letting Garrett live above justice?" I asked.

"Listen and I'll tell you," he said, and I grimaced. "I was far into my apprenticeship when I decided I wouldn't use aggression to increase my sovereign's standing. I wanted to try commerce. My master and I argued, and he tried to kill me when it became obvious I wouldn't continue his plan of conquest by sea. I barely escaped him, exchanging his life for mine."

I stifled a tremor, imagining the terror of finding someone I trusted trying to kill me.

"Once my peers found out I had killed my master, it took all my cunning to convince them I wasn't going to manipulate Costenopolie's king to directly threaten their individual games. They thought I was staging a continent-wide takeover, not believing I had killed my master to prevent him from doing the same.

Someone, I haven't figured out who, yet, started the Red Moon Prophesy to try to end Costenopolie's royal family line and set me back."

"Then it's fake?" I asked in disbelief, my feet scuffing to a halt. "It's all been a lie?"

His apologetic look was obvious, even though it was fully dark. "Most prophesies are continent-wide statements of a player's future intent."

As I stood there, trying to take that in, Kavenlow took my shoulder and moved me to the horses. They were watching us, Jeck's horse tossing his head in impatience. "I wasn't unhappy when Misdev's player died of consumption," Kavenlow said. "I only know Captain Jeck by reputation, seeing traces of his will in the upcoming marriage plans."

I was silent as we loosely cinched riding pads and draped packs on the horses. There were too many thoughts swirling through me, most circling back to the Red Moon Prophesy. The burning-hell thing had been a fake? What had all my misery been for?

"Where did you get these horses?" Kavenlow asked as he looked at the underside of Pitch's hoof. Blinking, he set it down and patted her hindquarters.

I turned from knotting a pack onto Jeck's horse, glad the moonless night hid my face. "The gray is Duncan's. The other two—" I warmed. "Why?" I asked. If he knew where I had gotten them, he would make me give them back and the *princess* would have them.

Kavenlow looked at me over the back of Jeck's horse. "These are my horses."

My face went empty in dismay. Kavenlow had bought them? For her? "You bought her horses?" I said, hearing the smallness of my voice. "As a betrothal gift?"

"No!" Kavenlow came around the back of the horse and gripped my shoulder. I looked up, hating the warmth of unshed tears in my eyes. "They're yours, goose," he said softly. "I bought them for you. What would a princess do with two black horses she can't even ride?"

"B-but the stableman," I stammered. "He said they were a gift for the princess."

"I couldn't tell him they were for the princess's changeling, could I?" he said gruffly. "How on earth did you end up with them?"

"Thank you, Kavenlow!" I said, giving him a hug. *They were my horses.* It seemed like such a foolish thing to cry over, but I had so little left.

"I take it you like them?" he asked, awkwardly patting my back. He gripped my shoulders and set me back upright. I wiped my eyes with the inside of my sleeve, and he turned away, clearly uncomfortable. "How did you get them?" he asked again. "I told that man to keep them until I sent for them. They were going to soften the blow of, er—"

"Of me not being the princess," I said, imagining the news would have spoiled my delight with them quite thoroughly, even if his intentions had been good. "I sort of stole the mare, and Jeck stole the gelding, though in actuality I paid for mine—well, I paid for a horse, but the girl ran away with it, so you see I had to take one of the others—"

Kavenlow waved me to silence, and I winced. I thought he would be angry, but his look was of concern. "Captain Jeck stole one?" he asked. "He's not at the palace? He's is out here?"

I nodded, suddenly worried. "Garrett sent him to find me. He caught up with me two days out from the capital. That's when he let it slip about players. He was going to take me back, but I escaped with his horse." Embarrassed at my double thievery, I dropped my gaze. "I left his pack in Saltwood for him, except for his knives. I kept those. He's either behind us or ahead, depending on whether he cut across the bay like I did."

Kavenlow went still, as if looking for strength. "You escaped him, stole everything he had, then left most of it for him to find a day down the road?"

"Yes." My voice sounded defensive, even to me. "I didn't need anything he had."

Kavenlow silently untied Pitch and Tuck and led them to the path, leaving me to wonder if I had done something wrong. "Let's get back to the others," he said, his thoughts clearly on something else. "As you say, he might be before us, or behind. Either way, we will want to meet him together."

I followed with Jeck's horse, my thoughts uneasy at his continued silence. We were nearly back to the camp when I scraped up enough courage to break into the noisy frogs. "Kavenlow?" I questioned, his dark shadow beside me seeming suddenly foreign. "Did I do something wrong?"

He was silent for so long I was sure I had, but then he shook his head. "I don't think so. Have you . . . told anyone?" he asked, his tone carrying a forced casualness. "About players? Duncan, perhaps?"

"No." I took a long step to match his pace. "But he accidentally darted himself and now thinks I'm an assassin. I told him I was the princess's decoy, but he doesn't believe me."

His motion hesitated for an instant so brief I might have imagined it. "Ah, how did you explain the venom?" he asked guardedly.

I met his eyes, black in the dusk. "I told him you made me immune to it so I could defend myself from assassins. It only enforced his belief that I was one."

"And he probably thinks I'm the same," Kavenlow said around a sigh. "No," he said, raising a hand as I took a breath to apologize. "It's my fault. It's not against the rules for someone to know about the venom, but it's risky. They might jump to the proper conclusion." His head drooped. "I'll try to reinforce the idea that I've been training you to be the princess's armed chaperone. It'll be all right."

"I'm sorry," I said, really meaning it.

Kavenlow smiled thinly. "He hasn't had much opportunity to tell anyone else. And it's only been a few days. It shouldn't be too hard to cloud his thoughts."

"But he nearly died!" I exclaimed.

"Really? I'll make it food poisoning so it's a small shift of his memory."

I frowned, not liking that I had cooked dinner that night and would be blamed for it. But a thought stopped me cold. "What do you mean by *shift of his memory*? Duncan's memory?"

We rounded a turn and found camp. Duncan stood up from beside the fire as the sound of the horses reached him. The princess was still crying, but at least she was being quiet about it. "Kavenlow, what did you mean by shift of his memory?" I asked again.

Kavenlow waved a distant greeting to Duncan. "Did Jeck tell you about the venom?" he asked, his eyes bright.

I made a small face. "He implied it came from an animal of some kind."

He nodded. "It does. But he didn't say anything else?" I shook my head, and he leaned close and whispered, "It's rather special, Tess. I said I will shift Duncan's memory, and that's exactly what I can do."

Twenty-three

❖

I pulled my cloak tighter against the cold. My bedroll was some distance from the fire, and the dampness of the ground had soaked into me. The princess was sleeping sweetly right before the coals, her sundry blankets—which she had haughtily told me she had purchased in Brenton—were strewn in a careless disarray. Kavenlow sat upon the log across the fire from her drinking his tea, keeping watch over us as we tried to sleep through the freezing spring night.

Everyone had agreed a watch was necessary. Duncan and I were slated to stand together later, Thadd and Kavenlow again just before dawn. The princess had protested she could stand guard as well, and I found a perverse satisfaction in that Kavenlow told her to sleep. Only Kavenlow and I were resistant to Jeck's darts; one of us would remain awake all night.

I pulled my blanket to my chin, accidentally exposing my feet. I still had on my boots—just the thought of which made my lips curl—but it was either that or suffer all the more from the cold. My evening had been a frustrating mix of awkward hesitations and Kavenlow's put-offs. All my requests that he explain his last words before we rejoined the camp had been brushed away with an infuriating, "Later." Depressed, I sat up to tug my blanket down over my feet.

"Can't sleep, Tess?" Kavenlow said softly, and I met his eyes over the fire. "Come sit."

Freezing, I rose and, draped in my blankets and cloak, shuffled to where he made room for me on the log. "Is it later now?" I asked dryly.

Kavenlow's salt-and-pepper beard shifted as he smiled. Pulling a sheaf of wormwood from behind him, he threw it on the fire. A musty smell came up, tickling my nose and memory. My eyes shifted closed, then jerked open. "You didn't burn it," I said, snapping full awake.

"Beg your pardon?"

"The gypsy. You didn't beat her, you didn't kill her horse, and you didn't burn her van."

"No." He poured a second cup. "Have some tea. It will help keep you awake."

I almost slopped the dark brew in excitement as he handed it to me. He wasn't trying to lull me to sleep; he was making sure no one else woke up! "The gypsy is a player, isn't she?" I asked, not caring to get my jar of honey for fear Kavenlow would make me share it with the princess in the morning.

"She used to be." Kavenlow watched the princess's slow breathing. "She willingly handed her sphere of influence to her successor almost a decade ago. Now she wanders, acting as an arbitrator and judge over the rest of us. I don't like her. Players don't ever stop playing. They just use more powerful pieces."

I pushed my frozen toes up almost into the coals. "You took me to see her. Why?"

He sipped his tea, his fingers still showing the ink from my last history lesson, black shadows the firelight flickered against. "I took you as my apprentice long ago, but I never cared to present you to her before. It was nothing. Don't waste time trying to find significance in it."

"She tested me," I said, remembering it now. A shaft of anger colored my words. "She said I was lacking."

The wrinkles across his brow deepened, and he looked pained. "By her definition, you are lacking: you'd rather work to find a compromise than face a conflict directly, and though you can defend yourself, you can't bring yourself to kill, even when you think it's deserved."

Miserable, I lowered my cup to rest on my knees. *How had he known I hadn't been able to kill Garrett?* "I'm no good at this, am I? That's what she said. That you should start over."

Much to my astonishment, he put an arm across my shoulders and gave me a sideways hug. "Tess, you lack those abilities because that's what I wanted my successor to be. I didn't want a soldier. I wanted an intelligent, sophisticated, beautiful woman who would search for an answer rather than go in with arrows flying and swords flashing. Someone who could enslave with charm instead of chains."

I smiled weakly, and his arm fell away. "The game is changing," he said. "The old methods aren't going to work much longer. When opposing forces fight, there're no choices. When one side refuses to fight, they have all the options. Your skills give you possibilities your competition will only wonder at. That bitter old woman doesn't see that. She never will."

I failed to see it either, not reassured at all by Kavenlow's proud smile. Despite what he said, I knew I had no skills. But then I wondered. Kavenlow had said he could shift Duncan's memory. The gypsy had said the same about me, and Kavenlow had told her it wouldn't work.

Curious, I pulled my toes from the fire before my boots caught. "The gypsy," I said, not sure I was remembering everything properly. "She asked me if I could ride a horse? And—if I had dreams? No. If my dreams came true."

Kavenlow started. "You remember all that? Tie me to a stake at low tide, I warned her you would." Smiling past his beard, he threw a second sheaf of wormwood on the fire and fanned the smoke away. From behind us came a stomp from the horses.

"It's the venom," he finally said. "It's a player's first weapon, yes, and I imagine players began strictly as assassins. But it was found long ago that if one increased their natural immunity by repeated exposure to the venom as a way to protect against a rival's dart, they were able to take on the abilities of the animal it came from."

I stared at him, not understanding. "Abilities?" I prompted. "Like what? What animal?"

He leaned closer, his eyes catching a glint of the fire. "A punta," he said, deadly serious.

My mouth dropped open. "A punta?" I finally said. "They're all dead."

He straightened. "No, they're not, and the next time I need to replenish my venom, you're going to help me. It's about time you start earning the poison I've been giving you."

"They're just stories," I protested. "Big magical cats that . . ." My words trailed off, and my breath caught. *Magic?*

Kavenlow grinned through his beard. "I've waited so long to tell you. Every player has cheated death, surviving a killing dose of venom to balance on the edge of oblivion, returning with the magic puntas possess. You were three months old, struck by an assassin's dart. I think it ironic that a rival player found my successor for me. I'd thank him, if I knew who it was."

He had to be jesting. "A punta?" I looked at him quizzically. "I can't do anything a punta can do. Neither can you." I hesitated. "Can you?"

"I'll show you," he said. It was just what I was going to demand, and it took me aback. "See Pitch over there?" he asked, pointing with his chin. "Try to get her to come to you."

Pitch had wandered from the other horses, trying to get at the hay in the wagon's bed. My eyebrows rose, giving him a pained look. "You mean, here, horsy, horsy, horsy . . ."

He gave me a severe look, but his eyes were glittering in a repressed amusement. "Don't be impertinent. Put the thought into her head that you have a handful of grain in your pocket."

"Like calling wandering sheep . . ." I said, and he inclined his head as if I had said something wise. He was in a grand mood despite the cold pinching his cheeks red.

I took a deep breath and slowly let it out. I stared at Pitch, thinking thoughts of grain overflowing my pocket. My heart pounded when Pitch swung her head and looked at me. She didn't move, though. I flushed, and a whisper of vertigo swept me. My knees started to tremble from the cold, and I felt nauseous.

Kavenlow silently eyed me rubbing my knees. Reaching up, he plucked a dart from my topknot. Before I knew his intent, he stabbed it through my blanket and cloak and into my thigh.

"Ouch!" I cried, shaking the spilled tea from my hand. "Why did you do that?"

"Try again," he said as he set the dart on the log between us.

My leg throbbed—from the needle, not the venom—and I rubbed it. Irate, I nevertheless imagined a juicy apple. My dizziness eased, and I stared at Pitch, feeling like an idiot. "Nothing is happening, except my leg hurts," I said sourly. In fact, Pitch seemed utterly sleepy, her tail going still and her head drooping as the wormwood smoke swirled about her hooves.

Something shoved me from behind. Cup dropping, I spun on my seat to find Jeck's horse. Frightened, I raised my hands to touch him as he dropped his head and snuffed at me with his prickle-velvet nose. "Kavenlow?" I quavered, frightened.

He chuckled, pushing the horse's head out from between us. "That wasn't quite what I had envisioned, but you did it."

"I did it?" I said, not really believing. Jeck's horse stomped impatiently, waiting for the nonexistent apple. I rubbed his ears in apology, thinking I'd have to get him an apple as soon as we got back to the capital. Much to my amazement, he blew heavily and turned away. *Chu,* I thought. I not only enticed him to me but told him to go away, as well! "Is that why I've been so dizzy?" I said, pulse hammering. "Saint's bells, I almost passed out the night I got over the palace wall when I told Banner to stay. Was that magic? I thought he was just obedient."

Eyes catching the amber light, Kavenlow picked up my cup. "He is, but a portion of that is because he's used to taking venom-induced direction from me. Animals become sensitive to it and respond better. And your abilities gain strength as you build up your resistance to the poison. You can also find a temporary boost by taking some, such as I did here, though that's a good way to end up unconscious on the floor and vulnerable. You might get dizzy when you try to do more than your skills have risen to, or your muscles might spasm—just as if you had an overdose of venom. Your knees were shaking before I darted you, yes?"

"Oh!" Excited, I turned to snatch a glance at Jeck's horse. "Is that why my hands hum?"

His eyes widened. "Your hands . . ." He grabbed one, alternating his attention between my eyes and my palm, looking small in his. "Oh, Tess," he said softly, frightening me. "I had no idea. They really . . . How long have they been doing that?"

"Since Jeck tried to down me with about six darts. Why? Is it . . . wrong?"

His smile went proud. "No. It's right. Maybe it's because you were first darted so young, but it's rare to come back from the brink of death with that particular ability." He swallowed, his brow furrowing. "You say they hum? Does it hurt?"

"Not . . . really." He said nothing, pressing his lips so his mustache stuck out. He looked almost worried. "Kavenlow?" I questioned. "Is that all right?"

He flashed me a quick smile that did nothing to ease my mind. "Yes, yes of course. I'm trying to figure out how I'm going to teach you something I can't do, is all."

I didn't like seeing him feel inadequate, so I smiled—though it probably looked rather ill. "What else can I do? Vanish in a whirl of wind like a punta in one of the stories?" I jested.

He chuckled. "No. As a novice you can nudge thoughts into quiet animals with nothing on their minds—like that black gelding there. I have a greater span." He sifted his attention to the trees, and I listened to the night, waiting for something to happen. My breath caught as a black shadow ghosted over the camp and an owl dropped to my abandoned bedroll.

"Oh, isn't he grand?" Kavenlow whispered, a delighted smile making him look younger as the horned owl shifted on his thick talons, hissing at us. "When there is a good match between player and animal, it's almost as if you can speak to them." Kavenlow reached out to the owl, and with three heavy beats, it took to the air and vanished. We both sighed.

"People are too complex to manipulate like that," he added, his voice still soft with wonder from the owl. "But you can cloud a person's memory and sight. And from that stems your wonderful ability to play hide-and-seek."

"I knew it!" I exclaimed, then covered my mouth, looking over the silent bumps of the people sleeping around us. "You were teaching me how to get out of the palace, weren't you?"

He nodded. "Magic or not, puntas aren't any faster than any other animal; they just seem to appear and disappear from nowhere because they can cause a person to not see them until they want to. The venom gives you the same ability. Right now the best you can hope for is to keep from being seen if you're trying to hide. I can walk the streets unnoticed if I work at it."

I slumped on my log. "So all those times I won at hide-and-seek it was the venom?"

Kavenlow took a finger and raised my chin. "Tess, it was never a game to me. It was practice. Don't think of it any other way."

It didn't make me feel any better. It seemed like cheating to me. "Have you—ever clouded my memory?" I asked, afraid of the answer.

"If you remember the gypsy, then you remember what I said."

"You said you couldn't. But she did," I blurted.

"She's stronger than me. Apparently, though, even her skills aren't infallible. Some of that is your will, but most is because of the venom slowly building up in you gives you some protection against venom-induced trickery. That's why she used wormwood to reinforce her attempt to cloud your memory. That you recalled so much tells me you've been sandbagging, my girl." He patted my knee. "I had no idea I had built up your resistance so high. It's past time I start teaching you how to consciously draw upon your talents and find out what you're especially good at." He hesitated. "Besides healing."

It was almost a mutter, and I heard the concern he was trying to hide. "The gypsy," I said, reluctantly. "She asked if my dreams ever came true."

Kavenlow's eyes went worried in the flickering light. "Be careful, Tess. Even a novice can have prophetic dreams, especially when under an overdose of venom needed to build their resistance. But dreams can be manipulated by your own feelings, giving you false truths. The gypsy has so much venom in her she can see the future even when awake. I don't trust dreams, and neither should you."

An uneasy feeling took me. "She forecasted for me. Before you came in," I said softly.

Kavenlow stiffened. "What did she say? Did she say anything about war?"

I shook my head. Everything she had said had happened. I had just been interpreting it wrong. "She said I would be traveling with a man who had dark hair." I looked over the camp to Duncan. "The rest was fluff and patter," I said, not knowing if it was or not.

"Good," he breathed. "It's no guarantee we won't find ourselves there, though."

I nodded, my attention on the coals. My eyes rose to the sleeping princess. The gypsy hadn't said anything about her. What else had she left out?

"She really isn't a bad sort, is she," I said, gesturing to the sleeping woman with my eyes. "Just rough. How is she ever going to learn the polish she needs to survive?"

There was a creak of leather as Kavenlow turned to me, seemingly surprised. "I was hoping you'd be able to help her with that. She didn't know who she was until last year, and I'm afraid she is very—ah—provincial in her reactions and expectations. I think the nuns realized who she was and let her have her way in everything."

I cringed, thinking of the political retaliation if her mouth ran amok with a visiting dignitary as it had with me. "She has no idea how many disappointments a princess must swallow with a smile, does she?"

He shook his head. "She thinks being a princess means doing what she wants."

"It's the exact opposite." I hesitated as my brow smoothed. I wasn't the princess anymore. Perhaps this was a good thing. "What is going to happen to me?" I asked, warming when my thoughts drifted to Duncan and that kiss. "Now that I'm not the princess?"

Chuckling, he downed the last of his tea. "I wanted her to take you as her attendant guard, though that might be difficult since you thrashed her."

I was quite sure I didn't fancy the idea of being a member of *her court*. It was insulting, and I would probably be stuck behind walls sewing all day. God help me, I would go insane if I had to make one more useless doily. Kavenlow refilled my cup before doing the same with his. He set it in my hands, and my fingers tingled at the new warmth. "Kavenlow," I mused aloud. "Just how strong can you become? Do you just keep dosing yourself to increase your strength?"

His head shook an emphatic no. "There are two reasons not to. One, you have to kill the punta to get the venom, and they are hard to find and devilishly harder to subdue. And two, players that push themselves beyond a reasonable level tend to die quickly. Though you were born with a natural immunity to the venom that most people lack, there are limits. Oddly enough, it takes more venom to kill an apprentice than a master, but an apprentice will pass out sooner, saving his life. A master won't, giving the impression that they're safe, which leads to the dangerous assumption that they can tolerate more than they can."

"Meaning . . ." I prompted, not understanding.

"The more venom you're able to tolerate before passing out— or the stronger you are, rather—the more careful you need to be about reaching your death threshold. An apprentice may fall unconscious after three darts, but it might take ten more to kill them. That's ten darts that no player will waste upon someone who is down. A master can stay active after as many as eight darts, but one more after he falls unconscious might be enough to kill him or her."

"With more power comes more risk and a lower threshold," I murmured. My head rose in a sudden alarm, and I searched Kavenlow's face. Was he in danger?

"Look at you!" he exclaimed, teeth glinting in the firelight. "I'm nowhere near overdosing on venom. I'm very careful to keep a safe balance of strength and safety. And speaking of that, here. You need these more than I do." He twisted to reach his pack behind him. Silently he placed several palm-sized darts in my hand. They were made of metal instead of bone, looking like wickedly long needles as they glinted with a gray sheen of oil.

"I had them made almost ten years ago," he said, his gaze on the fire. "These three are all I have left. Be careful. They hold a great deal of venom and will kill a large man very quickly. They're used to bring down a player," he finished, and my eyes widened in understanding.

"These are for Jeck," I said. Lips pursed, I extended the darts to him on the flat of my palm. "I don't want to kill him. I just want him to leave me alone."

The wrinkles about his eyes deepened as he curled my fingers over the darts. "I'm sure there isn't enough there to kill him—unless he makes a practice of dosing himself up to temporarily increase his skills. Use them to knock him unconscious."

Reassured, I obediently tucked the lethal darts in my topknot.

"Tess," he said slowly, a new hesitancy to his voice, and I put my hands between my knees to try to warm them. "There's a price for this. And I wanted to tell you before it's too late. The venom—it takes away your ability to have children."

Eyes wide, I stared at him, reading the truth behind it in his sorrowful gaze. "No children? Ever?" I asked, hearing the smallness of my voice.

He looked pained. "It's not too late. I think you have a few years yet before the venom asserts itself so deeply inside you that it would be difficult to carry a child full-term. It's one of the reasons why players can't rule. There would be no heirs."

Turning away, I clenched my blanket to me, colder than the night warranted. I rubbed at my thigh where the dart had penetrated. Magic—real magic—or children. "None?" I asked.

"No." His gaze was weary as he stared at the coals. "But it's not a bad option to take a child from the street as your own. They're full of surprises—like you." He cupped my chin and made me look at him. "Tess? I forced this beginning upon you, but it's not too late."

My gaze fell from him. I felt an unexpected tingle of tears. No children of my own? Probably not even a husband, as I was sure anyone close to me would be a target for player-sent assassins, just as I had been.

"Most apprentices are given no choice," he said, "but you're a woman, Tess. The decision should be yours. There aren't many women players, but what you can bring to the playing field— compassion, empathy, and the ability to compromise—are desperately needed. You can't be a player without the strength of the venom. If this is something you don't want, I'll find another. But, please. You could hold the future of thousands of children in your choices. You would be a magnificent player."

I said nothing, putting an elbow on my knees and dropping my forehead onto my stiff fingertips. *No children? Ever?* Why was he asking me to choose? I had always known what to do when I had been a princess; there never *were* any choices.

Kavenlow shifted his yellow-lined cloak about his knees, clearly uncomfortable at my distress. "Get some sleep," he said gruffly. "As I said, you have time to decide. Years. I'll wake you when it's time for you to stand watch."

He took my cup from my fingers, replacing it with the bone dart he had stuck me with. Not looking at him, I slowly tucked the spent dart away and rose. Edging around the sleeping princess, I numbly went to my bedroll. An owl feather rested on it. I picked it up, gripping it as if it were a talisman. I lay down with my back to Kavenlow and stared unseeing into the night.

A child of my body, or a lifetime manipulating vast forces and hidden agendas. A husband to grow old with, or a kingdom. I recalled my delighted shock when Jeck's horse bumped me, looking for an apple that existed only in my thoughts. The owl's feather was softer than silk as I brushed it against my chin. My children taken from me before I had begun to think of them?

But there really was no choice to make. I knew my answer. If I wanted a husband, I'd find a man able to defend himself from assassins. If I wanted a child, I'd take one who needed me as Kavenlow had. To do otherwise would say he had been wrong, that he loved me less because I wasn't of his body. And to say that would be a lie.

"Kavenlow?" I whispered, knowing he could hear me, "I'll stay your apprentice."

Twenty-four

❖

It was the sound of someone rustling in their pack that woke me, and I knew we had made it through the night without Jeck finding us. The birds were clamoring again, and faint through the twittering uproar were Duncan and Thadd's whispers. My eyes opened, and I stared at my odd view of matted leaves and grass, dim with the scarcely risen sun. I was finally warm, so I didn't move, hoping everyone would leave me alone and perhaps make me breakfast.

Sighing, I closed my eyes. It felt good to be hungry. It felt good to be warm. It felt good to have a purpose. I was a player, and not the princess—not anyone—could take that from me. *This,* I thought, *would be what I shape myself on, now that I'm not the princess.*

My eye opened at a crackle of leaf litter. It was a mouse, silver and small, hardly big enough to be out of its mother's nest. Creeping forward, it pushed its way over and under the sticks and leaves looking for food. A smile curled the corners of my mouth.

Steadying myself, I tried to put an image of a pile of seeds into the sweet-looking rodent's thoughts. The mouse hunted on, seeming unmoved by my attempt. My vision swam, and vertigo took me as I tried to use my skills past what my venom levels would allow. Ignoring it, I tried again, squinting as I tried to imagine a link between my thoughts and the mouse.

From my stomach came a pang of want so strong and fast, I almost bent double. I clutched at my middle, breath catching when I realized it wasn't my hunger but the mouse's! Thrilled, I shuddered as the eerie feeling of emotions-not-mine trickled through me. It was fascinating, and not at all comfortable.

Slowly I found the emotions that were mine and focused on them. The pained hurt in my belly grew less, making it easier to sense the mouse. He was hungry and cold, confused by the absence of his littermates. More confident, I again tried to put a thought into his head, overpowering his hunger with the idea that over here, inches from me, was a pile of seed.

The background noise of the birds disappeared, the scent of earth grew strong. My pulse pounded as the mouse rose up onto two feet and tested the air with his shifting whiskers. He took a humping step, then paused. I forced my excitement down, imagining the pile topped with a strawberry. My mouth watered with the memory of its tart taste.

The tiny mouse was clearly not old enough to have seen a strawberry before, but it hastened forward, scrambling carelessly toward the nonexistent seed. It halted when it got to the point I had imagined the food, sitting up and twitching its nose. His confusion poured through me, making the space I had put between our emotions turn blurry. Pity went through me, and I was sorry I had tricked it.

"A mouse!" shrieked the princess, sending the rodent into a crouch. "Thadd! Get it!"

I sat up. Thadd was standing with his long shirt untucked, wide-eyed and alarmed as he tried to spot the small shadow the princess was pointing at. I sent a thought of safety from birds and nasty princesses under my cupped hand. The mouse darted under the dome my palm made, shocking and delighting me. I could feel him, warm and shivering.

"It's in your blankets!" she wailed, twisting her skirt up to show her tiny ankles. God save me, they looked so thin they might break. How could she walk about on them without falling down?

"I know," I said, sending soothing thoughts as I cupped my hands to pick him up from the damp ground. "Would you stop shrieking? You're scaring him."

"But it's a mouse!" she cried, then hesitated when she realized everyone was staring at her. Duncan chuckled. Going red, she spun and stalked into the scrub, balancing perfectly on her tiny, thin, perfect little ankles wrapped in homespun wool.

"Princess," Kavenlow called. "Take someone with you. We stay in pairs from now on."

"But I need to—" she stammered, her eyes going from Thadd to me. "Come on, Thadd," she said, flushing even more. "You'll just have to look the other way."

I made an ugly face at her back and cuddled the mouse close. What did I care if little princess perfect ankles would rather have Thadd accompany her for her morning ritual than me, another woman? The mouse nibbled on the flat of my hand, and I cracked my fingers.

Kavenlow shook the leaves from the princess's thick bedroll and folded it. He looked fully rested and tidy, though he had slept less than anyone. "A mouse?" he questioned dryly.

"I want to keep him," I said, and he sighed as if gathering strength. "It's not as if he's going to eat much," I protested.

"Let it go, Tess," he said. Showing me his back, he went to stack the princess's blankets in the wagon, but my bad humor eased as he muttered, "I suppose I ought to be glad the first animal she charmed wasn't a moose."

I opened my hands, and a whiskered nose poked out, then withdrew. Duncan's shadow fell over me, and I squinted up. "Let me see?" he asked.

I smiled, and taking that as an invitation, he dropped down beside me on my blankets. The memory of our kiss shocked through me, and I searched his face with a feeling of guilt. I flicked my attention to Kavenlow, seeing his brow furrowed. Duncan took my cupped hands in his, and jolted, I opened my palms. The mouse sat unmoving for a moment, then washed his whiskers.

"He's a sweet little thing, isn't he?" Duncan said, and I nodded, tense as I noticed how warm his hands were under my fingers. My breath caught, and Duncan's eyes met mine, drawn by the sound. I froze at the intentness of his gaze. *When, then?* his eyes seemed to ask.

"Don't ask me that," I whispered, closing my hands to hide the mouse.

Eyebrows high, he said nothing. His hands cupping mine were very still, and I couldn't find the will to pull away. My thoughts spun back to his touch, rubbing my shoulder in time with the waves' motion, and then that kiss pulling from me a want I'd never let myself feel before. My heartbeat quickened. How could I have been so foolish? Why did I hesitate now? Why didn't I pull my hands away? *Chu pits, I'm not the princess anymore. I can do what I want.*

Kavenlow cleared his throat, and my hands slipped from Duncan's. Unable to bring my eyes to meet his, I opened my hand and watched the mouse dart into the leaves. Duncan rose, and I refused to look as he stretched. How had my life gotten so muddled? No one told me being able to make your own choices would be so . . . so confusing.

I slowly stood. My back was sore, and my eye where the princess had hit me was tender to the touch. "Pairs, Kavenlow?" I asked. I had my own morning ritual to attend to, and I could do it alone, thank you very much.

"Even you, Tess," he said. I looked at Duncan, then sent my eyes pleading to Kavenlow. His jaw grew tense, and his brow furrowed. "Be quick," he added, and my shoulders eased.

I touched my topknot, then my whip on my belt, then finally one of the knives that I had taken from Jeck at the small of my back. Reassured, I gathered my skirts and crossed the path to find some privacy.

My thoughts were a slurry of emotion, giving my steps only half my attention. Duncan was far away and distant from the safe, tidy, fumbling nobles with cold lips and light hands that I had spent time with. He smelled. He was prickly. He shouted at me and told me I was wrong.

And he pulled from me feelings I thought I had control over with no more than a look. I didn't know what I was feeling. It wasn't love. I wasn't that foolish. Duncan was a cheat—not that it mattered. Did it?

Almost under my feet, a duck exploded into the air. I gasped and reached for my topknot, then burst into laughter as all thoughts of Duncan were driven away. "Oh, what luck!" I said as I spotted the nest at my feet. Crouching, I felt the warmth of the eggs, wondering how long she had been sitting. It couldn't have been long; it was early spring. Thinking I'd found a capital-fine breakfast, I piled the eggs into the fold I made of my top skirt, leaving five for the hen.

"Eggs!" I cried triumphantly as I crossed the trail again and entered the camp. "I found a nest of eggs!"

The princess had returned with Thadd and had already claimed my usual spot before the fire. "Let me see?" she asked, somehow making it both mocking and demanding. My good mood faltered, and my mood soured. I felt like a beggar beside her. She had been sleeping on dirt same as me. How could she look so clean after sleeping on dirt?

Sore eye pounding from my tension, I knelt beside her, intentionally putting myself too close to make her move away. She didn't, but a new color rose in her cheeks as she watched me carefully unload the eggs on my far side. With a hurried quickness, she reached across me for one. "They're fine," she said as she gave it a tap with her fingernail. "The hen had just started to sit."

I frowned in disbelief. "How can you tell?"

She ran a quick gaze over me, making me feel even more dirty. "By the way the weight shifts inside the shell," she said, her scorn thinly veiled. "I grew up on Bird Island. I'd find nests all the time. There's nothing worse than cracking an egg to find a nestling. Learning what a good egg feels like is easy."

I watched, unbelieving, as she took the eggs one by one and set them on her other side. "What are you doing?" I asked, affronted.

"I'll cook them with some of that watercress I saw by the river. Thadd? Would you fetch me some?"

"Yes, Contessa." The short bear of a man got to his feet and gestured for Duncan.

"I can cook them," I said indignantly.

Duncan jerked to a stop, halfway out of camp with Thadd. "No, you don't!" he cried. "Princess? Don't let her touch those eggs. You cook them. I've had Tess's cooking. Made me sicker than a dog eating five-day-old carrion."

Appalled, I looked at Kavenlow, and he shrugged. Apparently he had been successful in clouding Duncan's memory of the true reason he had fallen into convulsions. But why did my cooking have to be the scapegoat? I turned back to find the princess humming, her motions vindictive as she rubbed a flat rock clean with the water I had been planning on using for my tea.

"Kavenlow?" I complained as I rose and strode to him. "I want to cook the eggs. I found them."

He folded up my blanket and set it beside the princess's in the wagon. "Do you know how to cook eggs?"

"It can't be that hard," I said. "I eat eggs."

He flicked his gaze to the sickening picture of domestic bliss the princess was making beside the fire. "Let her do it," he said. "She seems to know what she is doing."

I turned with a huff and went to brush the horses. I'd let the princess cook the fool eggs. I was willing to wager she'd burn them—or do whatever you do to eggs to ruin them. What would she know about cooking? She had been raised in a nunnery.

Twenty-five

❖

The heavy smell of eggs rose thick as I sat under the wagon and sulked. *The princess can cook,* I thought bitterly as I choked down the last fluffy, mouthwatering piece of egg. Not only could she cook, but she could cook well, having fashioned a pan from a flat rock and plates from the tightly woven reeds she had sent Thadd to gather while the cattail roots Duncan had dug softened. "The next thing you know," I grumbled, "she'll make us forks from sticks and leaves."

Kavenlow made a choking cough, and I glanced up. He was tending the horses, and I hadn't known he was close enough to hear. My attention went back to princess perfect ankles. Duncan was sitting at her elbow, his brown eyes bright and eager as he entertained her with a bit of card play. While she had been cooking, he and Thadd had gone to the river, both coming back refreshed and suspiciously clean-shaven.

The princess was duly appreciative of Duncan's sleight of hand. Thadd, too, seemed impressed. He had quietly tended to the princess all morning, treating her as if she might break. The two men had hardly left her side since she cracked the first egg, and it sickened me. Kavenlow didn't seem to notice them fawning over her, apparently not caring that Jeck might find us at any moment. The sun was well up, and no one showed the slightest concern. It was if we were out for an afternoon of hawking, not running for our lives.

The princess laughed, and I grimaced at the pleasant sound. I could take no more. Standing, I stalked out of camp, ripping my skirt as I jerked it free from a briar.

"Tess?" Duncan called. "Where are you going?"

"To the river," I said, never slowing.

"Pairs!" Kavenlow called. "We stay in pairs!"

Ignoring him, I stormed across the path and into the woods. I bullied my way through the brush, coming to an abrupt halt at the water's edge with my arms about myself.

It was quiet, since the morning birds had finally ceased their noise. The sound of the current against the rocks was soothing. Morning air, cold and biting, cooled me. My shoulders eased. I wished I was on the *Sandpiper*. I would've enjoyed seeing Lovrege's hillsides wreathed in fog.

Finding peace in being alone, I took off my boots and gathered my skirts. I waded into the river, shocked at how cold it was before remembering it was running with snowmelt. The rocks were slippery, shifting under my toes without warning. I looked toward the unseen camp and wondered if I might chance a bath—seeing as we weren't going anywhere soon. An urgent need to be clean had filled me. There wasn't a smudge on the princess. I didn't understand it. She was the one who had been pounded into the dirt, and I was the one who was filthy.

Brow furrowed, I decided I'd take a bath even if they were packed and ready to go when I went back for my clean dress. Feeling a stir of self-worth, I waded to the bank.

There was a rustle in the brush and my head snapped up. My skirts fell as I reached for my dart tube. I had it to my lips when the bushes parted to show the top of the princess's fair head. Her attention was on the ground. *One dart,* I thought bitterly. It wouldn't kill her, but rolling about on the ground in convulsions would get her dirty. I could say it was an accident.

She looked up. Fear flickered in her blue eyes. They looked like Mother's.

Shame filled me, and I tucked the tube away. "Sorry. I didn't know it was you," I lied. I pulled my dripping skirts from the water, then let them fall in disgust. Now I was dirty *and* wet. I looked to the sky and the clouds that ought to be threatening. Rain would top this off nicely.

"It was my fault," she said as she stepped to the bank. "I should have let you know I was coming. The chancellor says no one should be alone."

My first caustic retort died at her hesitant admission of blame, and I said nothing as she picked her way to the water, mincing in her little black boots. Her heart-shaped face and transparent skin made me feel like a crass bumpkin. I wanted to tell her I never dressed like this, that I normally wore silk and a circlet, that I usually had clean hands and face, that I could do sums and read—that I wasn't the gutter trash that she thought I was.

My skirt dragged in the current as I lurched to dry ground. Ignoring her, I picked up my boots to return to camp barefoot. I was as clean as I was going to get. *Why wasn't it raining?*

"Would you—like to use my soap?" she said, and I froze.

I hadn't any soap. I had used the last of mine on the *Sandpiper.* I met her eyes. "Yes," I said warily, wondering why she was being nice. "Yes, I would. Thank you."

Unfolding a cloth, she revealed a thick cut of brown soap, its edges smoothed by use. She set it on the bank and stepped away. I eyed her suspiciously as I took it. Knotting my wet skirts up, I waded back out to wash my face. I set the soap on a rock as I scrubbed, jerking in hurt when I touched my eye. The soap smelled of mint, and I wondered if the nuns had given it to her or if little princess pretty ankles had made it herself.

Though unable to watch her with lather threatening my eyes, I was painfully aware of her as she took off her boots and stockings to step-hop out over the river across a path of dry rocks. Sitting on the largest, she dipped her feet in. The silence grew.

The water dripped from me, and the current pulled the ripples away. My face tightened from the cold as I snuck a glance at her. I had escaped guards and a rival player, crossed the bay with money *I* earned, and made the mistake of kissing a cheat and learning what a real kiss could do to a person. I could pretend to be nice to her.

I lurched closer, holding the soap like an offering. Her narrow chin looked tense as I set it beside her and backed away. "Thank you," I said, trying to keep it unsullen. She gave me a nervous smile and started to wash her feet. They were tiny, and turning blue with cold.

I shifted to find better footing. My toes were going numb. "I'm sorry for—uh—slapping you," I said, thinking I should exert myself lest I end up making doilies the rest of my life.

"It wasn't all your fault." She didn't look up, and I wasn't sure how sincere she was. "I shouldn't have called you a beggar, and I'm—" Her expression went anxious, looking almost frightened. "I'm sorry for saying they didn't love you," she blurted. "It was cruel and untrue. But I . . ." She looked into the woods, her blue eyes going wide. My lips parted in surprise as she pulled her knees to her chin and wrapped her arms about her legs. Her eyes went dark and watery, and I realized the young woman was on the verge of tears.

"I was jealous," she whispered, "and afraid. I wanted to hurt you. You had everything. You knew everything. You came into camp looking so strong; I got frightened. I don't know how to be a princess. And when I saw you standing there, I realized I can't do it!"

I stood, shocked by her admission. She wiped her eyes, the pale skin around them flashing into an ugly red. Sniffing, she managed a weak-sounding bark of laughter. "I was going to marry Thadd, you know. And have children with him, and live in the house his grandfather built for his grandmother, and die there happy. And then last year, a man riding a beautiful horse and wearing the finest clothes I'd ever seen comes to my room and tells me I am a princess? That I have to leave my mountains and go to a city? That a prophesy said I might cause of a war if I didn't! Do you know what that's like? To have the fate of the world take your life away from you?"

She wiped her eyes on her sleeve in a very unprincess-like manner, and my heart went out to her. My throat closed in sympathy. I knew. I knew all too well.

"And then you walked into camp," she said, her voice bitter with self-incrimination as she looked at the moisture on her sleeve. "I'd never seen anyone like you." She met my eyes, and I saw the misery in them. "How am I supposed to be like you? You're so tall and graceful. Even when you had dirt on your face and had torn your dress, you looked like a princess, proud and calm. And you spoke so well. I could tell you were angry, that I was hurting you, but you stayed civil as long as you could. I hated that you knew everything that I didn't. I had to prove I was better than you, and when I tried, I only proved how low and common I was." Her gaze went across the river and into the woods. "I can't do this."

"Yes, you can," I said, shocked to hear the words come out of me.

She sniffed, looking up. "Chancellor Kavenlow said you could help me." Fear flickered over her as she met my eyes. "Will you? Please? I can't ask anyone else. I don't know what to do. I don't know how to act. I don't know anything, and I'm scared someone will find out!"

My eyes went to the water swirling about my shins, shamed for how I had treated her. Bringing my head up, I gave her a weak, comrade-in-arms smile. Her pinched face melted into relief as I nodded and sloshed to the rock beside her. Silently I sat down and arranged myself, finding the stone only marginally more bearable on my bare feet than the cold water. I looked at my toes, then shifted my dress to cover them, thinking they looked ugly.

"Do you want our name?" she stammered in a rush. "We can't both be Contessa. And since no one but you has the right to call me by my first name, you may as well have it . . ."

I looked past her fear and worry to the simple woman beneath. The tips of her fair hair had slipped into the water to make her look guileless. She utterly lacked the polish and sophistication of the people I grew up with, her emotions—good and bad—shining like stars in winter. If I didn't help her, she would be eaten alive. "You can be Contessa," I said. "Unless I'm in trouble, everyone calls me Tess or—um—Princess." My gaze dropped.

She shifted uncomfortably. "What were they like? Our parents?" she asked hesitantly.

Our parents? I mused. I really didn't want to talk about it, but I knew I'd be asking the same thing. "Father was nice," I said, my eyes on the opposite shore. "He was losing his hair, but it used to be black. Blacker than Kavenlow's. He was loud in the morning, deliberately shouting for everything, waking me and anyone else sleeping beyond the sunrise." I was surprised to find a faint smile coming over me. "Mother was very stern," I continued. "But if she said no, I could usually get what I wanted from Father . . . eventually."

It felt odd, referring to them like that: Mother, not my mother;

Father, not the king. "She taught me how to sew," I said, warming to the task. "She would never miss our appointments where we would talk as we sewed or collected flower seeds for next year."

"Appointments?" The princess looked shocked. Perhaps even appalled.

I shifted my shoulders. "She was very busy. Both of them were. But I never felt as if I couldn't interrupt them if it was important."

Contessa grimaced as she realized the tips of her hair were wet. Taking them in hand, she tried to pinch the water out. "Appointments," she said, her eyes on her pale fingers.

"Have you known Thadd long?" I asked, thinking it was my turn.

The anxious expression she wore eased, and it was with a flash of worry that I recognized the same look my father had for my mother. She loved him. It would make things difficult, but by no accounts insurmountable with discretion, something I imagined they both utterly lacked. "I grew up with him," she said softly.

My eyes widened. "In the convent?"

The princess flashed me a smile to make her a vision of my mother. *No, our mother.* "His father sculpted the saints and angels," she said. "When his father was on the grounds we played together."

"I grew up with a girl named Heather." I pulled a leaf from an overhanging branch and shredded it. The pieces fell to the current and scattered. "You'll like her. She can make daisy chains and steal an entire pie from the kitchen without getting caught." I sent a silent prayer that she be all right. "And the guards are nice," I said, sending a second prayer for them.

Her attention jerked up from the leaf I had thrown in. "Guards?"

I smiled to ease her thoughts. She was wary enough of the palace. The least I could do would be to try to make it less forbidding. "Yes. They have to do everything you say, you know. Once, I had one stand below my window and catch me when I jumped out."

"No!" she cried, clearly shocked.

I bobbed my head, grinning. "Three stories down. I broke his arm. It was the autumn star shower, and I wanted to get past the smoke from the city to see it. My—our parents wouldn't allow it, even when I sulked for two days. Kavenlow was furious. He wouldn't take me out to buy anything for two weeks. It was terrible."

The princess silently took that in. "Is the city large?" she blurted. "I've seen Brenton."

I tore another leaf and tossed it into the current, realizing how sheltered a life she had led. "It's ever so much larger than Brenton. And it doesn't smell like fish." I wrinkled my nose.

"How much bigger?" she asked, looking frightened but anxious to not show it.

"Lots," I said, starting to enjoy myself. "You could get lost in the streets there are so many, but you'll never be alone, so don't worry. Some of the buildings have three stories. There are several liveries, bunches of inns, and two markets, one by the docks and the other up in the high streets. We have twelve docks in the harbor. One is reserved for the palace. I've been down there with Kavenlow. And the markets are open until sundown every day but Lastday. On festivals, they stay open all night."

She was silent, her eyes on the bubbles trailing from her rock. "I went to a festival once," she finally said. "I'd dearly love to know how to dance."

I turned in surprise. "You don't know how?"

"The nuns were very reserved."

And probably boring, I thought. "Oh. Well, Kavenlow can show you. He taught me."

Much to my surprise, she shook her head. "No," she said, and when I didn't say anything, she added, "What if he laughed at me?"

I felt a pang of sympathy. "I can show you," I offered, not knowing why I did.

Spots of color appeared on her cheeks. She was the image of our mother, and grief stabbed into me. I couldn't help but feel my dark skin and narrow hips were wrong compared to her. I pushed the ugly thought away.

"You'll teach me?" she asked, clearly relieved.

I nodded, refusing to feel sorry for myself that she looked like Mother and I didn't. "I can teach you a little, and when you think you know enough, Kavenlow can teach you the rest. He's better than I am."

She smiled, and I found I didn't mind that she looked like an angel. "All right," she said, eyes eager. "And I can teach you a crochet pattern Thadd's grandmother taught me. It's a secret."

I froze, cringing inside. "Oh . . . how wonderful," I lied.

A twig snapped behind us, and I twisted, my dart tube to my lips. My heart pounded hard enough to make my head hurt. But it was Thadd, and my held breath exploded from me in a relieved rush. "Will you people stop creeping up on me!" I shouted, trying to burn away the flush of angst. "One of you is going to end up convulsing on the ground!"

Thadd's eyes narrowed suspiciously. His broad shoulders hunched. "Contessa?" he said in a slow, country drawl. "You should come back to the fire."

Head bobbing, she dried her feet with her white underskirt.

"You don't have to do what he says, you know," I said, surprised to find I didn't like him lording over her.

She smiled lopsidedly to make her look simple. "I know." My eyes widened as she leaned across the narrow band of water between us and gave me a hug. "Thank you," she whispered. "I don't think it's going to be as bad as I had feared."

My mouth hung open as she stood and hopped from rock to rock to the shore. Thadd extended a hand to help her onto the bank. He gave me a jealous look as she leaned comfortably against him to slip on her stockings and boots. I didn't know what to think. I had been ready to hate her from this lifetime and into the next, and here I was starting to like her.

"Are you coming, Tess?" she asked as she straightened. Thadd stood beside her, his squat bulk just besting her petite height. "We can wait if you aren't done with your wash."

Her question caught me off guard. I was safe enough, but if I didn't go back, Kavenlow would come looking for me with a lecture. "No. I'm coming." I stood and gathered my wet skirt up, lurching across the rocks to shore. Putting my back against a tree, I brushed the dirt off my feet and struggled to put my boots on without stockings.

Thadd took Contessa's elbow and started to lead her away before I had finished. "Why are you being nice to her?" he said in a too-loud whisper. "She tried to pull out your hair."

I flushed, my chagrin not abating even when the princess said, "I deserved it after what I said. And I like her. Leave her alone."

His shoulders tensed, and he held a branch out of her way.

"You can't trust her," he said, his low voice carrying better than he knew. "She could have killed you."

"Thadd," she said, the new sharpness of her voice bringing my head up. "She's my sister. She's all I have left of my kin. And I don't want to talk about it!"

I blinked, taken aback at how quickly she had gone from pliant friend to angry fishwife in three heartbeats. Giving him an irate look, Contessa tugged from his grasp and stormed away. A cry of frustration slipped from her when she caught her skirt on a stick. Thadd scowled at me as if their argument was my fault, then hastened to catch up. "Contessa . . ." he pleaded. "Please. I didn't mean it like that."

I smoothed my brow and started after them, wondering if turning Contessa into a proper princess might be harder than I thought. Their short exchange had the sound of an old pattern.

"Thadd?" I heard the princess say loudly from up ahead. It sounded as if she had gotten over her temper already. "Thadd!" she shrieked.

My head came up. There was a blur of a brown horse running through the woods. A black-cloaked rider was on it. *Jeck!* "Contessa!" I shouted, panicking. "Get down!"

She didn't. Thadd was weaving on his feet. He had been darted.

Jeck thundered down upon them. Jolted into motion, I ran.

Jeck picked the princess up and flung her shrieking over his horse's shoulders. Thadd fell as his support was ripped away. I stumbled onto the path, then flung myself back into the scrub as Jeck wheeled the animal into a two-legged turn right before me. He gave me a wild grin as his horse screamed. Tuck answered.

I scrambled for my dart pipe. Heart pounding, I aimed for the horse. Either I missed or one dart wasn't enough to affect the heavy animal. His gray cloak furling, Jeck put his heels to his horse and bolted down the path in a wild cadence of hooves.

I stared across the open space at Kavenlow. For a heartbeat, our eyes locked.

Kavenlow lunged for Pitch. "Watch them, Tess!" he exclaimed as he swung onto the horse and shouted Pitch into a wild run. The thumping rhythm of hoofbeats faded to nothing.

My astonished gaze fell on Duncan. He was sitting dumbfounded by the fire, not having had time to even rise to his feet.

"Angel's Spit!" he swore, throwing a pot of water across the camp to slam clanking into the wagon and send Tuck shying. "I've lost another princess. The same way as the first!"

Thadd was clenched into a ball, still conscious under Jeck's weaker darts. I crawled to him and felt his pulse. It was strong and steady. His eyes were closed, and his face was lined in agony. "Oh God. No, no, no," he moaned. "I lost her. I'm going to die. She'll be all alone."

"You aren't going to die," I said harshly, remembering his mistrustful words. "And we'll get her back." I turned to Duncan. "Help me get him in the wagon." I pulled at Thadd. "Get up!" I said, trying to drag him. "It will wear off. Get up, you lout! If you love her, get up!" *Where is the rain? It ought to be raining.*

Thadd lurched to his knees, doubled over in pain. Duncan took his other arm, and together we lifted the short but hard-muscled man into a staggering walk.

"Wagon!" I gasped, struggling to keep him from falling on me.

"Chu, Tess," Duncan muttered. "You might be nicer. Those darts hurt."

"I know," I said belligerently, surprised that Kavenlow's blurring of Duncan's thoughts hadn't taken. But my anger slipped into a grudging empathy as I helped Duncan move Thadd to the wagon. Jeck's darts held half the venom I used. Goat Boy probably wouldn't even pass out.

Thadd collapsed heavily into the wagon's bed beside the long box. "Harness the horse," I said tersely as Thadd groaned, his thick shoulders hunched and trembling.

Duncan jumped from the wagon. I listened with half my attention as he coddled the frightened draft animal into position. Jeck's old horse nickered in recognition, and I spun.

I loosed a dart, my hand covering my mouth when I hit Kavenlow. "Be careful with those," he said in annoyance, plucking the bone needle from his shoulder and frowning.

"Kavenlow, I'm sorry!" I cried, embarrassed.

Scowling, he nudged Pitch closer and handed me my dart back. He glanced at Thadd. "Is he going to be all right?"

I nodded, then scooted across the hay-strewn wagon and back to the ground. I wildly threw everything that wasn't packed in beside Thadd. *It's my fault. I should have been with her. I should have been closer.*

Kavenlow dismounted and tied Pitch to the back of the wagon. He levered himself up on the bench and slapped the reins. I joined him, gripping the bench as we rattled and bounced back onto the trail. Duncan mounted Tuck and paced in front of us down the path. The flighty gray arched his neck and pranced as if on parade.

"He must have been watching us for hours," Kavenlow said tersely. "Perhaps as early as last night. I thought we'd have more time."

My stomach clenched, and I felt ill. "It's my fault. I should have walked her back to camp," I whispered, and Kavenlow gave me a grunt and a sideways look.

"Your fault? No." I said nothing, and Kavenlow's frown deepened. "Leave it be, Tess," he said. "Jeck made a move. Now we counter it. We're going to the palace; he's going to the palace. It doesn't matter whose company she arrives in. Garrett won't harm her."

"He might marry her," I said, realizing I had worsened the tear in my top skirt. I glanced behind me at Thadd. His eyes were unfocused, but he seemed to be gripped more by remorse than pain.

"Not until he can prove to the people that she is the real princess," Kavenlow said. "He can't pass her off as you. The people know you, especially the merchants." He made a short, mirthless laugh. "This is the middle game, Tess, not the end. It's not over."

His voice held an eager, intent tone, and I watched him chew his lower lip as we jostled down the path at too fast a gait. A familiar light was in his eyes. It was the same I had seen when we stayed up late to finish a game of thieves and kings. Though worried, a tension that had been building in me since yesterday began to unravel into a steady anticipation.

Jeck had taken Contessa, but that didn't mean we would let him keep her.

Twenty-six

❖

Kavenlow pulled the draft horse to a stop where the trail branched. I leaned past him to see the hoofprints pressed deep in the soft earth. From atop Tuck, Duncan came to a halt. I looked from the tracks to Kavenlow. "He went straight," I said. "He's still carrying her."

A frown creased Kavenlow's forehead, and he ran a hand across his trim, graying beard. "If I remember, there's a river ahead. I'd be willing to wager the crossing is too difficult for a wagon the way Captain Jeck took. That's why the two paths. See?" He pointed straight ahead. "It tapers down to little more than a horse path that way. I think we should go left, but I don't want to diverge from Captain Jeck unless we have to."

I glanced behind me to Thadd sitting miserably in the wagon's bed beside the long box. He had quickly recovered, his squat bulk throwing off Jeck's weaker venom faster than I would have imagined possible. But he had yet to banish his depression. I felt bad, as nothing was his fault. Duncan had repeatedly told him so, but Thadd might not believe it until Contessa said the same. Even then, I didn't think he would.

"Duncan," Kavenlow continued. "Go see if the water is too high for a wagon crossing."

"Let's leave the wagon," I complained. "We've enough horses to follow on horseback."

It was the third time today I had suggested it, and Kavenlow grimaced. "Duncan?" he prompted. The cheat grinned at my impatience from under his grimy hat. Pulling Tuck's head up, he gave his flanks a smart kick. The flighty horse bolted down the thin trail. I would have liked to follow him. The slow pace the wagon had reduced us to had me almost frantic.

We had been steadily falling behind Jeck. Kavenlow wouldn't leave the wagon and its heavy load. Thadd's statue couldn't be that good. He wasn't much older than I was.

The draft horse's ears pricked, and I wasn't surprised when Duncan and Tuck slid back around the corner faster than they had left. "He's at the river!" he said as he reined up. "Captain Jeck is on the other side sitting on his horse waiting for us. I think he wants to talk."

My heart jumped into my throat. Jeck was waiting.

Thadd lurched upright in a clatter of noise. "Contessa! Did you see her?" he exclaimed.

Duncan shook his head, and a severe determination came over Thadd's square face. Bare feet sliding in the bed of the wagon, he pushed a spot for himself between Kavenlow and me on the bench. Snatching the reins from Kavenlow, he clicked at the horse. The sedate animal flicked an ear and rocked into motion.

"This is what I was waiting for," Kavenlow said, peering at me from around Thadd as we rattled forward. "It's a game, Tess. One where the pieces don't always do what you want."

I grasped the bench as the pace grew fast. "He has Contessa. What else does he need?"

The river wasn't far ahead, and Thadd kept us to a fast clip. The edges of the wagon began scraping the encroaching branches with an alarming amount of noise. I wondered how we were going to get back to the main trail if we couldn't cross here. Thadd's pace was substantially faster than Kavenlow's, and I started to feel queasy as we rocked and lurched along.

I heard the river before seeing it. My first glimpse of it did nothing to instill any confidence. It stretched before us, a rumbling icy tumble of water running high with snowmelt. It would be foolish to cross here if there was an easier way upstream.

My gaze roved the far bank for Jeck. I pulled my cloak tighter about my shoulders as I found him at a small rise in the trail atop a brown horse. He must have gotten it at Saltwood. He sat tall, unmoving but for the wind shifting his cape. Like a mysterious figure from a story, he tipped his hat and waited.

Contessa wasn't with him. I was willing to wager she was tied to a tree out of shouting distance, her hair down and her boots and stockings off for whatever reason. I didn't think Jeck would hurt her, but if he had, I would see he got twice what she received.

Frowning, I wondered where my loyalty had come from, finding it odd she should have earned it so quickly with her offer to share a sliver of soap and her honest plea for help.

Kavenlow took the reins out of Thadd's hands and pulled the horse to a stop before the man could drive the wagon directly into the river. Immediately I swung to the ground and reached for Jeck's horse tied to the back of the wagon.

"You're not going," Duncan said as he wedged Tuck between the black horse and me.

"The devil I'm not!" Shoving Tuck out of my way, I glared up at Kavenlow still on the wagon's bench. "And don't give me any chu pit of an excuse like I have to stay behind and guard the wagon. Someone has to watch your back."

Kavenlow took his eyes from across the river. He looked grim and uncertain. "I'm going alone. Duncan? Off your horse."

"What?" the cheat exclaimed.

"I need a horse. Yours is the only one ready to ride."

He shook his head, slow and controlled. "I'm coming with you. Tess is right. You can't go alone."

My shoulders tensed. "I'm the one going. And neither of you can stop me!"

Kavenlow's face darkened, and he gathered his breath to protest. I raised my chin, and he frowned. "All right," he said. "But I want your promise you'll do everything I tell you."

"Don't I always?" I countered, wanting to keep my options open.

He hesitated, knowing I hadn't said yes.

"I should go, not her," Duncan said as he tried to still Tuck's nervous sidestepping. "What's to keep him from knocking you on the head and taking you again, Tess? Then he'd have both of you. It's a trap."

Kavenlow jumped to the soggy ground. "She escaped him

before," he said. "She could do it again if she had to. I'll take Tess."

My flush of pleased vindication shifted into excitement. Duncan slipped reluctantly off Tuck and held the horse's head as Kavenlow took his place. The horse shifted at the heavier weight. My brow furrowed as Kavenlow held a hand for me to ride before him.

"One horse?" I said. "I've got my own, thank you."

Kavenlow's eyes looked tired under his eyebrows streaked with gray. "You want to put the animal you stole from him back within his reach?"

Sighing, I accepted his hand and arranged myself before Kavenlow like the princess I used to be. Thadd was scanning the shore, his expression of hope waning.

"Be careful," Duncan called as we splashed into the shallows. "Tuck doesn't like water."

"Tuck doesn't like anything," I said softly. But either the weight of an extra person was enough to calm him, or the soothing thoughts I was attempting to wedge into his foolish head were getting through, and we started the crossing without difficulty. It wasn't as deep as it looked. The statue-heavy wagon should be all right.

I kept the stained hem of my dress out of the water and my eyes on Jeck. The powerfully built man looked nothing like the captain of King Edmund's guard anymore. The lack of a uniform and overdone hat left him all the more dangerous, dressed in his simple but well-made black shirt and trousers. Even his thick-soled boots were black. He sat atop his horse, unmoving, with a sure confidence, his cloak drifting about his stirrups.

The memory of the firelight flickering against his damp skin as I sponged the blood from his back made my stomach clench. My hands had tried to heal him. His had warmed in return. Flushing, I put the back of my hand to my cheek to cool it. Of all the things I should be thinking about, this was the last.

We neared the bank, and Tuck heaved out of the water, blowing hard to take in the scent of the other horse. Seeing Jeck so self-possessed, I had a stab of doubt. Regardless of what Kavenlow said, I knew Jeck held all the cards. Together we might subdue him with venom, but I knew that Kavenlow wouldn't violate the truce of a parley.

My eyes widened as I realized Jeck's saddle was the one I had sold in Saltwood. The packs behind it were his own, and I was glad the innkeeper had been honest enough to give them to him. We came to a halt before Jeck, and I felt Kavenlow shift in a sigh.

Jeck's eyes flicked briefly to Kavenlow, then fastened on me. "Good to see you again, Princess," he said, his resonant voice lacking even a hint of malice or sarcasm.

I flushed deeper, the memory of his smooth muscles slick with ointment under my fingertips coming unbidden to me. "Captain Jeck," I said, sure Kavenlow had noticed my red face. My eyes lingered on my bag still fastened to Jeck's belt.

Seeing where my attention was, Jeck unknotted it and extended it to me. "I believe this belongs to you," he said. "You forgot it in your rush to leave my company."

I carefully accepted it and looked inside to find everything there but my bone knife and venom. "Where's the rest?" I asked, very aware of one of Jeck's knives at the small of my back.

"Where are my knives? My horse?" he drawled, his gaze drifting across the river.

Kavenlow cleared his throat, and I grew nervous. "You'll get them back later," I said.

"As will you." Jeck turned to Kavenlow and inclined his head in a respectful greeting. His eyes never shifted from Kavenlow's. "She ought not be here," he said, clearly having turned to the matter at hand. "Technically, she's still a piece, not a player."

"She would still be a piece in truth if you hadn't opened your mouth," Kavenlow said, anger in his usually calm voice. "What am I supposed to do? Pretend she knows nothing? You forced my hand with my apprentice; you will tolerate a few irregularities."

Jeck's horse shifted, and he took up the slack in the reins. "You have my formal apology for having interfered with your student. My inexperience misled me into divulging her status. I apologize. It wasn't intentional."

My eyebrows rose. Jeck sounded not only sincere but also meek. That wasn't the captain of the guard I had known. I turned to Kavenlow, surprised at the deep look of anger on him.

"You have severely compromised my game," Kavenlow said. "One of my most valuable pieces—I'm sorry, Tess—has lost her versatility because of you. It has furthered your position tremendously. Unintentional or not, you broke a rule. Your comparatively new status of player is no excuse. If you can't play properly, you will be removed—Captain."

Jeck reddened. "I made an error," he said, his meekness gone, "but it was an honest one. I won't make any large concessions for it. The only compensation I'll give is to help insure the rightful heir gains the throne, thereby eliminating the possibility of you and your apprentice being persecuted for putting a player in a direct position to rule."

"As if that makes up for it," Kavenlow growled.

Jeck's jaw tightened behind his black beard. "It's all I'll give you. You bear some of the blame, teaching her to use the venom before giving her the wisdom of what it meant."

I felt Kavenlow relax. "I'll accept that. Yes. I will refrain from lodging a formal protest, providing the proper Costenopolie princess gains the throne. Agreed?"

Jeck nodded, the tightness in his eyes easing. I wasn't sure if I should be happy or not.

Kavenlow whispered in my ear, "Good. We will at least walk away with our lives."

"Our lives?" I questioned. "What about Costenopolie?"

His gaze flicked to Jeck and back to me. "Kingdoms rise and fall, Tess. Only the players endure, their teaching lineages stretching back farther than most royal bloodlines. We'll simply begin again if worse comes to worst. But I don't think it will."

Jeck cleared his throat to bring our attention back to him. "The reason I asked for this meeting was to try to eliminate unnecessary loss or injury for the next few days."

I sniffed, taking on a haughty expression. "And what is that supposed to mean?"

"Tess . . ." Kavenlow warned, but Jeck seemed amused.

"I'm saying that having Costenopolie's princess does me little good unless I have someone to verify to the populace that she is the legal heir, not Tess."

"Is that you speaking or Garrett?" I asked tartly, and Kavenlow nudged me to be quiet.

"I'm going to take both princesses back," Jeck continued. "It's the only way I can ensure the proper heir gets the throne. Rather than expend a lot of wasted effort, I propose you simply give Tess to me."

My breath hissed in. Frightened, I forced my hands to stay in my lap instead of reaching for my darts. I would make it one of the metal ones. See how much venom the wicked things held. Garrett would kill me. I knew it. "That is ridiculous," I said boldly to hide my shaking voice. "Expecting us to believe you're doing us a favor. Taking me by force is more than you can manage. And you know it."

"Care to wager your thief's life on it?" He moved his brown horse closer, circling us to turn the ground where Tuck had dripped into mud. My pulse pounded as I felt his eyes on me. I remembered my missing venom, wondering if it was on his darts now.

"I will harry you, Princess," he said, his low voice and the intensity of his brown eyes pulling a strike of fear through me. "Pick you off one by one. I'm giving your master the chance to save himself and you a lot of unnecessary pain."

My heart hammered. "I don't think you can do it."

"Enough," Kavenlow said tightly, backing Tuck away and out of his circle. "Stop arguing with the captain, Tess. He is simply looking forward. We're all going to the same place. I'd rather get there unwounded. I'm going to take him up on his offer."

I spun to face him. "But Garrett will kill me!" I cried, uncaring if Jeck saw my fear.

Kavenlow's gaze was decidedly apprehensive. "Which is why I'm going instead of you."

Jeck started. "You!" he exclaimed. "I won't take a player when a piece is available. I want her."

"Then I step down," Kavenlow said. "I give my position to Tess and become the chancellor in full. She's the player; I'm the piece." He put a hand atop my shoulder, fixing an aggressive look upon Jeck. "You won't have her, Captain. In any way."

"Kavenlow!" I cried. "Don't!"

"Hush." His teeth gritted and his eyes went fierce. "This is not what I had planned, but if Garrett gets you under his thumb, he will kill you."

"Which is exactly what he will do to you!"

He shook his head. "I'm not the one who made him into a fool. I'm a mild man who does the books. Jeck can't breathe a word otherwise. There is little honor among players, but on this, we hold tight." He turned to Jeck. "Promise me you'll tell her how to kill a punta if I don't see the end of this. She also needs to know the formal rules."

I could say nothing. My mind was empty in panic. *He is going to leave me? Kavenlow is going to leave me again?* The thought I should have just killed Garrett flitted through me, taunting. Jeck's horse shifted nervously. Jeck's expression was dark and irritated.

"You're putting your entire game in jeopardy," he said. "She's a novice. Your game is mature, and only you know it. She will break a hundred rules."

Kavenlow was unperturbed. "There aren't a hundred rules. There are only six." His eyes went to mine. "Trust your feelings, Tess, and you won't break any."

"Fine," Jeck said tightly, pulling his horse's reins to make the animal prance and arch its neck. "Bring your horse. I have only the two."

I stared blankly, not believing this was happening.

"Down you go." Kavenlow offered me a hand to descend with. Frightened, I shook my head. "No. He'll kill you!"

"Here." Kavenlow twisted an unadorned ring from his finger. "It's just a ring, but with Jeck as witness, it serves as proof that I give my game to you willingly."

"Kavenlow, no!" I cried, clenching my fist when he tried to force it into my hand. "I don't know what to do. Garrett will kill you!" *Don't leave me again!* my thoughts screamed.

"Garrett won't kill me," he said. "You, though, he will. This way we're all alive to see the end of the game." He kissed my forehead, and my fist loosened from surprise. The smooth shape of a ring fitted my palm, and he closed my fingers about it. "You can't do anything when you're dead. Keep to your heart. I know you'll bring us through with more than we went in with, my little thief." He leaned close and whispered, "I've venom in my saddle-bags. And if I don't see the end of this, stay away from Jeck."

"I won't get down," I said belligerently.

"I'm sorry," he said, and he pushed me off the horse.

I hit the muddy ground with a gasp. Both horses jumped. I scooted backward as Tuck shied. "Kavenlow!" I cried, sprawled on the ground. "Don't leave me!"

He never looked back. Jeck touched his hat and followed Kavenlow in a slow canter.

"Kavenlow!" I shouted, stumbling to my feet. "Kavenlow. Don't!" But he was gone. I looked over the river to Duncan standing helplessly on the bank.

What was I going to do now?

Twenty-seven

✦

I stood beside the wagon, a hand over my eyes as I squinted up. The tree Duncan was climbing shivered, and a green leaf drifted down. We had been following Jeck for two days with hardly a rest. Our frantic pace had put us outside the capital's walls in record time. We had been meeting an increasingly small stream of refugees. None had any real news, simply running from rumors. It was fortunate we had hay within the wagon, or the horses would be ailing. I hoped for Duncan's sake that Tuck was all right.

"Well?" I shouted up. I was nervous and ill-tempered, and I impatiently tugged the hem of my gray dress down. It was now too tight as well as too short. I had shrunk it in my laundry aboard the *Sandpiper*. My ankles showed, and it bothered me.

"They're stopping everyone at the gate," came Duncan's voice. I craned my neck to spot him. "They're looking for us, sure as rain is wet and the sea is salty."

Frustration and anger spilled over. Mostly frustration. "Curse you, Kavenlow!" I shouted, kicking at a wagon wheel. "Why didn't you tell me what to do?"

Thadd looked up from the front bench, his round face depressed.

Branches snapped as Duncan slid down the tree to land lightly on the path. "Chu, Tess," he said. "You didn't expect us to walk in the front gate, did you?"

Not wanting to hear his opinions, I kicked the wheel again with a cry of frustration. It hurt, and I decided to find something else to abuse. Duncan, maybe.

"How about that?" Duncan said to Thadd, his hands on his hips. "A princess with a temper. I never would have expected that."

A rare smile crossed Thadd's stubbled face, vanishing quickly. Duncan brushed the bark and needles from himself, chuckling. I wanted to pace but forced myself to be still. "All right," I said, thinking aloud. "We can't walk in like this. Jeck knows everything: our horses, the wagon, everything." I found myself moving and stopped. "Duncan, you go in first with the two black horses. When you get inside, take them to the dockside stables and leave them there. Meet Thadd and me at that inn we played cards at. We'll come in with the draft horse."

Duncan looked up from rubbing the dirt from a boot. "Take them back?" he said, his face empty. "You want *me* to take the horses *you* stole back?"

I nodded. "I'm not going to risk everything coming down around us because someone recognizes them."

"I'm not taking them back!" he exclaimed, surprising me with his sudden vehemence.

Hands on my hips, I strode to him. "They aren't mine yet," I said, almost in his face. "And I'm not a thief. Leave them in the yard if you like. Take Thadd with you if you're afraid."

Duncan's jaw clenched and he pointed at me. "I'm not afraid," he said in a low, forced voice. "And *I'm* not a thief, either."

I backed up a step. "Don't point your finger at me!"

"I'll point my burning finger at you whenever I damn well please!" Duncan shouted. He took a step forward, and I backed up, finding myself against a tree. My eyes were wide, and I didn't know what to do. I wasn't used to having someone shout back at me.

Angry and red-faced, Duncan jerked his shirt from his left shoulder. A thick, raised scar in the shape of a circle—God no, it was a crown—was branded into him. "If I'm caught with those horses, they'll hang me!" he said, screaming though his voice was just above a whisper. "If you want to risk a hanging by taking them back, fine. But don't ask me to do it—Princess."

My face went cold. I'd forgotten. "Duncan." My anger turned to shame. "I'm sorry. I forgot." *Damn my mouth,* I thought in harsh guilt. *Why can't I keep it shut?*

Duncan spun on a heel and went to rummage in his pack in the wagon. "Here," he said, tossing me a wad of clothing.

I shook it out, finding it was his spare shirt and a pair of trousers. My face flamed. "What is this for?" I said tightly as I threw it back. What he wanted was obvious.

Duncan grimaced. "I'm going to cut your hair, too. They're looking for a woman. You're going in as a man. You almost look like one."

Jaw dropping in outrage, I glanced down at my straight hips and nearly flat chest. "I am *not* going to wear your disgusting clothing," I said hotly. "And you aren't coming near me with a knife." If I cut my hair any shorter, I wouldn't be able to use it to hold my darts.

Duncan took a step forward. "Thadd, grab her arms."

My breath quickened as I retreated, hand atop the knife at my back. "Stay away. Both of you!" I demanded. The pounding of my heart was so loud, I was sure they could hear it.

Thadd snorted. "I'm not touching her," he said in his slow voice. "You're on your own."

Duncan stopped his advance. "Well, she can't go in like that," he said, gesturing.

Watching them warily, I relaxed. "The woods are rife with black string," I said, recalling having seen the thorny vine in the brighter patches of forest. "It will dye anything black. I'll go in with black hair . . ." My words trailed off as a thought took their place. "I could go in as a gypsy. We all could. Gypsies come into the capital to sell horses all the time, especially matched pairs."

"You don't look like a gypsy," Duncan protested. "And neither do I."

"Thadd almost does," I said. "Give me a hot fire and three hours, and I'll be a raven-haired beauty with a bad temper."

"You're halfway there with the bad temper," Duncan muttered, crossing his arms before him and taking a stance to look nearly unmovable. "And I'm not going to dye my hair to play gypsy. If you don't put on those trousers, I'm not coming in with you."

"I don't care if you come or not," I lied, feeling a stab of worry. "Thadd and I can do this on our own. You can stay here with the wagon where it's safe."

"Oh, I'm coming," he said tightly. "But I'll be behind you. You're going to get caught if all you do is dye your hair and fake an accent, pretty little thief. I want to see that."

My eyes narrowed, but before I could say anything, Thadd interrupted. "Um, I'm not leaving Contessa's statue," he said in his somber voice. "We're bringing the wagon with us."

I closed my eyes and rubbed at the beginnings of a headache. Neither man was capable of taking direction. I would be better off darting them and tying them to a tree like goats than trying to find a plan that satisfied all their inane, sundry requirements.

Ignoring Duncan's increasingly barbed comments, I spent the remainder of the afternoon dying my hair and weaving strips of my red underskirt into it and the mane of the draft horse. It emulated the younger gypsies I had seen perfectly. I tied my two black horses to the back of the wagon with ropes stained red to signify they were for sale. I'd probably be all right unless I ran into real gypsies.

Thadd was frantic about his statue, insisting he sit in the back with it instead of up front where he ought to be. I had found some prickle stick in my search for hair dye, and after rubbing it on his foot, he developed swollen, itchy welts. No one would be poking about in our wagon with his foot looking like that, and it was a good excuse for me to be driving.

Surly and bad-tempered, Duncan watched us prepare to leave, claiming he would visit our heads on the palace gate tonight. And it was well past noon by the time I drove the wagon out from under the woods. The sun pressing down felt heavy after the chill shade of the trees. My toes were cold. Gypsies wouldn't have boots, and I'd hidden mine under the hay with the statue. The closer we rattled to the sentries, the more nervous I became. I had my handful of darts, but the entire point was to get in with no one the wiser. The stone walls of my city loomed gray and cold. My pulse hammered. *This isn't going to work,* I thought. Jeck would come out of the guardhouse, pin my arms to my sides, and drag me away.

"Are you ready?" I asked Thadd as we neared the gates. He said nothing, and I turned to find the man gaping at the walls like a peasant. My shoulders slumped. I was on my own. I'd have to talk to the guard myself. If he had any brains at all, he would know my accent was false.

"Ho there," I murmured, pulling the horse to a stop as the guard came forward. He had dried food on his jacket, and I frowned. He wore my father's colors, but I didn't recognize him.

"First time to the capital?" he said, his gaze flicking behind me to Thadd.

Heart pounding, I turned in my seat. The sculptor was staring wide-eyed at the buildings, the people, everything. "For him," I said, wrangling my tongue around the *R*s. "He wants a surgeon to look at his foot afore Momia chops it off."

"It isn't catching, is it?" the guard said, backing up.

I shook my head, tucking my feet under my skirt as I realized they were a shade whiter than the rest of me. "Momia can't cure it. Which street has a surgeon?"

The guard smirked. "Five coppers," he said, and I stared at him for a heartbeat before remembering to keep my eyes down. "Trading tax," he added, grinning as a second guard came out of the guardhouse, blinking at the brighter light. "You want in, you pay the tax."

My stomach clenched. I had no money. "I burning-well told you I was here for a surgeon, not trading. The horses are for fetching city medicine."

Thadd threw five coins on the bench, and the guard took them, his grubby fingers grasping. "Go on," the thieving sentry said. "You're blocking the road. Stinking gypsies."

Nervous, I clicked at the horse and slapped the reins a shade too hard. Head bobbing, the animal ambled peacefully forward. *Trading tax?* I questioned as we passed the gates. Right into their pocket, I'd wager.

"Does Duncan have money?" I asked as soon as we were out of earshot, not knowing why I cared. Thadd grunted an unknowing answer. I longed to turn and watch the gate but didn't dare. Taking the first right I came to, I halted beside a smithy. I had made it past the gate despite Duncan's dire predictions. Now, would he?

The hot smell of the forge tickled my nose, and I wiggled my fingers at Thadd for my boots. His somber gaze roved over the narrow houses, the people, and the few open shops. There should have been masts showing above the roofs, but there were none. I felt sick, wanting to drive to the docks and see if Garrett had burned them to the waterline or if they had simply abandoned the harbor because of rumors.

"I didn't know you had money," I said as my second heel thumped into a boot. "I'll get it back to you when I can. There's no such thing as a trading tax." I reached for the water bag and handed it to him. "Better wash your foot. If you keep scratching, those welts will turn real."

He accepted the water, his wide back hunched as he sponged the irritating sap from him. I anxiously watched the top of the road for Duncan. The foot traffic was thin. Shops were open, though the stock looked scanty. The few people about were tense, getting what they needed and moving on. There was very little banter. The veneer of normalcy was thin.

My nerves had me ready to bolt when I spotted Duncan's jaunty profile at the top of the road. Relief slumped my shoulders. I whistled, and he turned on a heel to make his unhurried way to us. "Since when does the capital have a foot tax?" he asked when he was close enough.

"Why didn't you tell me you had money?" I answered.

Duncan froze. "Because you would have spent it on something stupid, like a bath."

"Baths aren't stupid," I snapped. "They keep your hair from falling out."

"Look," he said belligerently, tugging on the hair showing from under his begrimed hat. "No bath."

My hands trembled. "All right," I said through gritted teeth. "We're here. Let's get something to eat while I decide how to get into the palace."

Thadd silently dumped his water over the side of the wagon and shifted his work-hardened bulk to the front bench. He took the reins from me and got the horse moving. Duncan gripped the side of the wagon and, with a graceful motion, pulled himself over the edge. "Don't you have a plan already?" he said as he knelt in the wagon's bed behind Thadd and me.

"Not yet," I admitted. I felt my stringy hair, hating the greasy texture. I thought longingly of the bath I had bought but never gotten. "How much money do you have?"

Duncan grew wary. "I'm not buying you a bath. It's my seed money. I can't start a game without it."

His words were laced with spite, and my worry flared to anger. "Why are you being so mean to me?" I asked, turning to see him.

"Because this stinks like a chu pit!" he exclaimed under his breath, brown eyes narrowed. "You should have gone with me and left this to sort itself out."

My brow rose. "That's it?" I exclaimed. "That's why you've been badgering me all day? You're angry because I won't leave her to be raped and killed so I can pursue a career cheating people with you?" Thadd clenched his jaw in mental anguish, and I added, "Pardon me for having a whisper of morals, but there's nothing stopping you from leaving. Go on. Leave! Thadd and I will be fine."

I spun from him and stared straight ahead. My hands were clasped tight in my lap, and my throat closed. I didn't need his help.

I sensed, rather than saw, Duncan look between Thadd and me. "That's not what I meant," he finally said.

"What did you mean, then!" I exclaimed. "Stop questioning my decisions or come up with something better!"

"Contessa?" called a feminine voice across the street. "God save us. Tess?"

My head turned. "Heather?" I cried, wiping my eyes and standing up as I saw her.

Thadd pulled the horse to a stop, and Duncan grabbed my arm to keep me from falling.

"Look at you!" my friend said as she ran across the street. "I was coming to see if anyone had picked up your circlet. I do it every day, hoping for news. Oh, pig feathers! You have a black eye? And what are you doing in the streets without Kavenlow—and in a *wagon*?"

I lurched to the hard cobbles and touched my cheek. *I had a black eye? Why hadn't anyone told me?* Heather reached us, and I gave her a hug. "Heather!" I exclaimed, almost crying. "I'm so glad you're all right."

She pushed away, her red cheeks bunched as she beamed. "Well, why wouldn't I be? I heard you arguing with"—she looked Duncan over appraisingly—"this man," she continued, "and I knew it was you. I've heard you put a servant in his place enough times. Lord help me, who did that to your hair?"

I glanced up at Duncan's scowl. "He's my friend, not a servant," I said softly. She went to touch my eye, and when I pulled away, she plucked the sleeve of my dress instead.

"I thought I threw this away," she chattered, then gave me another breath-catching hug. "I've missed you," she said as she pulled away, her eyes bright. "Why won't they let anyone into the palace?" She ran her fingers over my greasy hair in dismay. "They said you're getting married next month. I knew you weren't. You can't get married without me. And so soon!"

"This is Duncan," I said when she paused for breath. "And Thadd."

"Pleasure," she said, her eyes darting from them to me. Then her eyes went back to Duncan, and I sighed. "Why won't they let anyone in or out of the grounds?" she asked again. "The rumors put the king and queen dead. Then the next day they're alive but you're dead. But here you are! I don't recognize any of the guards on the gate. They tried to tell me it's practice to lock the gates when there's foreign royalty on the grounds. I told them that was chu on my shoe and gave them what for. But you look all right, except for your black eye. Who hit you? Saints preserve you, you're filthy! I hardly recognized you. How did you get that dirty?"

"We need a place to rest," I wedged in, starting to get depressed. "Do you know somewhere?"

"My house," she said breathlessly, touching my hair and making a face. "Oh, Tess. I don't know if this will come out. It's my parents' house, actually. I'll get you a bath. And a good meal." She glanced at Duncan and Thadd. "And your man-friends, too. They both have horses, do they?" She gave me another hug. Her blue eyes were wide as she put me at arm's length. "Heaven save you. Is that your red underskirt in your hair?"

"Heather!" I exclaimed, embarrassed. "Can we go? We don't want to be noticed."

Her mouth made an *O* of understanding. "You ran away? Shame on you! Prince Garrett was handsome enough." She hesitated, dismay coming over her. "He wasn't the one who hit you, was he? Why is it always the pretty ones who have the worst tempers?"

"Um, it wasn't him," I said, and she looked at Thadd. "It wasn't either of them, either."

"Help the princess into the wagon," she said pertly, as if Thadd should have already.

"Burning chu pits," Duncan muttered. "Does the woman ever shut her mouth?"

Thadd extended a thick hand, and I lurched up to sit beside him. Heather held a hand to her fair hair and pursed her lips until he offered her a hand as well. She sat next to me, adjusting her dress and she glancing at Duncan with the edge of her attention. "How long have you been out of the palace?" she asked again. "Thank heaven I found you. You shouldn't be out alone." She looked at Thadd. "Though I see you have a guard—of a sort."

"They aren't guards," I said dryly. "And I would have found you sooner, but I was at Saltwood and then Brenton." She gasped, and I glanced behind us. The few people who had seen our reunion didn't seem interested. "I was chasing Kavenlow and the real princess."

"Real princess? How . . ." Heather's blue eyes opened wide, and she put her hands to mouth. "Oh, Tess," she wailed. "You're the real—"

"No!" I cried, reaching past Thadd to cover her words. I felt the prick of tears. This was not what I needed.

"But, Tess," Heather said in a hushed voice as I pulled my hand away. "How?"

I shook my head. "It doesn't matter. I just want to take a bath and eat something. The horses have to be returned to the stables before someone recognizes them, and I have to figure out what Kavenlow would do."

Heather took a breath to demand I answer her, but years of taking direction were hard to overcome. Swallowing, she pointed down the street with a quivering finger. "There," she said. "Turn left down there." She forced a nervous smile. "I'll get you a bath. And see you in some proper clothes, though I don't know where, since the shops close early now. I'll get you cleaned up, and you'll see. You're the princess, Tess. You are."

I closed my eyes as her prattling washed over me, both comforting and irritating. I could smell the smithy going distant behind us. The scent of cooking potatoes and fish was making me dizzy with hunger. I didn't mind the stink of people, or that my dress was too tight, or my feet hurt from the pinch of my boots without stockings.

It was hard, though, seeing Heather as I last saw her, rosy-cheeked and dressed in white. And even harder that she was treating me as if I was still the princess. Deep in my heart I knew I wasn't.

Twenty-eight

❖

The water was blessedly hot, and I slid downward until it threatened my nose.

"Sit up, Tess," Heather complained. "I'm not ready to rinse your hair yet."

My breath bubbled out as I straightened. Heather scrubbed at my scalp with a vengeance until it hurt. "What were you thinking?" she scolded. "You should have used that new dye from the docks. I would have picked some up for you. You had such nice hair. I may as well finish cutting it all off for you, now. We can say you had a fever. That, at least, is romantic."

"Mmmm," I murmured, knowing her threat was idle.

She wiped her hands on her skirt and turned to a bucket of waiting water. "Hold your breath," she said as she dipped out a ladle.

I leaned forward and closed my eyes as it cascaded over me, making me shiver.

"Oh . . . dear," she said slowly, and my eyes opened.

"What?" I asked as the soap dripped into them. The harsh bubbles stung, and I waved my hand frantically for a towel.

"Nothing," she warbled, her voice a shade too high.

A towel hit my hand, and I wiped my face. I squinted up at her. Her brow was pinched, and her blue eyes looked worried. A strand of my hair lay in the water, and my breath hissed in. It was red. The black had washed out to leave my hair the color of a fine roan horse. My eyes closed in misery. "It's all right, Heather," I said, trying to find the strength to deal with this latest indignity. "Just rinse it the best you can."

Heather's hand shook as she tilted my forehead back and poured a second ladle of water over me. Apart from her horrified silence, I could almost believe the last thirteen days were a nightmare and I was in the bathing room in the palace. My eyes opened. The sight of Kavenlow's ring on a cord hanging from a hook brought it all back, and I slumped.

Heather's parents lived in one of the better sections of town, in a house, she had proudly explained, that she bought for them with her palace stipend. Right now, the two-story home was empty, since her parents had left the third night Prince Garrett's guards had taken the streets. They had tried to convince Heather to go with them, but she stayed, claiming I'd need her.

A flock of children ran chattering down the narrow lane between the houses, and I smiled. That was a sound I hadn't heard in ages. A dog was with them, adding to the happy confusion. There had been no children in the palace since I had grown up. I thought the princess should do her best to remedy that. There should be laughter in the garden again.

Heather dumped a third ladle, and I wiped the water from my eyes. "What's the news from the palace?" I asked. Heather had pointedly kept to frivolous topics since I told her about Garrett killing my parents and my escape. She dealt with the uncomfortable by ignoring it—unless it was gossip, which she then talked about until everyone believed it true.

She shook out my old dress, her pursed lips making it clear she wanted to throw it into the fire. "Officially?" she said as she folded the filthy thing up and set it carefully aside. "The Costenopolie guards that are usually in the streets have gone to inform the summer-festival guests that it will be a wedding instead of a betrothal. Unofficially, Prince Garrett has killed everyone and taken over the palace." Her eyes dropped. "His guards are scavenging for livestock and food since the regular vendors aren't coming in anymore. Most of the ships have left, too. The harbor's almost deserted. There's to be an announcement tonight in the large square."

My eyes dropped to my torn and ripped fingernails. Thirteen

days of grime couldn't be washed out. "Then that's where I'm going," I said, gripping the sides of the tub and standing.

"Tess!" Heather wailed, rushing to a towel. "You can't go out. I haven't had time to find a proper dress for you!"

The rough towel smelled of lavender, and I breathed the clean scent in, relishing it. "I can wear one of yours," I said, then hesitated. "If you'll loan me one?" I asked in a small voice.

"I—I've nothing good enough for you," she said, taking a panicked-looking step back.

I waited until her frightened eyes met my gaze. "I'm not the princess," I said evenly, finding no pain in the statement for the first time. "I'm a beggar's child." Heather took a breath to protest, and I frowned, halting her words. "I'd rather not put either of my old dresses back on until I've a chance to wash them," I said, finding it ironic Heather would be the first person I begged from. "Do you have anything that might fit me?"

Heather's eyes filled. Her hand went to her mouth. Hunching into herself, she ran from the room. She didn't shut the door, and I heard her shoes whisper on the wooden floor. A door slammed, then nothing.

"That went well," I said to the walls. Dripping everywhere, I reached to shut the door, hoping she'd bring a dress back with her. I toweled off, giving my black eye a close, unhappy scrutiny in the flecked mirror. My red curls were ghastly, and I arranged them, still damp, atop my head in a topknot. Thadd had brought up my things before he had left to return the horses. Duncan had gone with him, saying he'd stay ten steps behind in case there was trouble. Kavenlow's small bag with the venom looked dirty and out of place, tossed aside against the wall. Beside it was my coiled whip. I felt just like them, worn, tired, and abandoned.

I glanced at the shut door before I dug through the bag for more darts. Testing the potency of each with the flat of my tongue, I added a veritable plethora of deadly ornamentation. I was setting Kavenlow's three metal darts in place when Heather's hesitant knock startled me.

"Come in," I said, tightening the towel around me as the door creaked open.

"I think this one will fit you," she said. Even with her head lowered, I could see by her splotchy cheeks that she'd been crying. My heart went out to her.

"Your yellow one!" I said, forcing a cheery tone. "I always liked that one. Thank you."

Silent, she miserably helped me into the clean undergarments she had brought with her. I remembered the last time she had worn this dress: a picnic in the garden last spring. It hung rather loose in front no matter how tight she tied the bodice, and I grimaced at my slight figure.

Heather sniffed, and I had caught her twice wiping her eyes. "The overskirt needs a dunk in fresh dye," she said as she adjusted the lace around the collar. "And the trim has frayed around the underskirt hem. I had to put a new cord in the bodice, so they don't match—"

"It's the nicest thing I've had on all week," I said, giving her a quick hug. "Thank you."

"But, Tess, it's one of mine," she wailed as her composure broke. Standing miserably before me, she started to cry. Her shoulders shook, and her hands helplessly gripped her elbows. "Don't let them take your place," she sobbed. "She can't be nicer than you, or prettier."

I gave her shoulders a squeeze. "Heather? Heather!" I exclaimed, forcing her to pay attention. "It's going to be all right," I said, quieter, as her red-rimmed eyes flicked to mine. "She's nice—in a backwards sort of way." *That was putting it mildly.* "You'll like her. I promise."

Heather hiccupped. Encouraged, I wrangled the corner of my hem up and dried her tears. "I told her about you. She's going to need so much help. You'll have to give her advice and tell her which of the guards will let her walk in the garden in the moonlight and which ones won't. You're going to teach her to dance, and make cut-out snowflakes, and how to plan a dinner. Heather?" I squeezed her shoulder until she looked up. "She's going to need you."

"But what about you?" Heather warbled.

From somewhere inside of me I managed a smile. "I'll be all right. Kavenlow thinks she will take me as one of her advisors, and she's asked me to help her learn how to act properly, which she desperately needs. But she's going to need a friend, too."

"I'm *your* friend," she said, dropping her gaze.

My chest hurt, and hot tears filled my eyes in that she hadn't shunned me after learning the truth. "You're my friend, too," I said, giving her a hug. "Give her a chance?"

Heather took a breath as if readying herself for a chore. A familiar tightness came into her expression. "If she tries to push me around, she'll be sorry."

Her voice had its more familiar bossy tone, and I smiled thinly, thinking Heather could do more than I to put an uppity princess in her place and tame a ferocious temper. An unhappy staff made for miserable living, and an arrogant, overbearing royal usually caught on quickly when dinners were served cold and fires were neglected.

"I'm sure she will be nice to you. She was raised in a nunnery," I hedged as I put on my boots. Heather had oiled them, and they looked almost presentable, peeping past the yellow hem. My whip was next, and Heather watched with wide eyes as I coiled it about my waist, hiding it and the handle beneath a scarf. I tucked one of Jeck's throwing knives behind the impromptu belt at the small of my back. Her brow pinched in worry at the weapons, and I shifted my shoulders in a sheepish appology. The thump of a downstairs door shifted the air.

"We're back!" Duncan shouted, his voice muffled.

"Oh, good." Heather spun to the door, clearly ready for a distraction. "The men are here. Let's get downstairs before they eat everything I left out. You need to eat, too, before we leave for the square. Why you wanted to return those horses was beyond me. We could have ridden in style. Now we have to take the cart so we don't get crushed."

I preceded Heather down the stairs, and she started in on one of her prattling commentaries about the dangers of the street, bringing up past calamities and near misses that crowds just seemed to attract like wasps to an orchard. I relaxed in the sound of her voice, making the expected ums at the appropriate places as she led the way to the dining room.

As promised, a cold supper had been laid out. My stomach rumbled, and I remembered how long it had been since I had eaten real food instead of whatever Duncan dug out from the bottom of his pack. Thadd and Duncan were already filling their plates. The squatting sculptor looked up as I entered, then hastily got to his feet, his eyes wide. I warmed, thinking I must look better than I thought. Thadd kicked the leg of Duncan's chair, and he glanced up.

"Oh, hey. I like the red hair, Tess," he said, stuffing a piece of meat into himself. "Good disguise. Move the potatoes over here, will you, Thadd?"

My glimmer of self-worth vanished; Thadd's gaping stare was due to my hair, not my clean dress. Thadd awkwardly held a chair for me and then Heather. Duncan piled more than his share of cold potatoes on his plate. "Does anyone else want these?" he asked.

No one spoke a word, so I raised my eyebrows and said, "Go ahead." He fell to with a grunt of satisfaction. Rubbing my forehead, I gestured for Heather to fill her plate as well. Hesitant and unsure, she reached for a bowl. We had eaten together before, but never at a table. Her habits with me were going to be hard to break, and I didn't think she would ever see me as anything other than her fallen princess, unjustly robbed of her throne.

"Thank you for taking the horses back," I said, and Duncan paused in his chewing.

"Mmmm," he grunted around a full mouth. "We left them in the yard." He smirked as he wiped a smear of grease from two days of stubble. "We were three streets away when the stableman found them. You'd think an angel had left a bag of gold on his doorstep."

"An angel did," Heather said primly, and Duncan made a scoffing bark of laughter. His eyes were on his plate, so he missed her murderous look. I thought I would have to watch them both. Heather was likely going to kill him or marry him.

Indignant, she stood with a scraping of her chair. Thadd hastily got to his feet. Duncan did not. "I'm going to harness the pony," she said. "Prin—" She bit her lip. "Tess would like to take some air this evening and listen to the palace announcement."

"Take some air," Duncan mocked, and Heather's eyes narrowed.

Thadd put his napkin on his chair. "I'll help you, ma'am," he said, his slow drawl seeming deeper in the close confines of the room.

"Thank you." Heather raised her chin, her cheeks flushed. "I would appreciate some assistance from a gentleman." Heels thumping, she stalked out with Thadd a pace behind. My shoulders shifted in a sigh. Heather needed a husband—badly.

The meat was cut thin and ran with its own juice. It was just as well Heather wasn't here since I ate with little regard to manners. Stretching halfway across the table, I wondered if there might be something to this commoner birth if I was allowed to jam as many sweet roll tarts in my mouth as I wanted.

"So-o-o-o," Duncan drawled, leaning back in his chair. "What's your plan?"

I put my elbows on the table, enjoying that no one frowned at me. "I want to hear Garrett's announcement before I decide anything."

His eyebrows rose, and he looked at me as if I was insane. "Angel's Spit, I knew it. You've been soaking in a bucket of hot water for over an hour, and you still don't have a plan?"

"I have a plan." I kept my eyes firmly on my travel-torn nails as I peeled a green fruit, but I could feel his disbelief clear across the table. "I'm going to get into the palace, kill Garrett, and free Kavenlow and Contessa." I hesitated. "Not necessarily in that order."

"That's it?" he said. "Chu, Tess. If you want ideas, I have them."

I took a bite of the fruit, only to nearly spit it out when I found it to be exceptionally tart. Swallowing, I looked for the honeypot, not finding it. "I told you, I want to hear what Garrett says first. Or we could do what Thadd wants and storm the front gate and die with swords stuck in us after three steps. But I've seen that," I said, feeling cold. "I'd rather avoid it if I can."

Duncan scowled, his hair flat where his hat had been all afternoon. "You aren't getting me in there without a plan on how to get out."

"You aren't going in anyway," I said, setting the fruit aside on the rim of my plate.

His jaw clenched. "Like hell I'm not!"

There was a clatter of small hooves in the street, and I guessed Thadd and Heather were ready for us. A thrill of excitement went through me when Heather burst in through the front door. She went directly to a trunk against the wall in the hallway, rummaging in it to pull out two shawls and a yellow hat to match my dress. "Leave everything on the table," she said as she clattered into the dinning hall. "Here, Tess. I have a wrap for you. It's going to be cold. People are in the streets already. If we don't leave now, we won't get close enough to hear."

"Right," I said around my full mouth as I got to my feet and brushed off my front. Chu pits, I had gotten it dirty already. But at least I had stockings again.

"Thadd?" Duncan said as the squat man anxiously hovered in the archway. "You owe me a copper. She doesn't have a plan."

An indignant sound escaped me, and I spun. "I just told you I can't make a decent plan until I know what Garrett is doing!"

I waved Heather away as she tried to put her best shawl over my shoulders. Dodging me with a grace born from long practice, she darted close and fastened it about me with a decorative pin. I glanced at the mirror over the hearth and touched my topknot. My black eye looked atrocious, and I'd grown thin. But excitement made my movements quick as I checked my darts. It was akin to the feeling that I had when I was finishing a game, moving my pieces to where my opponent had no choice but to lose. It was addictive, the feeling. I wondered if I should dart myself to heighten my abilities, then decided against it.

Duncan came to stand behind me as I primped in the mirror. The room had grown dark as we hadn't bothered with lighting any candles. "I'm going in with you, Tess," he breathed, low and threatening. "You can't stop me."

A flush of angst went through me. My thoughts returned to him shouting at me this afternoon, pinning me to the tree with only his voice. I met his eyes through the mirror. His stubbled jawline was tight with determination; shadows made him ominous. My heart thumped.

Thadd shifted from foot to foot in the doorway, his big hands clasped tight. "We all want to help, Tess. Tell us what we should do," he said slowly.

It was the first time he had used my name, and I hadn't realized until now how much his distrust had bothered me. I turned to face them with a sick feeling. I couldn't ask them to risk their lives. What if something happened to them? "I'm going in by myself," I said, and Duncan made an exasperated noise and half turned away. "I'll free Kavenlow and the palace guards. Unless Garrett moved them, they're in the cells under the guards' quarters. While they retake the palace, I'll find Contessa and keep her safe until it's over. If Garrett interferes, I'll kill him."

Heather gasped, a trembling hand to her mouth.

"That's not a plan." Duncan's shoulders were hunched, and his face was cross. "That's a vague idea. You go in there with nothing more than that, and you won't be coming out. And what about us? You can't do all that by yourself."

I cringed inside, certain he knew I was trying to keep him out of the way. "I need a distraction so I can sneak in over the walls," I said.

"A distraction!" Duncan's vehemence shocked me. "I'm no one's distraction, Princess. Not for you. Not for anyone! Not again."

I warmed as my anger grew. "There's nothing wrong with being a distraction. I was one for twenty years!"

"Yeah?" Duncan stood with his feet spread, solidly planted on the wooden floor. "You need us," he said, pointing at me with a stiff finger. "And for more than the time it will take for you to get over the walls!"

He was shouting at me, and flustered, I turned back to the mirror, pinching my cheeks to try to hide how pale I was. My knees were weak, and my stomach was in knots. "I need you to stay in the streets," I said to my reflection. "Stir up some Misdev-dog sentiment. Raise a fuss at the gates. Something to keep Garrett's thoughts off me. If the gates open, everyone leaves."

Heather's eyes were pinched as she came forward with a wide-brimmed hat. "What about me?" she said. Her chin was trembling, and the fear was so thick in her blue eyes I wanted give her a hug and tell her it was going to be all right. "I know the palace as well as you do. What should I do?"

I couldn't send her behind the walls. I couldn't send any of them. "Can you talk to the people?" I said hesitantly as I took her hands. They were trembling and cold. "I can't bear the thought they might believe I ran away."

She nodded. "I'll tell them," she said, clearly glad she wouldn't be storming the palace.

"Damn it, Tess," Duncan said as he crossed his arms. "You're going to need our help. Thadd and I will drive the cart in with the statue. He has a commission paper. What are they going to do?

Call him a liar? You can hide in the box instead of trying to climb that wall, and once we're free of the guards, we'll get you out."

Bile rose, and I swallowed it down. The box looked like a coffin. "No."

"You're afraid of a box?" Duncan mocked. "A strong, tall woman like you is afraid of being in a box?"

I stiffened, affronted. When I had been in the wilds, it had been easy to remember I wasn't the princess, but here, in the capital with clean clothes and Heather fussing over me, it was harder. Fingers trembling, I ran them over the blunt ends of my darts in my topknot. "Jeck knows about the statue," I said, fighting Heather's flustered attempts to put a hat on my head. "I'd be a fool to get in it."

Duncan snorted, earning a dark look from Heather. "You're afraid," he taunted. "But you go right ahead and climb that wall. Thadd and I will take the wagon in and wait for you."

"No." I pulled my shawl tight. Heather took the opportunity and covered my damp hair with that ugly yellow hat. But it hid my face, so I took it off for a moment to shift a few darts to my sleeve and tuck my dart pipe into my waistband beside the knife. The thought of being in that box made me shudder. "I'm surprised they didn't stop us at the city gate with that wagon," I said. "If you try to get in the palace with Thadd's statue, you'll end up in chains."

Duncan's face went empty, and for the first time, he seemed to hesitate.

"What's the matter?" Heather said with a sniff. "Big strong man afraid of a little iron?"

"No."

"Don't think your plan is going to work?" she mocked, and he reddened.

"Heather," I said, thinking Duncan had earned the right to be afraid of iron around his ankles. "Leave him alone. It's a bad plan, anyway."

Duncan regained some of his bluster. "It's a sound plan," he insisted. "Once we're all inside, Thadd can get the guards from their cells, and I'll help you protect Contessa."

Thadd cleared his throat and shifted uneasily from foot to foot. "I'm going to rescue Contessa, not you," he said, his voice thick with determination.

I made a small noise of disbelief. It was the same conversation that we had had this morning, all over again. I was in charge. Why the chu pits didn't they understand that?

"You?" Duncan glanced at Thadd. "You wouldn't hurt a fly, Thadd. And there might be swordplay."

I stared between them, appalled. As if either one of them had been in battle before. "Listen to me!" I all but shouted in frustration. "Garrett isn't playing a game. He will kill you! None of you are going!"

Duncan shifted into quick motion. He strode toward me, his face tight. Startled, I backpedaled. Thadd grabbed Heather's arm, keeping her from flying at Duncan as he all but pinned me to the wall. "I am not letting you go in there alone," Duncan said, the width of my hat between us. His breath stirred the wisps of hair floating about my face. I felt the heat from him through my thin dress as he came close, bullying me.

My breath came fast, and my heart pounded. Fists clenched, I refused to push him away lest he think his nearness bothered me. Which it did. "You're a branded thief, Duncan," I whispered, knowing it would hurt him but desperate for a way to get him to back up. "You can't risk it."

He stiffened. Jaw clenched, he dropped his head and took a step back. My hands were shaking, and I couldn't seem to get enough air. I felt guilty for having said it, but I wanted him—all of them—safe. I wouldn't risk his life. I wouldn't risk any of them.

"That was foul of you, Tess," he said tightly. Turning, his hunched figure moved soundlessly into the hallway. He slammed the front door as he went out.

Feeling like the bottom of a chu pit, I looked up to find Thadd and Heather both downcast and uncomfortable. The sound of excited people in the street was loud. I wished I hadn't eaten; my stomach had turned into knots. "We'd better get going," I said faintly, and Thadd and Heather silently followed me out.

Twenty-nine

❖

Duncan wouldn't look at me as I came out onto the stoop. I hesitated, wondering if we would all fit into the small city cart Thadd strode down to. A surly pony was harnessed to it, and I surmised Thadd's huge draft animal was busy churning up the tiny yard where Heather said she kept the pony in the rare instance it wasn't in the field.

With much shifting and broken comments, we arranged ourselves with Thadd and me in the back, and Heather and Duncan in the front, facing us. Thadd ran the reins between Duncan and Heather, and we started off after an initial balking from the pony at the heavy load.

Unhappy, I sat crammed into the small space, comparing it to the few times I had toured the city by coach. I was closer to the people in the cart—hearing the worry in their voices and seeing the excitement in their eyes—but still detached. I caught snippets of talk of war, and that the war was already over and we had lost. No one was even considering that the changes in the palace were due solely to my botched marriage arrangements. It was depressing.

Even worse was Duncan's continued stiff silence. I wished now I had never opened my mouth. Any appology from me would be rebuffed; he wouldn't even meet my eyes. But he had scared me, and I had lashed out. The memory of our kiss intruded, turning me even more miserable. At least I wouldn't have to decide what to do about that now.

"Turn around," Heather said breathlessly when we found the main entrance to the square blocked with people. "Go down that alley there, then up and to the left. We can get in through the smaller side entrance between the yarn shop and the confectioner's."

People swarmed to take our place as Thadd hupped and called, expertly backing the pony up. He kept us to a good clip, and we dodged around other carts and mounted riders bent on the same thing. "Is it too close?" I questioned as we slipped back into the square. We were almost next to the hastily constructed, raised stage. Misdev guards in Costenopolie colors stood three deep, making a ring nearly thirty paces from the scaffold's footing. The young soldiers looked tense, and the crowd was voluntarily keeping back from them. We were past accurate dart range, but I had known Jeck wouldn't make it that easy for me. A movement on the high stage incited the crowd into more noise, and I stared along with everyone else.

Garrett, Contessa, Jeck, and Kavenlow were filing into the small box atop the scaffolding, having just climbed the stairs. Dressed in furs and silks, they arranged themselves behind six sentries forming a living wall. A closed wagon waited nearby to whisk them back behind the palace walls. Thadd looked desperate, helpless pain thick on him.

Shouts of, "Where are the king and queen?" and, "Where's the princess?" were put forth. I shrank down on the bench, praying I wouldn't be recognized. It might start a bloodbath.

Clearly Garrett was going to begin Jeck's endgame, proclaiming he had the real princess and that he was going to marry her. Kavenlow's word would be sufficient to convince the crowd it wasn't a convenient lie. The real question was how the Misdev dog was going to explain our parents' death.

"Duck your head, Tess," Duncan murmured, and I glanced up to see a Misdev guard circling the crowd. My heart pounded and my fingers touched my whip as he passed us murmuring, "Proud beggar woman with a black eye and good boots," over and over like a litany. I was fervently glad I had come as middle-class, and I no longer minded my hair was red.

My gaze rose to Kavenlow's, willing him to look at me. He didn't. My brow pinched as he shifted with an odd, shuffling walk. He was fettered with chains. He looked weary, dressed in a black robe that hindered his motions rather than his usual form-fitting trousers and jerkin. I wondered if he had eaten today, feeling guilty for my full stomach. His hair looked freshly combed and his face washed. It was obvious someone had tried to disguise the abuse he had suffered. I was torn between my hatred for Garrett and my heartache for Kavenlow. The pain at seeing him like this and being helpless to do anything was unexpected, and my heart clenched.

"I'm sorry, Tess," Heather said, seeing the direction of my gaze. "I'm so sorry."

Garrett leaned to the princess and said something. She recoiled, her face aghast. Kavenlow's lips barely moved, and a sentry hit the back of his legs. I gasped. Duncan caught my hands as I reached out.

Garrett shouted something at the guard, and the sentry backed off. Duncan's grip tightened in warning, then released. Thadd looked as if he might pass out, so tense with the effort to not storm the scaffolding was he. Giving the sentry a barked order, Garrett moved forward past him, raising his hands to the crowd. The murmuring eased to a background hum.

"Where are the king and queen?" someone shouted, and it was repeated several times.

Garrett raised his hands higher. I could see—and hate—his beautiful, reassuring smile from where I sat in the pony cart. "I have answers," he said as his hands lowered and the crowd settled. He took a breath. "As you good harbor folk have surmised, I'm Prince Garrett of Misdev, come to beg your princess's hand in marriage and usher in an era of cooperation and trade between your kingdom and my father's."

"Where's the princess?" someone shouted, and several more took up the call.

Not distressed in the least, Garrett turned to the first voice. "She is safe beside me."

"Take your whore away," a voice bellowed. "Princess Contessa shops at my stores."

The crowd surged into noise, drowning out Garrett's words. My heart hammered, and I wondered if they would swamp him, forcing a battle they couldn't win. The ring of guards about the scaffolding braced themselves, and the angry crowd stopped shy of their reach.

"The woman you were betrayed into calling princess isn't one!" Garrett shouted over their noise. "She was a changeling, bought in your very streets to occupy assassins while the real princess was raised in safety."

The people at the front went silent, shocked. A slow murmur rose as his words were carried to the back of the crowd. I heard, "He's lying. The Misdev dog has killed them all," and Garrett surged ahead before he lost control.

"I didn't know, either," he said, allowing a hurt, innocence-wronged tone to enter his voice. "I was betrayed as much as you. But your true princess has returned, brought back by your chancellor and my captain of the guards in a show of solidarity." Jeck stepped forward and touched his hat before stepping back.

The crowd's voices strengthened.

"The chancellor will affirm this woman is the true and rightful princess, heir to Costenopolie," Garrett said.

My throat tightened as Garrett gestured to Kavenlow. He stepped forward, pride making him hide that he was shackled. His eyes roved the crowd. I willed him to see me, almost crying out as our eyes met and he forced himself to look away. *He saw me,* I thought. Tears threatened, and I clenched my fists. *Damn Garrett. Damn him for what he has done.*

"The woman standing beside me," Kavenlow said, his resonant voice, stilling the crowd, "is the heir to Costenopolie's throne. At the queen's request, I took her daughter upon her third month of life to safety, and upon her twentieth year, I brought her home again."

The crowd didn't like that. "Where are the king and queen?" someone said. It was repeated and taken up until Garrett raised his hands. Silence grew. Slowly his hands dropped.

"Your false princess has murdered them," Garrett said.

I gasped, turning to Duncan. His long face mirrored my own shock. The crowd roared, and I shrank down, feeling as if I was being beaten. I couldn't breathe. I couldn't think.

"She killed them," Garrett shouted. The crowd tried to listen, but their outrage wouldn't allow them to be still. "She killed them when they told her she wasn't the princess. She murdered them, then tried to murder me because I knew the truth. She left me for dead to find and kill the true heir so she could take her place."

I watched from under my hat, shocked as Garrett pulled the princess forward. "Tell them who you are and how she attacked you," he said, and the crowd went silent. I felt as if I was going to pass out. The princess's lips moved, and I heard nothing. "Louder!" Garrett demanded.

"I am Princess Contessa of Costenopolie," she said, her voice trembling. She looked like our mother, more so for being dressed in her clothes. It was enough to convince the most doubting citizen. "She did attack me, but it was—"

Jeck gently pulled her back, and fear paled her cheeks. Thadd groaned. Sweat trickled down his neck as he kept himself unmoving.

"Your false princess killed your king and queen, and tried to kill their daughter," Garrett said. "She is here now, in the city, plotting another attempt on her sister's life even as I speak. I will knight the man who brings her to me."

The crowd erupted into noise. I slumped onto the cart's bench, putting my head on my knees more to keep from passing out than to hide. Someone draped a lavender-scented blanket over my shoulders. I numbly stared at the yellow floorboards as the clamor shook the wood under my feet. How could he be so foul as to blame my parents' deaths on me?

"I will find your murdering, gutter-slime, false princess!" Garrett shouted over the tumult. "Your future queen has agreed to wed me at month's end, and with her, I will bring justice to Costenopolie!"

The sound of the crowd, fierce with its conflicting opinions of denial and acceptance, beat upon me. I felt the cart shift and heard the call of our frightened pony.

"Get her out of here," Duncan said. "Thadd, get down and lead the pony out of here."

The cart jerked, inched forward, then moved faster. The press of the people grew less. With a shocking suddenness, the noise dulled. It was replaced by the sharp clips of our pony's hooves against the cobbles when we found an empty street. There was a pause, and the cart shifted as Thadd lurched into it. I could hear the muted roar of the crowd come and go like storm surf as Garrett continued his lies. The air was cool with evening, and when

I pulled my head up, I saw Duncan sitting across from me, waiting.

"What are you going to do, Tess?" he asked. He looked severe, the tiny scar above his lip pale in the gathering shadows of the streets.

I remembered Kavenlow in chains and the princess's interrupted confession. A feeling of inevitability and determination pushed out my confusion. I couldn't afford it anymore. Costenopolie was mine, and I had to win my master's game for him. I took a deep breath.

"I'm going to need some rope."

Thirty

❖

The jostling of people looking for answers at the palace gate square was overwhelming. I couldn't even see the open lattice-work of worked metal. Putting my back against a lamppost, I shifted the bag that contained my rope higher onto my shoulder and tried to ward off my panic at the crush. It wasn't dark enough to go over the wall yet, and I had come to estimate the amount of distraction the crowd would provide since Duncan was sulking, refusing to help me. My people weren't angry yet, but they were working themselves up to it. Already the guards behind the gate had moved back, showing an increasingly uncomfortable indifference to the shouts.

My hands were damp, and I brushed them on the trousers I had borrowed from Duncan. I felt naked, as if I was in my under-things, and the trousers caught at my legs with every step. Thadd had covered my topknot with a cap and firmly pronounced me a fine-looking lad, but Heather's pinched expression had told me it was a thin disguise. For the first time, I was glad of my tall, less-than-womanly figure.

"Hoy! Make a way!" came a familiar voice, and I spun in sur-prise. My lips parted as I saw Duncan and Thadd in the wagon with the statue, forcing it through the crowd.

"No," I whispered, realizing why he had been so adamant he was staying behind and would have nothing to do with my plan. He was going in anyway. After I had told him not to!

"Get out of the way!" he shouted as he stood from the wagon's bench and waved a dirty hand at the people. "Official palace business. Make a path!"

His cursed pride led him to this, nothing more. Frightened, I avoided eye contact. He looked confident, having put his trust in a plan that was going to fail. Thadd, though, looked properly petrified, and I cursed Duncan for pulling him into this.

The sculptor's blocky hands gripped the reins with a fervent intensity. His attitude went perfectly with his story of artisan delivering a promised commodity, and I was sure it wasn't an act. Duncan shouted again, and heads began to turn, both guard and citizen. A reluctant path opened to show the palace gates and the peaceful grounds beyond. A sentry came forward. His hand was on his sword hilt. "No, no, no!" I whispered. I should have darted them all into unconsciousness! I should have locked them in a closet! I should have turned them in myself!

I elbowed my way backwards as the wagon creaked to a stop before the tall gates. "Sit down," Thadd said, yanking Duncan back down on the bench. The sculptor pushed the reins into Duncan's hands and slipped off the wagon. His fingers trembled as he passed a paper to the guard through the gate. The collective noise of the gathered people swelled in question.

"I have a delivery for the palace," Thadd said, his slow drawl bringing the murmur of voices to almost nothing. My people were curious, if nothing else. "My father received a commission to make a series of statues. I have the last here. It was to be an engagement gift for the princess from the king and queen."

I strained to watch the guard make a show of trying to read the note. He nodded as he folded the paper and tucked it behind his jerkin. "No one gets in," he said. "Go home."

"I can't take it back," Thadd protested, his thick hands clenching. "It's too heavy to get up the mountain. And give me my paper. I need that to get my money."

The crowd pressed closer. I was pushed almost to the front. Wiggling, I put a tall man between the gates and me. "Give him his money," someone called. "Let him in," another said. The phrase was repeated, becoming louder.

"The king and queen bought it for their daughter," someone cried. "Let him deliver it."

"The king and queen are dead!" the guard said. "All of you go home."

It wasn't the best thing for him to have said, and the crowd turned ugly. Duncan looked behind him as the once-sedate horse nervously tried to back up.

"Let him in!" the shout came again. "He has a paper. Let him do his job."

I shrank down. Curse Duncan to the ends of the earth. He was going to get himself killed.

The noise clamored. A sharp crack of a whip brought a temporary silence, then the crowd returned to a soft murmur. I put an unnoticed hand on the shoulder of the man in front of me to stand on tiptoe. My heart gave a pound and alarm rocked me back. Jeck.

The captain was behind the gate, still dressed in his smart uniform of black and green, again wearing that overdone hat with drooping black feathers. He was reading the letter. A guard stood with an uncomfortable stiffness beside him. Jeck's brow furrowed, then smoothed as he folded the paper. His eyes rose to Thadd and Duncan.

Duncan's casual stance flashed into a tense, dangerous pitch. My breath quickened as I saw his understanding that they were found already. The two men locked gazes over the crowd. Duncan's shoulders went stiff, realizing he would never be able to flee. Jeck's eye twitched, and Duncan's jaw clenched as he acknowledged whatever silent conversation had passed between them.

"Get them in here," Jeck said, his eyes riveted to Duncan, and the assembled people buzzed between themselves. I scrunched down.

"But sir . . ."

"Get them in here," Jeck repeated, aggressively shoving the note behind the guard's jerkin. "They have a paper signed by the late King Stephen. We will honor it. Use a detail of guards to keep the crowd back, but I want them in here." He leaned close. "Now."

They were caught. I had known this would happen, and my breath quickened in frustration as two ranks of sentries came out the guard door in the wall. The people voluntarily backed up, and

I was pressed to the edges. Their shouts grew loud when Jeck came into the streets with shackles. "What's going on?" someone called out as his intent became obvious.

I all but panicked, torn between my inability to help them and my need to try. Jeck raised a hand. "Assassins have infiltrated palaces through the front gates before," he said, showing a soothing smile. "If they are who they say, nothing will happen. If they're impostors, you'll find their heads on the wall in the morning."

My hand went to my mouth and Duncan was roughly pulled from the wagon. The clank of the metal was loud as his boots were pulled off and the rings were fastened around his and Thadd's ankles. Duncan's face was tight and angry. Thadd's fists were clenched.

Jeck made a show of tucking the shackles' key into his pocket, his gaze roving over the crowd.

The crowd's noise swelled as the gates were unlocked. A guard mounted the wagon and slapped the reins. Neck sweating, the horse bolted from the crowd and into the dusky palace grounds. The ring of sentries before the crowd backed up to follow the wagon in. Thadd and Duncan were roughly pushed into motion. Jeck was the last to return. He looked over the crowd as the gate swung shut. The clank shocked through me, and my face went cold.

"What do you want done with them, Captain?" one of the better-dressed guards asked.

"Send word to Prince Garrett that we have them," he said, his eyes on the crowd through the gates. "And find me a lever and hammer. I want to open that box." Saying no more, Jeck strode after the wagon, that awful hat crushed in his grip and his cloak furling behind him. The guard's fingers fumbled as he checked the lock on the gate and hurried to follow. Swords drawn, the remaining guards struck aggressive poses in the safety behind the gate.

As if Jeck's absence was a signal, the crowd surged past me. I stood rooted to the cobbles, bumped and jostled. Their noise grew ugly, and the soldiers threatened to stab through the bars. I backed up until the crush thinned. Almost unseeing, I turned and paced quickly down the road, feeling light and unreal. I had to get in there. Jeck would kill them both.

The tree overhanging the wall wasn't far, but it seemed to take forever. Shadows were thickening. The moon wouldn't rise until late, giving me a smothering darkness until then. My attention alternated from the cobbles to the unbroken line the top of the wall made with the sky. I reached to touch my whip and then my knife as I looked for my tree.

The lamps were being lit, and my feet slowed as I passed one. A bad feeling settled over me as I recognized this corner. I had burned Kavenlow's note here. Confused, I spun to the line the wall made against the lighter sky. It stood unbroken, cold, and empty.

My tree was gone.

Shocked, I stood as if frozen. *They had cut it down. They cut my tree down!* An unreasonable anger flashed through me. How dare Jeck cut down my tree! That was my safe tree, the heart of my games with Kavenlow. It was as if he had killed a favorite pet. And how was I supposed to get in now?

Frustrated and angry, I slumped against the wall, sliding down until I was sitting on the thin grass that eked out an existence where the stone wall met the cobbles. This wasn't fair. I had to get in, rescue Duncan and Thadd, and save the princess. Jeck was ruining everything!

I crossed my arms around my knees and fought between my desires to cry and rail at the wall. If I didn't get in, Duncan and Thadd were going to die. Why hadn't he listened to me?

A cluster of jabbering people passed before me, faceless in the waning light. They ignored me as they would a beggar, and if I didn't get over the wall, that's just what I'd be. But how? It was built to withstand short sieges. A hundred men couldn't take it.

Hopelessness turned my heart black, worse than the night I had left my dog, Banner, to be kicked and beaten for his steadfast obedience. My tree was gone, probably no more than a stump. I couldn't tie my rope around a stump.

My head came up. "But Banner could," I whispered. A hundred men couldn't take the wall, but a lone woman might—if no one saw her. My eyes flicked across the empty street. Heart pounding, I took one of my preciously few darts from under my cap and stabbed it into my thigh. I grimaced at the sharp hurt, hating it. One dart wouldn't lower my resistance too far, and I needed all the help I could find to remain unnoticed and convince Banner to do the impossible.

I tugged my hat back on and looked up and down the street. It was quiet this far from the palace gate. I pulled my rope from my pack and re-coiled it loosely. There was a knot every arm length, and they bumped through my fingers.

"Banner," I whispered as I stood before the wall and closed my eyes. Now that I knew what the venom did, I could feel it, trace the tingling flow from where I had stabbed myself. I followed the sensation as it ran through my veins, settling on the space behind my eyes. It seemed as if my nose burned, and I willed the sensation to grow. "Banner?" I whispered again, thinking of sticks and bones, and games of fetch. "Banner, I'm back. Come play with me." *What if they had killed him?*

A muffled whine and a short bark from behind the wall set my heart racing. He was alive and free—and at the foot of the wall. It was working. It was really working!

Remembering the quick feel of the mouse's thoughts, I tried to slip into Banner's. The impressions of the night seemed to fade, then strengthen when I found him, his paws shifting restlessly against the damp ground. Like a rising tide, his emotions ebbed into mine, twining in an uncomfortable slurry. I struggled to fit his impressions into a context I could relate to.

He was far more complex than the mouse. Making sense of his view of the world was very much like composing poetry while hovering on the edge of sleep. My concentration wouldn't hold, distracted by the process itself. Every time I managed to separate us enough to remember what I was trying to do, I would lose my place and have to start over. It was frustrating, and only the knowledge that I had done it before kept me trying.

Slowly I began to understand. He was hungry. Hungry and wet. His hip hurt where he had slept on it, and one of his paws had a torn pad. But Banner's drives were more complicated than a mouse's want for food and warmth. He had the ability to reason, to learn to expect an outcome from a seemingly unrelated action. It was the ability to play that I had to exploit.

He whined, and I found a twin sigh slipping from me. Frightened from so close a tie, my eyes flashed open. The sight of the smooth wall shocked me. I had half expected to see Banner's tangled beard and rough coat. Checking to see that the end of the rope would uncoil properly, I flung as many loops as I could at the top of the wall.

Grunting from the effort, I caught my balance and watched the rope arch up. It settled over the wall with a soft hush. "Take it, Banner," I whispered, hoping the rope hung over the wall within his reach. "Take it and pull. Let's play tug." My hands tightened on the rope's rough strands. "Take it from me, boy. Come on. Pull."

I held my breath as the knots bumped through my fingers in a series of jerks. He was doing it! Banner was a heavy dog, but his weight wouldn't be enough to hold me. I had to get him to wrap the rope around the stump, if the Misdev guards were lazy and had left one.

A faint roar from the gate rose, and I risked a glance at the street. I had my distraction, but what would be the price? Sealing my emotions away, I settled myself. This was going to be nigh impossible, even if Kavenlow had sensitized Banner to venom-induced instruction.

"Banner," I whispered to myself, imagining the shattered remains of my tree. "Bring me the rope. Come on, boy. I'm hiding behind the stump."

The thought of me crouched behind the stump made Banner go wild. He barked sharp and high in greeting. The rope went slack. I felt his paws shift in confusion, and his disappointment was so thick I felt guilty for trying to manipulate him. Shoving my heartache aside, I tried again. "Get the rope, Banner," I whispered, forming the thought he ought to be quiet and take it in his teeth. "I'm hiding. Just around the stump. Bring me the rope, and we'll play. Get your rope, Banner. Get your rope."

His confusion shifted to hope, and I reinforced the idea that only with the rope in his teeth would I praise him and tell him he was a good boy. I imagined he saw the corner of my heel disappearing just out of his sight around the stump. I heard an eager bark. My pulse hammered. He was so excited, I didn't know if he had the rope or not.

"Pull, Banner," I said. "Come on. Try to take it from me."

I gave a tug on the rope. My heart sank as it moved freely. I pulled again until it held firm. Elated, my breath caught. I had taken up the slack, that was all. Banner had wrapped it around the stump. I hoped.

My hands were sweaty as I gripped the rope. Lips moving in a silent prayer, I forced myself to trust Banner and my unseen work. The rope held as I put my weight upon it. I took a step up the wall, balancing against it and pulling myself up a step, then another. My arms ached at the strain and the faint lethargy from the venom, but I couldn't stop.

Up a man length, then another. My jaw ached from clenching it, and sweat dotted my forehead. My hands were cramping, and my arms felt like cloth. By the time I found the top, my pulse was racing. I tried to swing a leg over the top, but missed. The sudden pull of my weight on my shoulders drew a low cry from me.

Banner barked a frantic greeting. I took a breath, wishing he would be still. Holding it, I flung my leg up and over, bruising my ankle through my boot. My breath exploded from me in a sob, but I lay straddling the wall. My cheek pressed against the cool rock as I caught my strength. My legs felt useless, and my arms were numb, but I'd made it.

I looked down at the street, glad no one had seen me. Banner barked again—a playful, eager sound—and I turned toward the quiet palace. A stir of pride filled me until I saw my tree, cut and left to rot, its green leaves souring into decay. Nothing was left but an oozing three-foot stump—the stump my rope carelessly circled.

There were no guards. Duncan's distraction had worked.

"Hey, Banner," I whispered as he stood with his front paws against the wall. "Good boy. Just a moment. I'll be right down." The big dog's tail whipped the ground.

I pulled the rope up from the street, then dropped it into the garden. Taking a deep breath, I closed my eyes and slid from the top of the wall. It was the most frightening thing I'd ever done.

There was an instant of stomach-dropping motion. My eyes flew open as it seemed I should have hit the ground by now. With a shocking suddenness, the ground pushed my feet, jamming my knees into my chin. Stars exploded. I fell sideways. Pain throbbed in my hip and lip. I tasted blood; I must have bitten it. Banner covered my face with his tongue, and that, more than anything else, pulled me to a sitting position.

"Down. Down, Banner," I gasped, trying to fend him off. He would have nothing to do with my commands, both verbal and in his head. He covered me with his body, refusing to let me do more than sit up. My tears flowed as I gave him a long hug before I scooted backward to hide under a bush.

He whined and fawned at my feet, and I ran my hands over his ears, telling him he was a good boy, the best dog anyone could have. His fur was matted with mud. His paws were caked with it. He stank like wet dog, and I breathed it, knowing he had already forgiven me for everything. "Good boy," I said, wiping my tears away with the back of my hand. "You're a good boy."

Thirty-one

❖

Banner's hunger-thin form vibrated as he growled at the sight of Garrett's guards. I felt it through the arm I'd draped across his shoulders. He had clearly endured a hard time. His ribs showed, and his head looked too large for the rest of him. "Easy, Banner," I soothed as I peeked out from under the bank of shrubs we were lying under, and his rumble turned into a plaintive tail thump. My fingers felt for the smooth finish of my dart tube. Kavenlow's venom had filled very few of my darts, but I wouldn't let them hurt Banner again.

The palace grounds were a shambles. Garrett's stolen livestock had been given free pasture of the gardens, churning the grass into mud and digging up the roots of the rare and delicate plants I had spent years tending. It was appalling, convincing me further that Garrett was an ill-mannered barbarian.

Banner and I were overlooking a circular patio surrounded by budding roses. At the center stood the wagon and a flurry of guards. The horse had been taken to the stables, leaving Duncan and Thadd with their hands bound and metal shackles on their bare feet. There was no more pretence that they might be freed.

Jeck stood unmoving directly across from them, his powerful outline obvious in the flickering torchlight. He had that gaudy hat on again, and the black feathers draped brokenly across the back of his neck. Even as I watched, he took it off, crushing it in a gloved hand. He looked irritated.

In sharp contrast was Garrett. The prince's motions were quick with excitement as he paced from one end of the patio to the other. His cape furled about his ankles, showing flashes of his elaborate outfit as he moved. He looked every bit the prince and desirable husband. I bitterly thought of how innocent I had been.

My gaze rose to the dark tower. Kavenlow's window was black, but a faint glow of light shone from my sitting room. I was sure Contessa was there, and I hoped she was well.

A series of shouts and harsh scraping sounds broke the dusky silence, pulling my attention to the patio. Six guards wrestled with the box Thadd had carted halfway across the kingdom. It was heavy; Thadd worked in marble. Jeck stood well back. He was watching not the box but the surrounding area. I slowly let my held breath out, shivering in the chill.

"Be careful!" Thadd said, his bound hands reaching out when the box thudded to the ground. The stone pavement under it cracked, and I could see his distress even from here. A guard cuffed him to be quiet, and only Duncan's quick reactions kept the short man from going down. Another shove, and Duncan and Thadd were separated again.

Garrett strode impatiently to the box. Banner growled at him. "Be still," I whispered, thinking I'd like to bite the prince again, too, and his threat turned into a confused whine.

"Get back!" Garrett shouted at the three sentries trailing him. "Your hovering is going to drive me insane. Get away, damn you all to hell!"

The three men dropped back when Jeck raised a hand and took their place. "More torches," Garrett said loudly. "I want to see the guttersnipe's blood run when I ferret her out."

My face went slack. They thought I was in the box! That's why they had ringed it. I closed my eyes in a long blink, thankful I hadn't taken Duncan's advice.

Garrett paced as two sentries pried at the slats. "So this is how she planned on gaining the grounds," Garrett said, sneering at Duncan and Thadd. "Not very clever, is she?"

Jeck said nothing. His eyes continued to scan the surrounding grounds.

"I don't know why I pay you, Captain Jeck," Garrett taunted. "You spent a week chasing a fool slip of a woman and couldn't catch her. All it took me was some patience."

Jeck stiffened. His hand was never far from the opening of his jerkin, and I wondered if that was where he kept his dart pipe. The sentries returned with more torches, and Jeck pointed, placing them at the fringes of the circle. The patio was as brightly lit as if for a festival, and my stomach churned at the irony of it all.

"Please," Thadd begged as they levered the box upright. "Please be careful."

Garrett rubbed his hands together in anticipation. "See?" he chortled. "She's in there."

I watched breathlessly while the guards continued to pry at the box with little success. Unable to take the suspense, Garrett strode forward. Snatching up an ax, he pushed a guard out of the way. With a grunt of effort, he swung it at the thick wood.

"No!" Thadd shouted, lunging forward. I covered my mouth as four guards fell upon him, pinning him to the ground. Jeck didn't move. He wasn't watching Thadd, focused instead upon the edges of the circle. He was looking for me.

Thadd struggled until he had a view of Garrett. He watched, horror etching his face while the prince beat upon the box. "I am surrounded by fools!" Garrett shouted as he swung again and again. The front of the box splintered with a frightening crack. He dropped the ax with a cry of victory and pulled at the shards of wood. Several guards grasped the edges, and with a cascade of sawdust, the front of the box fell apart.

The patio went silent. The sawdust spilled from Princess Contessa's statue, falling to reveal Thadd's heartfelt tribute to the woman he loved. In the softness of evening, the pale folds of her dress looked light enough to drift in the breeze. She was holding a dove, her head tilted to show the graceful line of her neck and the fall of her hair. The vision held sway for three heartbeats as all took in the vision of grace and beauty.

Face ugly, Garrett drew his blade. "It's not her!" he shouted, swinging it.

"No! Don't!" Thadd cried, desperately struggling to rise.

Garrett's blade hit the statue with a dull clank. My eyes widened as a fold of exquisitely carved stone broke away to crack the paving stones. Shocked, I glanced at Jeck. His lips were tight, and he had his hands on his hips. He gestured brusquely to one of the guards, and the man came close, unable to tear his gaze from the prince's tantrum as Jeck whispered in his ear.

"It should have been her!" Garrett exclaimed. Thadd bowed his head as Garrett's blade hit the statue again and, with a sharp *ping,* broke. "Aargh!" Garrett shouted, flinging the broken hilt into the shrubbery. Furious, he strode to Thadd, still on the ground under the guards.

"Where is she?" he shouted, pulling the man up as the sentries got off him. "Where?"

"You're a murdering dog," Thadd said, almost weeping over the destruction of his life's work. "I wouldn't tell you before. I won't tell you now."

Garrett reached for his sword. His hand slapped into his empty scabbard. Clearly furious for having forgotten he had broken it, he swung his fist into Thadd's belly. The squat, powerfully built man doubled over, almost pulling the sentries down with his deadweight.

Enraged, Garrett strode to Captain Jeck. "I want them questioned," the prince all but spat. "Put the taller one on the rack first. We'll find out where the guttersnipe is."

I put a hand to my mouth, deathly afraid for them. Beside me, Banner's growling became audible.

"There's no rack, Prince Garrett," Jeck said. "King Stephen didn't use one."

"Then improvise something—Captain," Garrett said caustically. "You, though, will go into the city and burn it street by street until she surrenders herself. She isn't here."

"With all respect, Prince Garrett, I will not be leaving the palace grounds."

Garrett jerked to a halt. The surrounding guards glanced uneasily between themselves. "I gave you an order!" Garrett shouted, spittle glinting in the torchlight as his voice echoed off the distant walls. "Go and find her!"

"I will not leave the grounds—Prince Garrett." As I watched in breathless anticipation, Jeck stood before Garrett and defied him. "I told you she wasn't in that box. This was a distraction. Pulling the men from the walls was a mistake. If she isn't on the grounds already, she will be soon. I will take the prisoners to their cell, then return to look for her here."

"I gave you an order!" Garrett cried. "I am the king! You'll do what I say, or you'll hang with them!"

The grove of roses had gone deathly quiet. Stiff-necked and angry, Jeck said, "You are not my king. Your father is my king. I take direction from him. I was told to keep you alive. That is what I will do down to my last breath. If I leave, she will kill you— Prince Garrett."

"We are not in my *father's kingdom!*" Garrett said, his voice shrill. "We are in mine. *I am your king!*"

A shutter banged from the palace walls, and my gaze shot to the lit window. Contessa stood framed by the light. "You are not a king, Prince Garrett," she said, her clear voice ringing out. "This is my land. You are a second son and will never be anything more."

My breath escaped me in a frightened hiss. It had to be bravery. No one was that foolish.

Garrett went red with a fury so deep, it had to be born from insanity. "Get her back in her room!" he shouted, and a shadow pulled her, protesting, away from the window. Thadd groaned in frustrated anger. Garrett spun from the palace and back to Jeck. "Give me your blade, Captain," he said, his clipped words giving no clue as to his intent.

I watched, unbelieving, as Jeck reached for his sword. The smooth sound of it coming from the scabbard chilled me. Garrett's hand was outstretched. The flickering shadows from the torches glinted on the blade, making it flame. My pulse raced. Jeck handed it to him hilt first.

Garrett snatched it, slamming it into his scabbard to replace his broken one. My shoulders slumped in a relief I didn't understand. "I want them questioned," Garrett snarled. "I don't care if it kills them. I want to know where she is by dawn." The prince strode away, trailing the three unlucky guards that Jeck motioned to accompany him.

Jeck waited until he was out of earshot before muttering, "I'm sure she will tell us exactly where she is—Prince Chu-head— within half that time." Clearly angry, he turned to the statue and the ring of guards. "You," he said, pointing to one gawky in adolescence. "Give me your weapon." The boy did, and Jeck took it as his own. "Go to my quarters and fetch my second blade. I'll be in the cellblock or with the prince. Those of you on the wall, stay in pairs."

"Pairs?" a young guard muttered. "Who does he think is coming? The angel of death?"

Jeck spun, surprising the sentry. "That's exactly who I think is coming, and unless you want to meet her early, I suggest you treat every breath of wind as an intruder. Understand?"

The sentry stiffened. "Yes sir!" With a creaking of leather, all but six of the guards left the patio. They passed me, unknowingly. All I had to do was sit and be still. I placed a hand on Banner's head, and his faint growling ceased. He had been bred to hunt elk and wolf. He knew how to be silent, postponing the attack until a more favorable opportunity arose.

Jeck motioned for the remaining guards to escort Duncan and Thadd. The sculptor shuffled forward with his head down. Pity filled me as I watched his slow-moving shadow. There was nothing, save threatening Contessa, that would move him now.

Duncan was hunched with determination and anger as he was led away. He was a branded thief, risking death should he be caught thieving again. I had told him no, but he had done it anyway. And if I couldn't free him, he would die with that same defiance glittering in his eye.

Jeck looked back once as he followed the tight group across the grounds to the guards' quarters, his hat in his grip. The light from the torches went with them. The rose patio went silent. Thadd's dream stood alone and broken. I lay under the shrubs, knowing it was safe but unable to move.

What was I going to do? I had to have the key in Jeck's pocket to free Thadd and Duncan. I couldn't get the key until I retook the palace. I couldn't take the palace without Thadd and Duncan's help. It was a tight circle bound with iron.

"Why the chu pits isn't it raining?" I whispered. Depressed, my eyes lingered on the shattered remains of Thadd's statue. It had been beautiful. Even now I could recall the lovingly shaped curve of her cheek and the graceful line he had made of her dress. Garrett had damaged it beyond repair before his sword had broken. Thadd worked in marble, and his tools were made of stronger stuff than Garrett's sword.

Thadd's tools? I thought, my gaze shifting to the wagon.

I slowly backed up from under the bushes to sit upright. Thadd's tools were bound to still be under the wagon's bench. His chisels and mallets might be able to break locks.

Banner sensed my excitement and stood, his tail wagging. I glanced at the palace walls, imagining the eyes. I'd have to risk going into the open. It was dark enough now, perhaps.

Telling Banner to stay, I crept down to the patio, hesitating by a tall briar of climbing rose to gather my nerve. Down here, the chipped mutilation of Thadd's work was heartbreaking. Shards of stone and scuffed sawdust littered the ground. I took a deep breath and ran to the wagon. Standing upon the spokes of the wheel, I reached for the bag under the bench. My hand searched unseeing. A soft sigh escaped me when I found the fold of cloth and dragged it to where I could use two hands to lift it over the side.

It was heavy, and I held it close as I shuffled back into hiding. "Banner," I whispered. Before I could count to three, he had loped to me with his rolling gait. He pushed his nose into my hand and looked for approval, nearly as excited as when I had dropped over the wall and back into his world. "Good boy, Banner," I said, juggling the tools as I fended him off.

I'd have to do something with him, but he wouldn't stay for long with me out of his sight. Eventually he would come find me, his odd behavior leading Jeck to me. I needed a distraction for the loyal dog. A smile drew the corners of my mouth up. The kitchen was on the way to the guards' quarters.

"Come on, boy," I said, giving him a pat as I started into motion. A sense of purpose filled me. "Let's go get you a well-deserved bone."

Thirty-two

❖

"Come, Banner," I whispered as I slunk down the hedgerow.
The massive dog trotted beside me, happy to be moving. Banner's bone would have to wait, since I had found two sentries outside the kitchen door. It seemed Jeck was taking me seriously
now. As I made my sporadic way from tree to wall to rock, I
heard the occasional shout when a pig or sheep caught the attention of a guard. Having livestock on the grounds was an unexpected boon. I'd have to remember that.

The soft footfalls of two men brought me to a heart-pounding
halt. Hissing to Banner to follow, I flung myself off the sawdust
path to crouch at the foundation of the palace. Banner growled,
and I forced him to lie down. I hardly breathed as two men passed
within a stone's throw. Hands slow and careful, I checked my
topknot, then winced as Thadd's tools clanked. Kavenlow's three
metal darts felt cold among the bone needles.

"Put extra guards on the perimeter," I heard Jeck's intent low
voice say, and I jerked with a thrill of angst. "It'll be dark enough
for her to come over the walls until the moon rises." He looked
toward the distant, unseen city. "Are the off-shift sentries searching the palace yet?"

"Yes, sir," the other said. "Devil of a girl. Shall I double the guard on the princess?"

"And Prince Garrett. Keep him in his room if you can." Jeck's voice went faint as they passed me. I took a grateful breath and gave Banner a pat, excitement tingling to my toes. My heart slowed as the quiet reasserted control of the night.

Rising from my crouch, I looked toward the guards' quarters: a one-story building at the center of an open area. Underneath were the cells, dug out and lined with stone. I had used one once as a playhouse and remembered it was dry and smelled of earth. The guards still teased the poor unfortunate sentry I had drafted as my "husband." My face burned at my innocence.

I slunk the last few paces to the edge of the field. There was nowhere to hide, and even with the darkness, the idea of crossing it was daunting. Keeping to an even pace, I walked down the sawdust path as if I belonged. Either Banner and I would be seen or we wouldn't. A trembling in my legs quickened, the vertigo coming with it telling me I was drawing too heavily upon my venom-induced skills to stay unnoticed. The boost from the dart was fading already?

My stomach was in knots as my feet found the wide covered porch. Breath held, I stood in the entry room and listened for a call of question or recognition behind me. There was none. Worried, I looked at Banner cowering at the smell of Garrett's guards. I couldn't take him with me. "Stay," I said firmly as I made a tentative step from him, and he whined. I took his heavy jaw in my hands and put my face beside his. "Stay," I said, giving his head a small shake. A wave of dizziness took me, but he lowered himself to sit in the doorway.

My focus returned and I straightened, indecision pulling at me. Should I supplement my skills, making it easier for Jeck to dart me into unconsciousness should he find me, or should I keep my levels of venom low, relying on luck and chance? I had a feeling this was the question that haunted all players, and my fingers went to my topknot, counting what I had left. There weren't enough to reassure me, and since Banner seemed inclined to stay where he was, I gave him a final stern command and headed inside. With him sitting there, I'd have some warning if anyone tried to pass this way.

The stairway to the cells was in the common room in the

middle of the building. I'd have to pass a score of bunks. No one was here, though. Everyone was looking for me. I was sublimely confident the situation would be different below in the cellblocks.

My hair on the back of my neck rose as I strode through the open barracks, my dart tube ready. I was shivering when I finally gained the stairway. My nose wrinkled at the foul smell wafting up the stairs. There ought to be two sentries at the top of the stairs, but by the faint rumble of conversation, it seemed they had foolishly joined the others.

I took my cap off and stuffed it into the back of my trousers before I slunk down into the softer darkness. Only a faint shadow of light showed the way. The oil lamps had their wicks too low, and they were smoking. I eased my pack to the lowest stair. My hand shook as I checked my darts, then palmed another. As I passed the first cell, there was a quick intake of breath.

"No," I mouthed frantically at the grimy face pressed against the floor-to-ceiling bars. I shook my head, surprised to find myself grinning at the excitement in the guard's eyes. I recognized him. More men saw me, holding themselves still to keep me from being found.

I glanced up the dark corridor to the brightly lit alcove and Garrett's guards. "Two men?" I asked the man before me. "Are they here?"

"In the thell acroth from the thable," he intentionally lisped to keep the sharp sounds from carrying to the sentries.

I wanted to hold my breath against the stink of him. It was worse than a chu pit in summer. "Kavenlow?" I asked, my hopes plummeting as he shook his head.

"The Mithdev dog thaid you were a beggar, a thangeling. I knew he wath lying."

My eyes dropped. "He was telling the truth," I admitted. "But the real heir is here now." I bit my lip, wounded at his shocked expression. "I'm going to try to get you out. Be ready."

He nodded, pulling away from the light. I heard the barest whisper and felt the air change to one of repressed excitement. The word of my presence went faster than my progress, and eager, hopeful eyes silently watched me pass.

Boots a whisper, I crept forward until I was close enough for the guards to see me if they bothered to look up from their dice game. I cringed as I took in the six soldiers. They looked huge, crammed into a space designed for four. My chances of bringing them all down were slim to none. Futility slumped my shoulders, but an arm raised in encouragement gave me strength.

Trembling, I crouched. Why they hadn't seen me was obvious and an outrage. The cells should be bright so no one could hide in the shadows. That I could get this close undetected was atrocious, magic or not. I had yet to see Thadd or Duncan, and my fear for them tripled.

Three sentries sat on chairs, two on the edge of the table, and the last stood. He rolled a pair of dice, and rough condolences were made. Having them jammed together might be a boon. They'd get in each other's way while trying to reach me, giving me the time I'd need for the venom to work. Garrett may have been able to take the palace with such inexperienced guards, but to keep it with the same was a jest. Clearly his father had given him the worst of the lot.

Breath held, I pulled five more darts from my topknot to make seven, counting the one in my hand and the one in my dart tube. Inexperienced or not, they were big and armed. I felt a collective holding of breath from my father's men as I let the first dart fly.

"Ah," a guard cried, slapping at his calf beneath the table. "Damn fleas."

The second was away as he reached down and pulled the needle out for everyone to see.

The third found the neck of a guard when they realized they were under attack.

The fourth landed in the chest of the man who pointed at me.

My eyes widened as all six got to their feet. "It's her!" one shouted. Panicking, I couldn't remember if I had shot him already, and so put a dart into him. My precious moments of confusion were gone. No one had fallen. One man, perhaps two, was undarted.

The hall dimmed when they eclipsed the light. Frightened, I stood. My fingers jammed a dart into the pipe the wrong way and I pricked myself. Dropping it, I plucked a bone dart from my topknot and physically drove it into the chest of the guard grabbing my arm.

"Princess!" someone shouted. Panicked, I pried at the man's grip on me. I stumbled as a Costenopolie guard reached past the bars and yanked him backward. Gasping, I jerked away, backpedaling until my head hit a wall. Stars filled my vision. I couldn't breathe, it hurt so bad.

Struggling to stay upright and conscious, I saw that the guard who had grabbed me was moaning, curled up in a ball. I felt the back of my head to find a lump but no blood.

A single man was standing. His hands were raised in surrender. He was scared, not even old enough to have a beard. "You," I wheezed, catching my breath. "Put your back against the bars where one of my men can reach you." The young guard's eyes widened, and I gestured with my empty dart tube. "I can down you from here," I said. "Go stand by the bars."

White-faced, he did, and a hairy, eager arm snaked out and pinned him to the bars by his neck. My shoulders slumped. I had done it.

"She did it!" someone exclaimed in a hushed voice.

"Duncan?" I called, finding him pressed against the bars with his mouth hanging open.

"He's got the key!" Duncan exclaimed, pointing with a blood-smeared hand. "That one there has the key to the cell. But Captain Jeck has the shackle key." Hunched in hurt, he held one arm with the other. His face was bruised and swollen. "Leave us here, Tess. We can get out, but what good will we be with these?" He shuffled his feet, the iron at his ankles clanking.

I picked my careful way through the guards trembling on the floor to Thadd. The sculptor was slumped in a miserable huddle, clearly convinced he had failed his love. "Get up!" I whispered. "I think I can get those off of you. And you were right, Duncan. I needed your help. I never would have made it over the wall if it hadn't been for you."

"But we don't have the key for the shackles," Duncan protested as I crouched to pat the clothing of the guard with the cell key.

I grinned at the buzz of muted excitement from my guards. "But I have Thadd's tools."

Thadd's head came up, his hollow eyes flickering with hope. "You have my chisels?" he said, reaching out past the bars.

"And mallet." I lurched over a writhing sentry and shoved the key into the simple lock. The door swung open. The light fell upon them cleanly without the shadow of the bars. "Can you break the shackles?"

"I'll try." He emerged from the cell like a young bear, nudging aside a downed guard. I ran back to the foot of the stairs to get his tools. Duncan hovered beside the table, anxiously watching as I handed them to Thadd. I silently took in Duncan's bruises, feeling sick. In the bare minutes he had been out of my sight, they beat him for that defiant gleam he still wore.

The clank of clean metal as Thadd chose the largest chisel drew my attention. I was torn between watching and the hushed calls of men from the cells. They were shackled as well, but I could at least get them out. Thadd swung his foot up onto the table and positioned his chisel.

I was unlocking the first door when a sharp clank rang out. Thadd said nothing, and I handed the key to the first guard and returned to the table. Brow furrowed in concentration, Thadd shifted the chisel against the lock and raised the hammer again. His muscles tensed, and with strength and exquisite precision, he brought the mallet down. "Chu!" he exclaimed as the chisel slipped from the metal to tear a gash in his leg.

"You did it!" Duncan exclaimed in a whisper, and an excited babble rose behind us.

"Yes, but look what I did to my leg." Thadd pulled the shackle from his ankle and swung the other up onto the table. He began to hammer at the second ring of metal.

The Costenopolie guards blinked at the brighter light as they rattled out of their cells. Their smiles were grim but honest. With very little conversation, they moved the five comatose guards and the last frightened one to a cell and locked it. The feeling belowground had turned.

"Got it," Thadd said, the sharp sound of metal against metal breaking the tension. It sounded different. "Saint's bells," he swore. "I broke my chisel." Thadd straightened. His eyes were hopeful as he threw the chains into his empty cell. "Duncan?" he said, and the man carefully eased his leg up onto the table, his breath held against the pain. He wasn't using his left arm, holding it close and unmoving. His face was drawn, and bruises peeked from behind his shirt. Garrett was an animal.

While two Costenopolie sentries kept a hidden guard near the top of the stair, the rest of us watched with waning hope as Thadd broke every chisel he had. "I'm sorry," the sculptor said as the last cracked to a thin shaving. "Duncan, I should have done yours first."

I solemnly met the ring of determined faces. They were hungry. They were brave. They smelled. They would do anything for me. "We will retake the palace while shackled," I said.

Duncan went still. His bowed head rose in a smooth motion, fixing the brown of his eyes on me with a surprising intensity. His lips pressed together. "Thadd, give me that last chisel."

"I broke it." Thadd put the handle in his grasp. "It's not good for anything."

Duncan was silent for three heartbeats. His carefully empty face shook me. He'd shown me only what he wanted to before—and now I would see more. A spark struck through me, more potent than our kiss. He had seemed so safe. He wasn't. Seeing my breath catch, he nodded almost imperceptibly, as if agreeing with me.

A guard chuckled as Duncan carefully placed the chisel into the opening of the lock. His brow furrowed, and he twisted the metal until it was at an odd angle. "Hairpin," he whispered. His eyes were fixed upon the rusted lock balancing against his leg, and his voice demanded obedience.

Fumbling at my topknot, I handed him a hairpin—no venom, just a mundane hairpin. My hair was ready to fall about my ears, and I rearranged Kavenlow's metal darts to hold it.

"Do you think he can do it?" I heard someone ask.

"Look at his hands," another said. "He's a thief sure as chu pits stink!"

"I'm not a thief," Duncan insisted, his breath slipping from him in a rush as the lock clicked open. "I'm a cheat." He eyed me from under his brow. "There's a difference."

"You did it!" Thadd exclaimed, and Duncan confidently tossed the shackles aside.

Duncan nodded, his eyes still fixed to mine. The guards had clustered around him, but I couldn't look away. I saw him there in his dirty clothes and thick stubble, holding his beaten body at an awkward angle to ease his hurts, and my knees felt like water. The heat of our kiss washed through me. He wasn't who I thought he was. *God help me. What was I feeling?*

"Princess," a guard said, jolting my eyes from Duncan. "We heard Prince Garrett's men leaving upstairs. What's happened?"

I blinked as I recognized Resh, the captain of my father's guard. "I'm retaking the palace," I said. "Do you know where Kavenlow is being held?"

"No. I'll find him. You stay here." He gestured for two men to act as my guards.

"No," I said. "I'm not the princess. And I won't stay here when I can do something."

"Princess—" he started, halting as I frowned at him. Old habits die hard.

"I can't wait until you're all free," I said. "Princess Contessa needs me now. You retake the palace. Thadd and I will see that Prince Garrett doesn't escape with her before you regain the grounds." His brow furrowed, and I glared. "Until you get out of your shackles, there isn't much you can do about it, Captain Resh," I said, gesturing for Thadd to join me.

The man hesitated, and in his confusion, I broke away.

"You'll get them free?" I said, and Duncan looked up from a shackle. The gleam in his eye took me aback. Under it was the sly knowledge I had seen past his innocuous exterior to the real man beneath—and that despite the stubble and grime, I was attracted to him. *Save me from myself,* I thought, thinking my desire for men of power would be the end of me if Jeck wasn't.

"Save the princess, Tess," he said, his look warming through me, unexpected and surprising. "I'll do this."

Our gaze broke as Thadd handed me the jacket from the smallest Misdev guard. I shrugged into it, not liking how it smelled or that it fell almost to my knees. Thadd looked frightened but determined in his borrowed Misdev jerkin. Someone's boots were on his feet, and he moved with only a slight limp. He wasn't much taller than I was, but I felt safe with his powerful bulk beside me. Despite his earlier mistrust, I knew he would sacrifice his life for mine if he thought it would help Contessa.

Passing through my father's guards to reach the bottom of the stairway, I wondered if anyone would ever love me like that.

Thirty-three

❖

"Slow down," I said breathlessly to Thadd as he paced to the door of the guards' quarters and the lighter rectangle of dark. "And don't look around so much," I added. "Drop your shoulders, and swing your arms. You look as if someone is going to fall out of the sky on you."

Thadd caught his pace, and I came even with him. "I'm sorry, Tess," he said, his voice slow and worried. "I'm no good at this."

"Yes you are," I encouraged, thinking I wasn't either. Thadd said nothing, his grip tight on his heavy mallet. My pulse quickened as we neared the entryway, and I strained to see past the door. A savage growl brought us to a standstill. My panic melted as I recognized Banner.

"God save us," Thadd whispered, clutching my arm and pushing me behind him as Banner's large silhouette rose in the threshold. "What the devil is that monster?"

"Banner," I said, more for the dog than Thadd. "That's my dog. Stay here."

Thadd's head bobbed loosely, and I went to the agitated animal. It took more than a few moments, but with encouragement and a firm demand for obedience, Banner accepted Thadd as someone to be tolerated. It didn't help we both stank like Misdev guards.

"I don't know how we can reach Contessa," Thadd said, tentatively patting Banner. "They're looking for us. And no disrespect, Tess, but you don't look like a guard. You don't even look like a man."

"Thank you," I said as I peeked outside, meaning it. I felt awful in Duncan's trousers, and my borrowed jerkin stank so badly of sweat, I didn't think it had been washed since being taken off the loom. "But if we can gain the halls, I can get us into my room without being seen."

"What about the guards outside her door?" he protested.

I edged into movement. I had snuck in and out of my room so often, I had worn the stone clean under my window. "Even with the guards," I said, motioning for Thadd to follow.

We saw no one on the way to the kitchen. Most of the sentries on the walls had torches, and they were too distant to worry about. A loud, fire-lit commotion was at the stables. I heard a horse call and frowned. It sounded like Tuck.

The sentries were still at the kitchen door when Thadd and I eased into hiding nearby. They were eating something sticky by the amount of finger licking going on. My head shook in disgust at the quality of Garrett's men. They fell with a brief moment of confusion, each pierced with a dart. Thadd and I dragged the convulsing men into the shadows.

"What do you want to do with them?" Thadd asked, his voice shaking more than his thick hands. I knew I could count on him, but he looked ready to fly apart.

Banner had his tail tucked, looking both aggressive and afraid. It was a dangerous combination. I took off my pack and pulled out a length of cord. "Tie them up and put them in one of the cooking pits," I said as I cut it into usable lengths with my knife. "I'll be right back."

"Tess," he protested, but I slipped to the door of the kitchen. I peeked in to find it empty. A pot of water was steaming, and several beheaded chickens waited on a table. Garrett had to be eating better than that, though, and I found a flesh-strewn bone in the refuse barrel. *Banner wouldn't move from this for a week,* I thought in satisfaction.

A wisp of song brought my head up. Someone was coming. Face tight in alarm, I glanced at the door. It was too far away. I dove for a nook beside the pantry. Crouching, I pressed against the wall. The singing grew louder as a man entered. My heart pounded. "Stay put, Thadd," I whispered. "Please, stay put."

"Oh-h-h-h, I don't have to man the walls," the man sang heartily off-key. "I don't have to clean my boots. I only have to clean the chickens and pull out all their goots."

"That's guts," I muttered, "and it doesn't rhyme." It was the Misdev guard-turned-cook. Apparently he had been enjoying his change of profession from spitter of men to spitter of chickens. I cringed in tired weariness as he launched into a ballad of the warmth of entrails on one's fingers when it was cold. "You can take the man off the battlefield . . ." I breathed.

I peeked around to see the apron-clad, ex-soldier contentedly dipping a chicken in hot water in preparation to pluck it. "Kurt!" came a faint summons from what sounded like the banquet hall, and the cook looked up. "The chancellor wants some water!"

Kavenlow! I thought, tensing. They had him in the banquet hall?

The guard hummed happily. "Water for the chancellor, not rain upon my head. I'd rather be a cook than a soldier who is dead."

I crouched, torn with indecision, as the cook left with a pitcher. I wanted to see Kavenlow, but if I left Thadd much longer, he'd come looking for me sure as Banner would. There were scornful laughs from the banquet hall, and I wondered what they had done. Worried, I glanced over the empty kitchen and made a dash for the garden with the bone for Banner.

"Hey!" the cook cried, and I spun, my face warming. Setting his pitcher by the door, he wiped his hands across this filthy apron. "Aren't you the one—"

"Guts and boots don't rhyme." Pulling my dart tube to my lips, I made a puff of air.

He frowned as it hit him in the neck. "You little harlot," he said, plucking it out and stepping forward. A pained look crossed him. He groaned, clutching his shoulder. My held breath slipped out as he fell, out cold by the time he reached the floor. Heart pounding, I watched him. He wasn't even twitching. I hoped he wasn't dead.

Banner whined from the doorway. Thadd stood beside him looking whiter than I felt. Knees weak, I glanced from the empty doorway to the prostrate cook. No one was coming. No one had heard. "Come on," I hissed, grabbing the cook's arm. "Help me get him outside."

Thadd dragged him out by his heels and I gave Banner his bone. The huge dog promptly sat where he was and began gnawing. I joined Thadd at the pits, binding the guard's hands and feet and tying a rag over his mouth. Thadd shoved the unconscious cook into the pit atop the others, and I tugged the cover over it.

"Banner, come," I whispered, coaxing the massive dog to sit on it. "Stay." The dog's tail thumped hollowly on the wooden cover as he resettled himself. He was more interested in the bone than my praise. He would stay put, and when the cook and guards were found missing, no one would dare disturb the huge, half-starved animal that they had been tormenting.

Thadd took my arm as I turned to the door. "Here," he said, extending a belt and sword.

I stared at the length of steel, not liking it. "I can't use it," I protested in a hushed voice.

"Then it's for show," he said, draping the belt around my waist and frowning since there wasn't a hole in the strip of leather small enough to fit me. "Take your knife back, too," he added, and I shakily accepted it. I didn't like this. I didn't like it at all.

Armed with a weapon I couldn't use, I reentered the kitchen and skulked past the boiling water. "Wait here," I whispered. "I want to see Kavenlow."

"What do I do if someone comes in?"

"Hit them on the head with your mallet?" I suggested, and he looked at it in horror, as if never having considered it as a weapon before.

I edged into the small, unlit dining room. My gaze went to the tapestry that had saved my life. I swallowed hard as I found nothing left of the curtain but three rings and a scrap of cloth. Sitting on a stool in the hearth where the fire would be was a game of thieves and kings. My face burned when I realized it was the game I had left for Jeck on the inn table. Obviously he had guessed I had hidden in the fireplace. With a sudden determination, I went to the board and moved my thief. There were moves left in the game, but it was over. His king was mine. It wasn't smart. I knew with an undying certainty I'd pay for it later. But I couldn't help it.

An echoing conversation filtered out from the banquet hall. The lamps were high, and a rectangle of light made it to where I stood. Edging closer, I peered around the archway. My hand rose to cover my mouth in heartache.

Kavenlow was slumped on the floor in chains in the center of the room. His chin was on his chest. He didn't move when I willed with all my soul for him to turn and see me. Guards surrounded him, leaning casually against the walls. He was dripping wet. My shock turned to anger. How could they treat him like that? Leaving him in chains on the floor!

But then I realized Jeck's intent. In the center of the room, Kavenlow had little to work with to escape. Worse, if I wanted to help him, I'd have to show myself. Even trying to gain his attention might result in my capture. But if Duncan could pick locks with a broken chisel and a hairpin, I was willing to wager Kavenlow could do the same with two bits of fire-hardened needles. I had one that was empty already from taking the cellblock. And I didn't think dosing him with the venom from the second would endanger him since he couldn't have had any contact with venom for days. It might even help him escape.

It felt decidedly wicked to take aim at my instructor. He jumped when the first dart struck his thigh, pulling him into an alert readiness. I put the second right next to it, and he returned to his slumped position. I waited to be sure he wasn't going to pass out. The guards continued to talk among themselves, wondering if they should send someone for more lamps. Kavenlow shifted his hand and plucked the darts. They disappeared under the concealment of his palm. I smiled as his hands edged to the lock on his shackles. I only had one bone and one metal dart left, but having Kavenlow free was worth a hundred darts to me.

"Good luck, Kavenlow," I breathed as I left, knowing he wouldn't risk looking at me.

Full of a new and probably unwarranted confidence, I backtracked into the kitchen. "This way," I said, and Thadd lurched into motion. I appreciated him not asking anything. He looked frightened for such a powerful young man.

I was torn between skulking from spot to spot or trusting my thin disguise and boldly making my way in the open. We did a little of both as we rose two floors, seen from a distance but unchallenged. Some of the hallways were entirely unlit, and I frowned, thinking that if Garrett couldn't even run a palace, how did he intend to run a kingdom?

"No," Thadd said, drawing me to a stop at the base of the stairs on the third floor. "I saw her from the garden. She is on this floor."

I pulled on his sleeve at the shuffle of approaching boots. "Come on!" I pleaded, my efforts having as much effect as pushing on a tree. "My old nursery is up a level. We can rope down from there," I explained, and he let me pull him up. My pulse hammered as we reached the shadows of the next landing. We had made it just in time.

"You there!" a masculine voice below us called. "Have you been up to the tower yet?"

I looked at Thadd, panicking. "Answer him," I whispered, my heart in my throat.

"Uh, no," Thadd said, pitching his voice deeper than usual. "We're going to recheck the fourth floor. Uh . . ." He hesitated. "See any sign of her?"

"Naw," the man said, putting a foot on the first step. "She ain't here. I was supposed to be on leave, and I'm spending it searching for a damned wench I can't even take a tumble with." He took a noisy breath through his nose and spat on the floor.

Thadd moved a step farther into the dark. "Hard luck."

I eyed the two guards and drew back into the shadows, trying to hide my pack. Their light made it difficult for them to see us. My sword felt heavy, and my knife was cold at the small of my back. I fingered my whip. It had a distinctive noise, and I didn't want to use it.

The first sentry stared up at us, his stance sullen. "Captain Jeck has gone mad. Have you heard he's got six men guarding that chancellor? Why not make *them* search the palace? That old man is so meek, you could tell him to stay put and he would." The surly guard snatched the light from the first sentry and stalked away. "Come on, Wilk. The sooner we finish, the sooner we eat, though it won't be much, seeing as everyone is searching for a *fool woman*!"

The last was an angry shout, and I swallowed hard as it echoed. The other guard gave us a wave and cheerfully followed his dour companion. He was persuasively telling him that the captain knew what he was doing, and if the chancellor was under heavy guard in the middle of an empty room, there was a reason for it. Thadd and I let out our held breath simultaneously.

Thadd's hands were trembling as he shifted his grip on his mallet. I took his arm as if seeking protection, and he straightened. "Thank you, Thadd," I said. "I think you just saved my life." He said nothing, but his breath shook as he exhaled.

We continued. A wry smile crossed my face when we found the door to my old nursery and I ran my fingers over a nick in the doorframe. I had chipped out the sliver of wood when I was nine, hitting it with a sword while playing dragon and slayer. No one had ever mentioned the missing wedge of wood. I don't think the guard I had nearly decapitated told anyone either.

"Here?" Thadd whispered. He glanced at the end of the hallway where two guards stood in a pool of torchlight. They were talking among themselves, eying us.

"Yes, this is it. Wave at them before we go in," I said, and Thadd did.

I pushed open the nursery door, breathing in the familiar scent of old stuffing along with the smothering darkness. My mother had almost turned the chamber into a sewing room. Afraid I'd lose my second, questionable door, I had protested it should stay the same for my children. She had dabbed at her eyes and pronounced it would remain unchanged. Heartache took me, and I pushed it away. Children I would never have. Children she would never see.

Working in shadow, Thadd barred the door with his sword. Looking about, he shoved the heavy dress-up wardrobe in front of it. It wasn't much, but I felt better. He strode to the largest window and opened the shutters. A chill wind shifted my hair. The moon would be up soon. "We can get to her from here?" he asked, leaning out.

"Yes." I set my pack on the too-short table and pulled out the knotted rope. Striding to the westernmost window, I opened the shutters and looked over. Down and to the left, the window of my sitting room beckoned with a bright square of light.

"Good," I whispered. Tight with tension, I went to the wooden hatch in the wall that opened to a hollow chimney leading to the servants' kitchen. There was a box and pulley that I had once rode up and down in before Kavenlow found out and had it removed. I tucked the end of the rope behind the iron hook that latched it closed, drawing it through until one of the knots I had tied caught. I gave it a tug, and it bumped through. A frown crossed me. I hoped the knots wouldn't be a problem. Usually I shimmied down a double length of rope, then pulled the one end back through once I reached my room. The knots might make that difficult. Giving Thadd a worried look, I drew the rest through, knotting the ends together before I lowered it over the sill.

Thadd looked uncertain. "It will hold?" he said, and I nodded, giving it a tug. Unconvinced, he set his mallet down and took a long pull on the twin lengths as if he were trying to draw a net from the water.

A rattle at the door pulled our heads up. Thadd's hand went to his mallet. We stared at each other, afraid to speak. "Hey," someone called faintly. "You need help in there?"

"You go first," Thadd whispered, then louder, "The door is stuck!"

I bobbed my head and scrambled onto the sill. My sword smacked into my leg, and seeing as his was barring the door, I gave it to him. Excitement thrilled through me as I swung my legs over. There were lights at the rose patio and the mews. My breath caught when I thought I saw Jeck's silhouette by a bonfire where the gardener's shed once was. I started down, faster than usual because of the knots and Duncan's trousers.

"Hurry, Tess," Thadd called in a whisper as he leaned out the window. "I don't think they believe me that the door is stuck."

Swallowing, I turned back to the cold stone and shimmied down to the sill of my sitting room. No one was there. Not even a guard. Reassuring myself, I swung my leg over and dropped to the floor. Breath held, I listened. Nothing.

I sat up as the rope slipped from the sill and back into the night to hang from the nursery window. I peered out to find Thadd already on his way. At least the guards hadn't gained the nursery yet. A feminine sniff from my bedchamber brought my head up.

"Contessa?" I whispered, shocked when instead of her, an old guard bolted out of my bedchamber with his sword drawn. We stared at each other for a heartbeat.

I reached for my dart tube. He took a breath to call out. I darted his neck, hitting him perfectly. Backing to the window, I fitted Kavenlow's last metal dart into the tube. I had nothing left. He would call for help before the venom took effect. I had failed.

There was a dull thunk, and he groaned. Eyes rolling to the

back of his head, the man started to topple. Behind him with a fireplace shovel raised high over her shoulder was Contessa, white-faced and frightened.

I lunged forward to catch him. Any noise would bring more men in from the hallway. He was heavy, and I only managed to slow his fall. We went down together. My breath whooshed out as he pinned me to the floor, and I frantically tried to push him off. My dart tube rolled from my grasp, lost in the folds of the rug.

"Tess!" the princess whispered, setting the shovel down and pulling on the guard. "Are you all right? What are you doing here? Garrett wants to kill you! He's absolutely insane!"

"Is this the only one?" I gasped, struggling to get out from under him and sit up.

"The only one in here." Her eyes were wide, and a flush was on her cheeks. "There are three others outside the door," she said breathlessly. "Bird feathers! You're dressed like a man!" Her hand went to her hair, an unspoken question in her eyes about the new color of mine.

She gasped as her attention was drawn to the window and her face was lit by the sudden love in her eyes. Elation, hope, and desire all swirled together, making her look like her statue in the garden come to life. I knew without turning Thadd was at the window. Pain struck deep within me. I couldn't love anyone. They would only be used against me.

"Thadd!" she exclaimed in a hushed voice, rushing to him with a little sob. I was left to wiggle out from under the guard alone. I didn't watch, telling myself it was so they could have a moment of privacy but knowing it was because it would hurt too much.

"I thought I'd never see you again," Thadd said, his voice muffled. "Did he touch you? Are you all right?"

Trying to ignore her tear-strewn whispers, I crawled to the ends of the rope and struggled to get the knot out. I had to pull the rope through before the guards gained the nursery and followed it down.

Seeing what I was doing, Thadd put his hands upon Contessa's shoulders, firmly sitting her down upon my couch. As tears silently slid across her cheeks, he took his knife and sawed through the rope. It gave way with a snap. I backed up as Thadd pulled upon one end. It hesitated, then surged free. It caught again, and his muscles bunched.

"The rope!" came a faint call. "Get the rope!"

Frantic, I reached to help, but Thadd pulled as if heaven was on the other end, almost falling when the rope jerked free. It writhed past the window to hang to the ground.

From the nursery, the guards redoubled their noise. It wouldn't be long until they figured out what room we had entered and would be down here.

Heart pounding, I leapt to my door and carefully set the lock. It eased into place with a well-greased silence. Jeck would have the key, but we had a few moments more.

"Out the window, Contessa," Thadd said, and tied the remaining end of the rope to the leg of the couch. His eyes were wide and his thick hands shook. "Just a short ways down."

"Tess first," she demanded.

"Go to the cellblock," I told Thadd, ignoring her. "You'll be safe there."

Thadd scooped her up and set her on the sill. Giving him a dark look, the princess pushed him away, moving his compact bulk with a single finger. "You're coming, too," she said tersely to me.

I glanced at the door. Jeck was going to burst in at any moment. I knew it. "I said I was going to kill Garrett, and I will," I said, handing her my knife. She needed something, and I had my dart—somewhere. "Take this, and get out."

Her jaw stiffened as she refused it. "You're not going to kill that man, not even for our parents. It will start a war, and you know it. You're going to come with us until we can free the outer garrisons and retake the palace."

"If I had wanted to involve our army, I would have freed them ten days ago," I said sharply. "I can take back the palace with only one man's death. Get out."

"Please, Contessa," Thadd pleaded, his large hands opening and closing helplessly. "It was so hard to get to you. Please don't ruin everything with your stubbornness."

Her eyes flashed, and red spots appeared on her cheeks. "I'm ordering you as your sovereign," she said. "You will not try to retake the palace. You will escape with us."

I glared at her. *Who was she to tell me what to do?* Behind her, Thadd fidgeted. "Just say you will," he mouthed, his expression pleading.

Frustration fought with pride, and I drew my anger in. "I'll follow you," I said, and Thadd visibly relaxed. *When I'm good and ready,* I added silently.

She frowned warily at me, weighing the validity of my words against my defiant look. The expression would have looked cross on me. On her, it looked charming.

A soft conversation in the hall drew our attention. I recognized Garrett's voice, and my stomach clenched.

"Now, Contessa," Thadd said as the knob rattled. "If not for you, then your kingdom."

I couldn't have said it better myself. The princess's protest shifted to fear when the rattle turned into a pounding. Her leg went over the sill and she looked toward the dark ground. She gave me a last look, then bowed her head and started down.

"I'm not coming. Make sure she takes this," I said as I pressed my knife into his hands.

"Thank you," Thadd said. Then he was gone.

I anxiously watched them descend, going jittery when I thought I saw Jeck running from the bonfire. He must have finally heard the guards at the nursery window.

The conversation in the hall continued with terse answers to Garrett's barked questions. The pale face of the princess was a spot of white as she looked up. Thadd reached the ground and took her arm and ran her away. I silently pulled the knot free from the sitting couch, and the rope slid from the room. I wasn't going anywhere.

Thirty-four

❖

The sound of my lock turning pulled my head up. Garrett
had the key? I wasn't ready yet! For an instant I thought to jump
out the window but knew I would nearly kill myself. I had lost my
chance, and I panicked as the door opened to show a slice of
lamp-lit hall and Garrett's shoulder.

"I tell you what to do, not that damned-fool captain," he said
caustically. He was framed by the open doorway, his back to me.
"One of you in here with me is enough. Stay out."

He turned. Our eyes met. Surprise froze his fair features, then
a slow, wicked smile curved over him. *Chu pits,* I thought, but
Garrett said nothing to the unseen guards as he crossed the
threshold and confidently pushed the door shut with a single
hand. The latch clicked shut. He reached behind him and locked
the door, slipping the thick key into his pocket.

My fingers twitched to reach for my missing dart pipe. I
didn't dare even shift my eyes to look for it. My heart raced. This
was not what I had planned.

"Oh, this is nice," he said, his eyes going to the guard upon my
rug. "Is he dead?"

"No." I backed up a step. Where the devil was my pipe?

"The princess?" he questioned, moving forward to keep the same distance between us.

"Gone."

He nodded as if the news was neither unexpected nor bothering. "I like the red hair. And trousers?" He leered as if I was naked, and I felt as if I was. "I think I will dress you in them all the time. Such fun we will have, my play-pretty."

"You've lost, Garrett," I said with a false boldness. "The princess is gone. You can't marry me. The city knows the truth. Or at least part of it."

He shook his head, his dominating smile never faltering. "Why would I marry a whore's get when I have a beautiful woman of royal blood? She won't get far."

My legs turned to wet rags. Where was my pipe? I only had the one dart, but it was a metal one, carrying twice the venom; it would be enough for Garrett. I shifted backward to put more space between us as I fumbled at the knot holding my whip to me.

"What to do? What to do?" Garrett said in a singsong voice, stepping forward until his toes nudged the fallen guard. "Call for help, or kill you myself?" His jaw clenched and he reached for his sword hilt. "Oh, I do believe I'll kill you myself."

I thought of my taunts about his low worth, wishing I could take them all back. The sound of the metal sliding against the sheath paralyzed me. I froze where I stood. He had killed my parents. He could kill me just as easily. Where was my pipe?

Garrett took a sideways step, making a show of placing his foot. The sound of splintering wood cut through me like a pain. My pipe. "Oh," he said as he ground his heel. "Sorry. That was yours, wasn't it."

He unexpectedly took a deep breath and raised his sword high over his head, bringing it down like a pike into the helpless guard.

"No!" I shrieked, reaching out. Though unconscious, the man groaned as his belly was punctured. His eyes riveted to mine, Garrett twisted and pulled his sword free. I covered my mouth in horror as the guard's life spilled onto my rug. The stink of bile rose strong, choking me.

"Prince Garrett?" came a muffled inquiry from the hall.

"Stay out!" Garrett shouted at the locked door. His eyes were wild, the blue of them vivid against his yellow hair. "I'll kill the man who tries to get through that door!" He listened for a heartbeat, then flipped his hair back with a toss of his head. From the hall came a hushed argument. "Witnesses never remember things properly," he said calmly.

"No one deserves to die like that," I said, my voice quavering.

"I wouldn't expect a *commoner* to understand."

His barbs at my low birth meant nothing. If he had hoped to anger me, it wasn't working.

Eyes never leaving mine, Garrett crouched to take the dead man's sword. Flinging it into my bedchamber and out of my reach, he stepped over the guard. My heart pounded and I shook my whip out, the sliding hush as it coiled on the floor chilling me.

He paused in thought. "You don't know how to use that."

I licked my lips, trying to find enough spit to swallow. "Of course not."

His stance went casual, and he laughed. "Stupid woman. You're already dead. I have everything. The princess is very malleable. I only need to threaten an innocent to get her to do what I want." He smiled, licking his lips suggestively. "Anything."

Anger burned through my fear. "You won't touch her."

"Oh, I'll touch her," he said, eying my trembling hand. "I'll touch her all I want."

He lunged for me. Panicking, I flung my whip up and out, practice shifting me into a firmer stance. My muscles moved by rote. The crack shocked through me. I froze as Garrett cried out and lurched backward. He stumbled, never going completely down. Straightening, he touched his jaw, looking at his hand to find blood.

"You little trull!" he cried out, anger turning him pale and ugly. "You hit me!"

"I'm sorry," I said, my voice high-pitched and frantic. It was the most foolish thing I'd ever said. I'd never struck anyone before. "Stay back! Don't come any closer."

"No one hits me!" His hands clenched, and his teeth gritted. Blood dripping from his jawline, he took a step to me. Heart pounding, I extended my free hand, warning him to stop, but it was the rush of boots in the hall that stilled his feet.

"She's in there!" an approaching guard shouted.

I held my breath to keep from passing out as Garrett looked to the door.

"The false princess," he cried again. "They roped down from the third floor. She's in there."

"But Prince Garrett is in there!" the frightened guard gasped.

Garrett frowned, irritation pulling his brow into furrows. "Stay out!" he shouted, his eyes never moving from mine. "There's no one in here but me and . . . my love."

There was silence, followed by a buzz of intense, muted conversation.

"Captain Jeck," came a relieved cry from the hall, and Garrett's beautiful face twisted with a black rage. "Thank the Almighty you're here."

I locked gazes with Garrett as the sound of Jeck's running boots was eclipsed by the captain's shout, "Break it down! Now!"

There was a thunderous boom, and the door shivered. The doorframe shifted with a cracking splinter. Garrett's expression went furious. "Damn that farmer," he snarled. Wiping the blood from his jaw, he shouted through the door, "The man who lets Captain Jeck into this room will be quartered. And all of your heads will be on the wall tomorrow. Kill him!"

The hall went deadly silent. I imagined the exchange of nervous glances. It was eight of them by my reckoning to their captain's one. Even a player couldn't best eight men with swords. The silence ended with a fury-driven shout and the clang of blades.

Garrett straightened and smiled confidently, the bloodied score mark red against his freckled skin. "My late captain of the guard was never one to appreciate the precious time spent between a man and a woman," he mocked, having to raise his voice above the noise of battle in the hall. "He's always interrupting. Now, where were we? Ah, yes."

I backpedaled as he took three quick steps across the room. Again I sent my whip out. It scored on his arm, ripping his shirt. Jaw clenched, he swung his sword up into my next strike, and my whip coiled about his wrist.

"That's the bad thing about whips," he snarled. "They only work on animals and cowards!" He grabbed my whip and gave a firm yank.

A cry slipped from me. I dropped it lest he pull me into him. Red spots appeared on his cheeks, and he showed his teeth. "Come back here," he said, throwing it into a corner, and I ran for the shattered ruin of my dart tube. I fell beside the dead guard, grasping for the feel of metal among the slivers. My breath came in what sounded like a sob.

"Stand up so I can kill you properly." Garrett gripped my shoulder and pulled me up.

I twisted, trying to writhe away from him. Eyes fixed to his bloodied sword, I sent my free arm searching blindly behind me on my dressing table for anything. Bottles clattered and rolled. He drew back his sword arm, his eyes fervent.

"Let go!" I shrieked. My fingers found a perfume bottle. Gripping it, I swung at him. My closed fist hit him in the face. He loosened his hold and backed away. His look shifted to an affronted surprise. I threw the bottle at him. He ducked. It shattered on the floor. The smell of lilac overwhelmed the guard's blood and bile. Garrett felt his jaw, his expression growing murderous.

"You slattern!" he shouted over the sound of booming at the door.

Beyond him on the floor was the sheen of metal among my crushed dart pipe. I dove for it. My fingers fumbled in the splinters. My breath came in a gasp as I found the metal dart whole. Kneeling, I gripped it in my fist.

There was a thunderous boom as the bolt on my door gave way. My head jerked up. The door slammed into the wall. Jeck stood in the doorframe. His face was wrathful, and his jaw was set. Bodies lay beyond him, shifting in pained surges of motion. As I watched, a guard slumped against the wall and slid down to a crumpled heap atop his companions. Jeck had been using them as a battering ram.

Fear gave me strength. I lunged to the window. Jeck couldn't catch me! I'd risk the fall.

"I told you to stay out!" Garrett snarled.

"No!" Jeck shouted. "Prince Garrett! Get away from her!"

A hand gripped my shoulder and spun me around. Garrett crushed my back to his front, his arm wrapped around my neck. I grasped his wrist, trying to pull it away so I could breathe. He backed to the wall, dragging me. His breath filled my ear in heavy pants. His sword was pressed into my side. I closed my eyes, remembering the sound of the guard's clothing tearing. The memory of the knife across my mother's throat pulled tears from my eyes.

"I'm going to kill her, Captain," Garrett shouted, and my eyes opened. "Get out so I don't have to kill you as well."

Jeck stopped in apparent indecision. Beyond him in the hall, the moans became calls for help. My pulse hammered. Panting, I shifted my fingers to show Jeck the dart I had pressed against Prince Garrett's arm wrapped about my neck. A smile came over me when Jeck saw it and his face went still in understanding.

"Close the door, if you would?" I asked, seeming to be Garrett's prisoner, but in reality it was the other way around. "Or he dies. Right here."

Garrett laughed, squeezing my neck until it hurt. I gritted my teeth, and my fingers trembled, threatening to stab him.

"Wait," Jeck said, putting a hand up. "I have an idea."

Still not seeing his danger, Garrett snickered. "I don't pay you to think, Captain," he said. "She's worth nothing now but to my pride, and my pride will see her dead."

"The door?" I asked calmly though I was shaking inside.

Not taking his eyes from mine, Jeck nudged a guard's foot clear and shut the door.

"Bar it with your sword," I said, "and move away from it." And he did.

Garrett's grip on me faltered. "What the devil are you doing?" he asked Jeck. "Get out! Get out, or I'll have you strung up for sedition. The princess is on the grounds. Go find her, if you think you can manage it."

Jeck frowned, sending a leather-gloved hand over his beard. "You're making it very difficult for me to justify keeping you alive, Prince Garrett."

"Kill me?" he exclaimed, his breath shifting my hair. "I'm the one with the sword!"

Jeck's eyes narrowed. "And you're the one with the poisoned dart to your pulse—fool."

Garrett's breath was a quick intake of fear. He tensed to pull away, and I gripped his arm until my knuckles turned white.

"Don't move," I whispered, and the smell of his fear rose over the scent of lilac and bile from the dead guard. "Drop your sword."

"Drop your needle, sea whore," Garrett said. "Or I'll run you through right now."

Jeck shook his head. "That's my blade, Prince Garrett. It's a bone crusher. It doesn't have a fine enough edge to cut without a full swing behind it, and she knows it."

"Damn you all to hell!" Garrett shouted. "Get her off of me, Captain!"

I pushed my fingernail into him, and his breath quickened in fear. My back, pressed against his front, felt damp from his sweat. If he tried, he might get away, but I didn't think he would risk it. He'd already tasted the poison once. "Drop it," I said, and the blade hit the floor with a thunk. I took a shallow breath. "Let go of my neck." He did.

Easing myself away from his stink of fear, I shifted until I was behind him and had my dart to his neck. He held himself stiffly. His blood beat hard and fast. Striking him here would go right to his brain. He would drop in seconds, die almost as quick. "I'm listening, Captain Jeck," I said. "Though as you said, it's getting harder to put this off."

Jeck stood in the center of my sitting room, his toes edging the dead guard. "I'd just as soon see him dead, but there's no reason to kill him now and several to let him live."

Garrett took a shuddering breath. "You traitorous dog!" he exclaimed. "I'll have you before my father, and his wolves will rip your insides out!"

"Shut your mouth," I said, then softer to Jeck, "I promised to kill him, and I will."

Jeck smiled. It was an honest smile, very much like the first one I had seen from that very spot. "Let him live with the memory you beat him."

"Nothing I've done means anything," I said bitterly. "Not until I kill him."

Jeck shook his head. "You've convinced me you can keep what you hold," he said. "The rest will follow my lead."

I bit my lip, wondering if I could trust him. It sounded too easy. "The royals, then," I insisted, knowing Garrett was hearing too much, but he was going to die, so it didn't matter. "They'll tear Costenopolie apart if I let Garrett get away with killing my parents."

Jeck's face went grim. "It's always a risk, but—ah—no one of import will be actively plotting against you. If you kill Garrett, though, it will be impossible for me to keep King Edmund where he belongs. Thinking you can convince him you were justified in killing his son is a delusion. No matter how stupid Garrett is, he is still his son. It will start the war you wanted to prevent. You know it. That's why you didn't kill him the first time."

"But he murdered them," I protested. My grip shifted as I remembered he had buried them in the garden like animals. Garrett caught his breath, and the point pricked his skin, not breaking it. "They're gone," I said, hearing a plaintive, hurt tone in my voice and wishing I could keep it from me.

Jeck's eyes went cold behind his black beard. "Yes. They're dead when they could have lived for years more. But to make a kingdom suffer for your want for revenge? You've won, Tess. Don't make the next game take place on the battlefield."

Anger filled me, and Garrett gasped as I gripped him tighter. "You're telling me that revenge is wrong," I said. "That I should be above it, to let him live. Well I can't! I can't let him live, Jeck. I can't!"

Jeck raised his hands in placation. "Easy, Tess. You aren't listening. I'm the last person to tell you revenge is a wasted emotion. It's sweet and warm, and for a time, it was the only thing that kept me going. But there's quick revenge that's fast and ultimately unsatisfying, or there's the lasting, sticky-sweet honey revenge." He cocked his eyebrows, and Garrett's breath shuddered. "There are ways to wreak revenge other than death, and some can serve a purpose."

I hesitated, surprised he seemed to understand. My thoughts went back to our night together before his fire and him telling me of his past. "What do you suggest?" I said, hearing my voice as if it wasn't my own.

"Don't kill him. He's worthless."

"I am a prince!" Garrett shouted. "If you harm me, my father will descend upon you. Your homes will be burned. Your ships sunk. Your—"

"Shut your mouth," I said. I could smell his sweat and knew he was afraid.

Jeck clasped his hands behind his back. A faint smile hovered on him. "There are worse fates than death," he said. "And Garrett has made a very large, embarrassing mistake. If you let him live, he will be sent home in disgrace like a boy pilfering apples from a neighbor's grove." I felt Garrett stiffen. "Beaten by Costenopolie's false princess? A child from the gutter? I've walked King Edmund's halls, and Tess, it will be a living hell."

I hesitated, hearing the truth in what he said, but my soul begged me to not listen, to just kill him and deal with the consequences later.

"King Edmund has a third son," Jeck said. "He isn't a man of action but a son nonetheless. If your princess will consider him—"

"Alexander!" Garrett exploded. "You can't call Alexander a man. He's a worthless—"

"Shut your mouth!" I shouted. I tossed a curl of red hair from my eyes as my topknot slowly fell apart. "I wouldn't have one Misdev dog in my palace. Why would I trust another?"

Jeck shifted eagerly. "The union between Misdev and Costenopolie—"

My eyes widened. "This is to save your hide!" I interrupted. "If you go back to King Edmund with a dead prince, he will demote you to where you can't effectively play."

"Play . . ." Garrett whispered.

Jeck straightened, glancing uncomfortably at Garrett. "Tess . . ." he warned.

"That's if he doesn't outright kill you," I continued hotly, not caring that Garrett was hearing more than he should. "Here's my idea. I kill Garrett, and the princess won't wed at all. The Red Moon Princess will stay unwed, and that damned prophesy won't mean anything!"

Jeck's expression was open and honest. "You're right. I'm looking out for myself, and that could work, but Tess . . ." His words took on a conspiratorial tone, and I met his sly gaze. "Consider how strong we could be together. Misdev and Costenopolie can still make an official alliance by marriage as Kavenlow intended through King Edmund's youngest son. I've studied your master's past games. He does nothing without a reason. He sees farther ahead then I am used to. Just look what he saw in you. But now?" His smile went devious. "I see what he intended here. I wish he could have approached me openly, but I never would have trusted him. Killing Garrett will limit you to one option, and you don't want war. I've seen it, Tess. It will kill you slowly."

Garrett shifted under my fingers. "You think you rule us," he said in wonder. "The captain of the guard and a changeling think they rule us!"

I frowned, wishing there was another way to do this. Jeck took a small step forward, and I tightened my grip on Garrett, my fingers going slippery with his sweat.

"Your ships and harbors?" Jeck said. "My fields and men? No one would dare raise a finger to either of us. Your people would be free to extend their reach by commerce, and my people could devote themselves to working the land as they want instead of sending their young men to die in constant battle. And if the need ever arose for a force on the land, you would have a group of very easily trained men only a few weeks away. But for even a chance of it working, you can't kill Garrett."

Garrett trembled in his desire to move, knowing it would mean his death. "Players," he whispered. "I've heard of you," he said, his voice rising. "We will ferret you out and crush you as we did five hundred years ago!"

That didn't sound good, and I tightened my grip. "He knows too much. I have to kill him."

"Tess," Jeck protested. "Killing a pawn doesn't make you strong. Forging a peaceful union does. And that's what Garrett has made himself into. He has gone from a knight to a pawn in his failure. It's your decision, your move, but the way you win this game decides how the next will be set up."

Hands clasped behind himself, Jeck took a symbolic step backward. I hesitated, thinking. The pain in my soul demanded vengeance, that Garrett shouldn't be able to feel the sun when my parents no longer could. But knowing he had been beaten by a woman, one not of royal birth but a guttersnipe, would prey upon him. Having everything taken from him by a child from the streets might . . . be enough.

An unexpected relief came over me. My breath whispered out, and my shoulders eased. Jeck saw my decision to let Garrett live, and the tension slipped from him. "Alexander?" I asked.

"No," Garrett said, panic staining his beautiful voice. "You can't do that to me."

I smiled. He would be remembered as the pathetic son who tried to start a war and escaped with his life. The one who could have had everything but was beaten by a beggar's child. Jeck was right. Revenge made a warm spot that couldn't be put out.

"There will have to be a long courtship," I said. "I'll not rush her."

"Of course. I expect nothing else."

"And there will be the understanding I can back out at any time, right up to the I dos," I continued, not moving my dart from Garrett. "And if you are lying to me, I'll see you dead."

"As is always a woman's right," Jeck acknowledged, inclining his head.

His brown eyes glinted in the shine from the lamps, and I wasn't sure if he was commenting on backing out of a marriage or a woman's right to kill the one who wronged her. "So, how do we end this?" I asked. "You still have the palace."

Clearly pleased, Jeck raised a finger like a lecturing nobleman. We froze at the sudden cries in the hall. "Get the door open!" someone shouted.

Garrett twisted, gripping my hand with the dart and forcing it away from him. I cried out when bones ground together and pain flamed. "Stop!" I shrieked. He pushed me from him as my hand opened and the dart dropped to the floor. I hunched over my wrist and backed away, terrified, as he scooped up his sword.

"I'll kill you both," he snarled. "I will be king!"

Jeck pulled his sword from the door in a beautiful arc of motion, leaping to stand between Prince Garrett and me. *It was all for nothing,* I thought miserably as I held my numbed hand to me. *All for nothing.*

But it was Kavenlow who burst in, trailing a handful of dirty, smelly, unshaven, barefoot Costenopolie guards.

"No!" Garrett cried, diving at me.

"Stop him!" I cried, seeing the shimmer of my dart in his hand. Feinting with the sword, Garrett drove the fire-hardened needle through Jeck's jerkin. Jeck stumbled back. He fell to the floor, clutching his chest. Garrett shouted and leapt at me. His bloodied sword gleamed red.

I stood, horrified, as Jeck lay still on the floor. I couldn't move, couldn't take my eyes from Jeck, though Garrett was coming at me. The guards dove for Garrett, bringing him down three feet before me by sheer weight of numbers.

Terrified, I ran to Jeck. He wasn't moving. Had he put himself at the edge of his tolerance to best me, making this a killing dose? *He has to be all right,* I thought frantically. He had to be.

"Jeck!" I cried, falling to my knees before him. "Jeck! Look at me!"

His eyes cracked open, and I slumped. He swallowed and waved his fingers weakly. "I'm all right. Give me a minute. Damn, you pack a punch, woman."

Immeasurably relieved, I pulled my gaze up from his, finding Kavenlow watching me with an amazed surprise. I opened my mouth to explain, then shut it, shocked to realize I cared if Captain Jeck lived or died. Confused, I got to my feet and left him on the floor. Two guards descended upon him, pulling him roughly to his feet. I reached out in protest, then forced my hands to my side.

Duncan's low voice drifted into the room. ". . . and then he slammed the one with the pike into the wall headfirst. It made a dent the size of my fist." His lanky frame came to a halt in the doorframe, and he stared in at the chaos. Behind him was Resh, the captain of my father's guard. "Angel's Spit!" Duncan swore. Then his eyes rose to mine. "Tess!" Surging in, he moved through the guards as if unseen. He took my hand to pull me toward him, and I yelped.

"No, I'm all right," I protested as he leaned close, holding my arm carefully to look at my hand. His fingers were stained with rust and dirt. "Ow. Let it go," I insisted as I glanced at his bruised face. "It's all right."

"It's not all right," Duncan said, his breath warm on my hand. "I think it's broken." His gaze went hard and he looked at Jeck hanging in the guards' grip. "Did he do this to you?"

"No," I said. "Prince Garrett did. And it's all right. See?" Steeling myself, I tried to close my fingers. Nausea and relief swept me as they moved as they should. I looked up, my eyes probing his. "You're a thief," I whispered. "Only a thief could have done that."

He stiffened, then relaxed. A flash of hidden promise flickered behind his eyes. "Only if you're an assassin," he said.

Flustered, I pulled my hand from him.

"Get off me!" Garrett shouted, his voice muffled. "Give me my sword. They're traitors to the crown. Both of them. They rule, not the kings! It's a sham! A conspiracy! Get off!"

I glanced at Kavenlow with a sick look. He was grim, accepting Garrett's sword when someone brought it to him. "Let him up," Kavenlow said, his tired gaze going over the room. I watched his lips move as he counted the number of people. There were a lot, and all would need their memories clouded. He gave Jeck an angry grimace as if he should have known better. I got an exasperated sigh.

My face went cold at the princess's lyrical voice in the hall. She above all shouldn't hear what Garrett was saying. Kavenlow leaned toward a guard. "Keep her out of here," he said, his eyes falling to the dead guard on my rug. "She ought not see this."

The guard nodded and left. There was a murmur, and the princess's voice rang out, "My sister is in there. You said the room was secure; let me through."

Eyes wide, I looked at Kavenlow. "Get out," he mouthed. But I wasn't fast enough, and before I had pulled from Duncan, the princess entered with Thadd tight behind her. Her eyes went wide at the guard dead upon my floor, then filled with relief as she found me.

"She's a fraud!" Garrett said, spittle flying as he struggled to free himself from the two guards restraining him. "A fraud!" He started laughing. The high-pitched sound made my skin crawl. "The farmer," he gasped, "and the dock whore. They rule. Not you." He pointed a finger at the princess and laughed hysterically. "She doesn't rule. The whore does. You're a fraud. My father is a fraud. We're all frauds. The farmer rules. The farmer rules us all!"

I stared in dismay at Garrett laughing, held up only by the guards supporting him. Kavenlow couldn't cloud so firm a thought. I glanced at Jeck and read the truth of it. If we couldn't shut him up, he would have to die or risk us all being exposed.

I bit my lip in dismay. Garrett couldn't die. It would ruin everything!

The princess stood with her hand over her mouth as Prince Garrett laughed. He nearly pulled the guards down as they struggled to keep him upright. "He's mad," she said, her eyes wide in a fortunate misunderstanding. "He is utterly mad! First he kills my parents, then takes over the palace, and now he thinks my kingdom is ruled by a farmer!"

I blinked. My gaze shifted between Kavenlow and Jeck. Prince Garrett was mad? That would work. Sent home in disgrace as mad. He would never be taken seriously again. Garrett's life would be a living hell. The warm spot in me grew brighter.

The princess lifted her skirts to delicately sidestep the dead guard, the most disturbing thing being that the sight of a disemboweled man upon my rug didn't faze her at all. Her face was severe as she settled herself before me, her white dress somehow still spotless. *Chu pits, how does she do it?*

"You didn't listen to me," she accused. "I told you to follow me. You disobeyed the very first order I gave you. It was the very first order I gave anyone."

I shifted uncomfortably, caught in my lie. It didn't matter I was taller than her; I still felt like a child. "I was going to," I said. "After I made the palace safe for you—ah—Your Highness."

She smiled. All her ire drifted to nothing. "As if I could ever be angry with you, Tess. Come on. There's a fire in our parents' room. Let me look at your hand in the light. I often helped the nuns heal the lame and bury the destitute."

She took my arm and led me out. Duncan had Thadd's elbow, pulling the reluctant sculptor into a corner to tell him of his battle. I passed Kavenlow, his desire to demand an explanation from me heavy on him. I ignored Jeck's worried frown for whether I would hold to our agreement. It could wait. They all could wait. It would do the men good.

The air in the hallway was cool, and the Costenopolie guards had moved the battered Misdev men somewhere. "Put the captain in my old cell," I heard the captain of my father's guard say, and I drew to a stop.

"Please, Princess Contessa," I said, stumbling over the words. "Captain Jeck—this isn't his fault. He tried to protect me from Prince Garrett—at the end."

She smiled to look like our mother. "Call me Contessa," she said. "I hate the princess part, and since you're the only one who has the right to call me by my real name, I wish you would." She looked back into the room. "Captain Jeck is to be confined to a stateroom as well as Prince Garrett. The captain treated me with the utmost civility when he took me prisoner, and I will return his kindness. I want to hear what Tess says concerning what happened before I decide anything. Keep the palace gates manned from a distance. I don't want the streets to know what has happened until I do." She took my arm, her eyes worried. "Tess, I need your help in finding a way to tell my neighbor his son is insane."

Kavenlow caught my gaze and smiled. I couldn't help but grin back as the princess escorted me down the halls that were once again mine.

Thirty-five

❖

"Will you rattle your teacup a mite softer? You're going to wake her," Kavenlow said, his voice slipping from the next room and into my sleep to stir me awake.

"But the morning is almost gone," Duncan complained, his tone more conniving than respectful. "She's got to see them. If she waits, they might take them down."

Kavenlow chuckled. "They won't come down until she says so. She's behind them somehow. I know it."

Curiosity pulled my eyes open. "Behind what?" I shouted, staring at my wall. My beautiful barren white wall with no dirt or leaves or sticks.

"Tess!" Duncan called from my sitting room. "Get dressed. It's almost noon. Hurry up. You have an appointment with the princess."

I flung the heavy covers from me. I'd never slept so late. But then I'd been up half the night: ferreting out Prince Garrett's guards, freeing the cook and sentries from under Banner, telling Kavenlow of the agreement I'd come to with Jeck. "An appointment?" I called as I splashed tepid water on my face. "I didn't make an appointment."

"The princess did," Kavenlow said dryly. "She is slipping

into her new role with a frightening sureness. Put on something nice."

He sounded irate, and I dressed quickly, arranging my hair with my usual darts and a new dart pipe Kavenlow had given me. I fingered the bullwhip, then left it on my bedside table. It had failed me; the darts hadn't. The back of my dress half-undone, I went to the doorway of my sitting room to find Duncan and Kavenlow resting companionably at my small table.

Duncan had found his tattered boots, and his heels were among the empty dishes and plates strewn before them. Kavenlow gazed wearily out my window to the mangled gardens. A cow ambled across my line of vision, a sight both disturbing and amusing. There was a new colorful rug where the Misdev guard had been, and the scented candle still burned to cover the lingering smell of death. It struck me how easily the permanence of death could be covered up.

"Could one of you lace my dress for me?" I said, and they both started.

"Sit," Kavenlow said darkly to Duncan as the thief pulled his feet from the table.

Embarrassed, I turned so Kavenlow could reach the laces. He tugged gently as he moved upward, leaving me more room to breathe than Heather ever did. *Heather,* I thought. I'd send a runner for her. She was probably worried sick. "Thank you," I said as he finished.

He made a soft noise of agreement. "Sleep well?" he asked and held a chair for me.

"Yes, thank you." As I sat, his ring, still on its cord about my neck, swung into my sight. Eyes crinkled, I pulled it up and over my head. "I forgot to give this to you last night," I said, extending it toward him on my palm.

Kavenlow eased himself into his chair. Smiling from behind his graying beard, he reached across the table. The ring disappeared into his thick hands. "Thank you." He cut the cord with his dagger and replaced the band of gold on his finger, clearly relieved.

Duncan looked between us, clearly knowing something had happened but not what. His shirt was hanging out from the rope holding up his trousers, and his boots had clearly not seen oil in quite some time. With that nasty attempt at a beard, he looked like a vagabond. There was nothing in him of the dangerous man

I'd seen in the cells below the guard's quarters, even if his eyes were glinting rather roguishly. I wondered if I had imagined his hidden strength in the heat of the moment.

The light glinted on Kavenlow's ring as he poured a cup of long-cold tea for me. "If you will excuse me, Princess Contessa wanted to know when you awoke. She has requested to see you at your earliest convenience." His eyes tightened in warning. "That means now, Tess."

I nodded and sipped my tea. Saint's bells, but she could wait until I had breakfast.

"There's to be a coronation this afternoon in the city square," Kavenlow continued as he stood. "The official one will be during the summer festival when her neighbors will be here."

A coronation instead of a wedding. It would be the grandest event I'd ever plan. I would make Contessa shine. No gypsies, though.

"Other than that, your day is yours. I suggest you stay clear of the streets for a while."

Wincing at his wry tone, I took an apple from a bowl. I did have to collect my horses.

"I'll see you at supper, Duncan," Kavenlow said. He gave me a nod and left, having to use two hands to shift the door since it hung loose on its hinges.

Duncan waved a careless hand in dismissal and continued to shove cold toast into his mouth. The silence grew, and I became uncomfortable. Though the door was cracked ajar, I'd never had anyone alone with me in my room but for Heather and Kavenlow. I wasn't the crown princess. It was the small things that would likely take the longest to get used to.

"How's Tuck?" I asked, knowing Duncan had spent the night in the stables with his horse. It was his choice, not anyone's request.

"Fine," he said brightly around a mouthful, then swallowed. "He needed a solid brushing. And he's thin. That captain all but starved him on the way back." He hesitated as if I might say something, and when I didn't, he added, "but he's all right."

The tea was too cold to enjoy. Setting it aside, I tucked the apple into a draping sleeve for my new gelding. It was my first official day as a commoner; I didn't know what to do.

"So how about it?" Duncan asked.

I looked up in bewilderment. "How about what?"

"You're done." He propped his heels on the table and clasped his hands behind his head. "You saved the princess, rescued the kingdom, blah, blah, blah . . . Are you coming with me?"

Surprised, I straightened in my chair. "I—uh—thought you would stay."

Duncan shook his head, not looking at me. "No." A hint of shadow was in his voice, a hue of power, a whisper of a past unshared. It was there. I hadn't imagined it.

I slowly let out my breath. "I can't," I said, stifling a shiver when I found I was tempted.

He took his heels from the table and leaned across it. The brown of his eyes fixed on me. I knew he saw my fluster, and as I watched, his mien of capable but friendly cheat dissolved to leave a dangerous man I knew nothing about. "Why not?" he asked, his voice soft.

"I—I told you," I stammered. "I won't make my way by stealing."

"I'm not asking you to." The intensity in his tone pulled my gaze up. "You can do people's books, or write their letters for them, or nothing at all. You don't ever have to play another hand with me. I like you, Tess. I want you to come with me."

"Contessa needs me," I said, then my breath caught. "Y-you like me?"

Leaning back in his chair, he picked up the last piece of toast. His air of bound portent vanished like one of his cards. "Well, yeah," he said lightly. "I'm still here, aren't I?" He shoved the wedge of toast into his mouth and rose. He held out his hand, then drew it back and wiped it on the back of his trousers. "I want to show you something," he said as he extended it.

I stared. It was gone. He had let slip enough of his true danger to pique my interest, then hid it away. My words to Heather resonated in my mind. *A man of power, not necessarily wealth.* Saint's bells, I was a fool. A very confused fool who couldn't hide behind being a princess anymore.

Swallowing, I took his hand, not wanting to let him know how muddled I was. His grip was warm in mine, the calluses on his fingers soft. I remembered their strength on my shoulder and neck, and a warm tingle rose through me. "What is it?" I said as I got to my feet.

"You can see it from your window."

Curiosity overwhelmed caution, and I let him draw me to the window. He left his hand upon my shoulder as he stood behind me. My breath caught as I saw the city.

Flags. The city was draped with flags. From the tops of the buildings to the lower spires of the church, they hung from walls, and roofs, and trees. And they were all alike: gold with three black bars slashing diagonally across them. "Captain Borlett's flag!" I exclaimed, tearing my gaze away to look over my shoulder at Duncan. "Is he here? But how?" Amazed, I leaned forward to scan the harbor and the paltry few ships resting there. "And why?"

There was a scuffing behind me. I didn't turn, recognizing Kavenlow's grumble as he edged around my broken door. He settled behind me, and Duncan's hand slid away with a reluctant slowness. "We thought you might be able to tell us what they meant," Kavenlow said.

I shook my head, at a loss for words. Apart from the flag atop the *Sandpiper* there was only the one in my pack. And Heather had that. "Heather!" I cried, my gaze on the distant blur of streets. "Heather must have found Captain Borlett's flag in my things. I told her to rally support for me. To tell the people the truth, that I didn't run away. She must have told them to fly it so I would know they believed me. They believe me!" I said, elated. I stared at the scores of banners unfurled in the morning breeze, each one a shout that I was trusted, that my word was good enough for them.

"Of course they believe you," Kavenlow said gruffly. "Did you honestly think they would believe a Misdev prince?"

I suppose not," I said as I turned. "But look at all of them . . ."

Kavenlow made a worried sound. "Yes. I was going to put the crown on Contessa this afternoon, but perhaps you should so everyone sees you accept her as your sovereign."

"Yes, all right," I said, not really caring. I looked past Kavenlow at the scraping of boots in the hallway. It was a sentry. After over a week in a cell, his clothes hung loosely upon him, but he was clean-shaven and alert. "Kavenlow? Princess?" he said as he came to stand apologetically just inside the broken doorway. "They are ready for you."

"Of course." Kavenlow reached for my arm. So did Duncan. Kavenlow frowned and physically removed Duncan's hand from me. "It's a private audience," he said without a trace of apology, and Duncan shrugged good-naturedly. He remained with the guard when we left. It occurred to me that Duncan, a self-proclaimed cheat and probable thief, was in the unique position of being known by all the palace guards. Having freed them, he had their trust and could breeze freely into every part of the palace as if invisible. I wasn't sure that was entirely a good thing.

The hallway had been washed clean of last night's ugliness. The news of our retaking of the palace had gone out this morning, and from the looks of it, most of the usual palace staff was back. Every window was open, and the cool spring air swept to the corners. A bowl of uneaten, untrampled flowers was at the end of the hall. *Violets. My favorite.*

"Have you talked with Captain Jeck?" I asked as we went down the first stairs.

"Yes," he said, lips barely moving. "I don't like going into an alliance this openly. Trust doesn't come easily to me, Tess. Watch him closely."

I went silent, concerned. I had no delusions that Jeck's motives in saving Prince Garrett's life were anything other than to keep his own hide intact. Still, we were coming out of this better than I could have imagined. "Didn't he help you cloud Garrett's thoughts?" I asked.

Kavenlow ran a hand down his tidy beard in worry. "Captain Jeck and I worked until nearly sunrise under the guise of interrogating Prince Garrett. Neither one of us is good at manipulating memories. All we managed was to shift a few key thoughts so he appears to be more insane than a man lost at sea. There will be no breach of confidence."

"Good," I said, relieved. I didn't want the question of broken rules hanging over me. We continued throughout the palace, making brief greetings and assuring the staff that we were well. My face went cold as I found myself in the hallway leading to the solarium. "Why here?" I said, pulling Kavenlow to a halt before the guards standing at the door.

Kavenlow's eyes were sad. "It's all right, Tess. This is where she feels most at home. The garden is duplicated at the convent. Except the statues there are of you."

Surprised, I let myself be led in. My tension eased at the changes. The round table where my parents had died was gone.

Even the paving stones had been torn up, replaced with new plants too small for the space. I had been to my parents' grave last night with Banner, explaining everything to them by torch and moonlight, asking for their forgiveness. If it were up to me, I'd consecrate the ground and let them rest among the laurels and ivy.

Kavenlow led me to a distant corner where the sun shone dappled through large potted trees. The princess sat with Thadd at a table, her long, fair hair falling freely to rest amongst their clasped hands as they discussed a topic known only to them. The sculptor had shoes now, and a new shirt. It looked tight, but I was willing to wager it was the only thing to be found on such short notice to fit him. Several aides stood nearby, following their practice of staying in the background. I waved my fingers at them and got happy smiles in return.

My pulse quickened as I found Jeck standing a small distance apart. Though his Misdev uniform was clean, he looked irate. He had on his gaudy monstrosity of a hat, making him look foolish despite his trim and powerful build. Too many guards stood by him. He wore no chains, but he had no sword, either. I touched my hip where a sword would hang, and he shrugged.

The princess looked up when Kavenlow cleared his throat. "Tess," she called eagerly, and my heart ached at how much she sounded like our mother. "Come and sit. I've been waiting."

"Good morning, Princess. I trust you slept well," I said formally.

"Oh, don't," she almost moaned as she indicated a chair to her other side. "I am so sick of that I could throw my chamber pot out the window. Please talk normally to me? I can take it from the guards and such, but not you."

I grinned and nodded in understanding as the aides shifted uncomfortably. And whereas I always had to bow to proper decorum, she had a capital-fine excuse to ignore it, being raised by wolves, so to speak. The next few months were going to be rather interesting as she met her neighbors. "Good morning, Contessa," I amended. "Sleep well?"

Sighing in relief, she bobbed her head to look artlessly alluring.

Captain Jeck took a step forward to help me with my chair. The nearest guard half pulled his sword in response, and Jeck fell back in exasperation. Thadd got to his feet as Kavenlow helped me with my chair. All the men remained standing, Kavenlow pointedly putting himself between the princess and Captain Jeck.

"Thank you for coming to see me, Tess. I just don't know what to do," the princess said as she resettled herself, and I cringed inside at her admitting it where others could overhear. Maybe being a bumpkin princess might not be such a good idea.

Seeing my face, her eyes widened and she flushed. "I find myself in a somewhat tight spot, and I would like your advice," she amended, making her words clear and precise. She managed a courtly accent, and I wondered if she had been practicing. "I can't marry Prince Garrett. But if I remain husbandless, I remain an enticing target for the next Red Moon Prophesy assassin."

The guards stiffened, and Kavenlow frowned. "That won't happen, Princess," he said.

"I would hope not," she said tartly, then winced as she recognized she had misspoken again. "Perhaps," she added mildly. "But it's something I need to consider." Her blue eyes, so much like Father's, were confused, and I felt a wash of pity. It was easier to die from a prophesy than live with it.

"I talked with Prince Garrett this morning," she said. "The man is completely insane. There's not a breath of reason in him."

Kavenlow eased back a step. "I'm pleased you have agreed to begin a dialog with King Edmund's youngest son," he said to Contessa.

The princess's gaze on mine faltered as Thadd took a pained-sounding breath. "It is my duty to wed. I understand that," she whispered.

Jeck stepped forward. A guard reached out and pulled him back. Giving him a black look, Captain Jeck brushed the man's hand from him. "I believe you will find Prince Alexander to be an equitable match, Princess. May I be blunt?" He hesitated, then at her solemn nod, he added, "Prince Alexander has refused to consider taking a wife since he became fond of a commoner woman. Until now his father hasn't cared. That's going to change. I would wager Prince Alexander won't be opposed to a royal joining if he was allowed to, ah, bring his mistress with him."

Contessa stiffened, spots of color appearing on her sun-starved cheeks. "Have a courtesan under my roof?" she said loudly. "Eating my food? Bedding my husband?"

I put a hand to my forehead and closed my eyes in a strength-gathering blink. Did the woman lack even a hint of polish? She sounded like a fishwife who had caught her husband pinching the tavern barmaid.

"Your *legal* husband, Your Highness," Jeck said, amusement hinted behind his carefully blank face. "It would leave you free to find your own company."

Contessa bit her lip, and I vowed to never do the same again. It made her look like a girl. The blush that rose to turn her face red didn't make her look any more mature either.

"It's done more often than not, Princess," Kavenlow offered in a low voice. "It's a lucky few who marry for love, even among the meanest of your streets."

Her eyes were on her clasped hands, ignoring Thadd's distress. "I would like to meet Prince Alexander," she said hesitantly. "I will have a letter for him when Prince Garrett returns to Misdev."

"Of course," Kavenlow said, easing back in relief. "I'll see to the travel arrangements myself. Is next week too late for your liking? I would see the palace secure before I go."

"Go!" I exclaimed. I was the only one in the room who would dare interrupt either of them, and I was going to take full advantage of it. "You can't go."

Kavenlow's eyebrows rose in warning. "Someone has to accompany them to be sure they reach their borders safely, Tess."

"Yes," the princess said. "I agree. But you, Chancellor Kavenlow, will be staying here."

Kavenlow froze. I thought it was in shock. I couldn't be sure, since I had never seen the emotion on him before. "Princess?" he almost stammered.

Contessa smiled, turning herself into an angel that rivaled the surrounding statues. "The Chancellor's place is in the palace with his books and ink, not running my errands. I'll rely upon your advice, and I see no reason to change something that worked so well for my parents." Grief furrowed her brow at the thought of them. "Tess will escort Captain Jeck and Prince Garrett to their holdings as my ambassador."

My breath caught and my mouth dropped open. *Me?*

The princess was beaming. "Look, Thadd," she said, gripping

his arm and shifting in her seat in a pleased excitement. "Duncan was right. She can hardly wait."

"But . . ." I stammered, thinking, *Duncan? Duncan had talked to her? The snake! The devious, contriving, clever, wonderful, snake!* This was all a plot to get me out of the palace. "But I can't!" I said, wanting to shout out I would. "I said I'd help you!"

"Oh, Tess," she pleaded as she reached across the table with our mother's grace and took my hands. "Please be my ambassador. You'll be my ears and eyes. You'll carry my decisions and speak for me before kings and queens. You will have the courtesies and authority that you're used to and will be treated with respect." Her smile turned wry. "I imagine it will be like being the princess without the responsibilities."

I looked at Kavenlow. His face was creased with irritation. Contessa drew my attention back as she gave my hands a squeeze. "Tell me you will accompany Captain Jeck and Prince Garrett back to Misdev?" she asked. "Take the king my regrets. Explain what happened, that we're sorry, and would like to inquire as to the health of his son Alexander?" Her gaze flicked to Captain Jeck. Whispering, she added, "And when eyes aren't on you, cast about for any hint of betrayal. You're so suited for it, with your palace manners and," she hesitated, her eyes flicking to my topknot, "unique abilities."

Elated, I nodded. No walls. No doilies. New places to buy things. "Yes. Thank you, Contessa. I would be honored."

A distant commotion from the halls brought the sentries to a bristle, but I brightened as I recognized Captain Borlett's voice. He was here? He should be halfway to Lovrege by now.

"Leave me sitting in the hall all the morning while my flag is fastened to every last standard," he said loudly, as yet unseen. "I have a thing or two to put in your princess's ear I do, concerning the right and lawful property of a free man. That's my flag. And I'll not have anyone take it because it goes well with her burning hair."

He turned the corner, escorted by two sentries. Bluster and bother had reddened his round face, and his frazzled beard was more scattered than usual. Eyes flashing, he took in the princess and the score of guards. His anger vanished, and he snatched his faded hat from his head. "Uh, Your Highness," he said gruffly, his eyes fixed on her as he bobbed in an unaccustomed bow.

"Excuse my impertinence, ma'am. And I beg your pardon, but why is my flag waving from atop your tower?"

Contessa opened her mouth, and I leaned close. "You can't talk to him until you're introduced," I prompted.

"Oh," she murmured, clearly embarrassed. She turned to Thadd. "Please introduce us so I may address him," she said, squaring her shoulders to find an air of formality.

Before Thadd could move, I rose. "I'll do it," I said. "I know Captain Borlett."

"Tess?" The wrinkles about Captain Borlett's eyes deepened as he recognized me. Hands outstretched in greeting, he stepped forward only to be blocked by the sentries.

"Leave him be," I said irately. "Not everyone is trying to kill me." I pushed the sentries aside and took his hands, beaming into his startled eyes. I could smell the sea on him, and I breathed it in like a balm. "Captain, you have no idea how good it is to see you again. But I thought you were going to Lovrege."

Captain Borlett shifted his gaze from the princess to me, his eyes lingering on my red hair and my black eye. "I had to deliver my books before I was beached. But what are you doing here? Was it you who put up my flag?"

I grinned. "I think it was a member of my old court. I'm sorry. It was an accident. She found it in my things, and knowing I would recognize it, had the city put it up to show their belief that I didn't run away."

He bobbed his head in understanding, then he paused. "Your parents," he said. "That would mean . . ." His eyes grew wide and his fingers gripped his hat all the tighter. "The burning princess did my books. I made the burning princess sleep on my floor. Oh, Your Highness. If you would have said anything . . ."

Delighted at his fluster, I took his elbow and led him forward. "Princess Contessa of Costenopolie, I would be honored to introduce you to Captain Borlett of the *Sandpiper*. It was because of his fast ship and skillful reading of the wind that I was able to reach you before, ah," I glanced at Jeck, "anyone else," I finished.

Captain Borlett shifted his work-stained hat from one hand to another. "Your Highness. Forgive my harsh words earlier concerning my paltry flag. If you want it, I'll find another."

The princess glanced at me, and at my subtle prompting, she extended her hand.

"Take it," I whispered to Captain Borlett, and he jumped to do so. I fought to keep from rolling my eyes. I had never seen such a backward court. Not one of them knew what to do.

"A pleasure to meet you, Captain," the princess said. "I'm sure we can convince everyone to take your flag down once they see Tess beside me where she belongs."

Captain Borlett fidgeted as he let go of her hand. "It's only a bit of cloth, Your Highness."

I made a subtle gesture with my fingers, and the guards dropped back from him. Contessa saw the motion, and I smiled when she repeated the motion as if memorizing it.

"Perhaps you can help me," she said, keeping her pronunciation slow and precise, "being from the docks as you are. I have just asked Tess to be my ambassador. Unfortunately, it's a new position and lacks a few essentials. She is going to need a fast ship. One with a low draft to manage the rivers. It strikes me that the *Sandpiper*—"

"I'll do it," he interrupted, then reddened for his impertinence. My heart leapt. A ship of my own, to sail as I wanted. "That is if I can buy my backers out, and the princess—ah—your sister here . . ." His brow furrowed as he glanced at me. "Uh, Tess agrees," he said. "We weren't very gentlemanly. My crew, I mean. Tess and I, though, had a fine evening of cards."

I didn't look at Kavenlow, but I saw his stance turn disapproving.

"Then it's settled," Contessa said, clearly pleased. "I'll buy your backers out. The *Sandpiper* will be the ambassador's boat. My chancellor will see to your retaining fee, Captain."

I beamed at Kavenlow—a boat of my very own!—and he frowned, looking as eager as the time I told him I wanted to climb a cliff to catch my own peregrine chick.

The princess leaned close to Thadd. "How long until we have to go?" she whispered.

He glanced at one of her statues and the light falling on it. "A little over three hours," he said, starting to rise. "I'll see that the coach is ready."

She touched his arm, and he stopped. Head tilted confidently, she made a slight hand gesture, and the sentry closest to the door vanished, his place taken by another. *Chu,* I thought, both pleased and worried at how fast she was picking this up.

"Time enough to tell Prince Garrett of his return home," she said. "Or at least try to."

Captain Borlett shifted from foot to foot. "Ma'am, uh, Your Highness?" he stammered. "If it's all the same to you, I should get back to my boat before my men start setting the ships afire that have my flag flying from them."

Contessa's eyes widened, and I nodded, imagining Haron giving the order to start lobbing flaming tar. "Of course," the princess said, then motioned to Kavenlow. "My chancellor here can fund anything you need to outfit your ship for its new duties. And welcome to the palace, Captain Borlett."

Captain Borlett's eyes lit up with a sudden avarice. He made an awkward bow to the princess and beckoned to Kavenlow. "I've got a few things I've been wanting," he said.

Kavenlow gave me a pained look as he obediently followed Captain Borlett out. The short man grabbed his elbow, spouting phrases like a third lateen sail, and a new galley stove, and perhaps a coat of paint. Black if they could find it.

"That's the man who took you across the bay?" Jeck said as he leaned close, and I nodded. "I'm glad I was here to see this," he murmured. "Your new sovereign is rough but clever. King Edmund will be taken by surprise should he think to start mischief with her."

I smiled. "Did you expect anything less? She is my parents' daughter."

The remaining sentries shifted closer, and Thadd set a protective hand upon Contessa's shoulder as Prince Garrett was bought in. I straightened, nervous for what he might say.

His wrists were bound with a soft cloth. Metal hobbles were about his stockinged feet. He was dressed in the same rumpled uniform from last night. A whisper of blond stubble was on him, looking out of place. His mien was cold and stiff as he stalked into the informal court. Jangling his shackles as if they were a badge of honor, he came to a haughty standstill before the table, a red mark on his face where my whip had reached him. "Princess," he said, sweeping into an exquisite bow. Bringing his head up, he spat at my feet.

The sentry behind him grabbed the scruff of his neck and almost pulled him from his feet.

"No!" Contessa called, and the guard hesitated. The prince

hung in his grip, a taunting smile hovering about him despite the pain he must be under. "Put him down," she said, and the guard reluctantly did. My pulse slowed, and I settled into my seat. I hadn't realized I had risen.

The princess looked distressed at the haggard, innocence-wronged look he had draped about him like a cloak. "I told you to offer him food," she said. "He looks hungry."

"He won't eat, Princess."

Her brow pinched. "We will get him home as quickly as possible, then."

"You are a fool," Garrett said, his beautifully clear voice shocking through me. "I told you last night to kill her."

Contessa shifted uncomfortably. "I'm sorry, Tess. I didn't want you to hear this."

"They're going to kill us all," Garrett said loudly. "The farmers and the whores. They'll kill us all when it suits them. *They* rule the world from their rows of soil and beds of lust."

His voice had an eerie edge to it. The silky sound grated across the back of my neck, making me shudder. I wondered if Kavenlow and Jeck really had made him insane.

"I demand you return me to my father. He must be warned," Garrett continued. "He must slaughter all the farmers and unmarried women in the streets. They can't be allowed to live." His green eyes went distant. "No," he breathed. "That isn't right. Just the whores in Costenopolic. And only the farmers in Misdev." Garrett's brow furrowed. Losing his upright stance, he hunched in on himself. "But not all the farmers," he muttered. "Just those with swords. And the whores with red hair. The rest are just whores. Yes," he said, his voice going crafty. "Whores with red hair. That's what I'll do. Kill all the red-haired whores."

A wash of uneasy relief went through me. Clearly the blurring of memory was imperfect, but the indecision in his story and the muddled state of his words would make him seem all the more insane. Still, there was enough truth in his words to make my nights occasionally sleepless.

The princess looked pained. "I'm sorry, Captain Jeck. Be careful with him on the way home. I'm afraid he might hurt someone."

The sincerity behind her simple words outweighed their lack of tact. I wondered if I should give up on giving her royal polish and instead capitalize upon her earthy, honest nature.

Jeck gave her a bow. "Yes, Your Highness. I'll put him safely in his father's keep."

Garrett jerked out of his soft mumbling. "My father is a fool!" he shouted. "He will have me beaten. My brother will treat me like a child. I'll have to kill them all if I want to be king!"

The princess gasped, then steadied herself. "Please give my deepest regrets to King Edmund," she said, her eyes on Jeck. "I feel responsible somehow."

Jeck bowed again. "I will do my best to assure him it wasn't your doing."

Of that, I was sublimely certain, and I made a tight, mirthless smile.

"May I go rest?" Garrett asked, his beautiful face twisted. "I feel ill."

"Of course." Pushing her hair from her eyes, Contessa gestured for the guards to take him.

"Not them!" Garrett shouted wildly as he fell back a step. "Where are my guards? I don't trust you. Your red-haired whores will poison me."

The princess sat very still, clearly thinking. She looked to me, and I shrugged. "Tess, will you and Captain Jeck please accompany him?" she asked.

The captain of my father's guard stiffened. "Princess!"

She raised her eyebrows, and he fell silent. "Prince Garrett is mad," she said, "not his captain of his guard. But please, follow at a discreet distance."

Garrett made a mocking bow, almost returning to the man he had been. "Your Highness is gracious and kind," he taunted, making it an insult.

I rose and gathered my skirts as he strode regally from the room with Jeck at his elbow. I touched Contessa's hand in parting, giving her a reassuring smile. She hadn't done badly in her first formal court. She would be fine with Kavenlow, and I knew Heather would love Contessa with all her heart, finding her a suitable companion worthy of telling all her gossip to.

There were a slew of Costenopolie guards between Jeck and me, and it wasn't until I gained the hall that I managed to bully my way through them and catch up with Jeck and Prince Garrett. Jeck gave me a sideways look as I came even with him. Here in the hallways, I was reminded how tall the man was, standing over me by almost a full head. Garrett strode before us like an injured hero. The sentries followed obediently out of earshot. Jeck's brow was furrowed, and he kept a terse silence. I wondered if I had done something wrong.

We entered a hall lit from wide, interspersed windows, and Jeck muttered, "You managed to get yourself a devil of a fine position, Princess. Congratulations. It took me six years to get the ear of my sovereign. How nice it was so easy for you."

"Easy!" I said, offended, as I looked up to see his jaw clenched behind his trim beard. "You call the last week and a half easy?"

"The only thing that would have made it easier for you was if it had rained to cover your tracks," he muttered.

My anger swelled. "You don't want me to go, do you," I said in sudden understanding. "You don't want me in your lands."

Jeck's lips pressed together, going unseen behind his beard and mustache. "You couldn't be farther from the truth," he said, but he looked angry, and it confused me. His pace was stiff, and his neck was red. Reaching into an inner pocket, he pulled out my bone knife. "Here."

The knife thrust belligerently into my hand was warm from his body. He had kept it. I had thought he had sold it to buy a horse. "Thank you," I said sharply. "I thought Kavenlow searched you."

"That's what he thought, too."

I frowned, tucking my knife into the wide sash of my dress where it belonged. The weight of it felt comfortable. "Your knives are with my handmaiden. I'll get them when I can."

"I would appreciate that."

We continued. Confused and angry, I walked beside him, Garrett before us. Jeck took a deep breath as we passed a window, glancing up and down the hall. There were sentries at either end, but they were too far away to hear. "Has Kavenlow explained to you about your—hands?" he asked, and I started, shocked from my anger at the shift in topics.

I said nothing, looking at Garrett in concern as I came to a wide-eyed halt. Jeck stopped with me, and when Garrett continued Jeck pulled him back, pushing him roughly into the wall. The young prince's eyes narrowed, but he stayed put.

Frowning, Jeck took off his foolish-looking hat, his gaze

drifting over my shoulder to the sentries coming to a halt out of easy earshot. "It's just that . . ." He hesitated. "Oh, to hell with it," he muttered. My eyes widened as he made a fist. Drawing it back, he swung it at Garrett with a small grunt, as smooth and sweet as honey.

I gasped. The prince saw it coming but had no time to react.

Jeck's fist smashed into his chin. Garrett's head snapped back and hit the wall with a hollow thunk. Shocked, I gathered my skirts and stepped back as the royal crumpled.

Satisfaction heavy on Jeck, he shook his hand free of the pain. "You have no idea how long I've wanted to do that."

My gaze rose to the guards jogging our way. "It's all right," I called, and they hesitated. "We're fine. Prince Garrett is fine. Thank you." They came to an uncertain halt. "Go on back."

Laughing among themselves, they returned to a respectful distance, gossiping. I faced Jeck squarely, a quiver in my middle as I waited to hear what he didn't want Garrett to know.

Jeck rubbed his hand, meeting my gaze from under his shock of black hair. "Tess, Kavenlow is your master. And that he cares for you is obvious. But he . . ." His stance shifted from foot to foot, and his shoulders hunched. "Has he told you why your hands hum?" he asked.

"He . . ." I hesitated. "He said I returned from the dead with the punta's ability to heal."

He nodded, a tension easing in him. "Did he also tell you that you can kill with them?"

I took a step back, frightened. Seeing my cold face, Jeck nodded as if I had confirmed something. "No. He hasn't," he said.

"Why are you telling me this?" I demanded, my stomach light and my knees weak.

He leaned close, his brown eyes carrying a sly anticipation that settled over me like a chill. "I'm saying Kavenlow is your master, but nothing says it has to stay that way."

Shocked he dared make his offer a second time, I drew back. "Kavenlow is my teacher. I am young, Captain. Not stupid."

I turned with a flounce, gasping when he grabbed my upper arm. "Wait," he demanded.

I froze in fear as I heard the snick of steel from leather. It wasn't Jeck but the sentries at the end of the hall. Swallowing hard, I tugged free of Jeck's loose grip and waved the guards back. I was shaking inside, but if I was going to have this conversation, I wanted them close.

Jeck took a step from me, darting a glance at the sentries. "Tess, hear me out," he said softly as Garrett lay slumped between us. "You're young, and raw with talent. I can see why Kavenlow took you as a student. But you're just that. A student. What I'm proposing isn't uncommon. Apprentices are wooed from their original teachers more often than not. It's hard to trust the man who continually poisons you."

My anger faltered at the truth of what he was saying. Seeing it, his brown eyes probed mine. "That's why Kavenlow didn't have you recognized for so long. Your high tolerance to venom makes you extremely valuable. But, Tess, he can't teach you to heal with your hands. He didn't even recognize you had the ability, did he."

It wasn't a question, and he read my answer in that I was unable to look at him.

The tips of Jeck's black boots shifted under my gaze. "The force you can direct through you swings both ways, and willy-nilly experimentation is likely to get you or the one you are trying to heal killed."

I felt a stab of fear and I looked up. I wondered if that was why Kavenlow had been so worried when he told me why my hands hummed.

"I can teach you things he can't, Tess," Jeck said, his low voice running through me like ice in a river. "Things he won't. I know he has high ideas and plans for conquest by commerce. But he's wrong. The world doesn't change that quickly. Be my apprentice, and I will teach you things Kavenlow can't—or won't."

"Kavenlow knows what he's doing," I said, but even I could hear the doubt in it.

Jeck smiled, straightening to look over my shoulder. "Your loyalty suits you. But ask him . . . ask him if what I say is true. He has never been honest with you with about his past—your past. It's ugly, Tess, the things he's done, the atrocities he's capable of. He has outright lied to you. I never have. I never will."

My eyes fell from his as a seed of doubt wedged itself deep, buried under my denial.

"While you're in Misdev, let me at least teach you how to heal with your hands," he continued. "I'm sure once you know enough, you'll decide I'm right and stay. If not, return to Kavenlow."

It sounded too easy. But then I realized I could take him for all his knowledge and bring it back to Kavenlow.

A pleased expression was in Jeck's eyes when I met them. "You just had a thought to take what you could from me and leave," he murmured.

Fear washed through me, shortly followed by a flush. Jeck chuckled, making me feel foolish. "I'm better at this than you, Tess," he said. "Come and learn from me with the sole intent to steal, and I guarantee I'll come out of the arrangement better than you."

Though my knees were weak, pride narrowed my eyes. "You're mistaken, Captain Jeck. I accept your offer. Teach me what you will, but I will stay Kavenlow's apprentice."

There was a scuff from behind us, and we both spun. My hand was at my topknot, and Jeck's was tucked behind his jerkin. It was Kavenlow, his venom-induced skills allowing him to get this close without alerting either of us. He was better than both of us combined.

"What are you two doing in the middle of the hallway?" he demanded, ignoring Garrett slumped unconscious on the floor.

Squinting in the bright light from the window, I looked at Jeck. "He asked me to be his apprentice," I said, feeling vindicated when Jeck clenched his jaw and his eye began to twitch.

Tension pulled Kavenlow tight. "Chull bait!" he muttered. "You couldn't wait, could you," he said, his face red behind his salt-and-pepper beard. "You think you can come here and charm my apprentice from me? She spat in your face, didn't she?"

Jeck crouched, and grunting in effort, he slung Garrett over his shoulder. "She said she would take me as her instructor," he said, puffing as he rose to a stand and put his hat back on.

Kavenlow gripped my arm in sudden fear. "Tess!"

Face warm, I frowned at Captain Jeck. "I said nothing of the kind," I replied hotly, walking almost sideways as I followed Jeck down the hall as he carried Prince Garrett. "I said I'd let him teach me how to heal with my hands while serving as ambassador. I'm using Captain Jeck, and he knows it."

Jeck chuckled, and Kavenlow went white. "Tess, no," he said urgently as he paced beside me. "That decides it. You aren't going. He'll wring what he can from you, then use it to take Costenopolie. That is, if he doesn't outright kill you!"

"He won't kill me. He wants me to be his apprentice," I said, not caring that Jeck was listening. "And he can't watch me all the time. When will another opportunity to walk freely in King Edmund's halls come again? Let me go, Kavenlow. I'll be all right."

"No," Kavenlow said, sounding as if he had bit the word off, it was so sharp.

"But I want to go," I insisted. "Kavenlow, let me go!"

Under the weight of Garrett, Jeck laughed breathlessly.

"What the devil are you laughing about?" Kavenlow asked, his eyes angry.

Jeck shifted Garrett to a more comfortable position and started down the hall. *"Let me go. Let me go,"* he said in a high falsetto. "That's all she has been saying since I met her." He eyed Kavenlow from under his hat. "Let her go. Or don't you trust your own work?"

Hunched and muttering obscenities, Kavenlow strode down the hallway between us, the guards trailing behind. "I have a week before Garrett goes back," Kavenlow said. "You are not leaving with Captain Jeck, Tess."

I said nothing, smug in the knowledge that Contessa would listen to me before him. I was going. I would learn how to heal with my hands if nothing else. The other thing—the killing—I wasn't so sure about.

Duncan's raggedy silhouette appeared at the distant end of the hallway. Hands moving expressively, he talked with a sentry until the soldier gestured toward us. Duncan followed his gaze, an eager stance coming over him. "Tess?" he called from the top of the hall, "Do you want to go get your horses? We have a few hours before your sister's coronation."

I looked from Kavenlow to Jeck, feeling the weight of an apple in my pocket. I wasn't Costenopolie's princess—I was Kavenlow's apprentice—and I had a present to collect. "Yes," I called out as I slipped from them both and went to walk the streets with Duncan, free for what was probably the first time in my life. "I'm coming."

DAWN COOK

FIRST TRUTH

Alissa didn't believe in magic—
not until she was sent on a journey to an
endangered fortress known as The Hold.
There she discovered the gifts within herself to save it.

0-441-00945-X

HIDDEN TRUTH

Now, an ancient book calls out to Alissa…
and threatens those she loves.

0-441-01003-2

FORGOTTEN TRUTH

When a shapeshifting student is transported back four
centuries, she is in danger of remaining in her
dragon form forever.

0-441-01117-9

LOST TRUTH

In the magical land where Alissa should be welcomed
she is instead taken in against her will.
Now she will rebel, risking her magic—and her life.

0-441-01228-0

Available wherever books are sold or at
penguin.com

B039

The bestselling author of the *Lost Years of Merlin*
saga branches off in a new direction that
"will surely delight readers" (Madeleine L'Engle).

T.A. BARRON
Tree Girl

0-441-00994-8

A nine-year-old girl searching for her roots
must face a forest filled with tree ghouls—
and her own deepest fears.

"Sprightly, magical, and wise."
—Barbara Helen Berger

AVAILABLE WHEREVER BOOKS ARE SOLD OR AT
PENGUIN.COM

From the fantasy world of

Lynn Abbey

co-creator of *Thieves' World*™

Taking Time

0-441-01153-5

THE NOVELS OF LYNN ABBEY ARE:

"BRILLIANTLY CONCEIVED."
—C.J. CHERRYH

"ALL THE THINGS THAT MAKE
FANTASY WORTH READING."
—*BOOKLIST*

Available wherever books are sold or at
penguin.com

From national bestselling author

Patricia Briggs

DRAGON BONES

0-441-00916-6

Ward of Hurog has tried all his life to convince
people he is just a simple, harmless fool...And it's
worked. But now, to regain his kingdom, he must
ride into war—and convince them otherwise.

DRAGON BLOOD

0-441-01008-3

Ward, ruler of Hurog, joins the rebels against
the tyrannical High King Jakoven. But Jakoven
has a secret weapon. One that requires
dragon's blood—the very blood that courses
through Ward's veins.

Available wherever books are sold or at
penguin.com